Praise for
A HEART OF BLOOD AND ASHES

"Dark, brutal, bloody—and incredibly compelling, with brilliant worldbuilding and a romance that gripped my emotions. Milla Vane has created something extraordinary in this story of kings and war, gods and vengeance."
—*New York Times* bestselling author Nalini Singh

"An engrossing, epic story of warriors, gods, leaders, and lovers. . . . The characters walk through the pages with heart, soul, and courage, and are matched by Vane's equally stellar worldbuilding, which weaves seamlessly with thrilling action scenes." —BookPage (starred review)

"[A] richly imagined dark fantasy world."
—*Publishers Weekly*

"An engrossing tale of barbarity and treachery, of devotion and loyalty, and ultimately of love. Milla Vane knocks it out of the park with the savagely delightful *A Heart of Blood and Ashes*. Now I find myself desperate to get my hands on the next book in the series." —Fresh Fiction

"Worldbuilding with depth and complexity, wonderfully fleshed-out characters, and packed with brutal fight scenes and heartrending emotion. . . . *A Heart of Blood and Ashes* is epic fantasy romance at its finest." —Smexy Books

"This book is a lusciously brutal foray into romantic fantasy, with a love story that burns so hot, you might singe your fingers while reading it. . . . With *A Heart of Blood and Ashes*, Milla Vane has crowned herself as the new queen of the genre." —The Alliterates

Books by Milla Vane

A Gathering of Dragons Series
A HEART OF BLOOD AND ASHES
A TOUCH OF STONE AND SNOW

Novellas
THE BEAST OF BLACKMOOR

A TOUCH OF STONE AND SNOW

MILLA VANE

JOVE
New York

A JOVE BOOK
Published by Berkley
An imprint of Penguin Random House LLC
penguinrandomhouse.com

Copyright © 2020 by Melissa Khan
Excerpt from *A Heart of Blood and Ashes* by Milla Vane copyright © 2020 by Melissa Khan
Penguin Random House supports copyright. Copyright fuels creativity, encourages
diverse voices, promotes free speech, and creates a vibrant culture. Thank you for buying
an authorized edition of this book and for complying with copyright laws by not
reproducing, scanning, or distributing any part of it in any form without permission.
You are supporting writers and allowing Penguin Random House to continue to
publish books for every reader.

A JOVE BOOK, BERKLEY, and the BERKLEY & B colophon
are registered trademarks of Penguin Random House LLC.

ISBN: 9780593197165

First Edition: July 2020

Printed in the United States of America
1   3   5   7   9   10   8   6   4   2

Cover photo by Claudio Marinesco
Cover design by Rita Frangie
Book design by George Towne

For Kippy
You were the cutest of all cats.

A
TOUCH
OF STONE
AND SNOW

CHAPTER 1

LIZZAN

Many an innkeeper had woken Lizzan by tossing a bucket of water into her face. This day marked the first time she was doused awake by a tree.

She sat up sputtering and squinting beneath the morning sun. Or perhaps it was the midday sun. The source of the light filtering through the jungle canopy was too high for morning, and far too bright for eyes unshaded by sobriety. Judging by how it blinded her, she was *nearly* sober.

A sad state that Lizzan would soon remedy.

Of late, her flask was always as near to her hand as her sword. She uncorked the neck and was doused again when another broadleaf overfilled with rain and tipped out its burden.

The deluge poured over the top of her head. Sputtering again, her black hair hanging around her face, Lizzan contemplated the effort of leaving the base of the tree where she'd made her bed. All around her, the canopy dumped water as if making wet war on the world below. She would be no drier if she abandoned this spot.

And she would be no drunker unless she did. Only a few drops remained in her flask—and those tasted of rainwater.

Groaning, she shoved the cork into the neck. A fine day this was. Such a very fine day.

Whatever day it might be. The last she remembered, her flask had been full. Usually at least two or three evenings passed before she had to fill it again.

Head pounding, she unsheathed her sword. Bits of vegetation stuck to the blade, as if she'd hacked her way through the jungle foliage, but no blood stained the shining steel. She had not likely killed anyone in the time unremembered, then, or the blood would still remain. Lizzan was not the tidiest of warriors when drunk.

And now she was here. Beneath a tree. She had the vaguest recollection of a man with a gray curling beard saying that a band of thieves plagued the road between Ebrana and Oana. Perhaps she'd set out to hunt them.

If so, then a fool she was. Gladly would Lizzan collect bandits' heads. But she had no money and no horse—and now, no drink. Better to have waited until someone offered to pay for those heads.

At least her only foolishness had been chasing after brigands. She was still in possession of her purse—empty though it was—and her sword, which would fill the purse with coins again. She had not sold any more of her armor. Even with the sigil of the Kothan army scratched away, each piece was fine enough to fetch a fair price. Her mail tunic alone could buy a horse and a year's worth of drink. But she was not yet so desperate. Or so thirsty.

A sniff told her that she also possessed a rather unpleasant odor. But the rain would take care of that.

Mostly.

Her leathers and boots were sodden when the storm finally passed. Made from a northern falt's water-shedding pelt, her bedroll had been spared the soaking but was so muddied that nothing of the white fur could be seen under the brown. The cursed heat in this realm would dry them all soon enough, but still she stripped down to her underlinens and boots before starting out in search of the road, so that her squelching would not draw predators—whether human or animal—and to spare herself the chafing.

Some days it seemed that everything chafed. Not only what she touched. But all she heard, all she saw. All of it rubbed the wrong way. Yet only her clothes left blisters.

Soon she would remove her boots, too. Wet boots always meant lost toes—in the north, lost to frost; in the jungle, lost to rot. Yet she would wait until the road before taking them off, when she would be less likely to step on a venomous snake or a stinging vine.

Finding the road was a simple matter of following the path she'd slashed through the foliage. She slowed when the sound of voices told her that a group of travelers was already upon it.

Out of sight amid a heavy growth of ferns, Lizzan studied the procession. A few dozen families—men and women, young and old. A handful of carts drawn by oxen carried supplies and the weaker among the travelers, but most walked.

Except for the mounted figure at their head. From this vantage, Lizzan could not see her face, but the red cloak she wore identified her well enough. A Nyrae warrior—or so she would have everyone believe by wearing that cloak. Once, those roaming warriors guaranteed the safe passage of anyone who traveled the road with them, for only a fool would attack one of the goddess Vela's chosen. But few Nyrae warriors had survived Anumith the Destroyer's deadly march a generation past. Now, it was more likely a woman from the caravan had donned a crimson cloak in hope that bandits would not risk attacking a party led by a true Nyrae warrior.

The deceptive practice had become so common, however, that there was little protection in it anymore. Instead those who could afford the cost hired guards—which was how Lizzan earned most of her coin. She escorted merchants and nobles fleeing east, as rumors spread of the Destroyer's return from the west. From the east, she escorted merchants and nobles fleeing west to escape the tyranny of the warlords in Lith. And from the north came those fleeing unnamed terrors that haunted the ice and snow.

From every direction, everyone was fleeing some danger—only to find there was nowhere safe to go. So most remained in Krimathe, where the Ivory Throne offered protection to all who sought refuge. Those who didn't stay in Krimathe continued fleeing south.

This was the first party she'd seen fleeing north. Usually the only escort in that direction was for merchants' goods, which were a prime target for bandits. More than all else, the destitution of these travelers might be better protection than any red cloak. They had little to tempt thieves.

Unfortunately, thieves were often tempted by very little.

A few stragglers made up the tail of the caravan—likely those who had joined the group after it had already started out, for it was Vela's law that no one would be denied a Nyrae warrior's protection upon the road. Even if that warrior was in truth a farmer, she would not chase away the stragglers and risk her disguise.

Lizzan waited for the entire procession to pass, then caught up to straggle after the stragglers. With her sodden hair hanging over the left side of her face, armor and leathers wrapped up in her bedroll, she received little more than a curious glance or two from the others, and she remained far enough behind to escape any attempts at conversation.

But she did not escape notice. Lizzan had barely settled into the procession's slow pace when the quick tempo of hoofbeats announced the approach of the red-cloaked figure.

Oh, and no farmer was she. Not on a horse so fine. Sheer envy struck Lizzan's chest. Perhaps she would part with her mail tunic, after all.

Except this woman did not need Kothan armor, though she hardly wore any of her own. She was not a large woman, shorter than Lizzan and more finely boned. A thick braid swept her black hair away from the proud set of her face. Lizzan had never laid eyes upon that face before but had little doubt of the woman's identity. Lizzan could not step into a tavern without hearing of how Krimathe's future queen had set out on the sacred quest that would earn her the Ivory Throne—and all who quested for the goddess Vela also wore a red cloak.

But the woman eyeing her now was no mere princess. Legend was that Hanan had fucked one of her foremothers. Now that god's silver blood ran though her veins and his strength through her limbs.

So Lizzan felt a bit of a fool when she said to the woman, "I was told that bandits prey the length of this road. I offer my sword and assistance if we happen upon them."

The woman's dark eyes swept Lizzan from drenched head to wet toe, and Lizzan did not think that piercing gaze overlooked a single scar or battle-hardened muscle.

No response did she give, except to cock her head—as if waiting for more.

Lizzan sighed and scratched the side of her neck. "I would not ask these people for payment . . . but if the bandits are mounted, I would like first pick of their horses."

The Krimathean's eyes narrowed. As if she *knew* there was more.

And so there was. "Also their flasks."

The woman's lips twitched. Then she swept her forefinger over her left eyebrow.

Lizzan's chest tightened. Yet she could see no way around it. Had she still been in the north, or if it were winter, no one would think anything if she'd covered much of her face. Yet if she'd joined this procession wearing the mask she often used while working, she'd have immediately been thought a bandit. And her hair had not concealed her well enough.

With muddied fingers, she drew back the black strands, revealing the scars that raked down the left side of her face.

"Though it looks similar, it is not Vela's mark," she said thickly. "I am not cursed."

Of all people, this woman might know. If the Krimathean failed in her quest for Vela, she would bear that goddess's mark—and be shunned by all. Driven from every village and city to live forsaken and alone. A woman to whom even a Nyrae warrior would not offer protection.

With the tip of her finger, the Krimathean drew a line down the outside of her cheek from hairline to jaw.

Relief lightened Lizzan's heart. That line was where another scar would have been, had she borne Vela's mark. So this woman must have seen it before. So many others had not. And Lizzan had often known the weight of the curse that she hadn't earned.

She *had* been cursed. And shunned. But not by a goddess. Instead a bastard prince had been the one to steal everything from her. Her rank. Her honor. Her heart.

Oh, and now that she'd thought of him, everything chafed again, and her sword thirsted for blood. For not all thieves skulked in the forests. Some lived in crystal palaces.

But if bandits were to ambush her here . . . they would serve as a fine substitute.

The ambush came not from bandits, but from Lizzan's fellow travelers when the caravan stopped for a midday rest.

In a clearing bordered by a stream, Lizzan laid out her belongings to dry, then sought shade beneath a giant fern. Her head ached madly. The sun in this realm was never as bright as during a northern winter, where Enam's glare upon the ice and snow dazzled and blinded, but the god's eye burned so cursedly hot here that shade brought scant relief. And although she'd filled her flask with rainwater, every swallow seemed to immediately spurt from her skin as rivers of sweat, and her thirst never eased.

So it was there beneath the fern, in her barefoot and vulnerable state, that they ganged up on her in a party of three—an elderly woman, a younger woman, and a still younger man who was hardly more than a boy.

Through slitted eyes, Lizzan watched them approach. No fear did they seem to have of the disagreeable scowl she wore—and no respect did they seem to have for the sheathed sword lying across her lap. Probably because they were all under the protection of a Krimathean warrior who could crush Lizzan's skull between her bare hands.

In truth, it was only because of the Krimathean's presence that Lizzan had allowed herself to be in such a vulnerable state. Now she prepared to be ousted from the caravan despite the law of the road. Many ways there were to make a person feel unwelcome, until leaving a place was not forced but the person's own choice. Lizzan was familiar with most of those ways.

She sneered at most attempts to oust her. Unless her presence made these travelers feel unsafe.

Never could she stay if they did.

Under the bright sun, the older woman's snow-white hair was hard to look upon—and too similar to everything that Lizzan had left behind, yet would not lie still and unremembered in her mind.

Instead Lizzan focused on the other woman, who resembled the elder so fiercely that a family connection could not be mistaken. Solidly built, she wore her brown hair plaited into a simple braid that draped over her shoulder, with sweat-dampened tendrils curling at the edges of a round face. Her pale green tunic and loose brocs appeared homespun, yet lighter and of finer quality than Lizzan's linens—and though more of her brown skin was covered, the woman seemed less discomfited by the sweltering heat than Lizzan was.

She carried no weapons. Lizzan suspected she didn't need them. When the procession had passed earlier, this woman had walked near the head, and she had the air of a leader who could rouse a village—or a caravan—to action with a few words.

Years past, that was the sort of woman Lizzan dreamed of becoming—though she would have led an army, not a village. But that dream was dead. As were her soldiers and any future she'd once imagined.

Now Lizzan silently returned the woman's regard, chin lifted and her scars partially exposed, daring the woman to shun her for them. The Krimathean had already accepted

Lizzan into the caravan. Only if the goddess Vela flew down from the moon to cast judgment upon the markings would any opinion carry more weight. They likely still made this woman uneasy.

Yet no unease did Lizzan see when the woman gestured to her drying bedroll and asked, "Is that the hide of a northern falt?"

"It is not for sale."

Though she *should* sell it. The hide had once promised everything but now meant nothing. Lizzan should abandon it as easily as a bastard prince had abandoned her. But Lizzan could not.

Which did not make her entirely a fool. Like her mail tunic, which had also once meant everything to her and now meant nothing, the hide was useful.

The woman made a dismissive gesture, as if acquiring the valuable pelt had never been her intent. "You have spent time in the north?"

The pounding in Lizzan's head worsened. "I have."

"How far do you travel now?"

"Only as far as my next job demands."

"Have you one?"

"Not as yet." Lizzan's eyes narrowed with dry amusement. "Do you have need of another escort with a sword? It would be coin well spent. For certain, a Nyrae warrior with a god's blood in her veins isn't protection enough."

The woman gave a short laugh, and they both glanced toward the Krimathean, whose leather belt was studded with the eyeteeth of those who'd fallen before her blade. Fortunately it was a wide belt, or soon the warrior would need another one.

"We only travel the same route as the Nyrae until Oana. There our paths diverge."

As the road did, continuing north or forking east toward the pass over the Fanged Mountains. "You intend to hire a guard in Oana?"

"We have little coin."

Lizzan had already guessed as much. But their animals

appeared well tended and each traveler appeared well fed . . . and an unmounted warrior could not always be picky. Far fewer jobs were available to those without a horse. Her gaze touched on the forward wagon, where two casks were nestled beside bulging bags of grain. A meal twice daily—washed down with whatever they kept in those casks—seemed at this moment a very fair price. "And which direction will you go: north or east?"

"North," the woman said. "We hope to reach Koth."

A rotten stone shifted in Lizzan's stomach and threatened to expose a thousand crawling, squirming emotions lying beneath. Before they could wriggle up her throat and onto her tongue, she shook her head. "I can't help you."

"Then we would ask of the situation in that realm. Recently we have heard rumors that Koth has fallen and the people have abandoned the island."

As had Lizzan. So she drank enough to forget most of what she heard.

"I know nothing of how Koth fares," she told them. The old woman's hair seemed even whiter now, its wintry brightness driving a throbbing spike through Lizzan's brain. Desperate to escape, she gained her feet, towering over the women—and the young man, too. "I must hunt my midday meal."

"We would happily share ours with you here beneath this fine shade," the woman said, her voice steady and warm. "There is cheese and bread, and a bit of stewed boar."

But the sharing would not come without a cost. Lizzan would have to talk of Koth. So although her mouth watered, she shook her head. "There is no need—"

"And palm wine," the old woman said.

Lizzan sat again.

The younger woman's lips curved with amusement. "Sweet or sour?"

"Sour." It was stronger.

The woman turned to the young man. "Please fetch it for us, Bilyan."

"But first drag that pelt into the shade," Lizzan said.

"Your mother and hers will find sitting upon it more pleasant than the damp ground."

He did before loping off toward the wagons, all loose stride and lanky limbs. A boy who had not yet grown into his body. An awkward age for some men—and the finest age for others. Such as kind and generous young men who passed that awkward stage, only to become aloof, pig-swiving jackals.

And she had not yet made sense of this caravan. By heading north, they traveled in a direction that usually only merchants and traders went. But hearing them speak told her where they'd come from.

The goddess Vela had given everyone the same tongue so that all the realms might understand each other, but they did not all sound the same. Until Stranik's Passage beneath the Flaming Mountains of Astal had opened three years past, the fiery peaks had prevented easy travel between the northern and southern realms. The speech of the southern realms just beyond the mountains had an old-fashioned cadence to Lizzan's ear, as if she spoke to her mother's mother, or watched a mummers' play set in the near past. And those from the far south used heavy, ancient-flavored speech—and Lizzan had only heard it a few times, spoken by Parsathean mercenaries.

These people spoke as those from the near south did. And they did not yet possess the hardened, weary look of travelers who'd spent more than a full turn of the moon upon the road. A few of the stragglers who'd joined the tail of the caravan did—and they had been welcomed into the larger group for the midday meal, she saw now.

Sharing was a kindness woven into the fabric of the law of the road, yet one she rarely saw. Especially as travelers' supplies dwindled. This caravan's supplies had not yet.

"I am Mevida," said the brown-haired woman, taking her seat at Lizzan's left. "My mother, Carinea."

Whose skin seemed as fragile and crinkly as a fallen autumn leaf, though nothing else about her seemed frail. Her gaze was as steady and direct as her daughter's, though also sharper and brighter—as if the mind behind those dark eyes were an unsheathed blade.

Or perhaps by Carinea's age, whatever once covered the blade had simply worn away. Lizzan's own blade had been scraped clean by anger and pain, and was kept honed by all the chafing that followed, but she did not think the sharpness shone through her eyes as this woman's did. Instead every slice and incision was aimed at the foolish matter within Lizzan's own skull, delivered by too many thoughts with razored edges. The only thing that dulled them was enough drink.

Which the boy quickly brought in a clay mug with a rounded bottom that nestled comfortably in Lizzan's hand. Generous he'd been, filling it nearly to the brim.

Sheer relief lightened the urge to gulp the wine. Oh, and it was strong—as strong as palm wine could be without turning over to vinegar. The first sip Lizzan held against her tongue as long as she could, watching as the boy laid out the other provisions. Already the sun seemed not so bright, the air not so humid.

The women sipped from their own cups—of the sweet and mild variety, Lizzan noted, and theirs only containing a few swallows. Truly they must believe that Lizzan knew more than she did.

Though if they were from the south, they likely knew very little. "Why do you go north? Have you family in Koth?"

Which was so unusual as to be almost unheard of. Before the passageway had opened, Lizzan had personally known not one person who had been south of the flaming mountains. Tales she had heard—of the monoliths of Par and of the Dragon Sands, of the Farian savages and of the Bone Fields and of the Boiling Sea—yet much like Anumith the Destroyer, that was all they were. Tales and legends, something that occurred elsewhere and to people wholly unrelated to anyone she knew.

"No family." Mevida's smile tightened. "But surely you have heard that the Destroyer returns?"

It seemed that was all Lizzan had heard of late. "But are you not from Blackmoor?"

"Near to it."

"It was Blackmoor's king and queen who slew the demon from Stranik's Passage. You do not think that of all realms, Blackmoor is not the safest and their protection the strongest?" Most of those who traveled south seemed to believe so. "There is also word that a great alliance forms, and that the southern realms are uniting to stand against him."

Which sounded to Lizzan a marvelous idea. Especially if the realms in the north would create a similar alliance, but she could not imagine how that would happen. The smaller realms were in turmoil as everyone fled south. And the larger realms offered their protection, but with no agreement between them. Koth believed the only safety would be found on its island. The monks of Radreh spoke of using dark magics to fight the Destroyer on his own terms—a tactic that Koth and Krimathe vehemently denounced—and Lith was lost to the battle between its warlords. But even if it had not been, no alliance would *ever* form between Lith and Krimathe. Not after Lith's former king had invaded the broken realm and sought to finish what the Destroyer had begun.

"It's true that an alliance forms," Mevida said. "But what of it? They all fell before the Destroyer before: Blackmoor, the riders of the Burning Plains, every realm between the Fallen Mountains and the Boiling Sea. And so did Krimathe." Her voice lowered slightly, as if so the red-cloaked warrior would not be pained by her words, though that woman was too far away to hear. "But although he laid waste to these northern realms, neither he nor his warlords ever attacked Koth. Is that truth?"

Lizzan sighed. "It is."

"So if the Destroyer will not go to Koth, that is where we will go," Mevida claimed, determination ringing through her voice. "I was but a girl when the Destroyer's army came through our village. My mother hid me away but I remember the screams. I remember how many . . . how many were . . ." Words faltering, she reached out for the older woman's hand. "And how after the Destroyer's army left, the road was muddied as if a storm had swept through, but the puddles were all of blood. I will not see it happen again to those I love."

"And I would like to see a place untouched by the Destroyer's hand," the older woman said, her gnarled fingers tightening on her daughter's. "A realm that has not been wounded, and is not still a weeping scab."

Koth was wounded. But those who lived in the realm preferred to hide its scars.

Or exile them.

"You might also stay in Oana, then," Lizzan told them. "Though the Destroyer burned all that stood, the trees are fed by Nemek's healing baths. To look at them now, you would not know he'd ever been there."

"But he *was* there," Mevida said quietly. "And might be again. So we go to Koth."

"It is said that the Destroyer fears the ice and cold," Mevida's son broke in. "Because he calls upon Enam's strength for his own, and the sun god's power is weaker in the north."

"That is said," Lizzan agreed. It was said in Koth, too. But Lizzan was not so certain. The sun was not as warm in the north, true; but only someone who had never been blinded by the shine against ice would think Enam's power weaker.

Yet that thought Lizzan kept to herself. Mevida and her people had hope . . . which was more than most of those fleeing desperately through the realms did.

The boy continued, "It is said that the crystal palace is the finest of all palaces ever built."

The finest of all palaces. So Kothans said of much that was built or created in their realm—that they were the finest of all things—because those who lived there never stopped improving themselves or their craft, never stopped working and learning. When she'd been young, Lizzan had also believed it. Yet after seeing how Kothans treated those whose names were not written in the books, the cracks in that claim had begun to show through.

But she only agreed, "The palace is beautiful."

"It is also said Koth's mountain bridge is too well defended for any army to cross."

It was as if a knife sliced through Lizzan's chest. Heart bleeding, she replied, "That is also said."

"And it is said that, in Koth, a man might become anything he wishes to be. He might even become a king—or a god, as Varrin did."

"So it is said." Though that particular rank was a bit harder to obtain. "And what would you be?"

"I know not." Again his excitement shone through his face, bright with hope. "But that is the wonder of Koth, is it not? That I could be anything. At home, I could only be an innkeeper."

The old woman swatted his leg. "And what is a king compared to an innkeeper, eh?"

The boy grinned. "Richer."

Perhaps. But to Lizzan, there was no finer profession than to keep a place for those who had nowhere else to go. To the two women, she asked, "You are innkeepers?"

"And will be again, if we can build a new inn in Koth. There will be many more like us hoping to escape the Destroyer," Mevida said.

So there would be. "When I was last there, the villages on the windward side often lacked for accommodations."

Sharp gaze steady on hers, the old woman asked, "What of the rumors that the island has been abandoned?"

Chest tight, Lizzan shook her head. "I know not if they are true. Only that it seems impossible." But also deemed impossible had been the creatures of ice that had killed her father and slaughtered her soldiers. "The other rumors are true—that terrors haunt the northern forests."

"Better to face terrors than the Destroyer's army."

Perhaps. But Lizzan would not be in Koth to fight either monsters or the Destroyer. Deeply she drank, finishing the wine . . . already wishing for another.

But nothing was free, and Lizzan had told them all that

she could bear to tell. "I thank you for this," she said, placing the cup down. "I regret that I had nothing to tell you."

"You told us more than we knew before," said Mediva. "Perhaps at supper, you might tell us what supplies we will need for a winter on the windward side of the island."

The old woman gave the cup a sly glance. "Or perhaps you might stay with us through many suppers, and show us the windward side yourself."

Lizzan's throat closed. No, she could not do that. She had been exiled and her name had been struck from the books. To merely speak it was against Kothan law. And if Lizzan returned to the island, she would be killed . . . and worse, she would bring more shame to her mother and brothers than they already knew.

But more wine she would not refuse—though this time she would earn it. Gripping her sword, she rose to her feet.

"What shall I hunt for our supper, then?"

CHAPTER 2

AERAX

Many times since leaving Koth, Aerax's eyes had tricked him into seeing Lizzan where she wasn't. In the turn of a woman's head, the shape of a smile, the sound of a laugh. Never had he seen her in a footprint.

Or in two footprints—for it was the pairing that had made him stop to look again. The soft impression left by a leather-clad boot could belong to any number of women. But that stride was Lizzan's.

Aerax searched for more prints, but the Parsathean horses that passed down this road after the woman had obliterated most of them. He spotted a single print here and there. Not a full stride.

"How intently you stare at the ground," Lady Junica said as her periwag walked up alongside his mount. From her lounging couch atop the wide beast, she craned her head as if to examine the tracks—then winced and settled back on her cushions again, apparently thinking better of moving. "Does the rain make it harder to follow the Parsatheans' trail?"

Aerax shook his head. The rain made it easier. And better allowed him to judge how much time had passed since the caravan had come through, and then the Parsathean warriors.

But rain or sun, this took no effort. He had spent his early years hunting through the northern wilds. Yet even in this unfamiliar jungle, he could follow the trail of a red-cloaked warrior who had drawn notice everywhere she went—as could anyone. Reading the tracks only meant they did not have to continually stop and ask for the direction she'd gone.

"Our feral prince did not likely expect to be of much use on this journey." Degg spoke to Lady Junica, who rode between them, but his bland smile was aimed at Aerax. "You must be glad to have a purpose again."

Aerax grunted. He had a purpose. One that the king would kill him for and these councilors would put a stop to, if they knew of it.

And despite the title he'd been given, Aerax was not truly a prince. His uncle had only acknowledged Aerax's existence out of desperation after the red fever had torn through the realm, killing nearly every member of Koth's royal family—including Aerax's father, the king, and his legitimate heirs. But Aerax would never inherit Koth's throne; he would only know the burden of it, and the ink that finally added Aerax's name to the books had not yet dried when a sullen and resentful Degg had been assigned to act as Aerax's guide through the palace and to teach court etiquette to a coarse huntsman.

Aerax had never taken to those lessons, and Degg had never refrained from saying how badly he'd failed them.

So no diplomat was he. Aerax had only been sent on this journey for appearances' sake. The snow-white hair of Koth's rulers was legendary—and so was the rarity of any Kothan royal leaving the realm. His uncle had believed that Aerax's presence would communicate the urgency of their need to Krimathe better than any words could.

Of the words that needed to be spoken, few would come

from Aerax. Not when he might offend the High Daughter of Krimathe with his coarse manners and vulgar tongue.

When they had arrived in Krimathe, however, there was no High Daughter there to speak with—instead it was her cousin, Mala, who looked after the realm while their future queen was on Vela's quest.

And it was not only Koth that sought an alliance with Krimathe. From south of the Flaming Mountains of Astal also arrived an ambassador guarded by Parsathean warriors, hoping to unite all the western realms to stand against Anumith the Destroyer.

But the High Daughter's cousin had claimed that her role was to defend Krimathe while their future queen was gone, not to send away part of its army or to make important alliances. So Mala had given them a choice to wait in Krimathe until her cousin returned from her quest—or to seek her out, as she had only recently left.

As time could not be wasted, they had all chosen to follow. And since no one in Krimathe knew for certain where the goddess had sent the High Daughter on that quest, Mala had asked her Hanani companion, Shim, to lead them.

Over the past fortnight, the stallion had tracked her by scent far more quickly than even Aerax could have—until an injury had forced the Kothan party to slow while the southerners rode ahead.

They were not far behind, however. Perhaps a half day, and their slow pace was helped along by the even slower caravan that the Krimathean appeared to be leading. If the Kothans traveled late into the night, they might catch up again before making camp.

But only if all of their party could ride that far without needing rest.

He looked to Lady Junica. The graying curls that an inn's handmaid had meticulously twisted into a roll that morning had fallen prey to a rain shower and hung in limp tendrils around her shoulders. This long journey from Koth had taken a toll on her, though she'd held up well—until two days past, when she'd dismounted awkwardly and twisted her back. Now she was carried along by a periwag, a gray-skinned beast with splayed legs and a drooping snout. The litter strapped to its wide back allowed her to lounge upon cushions instead of straddling a saddle.

But even a smooth ride was not always an easy one. "How do you fare?"

She sighed, fanning herself with lazy sweeps of her wrist. "I may look like a queen as I lounge here amid my many cushions. But I feel like a fool."

"Then be at ease. You might be mistaken for a queen, but no one would mistake you for a fool."

A smile curved her lips. "I see those courtly lessons have begun to sink in."

Degg snorted. "Not far beyond his skin. His every conversation is still mostly grunts and growls."

Aerax shrugged. "In the palace, more response is rarely needed."

With eyes narrowing, Lady Junica said, "Do you suggest that we councilors blather on without saying anything?"

He would suggest sinking every councilor with the rest of the palace. Except for Lady Junica. "I would not suggest it of you."

She laughed lightly. "So you *have* learned well."

Aerax grunted. For he had not learned well enough. If he had any gift of persuasion, already his purpose might be done.

But it was not.

"Speaking of overlarge beasts that growl, where is your cat?" Lady Junica rose up slightly, her gaze sweeping the road ahead. "I have not seen him since midday."

"Hunting," Aerax told her.

After catching a scent that had excited Caeb so much that he'd nearly pulled Aerax from his saddle, trying to urge him along on the hunt. Almost anything Aerax would have given to join the cat . . . and then keep riding.

One day. There was work to be done first.

The councilor's gaze seemed suddenly intent and piercing, as if trying to see through him. "Do you not worry when he is gone?"

Always Aerax worried. Everything he'd ever loved, he'd lost—except the snow cat. But he knew the surest way to lose Caeb would be to leash the cat to his side. "He likely sleeps off a full belly."

"Hopefully that full belly will calm his foul temper," Degg said.

Aerax slashed a disgruntled look at the councilor. Caeb had but a snow cat's temper. And like every cat, he had little use for humans and wished to be left alone. So with a few exceptions, Caeb snarled at anyone who approached him.

Aerax only wished that a bastard prince's snarling were as effective as a saber-toothed predator's was.

"Though perhaps the foul-tempered one is the prince who loves him," Degg said, catching sight of Aerax's look.

Lady Junica speared the other councilor with a quelling glance, then sighed. "This heat makes us all foul-tempered."

It was not the heat that fouled Aerax's temper. Nor was it Degg, who had poked at him with smug, relentless jabs since leaving the palace. Never did such things touch him. Only someone Aerax cared for could affect him.

Those people numbered very few.

Instead what fired his impatience was this journey away from Koth. He had dreamed of leaving the realm since barely able to walk, and yet now his only thought was of returning to the island so he could truly be forever done with it.

And everything he saw was haunted by Lizzan. The loss of her was an ache that never eased. Every reminder was a knife in his chest.

It was she whom Aerax ought to have been with now, not these councilors and guards. He ought to be finding his way to her, not hoping to return to Koth.

If that made him foul-tempered, Aerax cared not. With Lizzan exiled, he had no friends left in the realm. And he was glad she was gone from that spider's trap of an island, though her absence was like an endless chasm within him.

Still . . . Aerax would have given anything to see her again. Which was likely why he saw her everywhere he looked.

The raucous calls from the trees around them quieted. Rare lightness lifted through Aerax's chest when Caeb prowled out of the tangled foliage and onto the road. The silver on his harness glinted in the sunlight, powerful muscles rippling under white fur dappled with pale gray.

"There he is," said Lady Junica, before adding with a soft laugh, "It seems that he was unlucky in his hunt—and you are spared a bath."

Amused, Aerax grunted his agreement. Usually after a hunt, Caeb returned with his muzzle and chest covered in blood. But no washing would Aerax have to give him this time.

Standing in the road, the big cat looked back over his shoulder and regarded the periwag. Nearly as tall as Aerax's horse, with a powerful chest and forelimbs combined with explosive speed, Caeb could easily take down even a beast of the periwag's size—and had, when he'd encountered herds of the untamed animals. Yet this one he could not eat.

Aerax gave a small shake of his head and the cat turned away as if he'd never given a thought to devouring Lady Junica's mount. Instead he batted a clump of grass, then leapt straight upward in an attempt to swat a brushfly from the air, its segmented body as long as Aerax's arm.

Caeb seemed more like a kitten than a fully grown snow cat on this journey. Away from the boredom of the palace, the cat explored and investigated everything—and hunted often, as he and Aerax once had.

Now Caeb trotted ahead, where the road widened into a clearing. Here the caravan had stopped, the travelers leaving a wider array of footprints that led to a stream and to the edges of the forest, where they'd waited in the shade until starting off again. Caeb sniffed at a few of the tracks—then rolled on them, as if covering himself in the scent.

Aerax watched him, frowning. Never had the cat done that before. Caeb took an interest in many scents. But rarely did he care for human odors, except for Aerax's . . . and Lizzan's.

Hope constricted through his chest. He urged his mount to the edge of the clearing, calling himself a fool. Everywhere he saw her. Because everywhere he *wanted* to see her.

Yet this was no trick of his eyes. Here was a print of a bare foot, and he would have known it was Lizzan by the shape of the heel alone. Or by the curve where the arch met the ball of her foot. Or by the sweet dimples that were impressions of her toes.

The first time he'd seen that print, her foot had been smaller—as had been his own. His voice had only recently deepened when he'd come across a dark-haired girl in a finely woven tunic and brocs, fiercely hacking at a tree trunk with a dulled sword. It had been a sight both unexpected and amusing, so he'd stopped to watch. He hadn't anticipated her speaking to him, let alone imploring him to take up one of the other swords she'd brought with her, so that she could practice fighting with it.

Aerax could not help her. But he had not told her why, at first. Instead he'd given other reasons.

He had said that he only knew how to hunt and had no experience with swords. She had said they would learn together.

So he had said that surely there was someone in her family who would help her. She had said they did not support her intention of becoming a soldier, because her older brother already had taken that path. And they believed that she was so softhearted, it was best for her to become a healer, instead.

So he had said that a softhearted girl would be better off tending to the sick and injured instead of fighting. She had said that she wanted to become a soldier to prevent harm from ever coming to anybody, and she could not imagine anything more softhearted than using her own body to protect those she loved.

There she had defeated him. So he had finally confessed that his name was not written in the books, and that it was against Kothan law for her to even speak with him.

Only criminals' names were expunged from the books. So she'd looked at him warily then, grip tightening on her sword. Her eyes had narrowed, and she'd tilted her head, studying him.

"You are hardly older than I am," she'd said. "What have you done? Have you killed someone?"

Better if he had. That might have been forgivable. "I did not die when I should have."

He hadn't needed to explain. His white hair spoke for him, and she was clever enough to understand that he was the king's son, but his mother was not the queen. So if he had died at birth, it would have been more convenient for everyone.

But he hadn't. And never would he forget how her wariness had vanished, how she'd smiled and said that they were both what their parents did not wish them to be. Then she'd asked for his name.

Only once had he ever heard it spoken, when his mother had whispered it into his ear. Never had Aerax said it himself. Yet he did then, for he could not deny her.

"Aerax," she had repeated boldly—and smiled while again extending a sword to him. "Will you help me practice?"

Of course he would. From that moment, Aerax would have done *anything* for her. He would have ripped out his own heart for her.

And he had. Years later, to save her—he had.

Now she was here. Protecting the caravan, no doubt. For that was who Lizzan was. Who she would always be. The brightest, most beautiful jewel that Koth had ever produced, with the softest heart and the bravest soul. Aerax had not deserved the happiness of a single moment she'd spent with him, let alone the years she'd given, along with the joy of every kiss and every touch. And he did not deserve to see her again.

Yet as a prince, even a feral one, he often got what he didn't deserve.

CHAPTER 3

LIZZAN

S nake. They had chosen snake for supper.

With the heavy carcass of a tree boa slung around her shoulders, Lizzan trudged onto the road where the caravan had made camp. They had stopped early, and at a location less than ideal for an overnight stay—there was no easy distance to a stream and, instead of circling their caravan in a clearing, the long train of wagons and carts was vulnerable to anything that might come out of the jungle.

But they could have gone no farther. Less than a sprint away, a herd of helmeted onks sprawled across the road and foraged through the ferns on either side. The brightly plumed reptiles usually gave passing humans no mind, but more young were among them this time of year. Charging onks had been known to smash carts and wagons to pieces—and to crush the people in them.

Just as they crushed all else in their path . . . such as the head of a slow-crawling boa. So that instead of hunting a snake, Lizzan had merely found one, but the result was the same. She carried the boa to Mevida's camp, where she heaved it off her shoulders to flop over the side of the wagon, flattened head dripping. Hastily she averted her eyes from the creature. No snakes lived as far north as Koth, and although Lizzan admitted they were good for eating, she couldn't see them as anything other than a giant, squirming gutworm. So she would not look at it again until it was chunks in a stew.

A large pot already bubbled over the nearby fire. Many members of the caravan were gathering around, settling in for the night ahead—which Lizzan knew from experience would mean plenty of talking and laughing.

She looked for the one person who would not expect a conversation and saw the Krimathean at the tail of the caravan. She had barely taken a step in that direction when the old woman's voice stopped her.

"Warrior."

Lizzan paused. Carinea held out two mugs of palm wine.

"One for her, as well." She indicated the Krimathean with a tilt of her snow-white head.

So Lizzan had assumed. Still she joked, "I risked life and limb for your supper and they are not both for me?"

The old woman scoffed. "The snake is not *that* big."

Fair enough, as it had not been hunted, either. Grinning, Lizzan gratefully took the cups and carried them past the train of wagons. The sun was low in the sky, the shadows long, but there was still enough light to see by. The Krimathean was sitting on her furs and sharpening her sword, her gaze sweeping the road behind them—the only direction from which attack might easily come now. Any bandits on the road ahead would have to make their way through the onks or circle around through the jungle, and they could do neither quietly.

But that was not the only reason to wait here instead of near the head of the caravan. The humid air did not stir much, but a herd of onks soon made a foul wind of its own. Best to be as far from it as possible.

"May I join you?" Lizzan didn't wait for a reply before sitting. Her own bedroll and belongings were tucked away on

Mevida's wagon, but the ground would do for now. The woman gave a nod of thanks when Lizzan passed her the mug, and though she'd hoped to escape conversation, she still found herself asking curiously, "Can you not speak or is your silence a condition of the quest?"

The Krimathean responded with an arch of her eyebrows and a tilt of her head to indicate the latter. Forbidden by the goddess, then.

And Mevida had claimed she would soon head east. "Your quest takes you to Lith?"

A nod, eyes narrowing.

Lizzan knew that look, as sharp as the blade the woman carried. "But not to kill King Goranik."

The king of Lith, who had served the Destroyer and had killed this woman's own mother. Supposedly the king was already dead—an event that had stirred the unrest in that realm now, as his warlords fought over Lith's crown.

Lizzan was not so certain of his death, yet a shake of the Krimathean's head confirmed that was not the quest, anyway. And it would be impossible to guess what her quest truly was. The goddess Vela might have given her any number of tasks to complete, and the only certainty was that it would be painful and difficult . . . but with great reward.

The timing of her quest, then, was not hard to guess. "Do you think the Destroyer truly returns? Or is it merely rumor and panic again?"

The solemn nod said that he truly came.

A dreadful fist seemed to clutch around Lizzan's heart. Koth had been spared a generation past but might not be this time. And she would not be there to protect her mother, her brothers. "You asked Vela for help to defeat him?"

Gaze steady, the woman nodded again.

"The goddess will not simply *give* her help?"

The Krimathean was not allowed to talk but apparently was not forbidden to make any sound. A short, stony huff of laughter matched the hardening of her eyes. So she must be wondering, too, why Vela would not offer assistance without demanding something in return.

But a future queen might question a goddess. Lizzan would not. Instead she hoped the goddess *did* give this woman the power to defeat the Destroyer. For if he was stopped in Krimathe, never would he reach Koth.

And Lizzan would not need to return home to save her family. "Will Krimathe accept outsiders into their warriors' ranks?"

With a faint smile, the woman nodded.

"Even a warrior such as me?"

Expression more fierce now, as if rejecting the *such as me*, Krimathe's future queen nodded again.

Lizzan concealed the sudden tightness of her throat and burning of her eyes with a sip of sour wine. All would not be well. Still her family would bear the burden of her shame. Yet she could fight. And even from afar, she could protect the people she loved.

Even the one who'd never deserved her heart.

At the thought of him, she sipped more deeply—and too quickly. Better to make this last. Yet it seemed only an instant later that her mug was empty, and she was staring sightlessly down the road.

Until the nickering of the Krimathean's horse brought her to full attention again. The gelding lifted his head, nostrils flaring. He had caught a scent, then—yet the air was so stagnant, whatever the horse smelled could not be far distant.

The road's meandering path through the tangle of trees and ferns only allowed them to see to the next turn. Holding her breath, Lizzan listened. The jungle was so chaotically loud that the steady rhythm of one sound set it apart. Hoofbeats.

Riders, approaching fast. Lizzan's armor was on Mevida's wagon, but the speed of those hoofbeats told her she had no time to collect it.

She gripped her sword and began to rise even as the gelding loosed a rollicking whinny—and was answered by a trumpeting neigh.

The Krimathean shot to her feet, staring ahead. Her

mouth opened on a deep breath before she snapped her teeth shut again. As if she'd meant to call out, but stopped herself.

A horse galloped around the curve ahead. *Only* a horse. No rider.

The Krimathean made a sound deep in her chest—then sprinted down the road. Heart jolting, Lizzan followed for two paces before spinning back to mount the Krimathean's gelding instead. Racing after the woman was like chasing after a deer. Even her horse could not keep up.

Perhaps the horse ahead could. Never had Lizzan seen a stallion so fine. Breathtaking in strength and speed, his long and swift strides crossed the distance in a quarter of the time the gelding might have. Another of Hanan's descendants, then. For that insatiable god had fucked everything, not only ancient queens.

The Krimathean seemed to know the stallion. They met in what appeared to Lizzan an urgent dance. The Krimathean threw her arms around his neck before pulling back to look at him, concern etched into her face as she glanced down the road. The stallion snorted and pranced, tossing a heavy mane.

Two creatures who couldn't talk, but desperately trying to. Perhaps because the Krimathean knew who usually sat upon the Hanani stallion . . . and who wasn't sitting there now.

Lizzan reined the gelding to a halt. There were more hoof-beats approaching—a large number of them. But were they chasing the stallion or traveling with him?

"The ones who come behind you," she asked him. "Are they friend? Or are they foe?"

The stallion tilted his head to indicate the first, in the same way the Krimathean had when answering Lizzan earlier.

Friend. Tension easing, Lizzan slid from the gelding's back. The animal promptly trotted forward to greet the stallion, nickering in the familiar way of horses who have been companions.

Despite the stallion's reply, still the Krimathean's features were lined with worry and fear. It was not difficult to guess why. If anyone from home sought out Lizzan, surely the reason would not be to deliver good news.

That news would be delivered soon. But if it were Lizzan, she would rather be prepared for it.

"Is Krimathe under attack?" Lizzan asked, and the stallion shook his head. "Has any of her family fallen ill? Or died?"

Apparently not. As Lizzan couldn't imagine what else might send friends chasing after a woman on a quest, she had no more questions to ask. The Krimathean's concern finally eased, at least. She gave Lizzan a grateful look before turning to face the length of the road again.

More riders appeared. Krimathean warriors, by the look of their dark braids and armored chests.

Splashes of crimson drew her gaze past them. Not only Krimatheans. A dozen Parsatheans followed, most of whom wore nothing over their chests at all, and their legs were only covered by a skirt of red linens folded over a wide belt.

The Krimathean rider at the head shouted out a joyful "Laina!" before signaling to everyone behind her. They all drew their mounts to a halt while the first rode ahead. She was a tall woman, with broad shoulders. Like the other Krimathean soldiers, the only armor she wore was a cuirass of molded leather. Her heavily muscled legs were bare from midthigh to her boots, her linen breechcloth covered by strips of leather—likely in deference to the heat, for in the cooler, higher altitudes of Krimathe, most of their warriors wore leggings.

She leapt from her horse almost before it stopped, and the two Krimatheans embraced. "Look at your face. All is well, Laina, I promise you!" With a hearty laugh, she drew back. "Your cousin sent us after you. She said that although you trusted her to look after Krimathe while on your quest, this was a matter too grave and too important to decide without your knowing. So she asked Shim to find you."

The Hanani stallion—Shim. And the red-cloaked woman was called Laina.

"What is too important?" Lizzan asked.

The woman gave her an odd glance. Perhaps because Lizzan had just spoken for a queen who was not even *her* queen. But Lizzan had already begun with the horse, so she might as well continue now.

Then the woman's lips rounded and she turned to Laina again. "Ah! I have forgotten you cannot talk." She snorted. "Has it been difficult?"

A withering glare was Laina's answer.

"The path is never easy." The woman recited what was often said of quests, but with a snicker instead of solemnity. "And the matter of importance is an alliance with these southerners, who wish to unite *all* of the western realms and stand against the Destroyer."

Lizzan sucked in a breath. She had just spoken of that alliance with Mevida. But she also thought one in the north was impossible.

"Blackmoor has already joined. Your cousin did not want me to tell you so, because she didn't want to sway your decision. But *I* will attempt to sway it," the woman said with a faint grin that quickly turned grim. "Because if Vela abandons us again, your quest might be of little help. But more warriors will be. If we can trust them."

Laina frowned at her.

The woman sighed. "They have not given reason to *dis*-trust them. These Parsathean warriors seem honorable, as do the other southerners who travel with them. But all that we have ever heard of Parsatheans is that they are raiders and thieves. And it is hard not to look to the past."

When Lith had promised an alliance, too—and then betrayed them.

"The path is never easy," the woman said again. This time, without the jest.

Sheer frustration pulled at Laina's expression as she gazed down the road toward the Parsatheans. Not only because she couldn't speak, Lizzan imagined. But because she might risk her people with a decision hastily made in the middle of a road. Yet she couldn't abandon her quest and return to Krimathe, taking as much time as the weighty decision deserved.

A weightier decision than a mere soldier would ever make. So this time Lizzan was more circumspect when she broke in with, "If you will allow it, I have a suggestion."

Eyes narrowing, Laina studied her face for a long moment before nodding.

"I have known Parsatheans in my own trade. I have seen them guard a noble's caravan, and when finished with the job, seek out a rich merchant to raid. They are warriors who pride themselves on their honesty and never breaking an oath . . . yet also lament that the Parsatheans who still live on the Burning Plains have turned away from raiding in order to make allies of their neighbors." Lizzan spread her hands. "If the Parsatheans who seek an alliance now are the lamented ones from the Burning Plains, then they might be trusted. And for certain they will keep any vow they make."

Laina nodded thoughtfully. Likely wondering what sort of promise she could extract from them that would best suit Krimathe.

But Lizzan was not done. "At the speed the caravan travels, Oana lies only one or two days hence. Tell them that you will meet them there to discuss the alliance, instead, for the road is no place to do it. Suggest to them that they ride ahead and enjoy the baths, for you cannot abandon the caravan when bandits might attack it. If they stay to help you protect the caravan, how will they treat the people who travel with you at this slow pace? If they ride ahead to the bathhouses, seeking their own rest and pleasure, will they treat the servants and the sick with care? You will be a queen, and they need something from you, so they will present to you their prettiest manners. But more time will help you judge whether they truly care about the citizens of other realms, or if they only seek an alliance to save their own skins."

Laina and the other woman exchanged a glance, then seemed to come to quick and mutual agreement.

"I will tell them that," the woman said, lips pursing as she gave Lizzan another long look. "You know this road?"

"I have passed this way a few times."

"Where is your home?"

"I have no home." Lizzan's throat tightened, and she would not have said more. But if she wished to join this alliance of warriors, more should be said. "Or rather, home will not have me."

"Why?"

That answer was complicated . . . yet also very simple. "I did not die when I should have."

The woman abruptly grinned. "A trait most vexing to enemies, but a fine talent in an ally. I am Riasa. She is Laina, because if danger approaches and you try to call out all of her true names and titles, you'll be long dead before the warning is finished"—a huff of laughter met that statement—"and this is Shim the Magnificent, who would as soon kill a human as look at one. Unless you approach him with a brush and a carrot, then he will tolerate you for a very short time."

The big stallion's snort sounded like amused agreement.

Lizzan smiled but only said, "We are well met."

"So we are," Riasa said. "Now I will tell these southerners they can hie off to the baths or travel with the caravan. If there were not another party lagging behind that is also seeking an alliance and who must be told the same thing, I would hie off to the baths myself."

Laina frowned. Lizzan asked, "Another party?"

"Kothans, seeking help from Krimathe. They are asking us to send warriors north."

Lizzan's heart stopped. "It is true, then, that Koth has fallen?"

The shake of Riasa's head left Lizzan dizzy with relief. "They have only said that their own numbers are low, and they need help defending the island against bandits."

They. "Who travels in that party?"

"A few guards, two high councilors, and their snow-haired prince."

Aerax. Lizzan's gaze flew down the road. He was not with the Parsatheans. Already she knew that. Even in the midst of a snowstorm, her gaze would find him before seeing anything else. Yet he was coming. The situation in Koth must be desperate if they'd risked sending him. If he'd risked leaving the island.

Because he'd not even risked leaving with Lizzan.

Oh, and she was a fool. Such a fool. Because even now, she had a moment's dream that he'd come for her.

But she was not why he'd come. And she could not be here when he did.

"I must go," she said, her throat unbearably tight as she began backing away. "Forgive me. I meant to protect the caravan, but you have more help now and . . . I cannot stay."

Brow furrowing, Laina glanced at her, then down the road.

But there was nothing else for Lizzan to say. She only slowed to collect her belongings. Running away. Not long ago, she'd been exiled from her home, branded as a deserter and a coward by an entire realm.

This was the first time she'd ever felt like one.

CHAPTER 4

AERAX

It was full dark when they caught up to the southerners and the caravan. The faint glow of multiple fires ahead cast shadows down the road. Immediately Aerax's gaze began searching for Lizzan amid the train of wagons, but the night and the distance did not allow him to see much.

The Krimathean captain, Riasa, came to greet them as Aerax assisted Lady Junica to the ground. The councilor's face was pale with fatigue and pain—and Aerax did not think he was mistaken in her relief when Riasa said that the High Daughter intended to travel slowly with this caravan to Oana, and it was there she would meet with them.

"So you will not have to negotiate an alliance while lounging aboard a periwag," Aerax told Lady Junica.

Even her laugh was tired and pained, so he left her as soon as the Kothan guards set up her tent. Caeb had already disappeared into the jungle for his nightly hunt, while Aerax went on his own.

With the onk herd preventing the travelers from reaching a clearing, where all might gather together, camps were instead stretched out along the road. Silently Aerax made his way past them. At some fires, southerners mingled with travelers from the caravan, sharing stories and food. Others already slept. Still others were in their furs for more active reasons. He passed two Parsatheans fucking a man from the caravan—the male warrior working him from behind while the female warrior worked his front, all muffling groans with teeth set into skin.

Aerax averted his gaze, but still the sounds followed him. Again he imagined Lizzan where she was not, until warmth pooled thick and heavy in his groin.

Then his arousal was banished in a dazzling flash of pain when, for the first time, Aerax wondered if he might find Lizzan in her furs with someone else. Someone who would know the sweetness of her kiss and the heat of her touch.

He only wished her happy. He only wished her love.

Yet he could not bear seeing her with another.

But nowhere did Aerax find her, and despite the full moon, the shadows beneath the trees made the ground too dark to search for her tracks. Instead he made his way back along the camps, drawn by the sound of a familiar, booming laugh. He had heard it often since leaving Krimathe—it was from Riasa, and that laugh was one she deployed often.

She sat with two others at a fire near the end of the caravan. At Aerax's approach, she was in conversation with one, and so it was the third who stood and invited Aerax to sit with them—Tyzen, the Syssian prince who led the southerners. Like Aerax, the prince was marked by his ancestry. Not with snow-white hair, but with eyes that were almost as pale, like moonstones set against the bronze of his face.

Tyzen was also all that Kothans likely wished that Aerax was. A prince with manners fair and who had been taught his role from a young age, instead of a bastard suddenly thrust into a cage and who had lashed out at everyone around him.

And the boy was so cursed young. Only a hint of a whisker had grown on Aerax's chin when the weight of every life in Koth was placed on his shoulders—and barely had

Aerax held up beneath it. Tyzen had only just reached the age that Aerax had been then, and he bore the weight not of one realm, but *every* realm west of Temra's Ocean.

With the prince and Riasa was one of the two companions who were often at his side. The young monk was missing, but the Parsathean warrior was here. She was hardly more than a girl—and except for the blackness of her hair, she was nothing like Lizzan at the same age. Around everyone but Aerax, Lizzan had been regimented in her appearance and precise in her behavior, and this girl seemed only a few steps away from possessing claws and fangs. More like Aerax had been.

Yet it was Lizzan's daring manner and bold amusement he saw in this warrior's dark gaze as she asked the Krimathean captain, "What would it take to lure Shim away from Queen Mala?"

Riasa scoffed. "That horse will never abandon the queen."

The girl was not thwarted. "How did she first persuade Shim to let her ride him?"

"She never asked it of him," Riasa said. "It was he who first urged her onto his back to save her life. She'd been stung by a river serpent, and he could carry her to a healer faster than her own mount could."

When the Parsathean warrior's eyes narrowed thoughtfully, Tyzen grinned. "Now Seri considers poisoning herself."

Riasa's deep laugh rolled out. "I advise against it, young one. Shim would leave you to die."

The young warrior scowled.

The captain raised dark eyebrows at Aerax, who had not taken the invitation to sit but still stood across the fire from her. "Have you escaped your minders, then?"

The other Kothans, who hovered around Aerax whenever he approached anyone not from their realm. Most outsiders saw their constant attention as protection for a royal, or assumed that he surrounded himself with courtiers who were always prepared to serve him. Instead Lady Junica and Degg made certain his vulgar manner did not offend those whose alliance they would rely upon. They would not risk putting Koth's fate in the hands of a savage bastard who had no one to love but a cat.

Since the Syssian prince sat at this fire, Aerax would not remain unattended for long. So he couldn't be subtle. "Does Lizzan protect the caravan?"

Riasa's brows drew together. "Lizzan?"

Of course she would not say her name. "A woman with black hair and of this height." Aerax measured on level with his chin. "One of the finest warriors ever seen, fierce when protecting anyone weaker than she. You might know her by the way she never fully smiles without beginning to laugh, or how she will say so much with her eyes that are the blue of a mountain lake, or that she favors her left hand when she uses her sword."

Recognition lit the captain's expression. "And a scar?"

"Likely a scar," Aerax confirmed. From an injury he had never seen healed.

"She was here," Riasa said, stirring the fire with a stick before lifting her gaze to his. "Then ran when we told her Koth's prince came."

Pain slashed through him, the hot agony of a gut wound. She had run from him. But Lizzan did not run from anything. She had stood her ground against wraiths and lies.

Yet she had run from *him*.

It was as if he'd stepped through a mist and into a hazy world that made no sense. As if in a fog, he looked to the others at the fire, the boy prince and the girl warrior. They watched him with such steady and sympathetic eyes that he did not know who they saw. Not a huntsman or even a feral prince, but a man utterly lost.

"Should we have detained her?" Riasa asked.

Like a criminal? His voice was a painful rasp when he told her, "Lizzan has done nothing wrong."

Slowly the woman nodded. "She claimed that she was unwelcome at home because she did not die when she was supposed to."

At the mere thought of her death, new agony wrenched through his heart and he shook his head. "She only spoke a truth that no one wanted to hear. She is Koth's shining jewel and was tossed into the mud."

"Now you are searching for her?" Riasa asked quietly.

"I doubt she would want me to." He'd done the tossing. Yet he needed to know: "Was she well?"

"She seemed well. From what she said of her trade, I gathered that she often provides escort to travelers."

Protecting them. Of course she would.

And she was well. Relief began to clear the fog that had smothered his mind, and he saw that Degg was on the approach.

"I thank you," he told the captain and, with a nod to both the moonstone-eyed prince and his warrior companion, took his leave.

Heart heavy, he made his way to the Kothan camp. He had barely laid out his bedroll when a rustle through the nearby leaves told him Caeb returned from his foray into the jungle. The cat nudged Aerax's shoulder before yawning, his curved fangs as long as Aerax's forearm. Making room for the cat, he shifted aside—then frowned when Caeb began to bat at the small leather pouch that hung around Aerax's neck with a paw as big as Aerax's head.

Aerax pushed the paw aside. "It is time for sleeping."

Caeb snarled.

Cursed cat. Throat tightening as it always did when he untied the knot closing the pouch, Aerax withdrew the braid that lay coiled inside. All who joined Kothan's army shaved the sides of their heads, then made braids of the shorn locks to give to their loved ones. So Lizzan had given this to Aerax, that he might always have something of her while she attended to her duties. After all these years, none of Lizzan's rosemary scent could he still detect on the black plait—but the cat must, because Caeb often made him take it out for him to sniff.

This time, Caeb's mouth gently closed around Aerax's entire hand and he tugged him forward.

The tightness in his throat became a raw burn. "We cannot go after her."

Caeb released his hand and snarled again.

"She does not want me to go after her," he said thickly. "She ran from me."

As if the cat intended to leave him, too, Caeb turned his back to Aerax and lashed his face with his tail.

"Lie down, you fool," Aerax told him, his chest aching, and the cat finally did—a white mountain made of fangs and fur at his side. Aerax tucked the braid away and lay back, scratching Caeb's ruff. And the cat's loud, rumbling purr concealed his next quiet words from all but Caeb. "Recall to me why we cannot abandon Koth and go after her?"

Yet the cat was not one to ask. He cared as little for Koth as Aerax did.

And it would be so easy to do as Caeb wanted. To follow Lizzan. Until she forgave him. Aerax had hurt her when he'd refused to leave Koth after her exile—and perhaps she hated him for it—but what he'd done might be forgiven.

What he soon must do could not be, because it would destroy everything Lizzan had fought so hard to protect.

So there was his reminder. The reason why he could not go after her. What he must do. One day, she would hear of it, and be grateful the world had gotten in the way of everything that she and Aerax might have been. So it was best that she ran away.

Before she hated him completely.

CHAPTER 5

LIZZAN

Lizzan did not make her bed until dawn, and rose not much later from a short and restless sleep. Head throbbing, she picked her way through the dense clusters of ferns until she was almost upon the Angot river. The ferry docking lay directly ahead—but the boat itself was anchored across the river. No one could she see on the other side.

So she might be here until midday . . . or until five days hence. With a party of Kothans close behind.

With Aerax close behind.

She would *not* be trapped like a rabbit caught in a snare until he arrived. She would swim the cursed river first.

Yet surely it would not be long before someone used the ferry—unless rumors of bandits had made travelers too fearful of taking this road without protection. If that were so, then she might soon find a job in Oana.

At the river, only one other traveler waited on the limestone shelf that formed a natural docking for the ferry boat. A woman sat with feet dangling in the water, a patchwork blanket around her shoulders and a fraying, homespun bag near her hip. Her eyes were closed and her face tilted toward the slanted rays of the early-morning sun, and the light picked out both copper and silver threads in her dark hair.

Deliberately Lizzan scuffed her boots against the ground, alerting the woman to her presence. The woman glanced back with the unconcerned manner of someone accustomed to traveling alone—or of someone who wasn't truly alone.

It *would* be a fine place for an ambush. What better time to attack than when travelers were congregated at the edge of a river with nowhere to run?

But if this woman were a bandit, most likely she would be seeking to distract Lizzan now. Instead she turned her attention from Lizzan and reached down to tug at a line.

Fishing. Well, then. Lizzan would happily join her.

She settled onto the shelf with an arm's length between them but didn't dangle her feet over the edge. It was said that no large reptiles hunted this stretch of the river because the current flowed too swiftly. Yet Lizzan wouldn't test that claim. Fishing, she enjoyed—but she preferred not to be bait.

"What do you use for a lure?" Lizzan asked. "Your toes?"

The woman's lips twitched. "The bottoms of my feet are so hard and thick that a fish could not tell the difference between my toes and the stone we sit upon. I used a grub."

With apparently no luck. "I have with me a hard cheese with a strong smell."

"We will try that, then."

While the fisherwoman drew up her line, Lizzan laid out half of the provisions that Mevida had shoved into her hands as she'd fled. If both fish and ferry failed to show, there was plenty for a midday meal—and the caravan would catch up to them long before their stomachs began crying for supper. Lizzan's thirst and aching head would not be eased so quickly. She ought to have filled her flask from one of Mevida's casks, as well. Knowing that Aerax was not far behind, never had she wanted a drink so badly.

With a word of thanks, the fisherwoman accepted her

share of their breakfast. Lizzan could not judge the woman's age. Her skin was as leather and deeply lined, as if she were a full generation older than the sparse silver in her hair suggested. "Have you been waiting long for the ferry?"

"I have no intention of crossing." She threaded the cheese onto the bone hook. "Instead I will wait here until I am dead. Which will be soon enough."

Lizzan grinned. Such a very fine companion this woman must be. Little wonder she traveled alone.

"Do you fear the ferry's lines will not hold? I assure you they are stronger than they appear." Lizzan gestured to the thin rope stretching from riverbank to riverbank, anchored on each side by a stone column depicting one of Nemek's two faces. "It is said that Nemek wove their hair into an unbreakable chain."

"It is also said the Destroyer returns."

Ah. "So he is."

"And so we will all soon be killed. Or violated again and left to bear that pain. Or see our children enslaved in his armies." She glanced at Lizzan's face. "You are too young to have known how it was."

That was truth. Lizzan had been born five summers after the Destroyer had razed Krimathe and continued west.

Yet she was here now. "A great alliance is forming to stand against him. On this very road come warriors from the south seeking to unite the western realms, so we might all fight together."

The woman seemed to contemplate that news. Finally a smile touched her lips. "That is a fine thing."

"It is."

"Then you will fight. I cannot." With a sigh, the fisherwoman lowered her hook into the water again. "My son was but four years old when he was taken. Now I would not recognize his face. How could I raise a sword against anyone in that army when I might cut down my own boy?"

Sympathy clutched at Lizzan's throat. "I don't know."

"I don't, either. So it is best that the young lead this fight. The rest of us might lose heart."

And perhaps that was why the Destroyer took the children. Not just to bolster his numbers but to weaken resistance before he even returned.

But he was not here yet. And might never be, if the alliance stood against him. "Where do you hail from?"

"Oana." The woman gestured to the other side of the river.

And she didn't intend to cross? But perhaps she would not need to. Everyone who traveled to Oana from the west would have to pass by her.

"Do you think that your son still remembers this place? If he escapes the Destroyer's army—or if the Destroyer is killed and his armies are freed—will he know where to return home?"

"Home?" Disbelief filled the woman's huff of laughter. "What home would he find here? What home would *any* of the Destroyer's soldiers find? After what they have done?"

"It isn't known whether they have a choice."

"That is true. But what does it matter? Whether they were taught to believe that slaughtering and violating so many is justified—or whether forced by the Destroyer's sorcery— who would trust them now? Even if his own soldiers rebel and kill the Destroyer themselves, who would welcome any of his ranks into their villages?"

But there must be one place they would be welcome. "If your son returned, would you not take him in?"

"I would."

"Do you think others who lost their children would not?"

"They would." A wry smile curved the woman's mouth. "And their own child might be forgiven. *That* child might have been forced. But everyone else's child? No pardon will be made. The only others who will be forgiven are the ones who didn't live to return home. For that is the way of people. They will claim their loved ones are an exception and deserve forgiveness. But anyone else will be cursed as a villain—and a villain's only redemption is death."

Lizzan only had to look to her own experience to know that for its truth. To remember how her mother and brothers had held her so tight, though their own husband and father was dead and Lizzan had been named the reason. To remember how she'd fled Koth with spit on her face and stones hurled at her back. To remember how they'd shouted after her the names of her soldiers who'd fallen, and how she hadn't deserved to be the one who survived.

Lizzan agreed with the last.

Quietly she said, "When the Destroyer is killed, there will be many with nowhere to go."

"The inns will be crowded," the fisherwoman agreed. For it was Vela's law that no innkeeper could turn away someone with a coin to pay, even if all they had was a copper smidge. A spot must be found for them—though Lizzan knew well that spot was often in the stable. Since leaving Koth, she'd made more friends with horses than people. "But perhaps my son will return, if only to see justice done. To him, I must be the villain."

Lizzan frowned. "How could he think so?"

"How could he not? He was so small and so afraid when they took him—yet trusting that I would save him. How many times did I say that I loved him? And I was the one to shelter him, to feed him, to protect him. What child would not believe that his mother would come for him?" Closing her eyes, the woman tilted her face to the sun again. The soft morning light gentled the harshest of lines in her skin but did not conceal the pained tightening of her lips. "And how long before his thoughts of me turned bitter, before his love became hate? Before he became grateful to the Destroyer for providing food and shelter and purpose? Before he believed a parent's love is a lie, and that the Destroyer's army freed children from that lie? Because he couldn't know that I searched for him."

"Did you?" Lizzan asked quietly.

"From almost the very moment he was taken." As if to delay speaking more, the fisherwoman took a bite of bread; but only a crumb, perhaps fearing she couldn't swallow a mouthful. "His armies left us bleeding in the mud with our legs spread. Mothers, fathers—though they killed most of the men after using them. But there were so many of us who immediately began to follow. My husband was dead, my home burned, my sisters . . ." Her voice faltered. "And they had taken my son. What else was left but following?"

Lizzan had no answer. She shook her head.

"Many were in a daze as we walked. Not eating, not sleeping. And those who could sleep were always awakened by the others screaming. Most died that first winter. We hadn't taken provisions. We simply followed." Her throat worked, and she looked down to tug on the line. "The Destroyer reached the sunset shore in five years. It took me seven—and by then, I was the only one of our group left. Though I have met other groups of followers since."

Chest swollen with emotion, Lizzan asked, "You followed your son to the edge of the continent?"

The woman nodded. "And farther. Though not as quickly as I wished. The Destroyer leveled a forest to build the ships that carried his army across the western ocean, and had also taken possession of every boat there already was. But eventually I found passage and began following them west again. I followed until I reached the eastern shore of Temra's Heart."

The ocean at the center of the world. Now she was here, not far from the western shore of Temra's Heart, and Lizzan was breathless with the realization. "You walked around the world? You must have seen so much."

"In the Destroyer's wake?" The woman shook her head. "There were only piles of rotting corpses."

"But you didn't follow when he marched east again?" Back the way he'd come.

"When I reached Temra's Heart, already I was years behind him. And when I learned that he had not sailed across the ocean but turned south along the coast, I thought he meant to return to the western realms by marching over the Bone Fields at the bottom of Temra's Heart. And I had been fortunate in my travels until then, but knew I would not survive through Farian lands."

The savages that plagued the far southern realms. "I

wish the Destroyer had taken that route. Perhaps they'd have eaten him."

"Or perhaps he would have enslaved them to his purpose, and they would soon be eating us, instead."

That seemed more likely. "You didn't know that he'd circled back east?"

Shaking her head, the fisherwoman finished her last bite of bread, then reached down to rinse her fingers in the river. "I crossed Temra's Heart, hoping to finally get ahead of him, and returned to the western realms near to the same spot where he landed with his army a generation past, at the far edge of the Burning Plains. All those ships still lie upon the sands, rotting."

"If that was where you landed, you must have seen the monoliths of Par." Giant structures said to be built by the gods themselves. Not even the corpses left in the Destroyer's wake could be piled high enough to obscure them.

"Only from a distance. That place is besieged by wraiths. But the monoliths are . . ." She tilted her head back, looking up, perhaps remembering their unimaginable height. "Extraordinary. If only because they were one of the few things he didn't destroy. Or couldn't destroy."

"I like to think he could not."

"As do I." A quick smile touched her mouth. "From there I walked toward the Boiling Sea . . . all the while, waiting to hear of the Destroyer's approach from the south. Yet that word never came, and I realized he'd not taken the route through the Bone Fields but intended to sail back across the western ocean, instead. I began walking north, so that if my son *did* return, I might meet him." She huffed out a soft laugh. "I hadn't heard that Stranik's Passage was open."

And she must have taken the long way around the flaming mountains, through the western passes. A two-year journey that was. Longer, if on foot.

Lizzan's throat felt thick, for beside her sat another marvel that the Destroyer hadn't been able to destroy. "*You* are extraordinary."

"I am *tired*," the woman said, then gave another quiet laugh. "But now I will have my rest. Nothing is left to do but to sit here and wait for the end."

For the Destroyer's return—or her son's. "That might be several years hence. If you stay here, how will you fend for yourself until then?"

"For nearly a full turn of the moon, I have been here." She gestured to the fishing line. "Always the river provides."

Perhaps it could provide more. "Become the ferrymaster," Lizzan suggested. "Then no one will ever have to wait for the boat—and you could earn bread or coin in trade."

"So that it might be stolen from me?" Shaking her head, the woman said, "I fare well enough under Vela's protection."

"Does that goddess protect you?"

"I believe she must. When I first began following, I had thoughts of taking the red cloak if I might have the reward of seeing my son again. But all of her temples had been razed, and her oracles and priestesses killed, so never could I ask for a quest. Yet I believe she still heard my prayers. Vela protects those who quest for her on their journey, and I have been hungry, cold, afraid . . . yet never suffered again as I did at the hands of the Destroyer's army. So I also believe that I will have my reward and see my son again. Even if it is only after silver-fingered Rani carries us both into the mercy of Temra's arms—or when my son sees me here so near to my home, as if I'd never left to search for him, and he strikes me down as the villain who abandoned him."

"You are no villain," said Lizzan fiercely. "And I will make certain your son knows it. At every village and tavern I will tell the story of a woman waiting by a river. By the time the Destroyer arrives, so many will have heard and retold your tale that it will reach your son's ears. What name does he know you by, so that he will stop to listen?"

Both laughter and moisture gleamed in the woman's eyes. "He would only know me by 'Mother.'"

"Oh." That name was not so unusual. "What is his?"

"Ilris."

"So it will be, then. Everywhere I go, I will tell the story of Ilris's mother. Word will spread, for I am always upon the road." Lizzan gave her a wry look before adding, "And I frequent many taverns."

The woman huffed a quiet laugh before wiping her eyes. "I do not know if Ilris will hear, but I thank you for your kindness." Her gaze slipped over Lizzan's face, a frown creasing her brow. "Why are you always upon the road? You are not returning home to Koth? I assumed you head there now."

"How do you know I am from Koth?"

"Your hair is a Kothan soldier's—very long at the crown, shaved on the sides—though grown out. How much time has passed since the sides were last cut?"

"Two winters," Lizzan said thickly. She could now tuck those hairs behind her ears. But she could not trim it all to a matching length. She needed the long strands to cover her scars.

"And your mail tunic. Koth's emblem is gone, but in all my travels, I have rarely seen any armor as fine as Kothan mail." Her eyes closed. "And I will never forget the first time I saw it—after the Destroyer had passed through this land, and your Kothan soldiers rode out from their island in their shining armor that had not seen a single battle. They came upon our group of followers and asked if we needed help. Some of us screamed at their captain that the time to help had been when the Destroyer was here, but instead of fighting, the Kothans had hidden away in their crystal palace and let their god protect them."

That was truth, and it wasn't. The Kothans hadn't known the Destroyer would spare their island, so they had shored up their defenses and prepared for a siege—just as every other realm had. But it was also true that Kothan soldiers had not ventured out until the Destroyer had left the western realms.

Lizzan's father had been one of those soldiers. And he had described to her the destruction he'd seen, and the guilt and relief he'd known that Koth was spared when no one else was. But by the time Lizzan was old enough to hear his tale, most of Koth seemed racked by neither guilt nor relief. Instead many believed that it was proof of the god Varrin's strength and Koth's superiority.

"What was the captain's response?"

The woman's face hardened. "That if we'd had the sense to walk north and seek Koth's protection before the Destroyer had come, we would not be walking in search of our children afterward. So *never* will I forget that shining mail."

Lizzan's face burned. Apparently not all of Kothan's soldiers had known guilt and relief, only superiority. "I am sorry that was said to you. It was cruel."

"It was not you. And your armor does not shine so bright." Her gaze slipped over Lizzan's scarred features. "You fought."

"And lost."

The woman laughed suddenly. "As we all have. So what is your story, that I might pass it on to all who travel through here?"

"It's not a tale worth repeating. I led my soldiers into a battle that we should have won, and they were slaughtered." And the river seemed so very loud, almost loud enough to drown her voice, for her words sounded so weak and watery. "But I alone survived. So I was named a coward, my family was shamed, and I was exiled from the realm."

"You are right," the woman said. "That is not a tale worth repeating."

It was not. Lizzan's throat ached and burned, but the water in her flask did nothing to ease the hot constriction.

"Do you know," said the woman, gesturing to the statues that stood on either side of the river, "the rope between them has never unraveled or broken, though the boat has been replaced many times. And over generations, as the faces wear away by wind and rain, they've been recarved into the stone."

"You think the rope is truly made from Nemek's hair, then?"

She shrugged. "Who can know? But it is said that Oana's baths are blessed by Nemek the Healer. Anyone who crosses the river in that direction is greeted by Nemek's young and beautiful face, so the traveler will know that healing lies ahead. In the opposite direction, as you enter the jungle filled with disease and wounds that fester, you see the withered and distorted face. But I have been to Nemek's birthplace. I have seen where Mother Temra erupted them into the world with two faces: the healer and the disease. And there I learned that everything I believed about Nemek was wrong. These statues are wrong. In truth, that aged face belongs to the healer."

"That cannot be." It was contrary to everything Lizzan had ever heard.

"It is truth. For who better knows the value of healing than someone who has been sick or wounded or old? And what is more unthinkingly cruel than disease—or someone who is young and beautiful and has never known pain? Perhaps when those statues were first carved, the faces were correct. But over time, as people began to say that Nemek's beautiful face was the healer, as that story was told again and again and as the statues' features withered away, the wrong faces were carved into them—and it became a truth set in stone."

Lizzan glanced from one statue to the other, trying to believe it. "Truly?"

"Truly. And that is why I will not repeat the story you just told me," she said. "Because I suspect it is not *your* story, but the story that was told about you. And I will not recarve your face."

"It has already been carved enough," Lizzan agreed with a laugh, though her eyes were burning. "And my story is also not worth retelling."

"Then is it worth hearing? Because I have little else to do now. And neither, it appears, do you."

Lizzan *did* have much to do. She needed to find a way to cross the river—though the rope between the statues had given her an idea. Perhaps a foolish one, if she fell into the river while wearing chain mail and burdened by all of her belongings.

But no need to rush. The caravan moved slowly. The ferry might still arrive before Aerax did.

And that, Lizzan supposed, was the place to start. "There is a prince—"

"Of course there is!" The fisherwoman cackled. "A handsome one?"

Unable to stop her own laugh, Lizzan nodded. "He is very fine to look upon."

"I knew this would be the better story." The woman checked her line before settling in again. "Is he a villain?"

"He is." Lizzan's grin faded. "Though perhaps only in my telling of it. And he did not start off that way."

"Then how did it start?"

CHAPTER 6

AERAX

With his task of finding the High Daughter finished, the Hanani stallion returned to Krimathe at dawn—and took all of the Parsathean mares with him.

Aerax woke to the sound of galloping hoofbeats and shouts from the warriors, yet the mood at the other camp seemed no darker for having half of their mounts stolen. Instead Aerax saw smiles and laughter as the southerners gathered their things and sorted out who would be riding and who would be walking.

Or riding double. Aerax had just finished saddling his own horse when Tyzen joined him. The young monk, who was more slightly built than either the prince or the Parsathean girl, was seated behind him. Seri was on foot.

And it was apparently she who had prompted them to seek out Aerax. Her eyes shone brightly as she asked, "Does Caeb let anyone ride him?"

"He does not."

"Has anyone ever tried?"

"Once." He could still picture Lizzan giggling wildly and clinging to Caeb's thick ruff while he sped across the snow. "She said sitting on Caeb was akin to straddling a log in water. Every movement would threaten to tip her off balance."

Tyzen grinned. "That will not put Seri off. She believes that she can ride anything."

"Parsathean warriors *ought* to be able to ride anything," she retorted. "We are as silver-fingered Rani. And a long-toothed cat seems more like a dragon than a horse is."

Silver-fingered Rani, the goddess who flew upon her dragon to deliver the souls of the dead into Mother Temra's arms. If Parsathean warriors were as Rani, then they were as near to the goddess as Aerax had ever been.

He mounted his horse, then held out his hand. "If you will settle for a mere Kothan steed, you can share my saddle."

Seri's wide smile appeared. As if in deference to his outstretched hand, she touched his fingers but needed no help to mount the tall horse. Nimbly she sprang up behind him, the red linens belted around her waist flaring out before draping over her legs. She did not grip his waist or his shoulders to steady her balance, and so lightly she sat that Aerax could hardly feel her presence.

"I like your Kothan breeds," she told him. "They are not as big as ours, but they are hardy and surefooted."

"So they are," he agreed. "And you do not seem upset that your mount has been stolen."

She gave a merry laugh, and it was the young monk who answered wryly, "The Parsatheans have been parading their mares in front of Shim since we left Krimathe."

"By the time we return south and retrieve them from his herd, they will all be heavy with his foals," she said. "And we will find other mounts that are suited to the cold climes in the villages ahead."

So the Parsatheans had not anticipated that Shim would steal their horses, but the outcome was exactly as they'd hoped. And the satisfied glance Tyzen gave to Seri made

Aerax wonder if his offer to let her ride with him was another hoped-for outcome.

He had the suspicion that these three young southerners were protecting him. It was an absurd thought, as Aerax was half again their age—also half again Tyzen's weight, a head taller than Seri, and was already protected by a cat that could tear apart a mammoth.

A cat that was uncertain about Aerax's new protectors, too. Caeb prowled up alongside his mount, his disdainful gaze on Seri before he rubbed his big head against Aerax's thigh. Only after Aerax scratched the cat's ears did Caeb continue forward, using Aerax's calf to massage the full length of his body, pressing so hard that his horse had to shift his stance to remain in place and leaving a covering of white fur on Aerax's leather boot.

Seri chuckled. "Is he telling me or telling the horse who you belong to?"

Likely both. Yet Aerax did not answer. A mounted Riasa approached them at a trot, tipping her head to indicate farther down the road. "The High Daughter requests that Prince Aerax and Prince Tyzen ride with her."

At the head of the caravan. Aerax spared a glance at Lady Junica, who was already in her litter, and Degg, who was scrambling onto his own mount, before following the captain. The travelers in the caravan watched them pass, eyes curious—and widening when they caught sight of Caeb.

Aerax's own eyes began to water as they caught up to the red-cloaked warrior. Before dawn, the herd of onks had continued on, leaving a swath of trampled ferns in their wake—along with piles of steaming dung and pools of rancid piss. He heard Seri's snort of a giggle, and then she pulled up the outer length of linen that hung from her belt. To cover her face, he realized when the young monk behind Tyzen did the same with the skirt of his robe.

Choking on laughter—or the stench—the Syssian prince caught Aerax's eyes. "This will be a fine part of the songs they will eventually sing of the Destroyer's defeat—the tale of an alliance struck amid onk shart."

Aerax only hoped that there would not be a verse about a giant cat rolling in it. Or about a bastard prince who knew not how to properly address the High Daughter of Krimathe.

But it mattered little if he did. No one possessed a lofty rank while wading through dung. Inclining his head, Aerax greeted her with a simple "My lady."

Holding the hood of her red cloak across the bottom half of her face, she nodded in return, then again in response to Tyzen's greeting before pointing down the road.

Aerax took the lead, guiding his horse between the pools of urine while they followed behind one at a time, spaced far enough apart so they would not catch anything flung from a hoof. His gaze remained on Caeb, who stopped to curiously sniff at a few piles but did nothing that required a bath.

Once beyond the night mud, they stopped to wait for the others. Raucous calls came from the ferns and trees, the jungle waking as the sun slowly rose. It wasn't yet high enough to glare down at them, but already the air was warmer, dew rising as vapor above the canopy.

Aerax's gaze scanned the ground, searching for a sign that Lizzan had come this way. There was nothing, but that was not unexpected. If she knew he was behind her—running from him—she might make her way through the jungle instead of along the road.

He glanced back. Riders were approaching through the night mud—Riasa and the Krimathean soldiers who'd accompanied her, Lady Junica and Degg, and a handful of mounted Parsathean warriors. The Kothan escort was followed by the caravan. Few among them seemed to be walking, and the noise through the jungle told him that the Parsatheans and travelers on foot had opted to go around the mess on the road.

To reach them first were the two warriors who led the other Parsatheans, and who served as Tyzen's guard—Kelir and Ardyl. People of the north were taller than those in

Krimathe and nearby realms, yet these riders of the Burning Plains were taller still. Most of the male warriors in their company were of a size with Aerax, and he was considered a large man among his own people. But he was not a large man next to Kelir.

Like Seri, their black hair was drawn back in multiple braids, and they only wore boots and red linens folded over a belt—though Ardyl had also bound her breasts, and silver piercings decorated her ears and eyebrows. At the Krimathean palace, their warriors' dress had appeared more elaborate—with armor bound in reptilian leather, their foreheads painted black, and wearing silver claws that rivaled Caeb's. Yet not until this moment, recalling how Seri said Parsatheans were as silver-fingered Rani, did Aerax realize how they resembled descriptions of that goddess.

Always before he'd seen Lizzan in them. She was nothing like them. Yet still these Parsatheans reminded Aerax of her, in brief clear impressions that faded too quickly.

Sweet and painful those moments were. To glimpse Kelir's quick grin and also to remember hers. To see the scars that raked down the side of the warrior's face—and to recall the slashes carving through Lizzan's. Red and angry they'd been when Aerax had last spoken to her, scabs newly forming. The injury must be fully healed now, though the marks left would not be as old and as white as the Parsathean's. Still Aerax saw those scars and saw Lizzan.

Just as he did when he looked at Ardyl, a woman who burned with a ferocity tempered by humor and pride. In Seri he saw the girl Lizzan had been, but in Ardyl he saw someone similar to the woman she'd become—and of a size she and Lizzan were, tall and lean. Nothing they looked alike. Ardyl had brown eyes instead of blue, features that were square instead of angular, and a smaller nose, and her chin did not possess the stubborn jut that had driven Aerax to madness time and again. Yet the way the Parsathean moved with deliberate purpose, with shoulders back and head high, with a look of utter confidence always in her gaze . . . that was Lizzan, too.

Every time he saw her in them, so quickly she vanished again. As if she haunted him. Yet she was no ghost.

Instead she was flesh and blood—and she had run from him.

Seri poked Aerax's armored ribs. "What has Caeb caught scent of?"

The big cat had been prowling ahead of them at a leisurely, meandering pace, investigating the jungle on either side of the road. Now his head was up, and he loped down the road in a direct path. Not hunting, for he was not moving stealthily enough for that, but with clear purpose.

The red-cloaked Krimathean watched him, too, her brow furrowed. She glanced over at Aerax when Riasa said, "Bandits plague this stretch of road."

Aerax frowned. "Caeb!"

The cat ignored him. Idiot beast. When Caeb hunted within the jungle, the foliage offered him cover and protection. Yet on the road he had neither, and Aerax did not know what would be more valuable to bandits—the silver of his harness or the white of his fur.

But Aerax knew exactly what the cat was after. He didn't know if Caeb would catch her, but if the cat did, Aerax would be right behind. Because if anyone traveling this road was in danger from bandits, then Lizzan was, too.

"I must follow him. Do you stay or do you ride with me?" he asked the girl, who looked over at Tyzen and back at the other Parsatheans before answering.

"We ride with you," she said.

CHAPTER 7

LIZZAN

How had her story with Aerax begun? Of late, Lizzan had not thought of the beginning much. Only of how it had ended.

Suddenly she was desperate for a drink. Anything to dull the razor's edge of remembering all that was lost as she told the fisherwoman, "It began with the two of us becoming the finest of friends—though we wanted to be more than friends. Wanted so badly. But my parents warned us it would only end in hurt."

"Because of his rank?" the fisherwoman asked.

"Because he had no rank. Nor even a name. He was a bastard born without acknowledgment—and he *hated* Koth." He hated everything his father was, and how the law allowed a person to be treated as nothing, for no other reason than by accident of his birth. "He stayed only for his mother. But always he planned to leave. And me . . . for as long as I could remember, my only wish was to become a soldier and protect the people of the realm. So when he asked me to go with him, I told him it was my duty to stay—and then

I tried, so very hard, not to love him as anything more than a friend. And he tried the same. So that when the time came for him to leave, it would not hurt so much."

"But it did?"

"Oh, it did." Lizzan laughed at the memory of how tormented she'd been . . . and how young she'd been. "So much. And even as I was packing my things to leave with him, he decided to stay—though it would still not be easy. His name was not written in the books. If it was discovered how close we were, I would have been expelled from the army. But there was talk among the nobles and councilors of doing away with the books, so we thought . . . maybe soon, all would be fine. So we pledged ourselves to each other. Yet not even a tennight passed before the red fever came and killed near to half of those living on the island."

"You lost him?" the fisherwoman asked gently.

"Not to the fever." Though Aerax had lost his mother. And Lizzan had lost her mother's parents, healers who'd tended to those stricken with the disease and succumbed to it themselves. "Nearly every member of the royal house was dead—the king and all his heirs, and so many others. All that remained were the king's brother, the brother's young daughter . . . and Aerax. You have heard of Koth's snow-haired kings?"

The woman nodded. "That they are descendants of the man-god, Varrin."

"They are. And legend is that Koth will sink if none of his heirs stands on the island. So the king never leaves Koth until he takes the King's Walk at the end of his life. And always, *always*, there is someone of at least a queen's age ready to step into the role. Aerax was barely more than half that age, yet they had little other option. The princess had not even seen three winters yet. So they wrote Aerax's name in the books and he began his lessons about how to be a Kothan prince."

"And now his rank stood between you?"

"Not truly." Not an insurmountable obstacle. "I could rise through the army's ranks, become a part of the high command—as my father was. It would only take time and effort, and was no different from what I'd always intended to do. And the way the red fever had torn through the soldiers' barracks . . . it was said the Destroyer had come at last. So there was no shortage of work." She had passed a full winter simply clearing houses of bodies. "And that was the true obstacle—how much work there was to do. I bore the duties of two or three soldiers, so it was near summer before I met with Aerax again. But . . . all had changed. *He* had changed."

"How so?"

Chest aching, Lizzan lifted her shoulders in a helpless shrug. She did not know. She *still* did not know. "There was . . . a distance between us. Never before had there been. And he seemed so very troubled. But when I asked what I could do to ease whatever he suffered, he said there were royal secrets to keep and he now bore burdens that I wouldn't understand."

The fisherwoman sucked in a breath through her teeth. "And you did not slice him open there?"

Though it hurt, Lizzan laughed. "I forgave him. I thought it was grief for his mother and his resentment at being trapped in a role that he'd always despised."

"But it wasn't?"

Again Lizzan gave a helpless shrug. "He never told me—and I had little time to dwell on it. There was so much to do. Marauders plagued the forests beyond the lake, there were tales of howling terrors and bramble beasts, and it seemed that my soldiers and I were always chasing after enemies that simply disappeared. And the number of soldiers we had was still so few. Dangerously few. But I still did not think that . . ."

"You would lose?" the woman said when Lizzan's voice faltered.

"None of us believed so. There were but fifty bandits who threatened to cross the King's Walk. It was laughable. But the army's high command thought it a fine time to give the bandits' leader a demonstration—and it was an opportunity for a promotion for me. Already I was a captain in charge of a company of soldiers. So I was to be tested, and my performance observed by all in high command. And it was a fine night for it. Cold and clear, the moon full. The first snow of the season had fallen during the day, so against all the white, nothing could move without us seeing it. So we saw the bandits coming." Lizzan paused on a hot, shuddering breath. "We did not see what came from behind us."

"What was it?"

"Wraiths, I think." Made of ice, and with fingers like knives. With her own trembling fingers, Lizzan touched the scars on her face. "They tore apart my father, my friends . . . the bandits. I fought, until I could fight no more. The next morning, it was Aerax who found me amid all those who'd fallen."

With his bloodbare face as white as his hair, until she'd breathed his name and he knew she still lived.

"How did he find you?"

"Aerax is the finest of hunters; he can track anything." But that morning, he'd likely had help from Caeb. "He took me to the palace, and there the questions from the councilors and the king's court began. I did not right away see where those questions were leading."

"To the first story you told me?"

"And I, a coward who deserted my soldiers," Lizzan said dully. "They said I panicked and imagined the attack from behind. They said Varrin's protection meant that a wraith could never haunt the island. They said either I was of unstable mind or I was a liar. Then I was exiled and my name was struck from the books."

"So no one could speak to you?"

"Or ever speak my name. Or acknowledge that I ever lived. But I did not care about that. Aerax had survived without a name written; so could I. Yet my family . . . they would bear all the shame that the people were not allowed to heap onto me, for I was not even supposed to exist. Execution would have been a better end, for at least then my name would be written in the books again, because you cannot execute someone who does not exist." She scrubbed at her eyes with the heels of her hands. "In truth, I expected death. But exile suited me. I was so *angry*. And not quite ready to die. So I left and will never return."

The fisherwoman nodded, then slanted a narrow glance at her. "You did not say how your prince became a villain."

"Ah." With a hard laugh, Lizzan swiped at her cheeks. "I was named a deserting coward, and called delusional, and a liar . . . and yet he had been there on the battlefield. He had seen the tracks. He knew that I spoke truth. But he would not speak to the council on my behalf." Her foolish eyes spilled more tears. "He said it would make no difference— that the court had already made up their minds and would dismiss the evidence he'd seen, because he hadn't witnessed the battle in person. He was likely right," she whispered painfully, shaking her head. "But it would have made all the difference to *me*."

"So it would have," the woman said, her voice deep with sympathy. "And then? For that cannot be the end."

Lizzan laughed again, because if not she would continue crying. It had *not* been the end—though it might have been. The royal guards had been instructed to take her across the King's Walk, but she had known what awaited her there. She had known it at her sentencing, when the outraged cries had drowned out her mother's sobs, when spittle and stones and threats had flown in her direction. Since the court had not killed her, either the soldiers who still lived or the families of those who'd been slaughtered would see the proper justice meted out.

So Lizzan had slipped away from the guards. She could not go home or to the docks; they would look for her there. Yet there was another way off the island—in a cave on the windward shore was a small boat that she and Aerax had used often when they were younger.

She'd barely made her escape from the guards before Aerax found her, emerging from the darkness with Caeb at his side—as if they'd already been following the prisoner's wagon. She'd still been angry with him. Angry, betrayed, hurt. Yet seeing him there, knowing he would have fought with her across the King's Walk, had filled her shattered heart with so much warmth. Then he'd swept her up onto his horse, and they'd ridden for the windward side.

That short journey she'd never been able to forget, though she'd tried. No wind had there been that night. Only the whisper of falling snow, the rhythm of his mount's hooves on the road, the gleam of Caeb's harness as he'd run silently beside them, and Aerax's arms holding her so tight.

It seemed the full distance she'd spent kissing him, though that could not possibly be true. She had been riding in front of him, so every kiss must have been swift and awkward with her head angled back against his shoulder. Yet so clear she could remember the frantic heat of his mouth, and the desperate sweetness each time she'd tasted his lips, and how each one had hurt—for the wounds on her face had barely begun to heal, and burned with the salt of her tears and at the slightest touch.

Yet if she could only strike one memory from her mind, it would not be the kisses or the pain. It would be that, for the duration of that short journey, she'd believed Aerax would go with her.

For so long, he'd wanted to leave the realm. And eight years had passed since the red fever. Eight years since they'd pledged themselves to each other but had not even been able to lie together on their moon night before being called to their duties. Eight years of devoting every waking moment to Koth.

But she was no longer a soldier, and the realm no longer needed a prince. The king had taken a half-dozen wives and produced other snow-haired babies since, so Aerax could leave the island safely—and the princess was still very young, but old enough to step into the king's role if she needed to.

So Lizzan had believed she and Aerax could finally be together. She had believed it when they'd reached the small cave, and she'd seen how he'd already filled the boat with provisions. She'd believed it as he kissed her again, so long and sweet and slow, as if he would never let her go.

She'd believed it until Aerax told her to continue on—alone.

And even then, *even then*, it had not been the end. Because she'd been such a fool.

"I asked him to come with me," she told the fisherwoman. *Begged* him, in truth, though she'd only asked the once. But the plea had been in her voice, in her eyes, in her heart. She knew Aerax had seen it.

And she would never forgive herself for giving him so much in that moment. Because by the time she got into the boat, she'd had nothing left.

"Temra have mercy on the young in love," the woman breathed on a heavy sigh. "As your prince is not here with you, I need not ask his reply."

That it was his duty to stay. Though Lizzan couldn't imagine what duty still kept him there. Never would she have asked him to go if he was still needed at the palace, just as he had not asked her to leave Koth when her dream had been to protect it.

Before the red fever, he had wanted her enough to stay. But after her exile, he had not wanted her enough to go.

Or he'd wanted something else more than he'd wanted her. If so, he'd never shared with her what it was. Just as he hadn't shared anything with her in the years following the red fever. If she had been less of a softhearted fool when he'd swept her onto his horse, she'd have realized that Aerax had exiled her from his life long before she'd been exiled from Koth.

"So that was the end," Lizzan said. Aside from memories that never let her be. Memories of sweet kisses, of screeching wraiths, of agonized screams. But there was enough drink in the world to drown those. All the rest had reached a finish that she was determined would *remain* finished. But it could not if she met Aerax again. "And is still not a tale worth repeating."

But it had been a fine thing to tell it. So often Lizzan tried not to think of all that had happened. Only pain lingered in those memories. And it *had* hurt to speak of them.

Yet it was also as if a great pressure within her had released.

Until sudden tension tightened the back of her neck. As if nudged by instinct, she and the fisherwoman went utterly still, listening over the burbling rush of the river. So different the sounds were in the jungle. In the north, everything howled and creaked and cracked. Here it buzzed and chittered and dripped.

Yet that was all she heard. Nothing that was unexpected . . . except that there was less noise than there'd been before. The jungle was falling silent in one direction. Lizzan's gaze fixed in the same direction.

There. The barest flash of white fur, the briefest glimpse of a prowling stride before the shadows between the ferns swallowed it from sight.

Lizzan had not yet seen anything white in the jungle. But people were not the only things desperately fleeing the places they'd once lived, and mountains lay both to the south and to the east. A long-toothed snow cat or an ice walker might be migrating across the valley to reach the eastern range.

Again, a hint of white . . . and the gleam of silver. Lizzan's stomach lurched up into her chest. Heart thundering, she unsteadily rose to her feet and called out, "Caeb?"

The ferns rustled. A big feline head poked out from the leaves, daggerlike fangs gleaming. Oh, she knew that face and the regally disdainful expression that he seemed to wear, even when at his most playful.

Laughing, she started forward. "If I had a bow and arrow, you might have got yourself killed, you fool."

An enormous fool. Though Caeb seemed nearly wasted away as he prowled onto the road, powerful muscles rippling beneath white fur. Around his broad chest he wore a leather harness studded with silver beads to alert anyone who saw him that he was a tamed predator—and that harness hung from his frame, when always before the thickness of his fur often concealed the leather and silver.

Though it was only the fur that made him appear so

thin, she realized. Even during the warmest summers on Koth, Caeb had never so shed much of his coat, so that he looked to her now as sleek as a seal.

And he looked like home.

A sudden constriction tightened around her heart. Not a word could she speak as he bounded toward her in great leaps, ending with a pounce that would have sent her flying backward had he not stopped short. As it was, the butt of his head into her chest sent the air whooshing from her aching lungs, and she clung to him, fingers burying themselves in his ruff. He lifted his face to hers and she rubbed her cheek against his muzzle, his velvety fur absorbing her tears.

"So you have not forgotten me?" she asked hoarsely. Feeling as if a hot stone were lodged in her throat, Lizzan scratched Caeb's ears, listened to the rumbling purr in response. But although she wanted to cling to him forever, she could not linger. Wherever Caeb was, Aerax could not be far behind.

With a kiss to his furred face, she whispered, "You cannot come with me. Go on back to Aerax, instead."

Never had she been so grateful that the cat, as clever as he was, could not talk. And she had not given Mevida or Laina or any of the others her name. If Temra was merciful, Aerax would never realize she'd been here.

And she could not bear to see him.

With a shuddering breath, Lizzan pulled back. Caeb followed and rubbed his face against hers again.

Foolish cat. And she was a foolish, foolish woman. Heart aching, she turned away from him, then nearly tumbled over onto her head when Caeb nudged her backside.

The fisherwoman watched them without the wariness and surprise that Caeb usually provoked. But perhaps after all of her travels, the sight of a tamed snow cat was an unremarkable one.

With an arch of her brows and a pointed glance at Caeb, she asked, "You are certain your prince does not follow you?"

Once, Lizzan would have believed it. When they'd been young, and she'd been ready to give up everything for him, and he had given up so much for her. Aerax might have followed her around the world then, as she would have followed him.

But the Aerax who had sent her off alone would not even follow her across a few realms.

"I am certain," Lizzan said, her voice raw. "He is only here to make an alliance with Krimathe."

With a sigh, the woman returned to her fishing.

Unable to resist the warmth one last time, Lizzan turned to wrap her arms around Caeb's thick neck and buried her face in his ruff.

"You cannot come with me," she repeated, and knew not whether she told herself or him.

And perhaps Temra *was* merciful. Across the river, a half-dozen riders approached, leading three more horses bearing packs.

The fisherwoman hastily drew up her line. "Come with me. Come with me now. We must hide."

"Hide?"

"Your mail armor does not shine, but they will still take it from you. Just as they will take that one's pelt."

Lizzan's attention sharpened. "They are bandits?"

Wet feet leaving clear prints on the docking, the woman quickly gathered her pack, her blanket. "If they do not see the snow cat or see what you wear, they won't hunt us down, and instead look for easier prey on the road."

No easy prey would they find on the road behind her. But Lizzan was not yet certain. At this distance, they appeared no different from any other travelers.

"They seem well supplied for bandits."

"Because they are back from Oana with the provisions they've traded for the goods they've stolen. They will steal your armor, then sell it, then eat well off it while the creatures in the jungle eat what remains of you."

Not driven to thievery out of desperation, then, as some

bandits were. Just greedy. "They do not let go the people they steal from?"

The fisherwoman shook her head. "They drag the bodies into the jungle to rot. We only need to wait until they pass us. Then you can take the ferry safely across."

Lizzan nodded. She *should* hide and wait. The bandits would pass by . . . and quickly meet their end when they met the red-cloaked warrior who led the caravan, or the Parsatheans who now traveled with them.

But once before, Lizzan had thought bandits would be easily and quickly defeated. If she hid and let these pass by, and anyone in that caravan was harmed . . .

She simply couldn't allow it.

She glanced at Caeb. "I need a mount, so try not to terrify their horses so badly they run away," she told him. Especially the horse that carried two small barrels. "Most of the supplies will be this woman's. But if you protect her well, any meat will be yours. So go into the trees with her and hide. Only come out when I call you."

After rubbing his head against her shoulder, Caeb prowled into the foliage.

The fisherwoman watched with wide eyes, for *that* was not likely something she'd seen before in her travels. "He understands you?"

"He does," Lizzan said. But understanding was not the same as listening—or obeying. "But he is a cat. So he'll still do exactly as he pleases."

She glanced across the river. The bandits had reached the ferry. No doubt they were looking back at her, thinking how swift and easy this would be.

They had best pray that it *would* be over quickly. Because Caeb only did what he pleased . . . and it only pleased Caeb to hide when hiding was prelude to stalking his prey.

Or playing with it.

CHAPTER 8

AERAX

A single body lay on the road ahead.

Aerax slowed his mount, heart thundering. But the corpse was not Lizzan's. Instead it was a man, his body mauled by bite wounds and long ragged claw marks.

Behind him, Seri sucked in a breath. "Caeb did that?"

"He did." Though the long-toothed cat had not done all of it. The evidence left in the tracks told Aerax that the man had been running down the road when Caeb caught up to him. Then the cat had played with him. But the footprints that overlaid the man's and Caeb's—and the slice across the man's neck—told him that Lizzan finished him before Caeb was done.

"Your cat will attack humans?" Kelir frowned at him.

"Only with permission."

"Who gave him permission?"

Without answering, Aerax urged his horse forward. More bodies were sprawled at the end of the road. Five men, killed by crossbow and sword. On a limestone dock, Caeb lay facing the water. Near to him sat a dark-haired woman, her hair too coppery to be Lizzan's.

That the woman sat so close to Caeb without fear said Lizzan had made a friend of her. She appeared to be unarmed—and unharmed—as she turned to watch their approach. Held in place by its tether, the ferry drifted slightly from side to side in the current, as if not properly tied to the dock's mooring post. Horses waited on the boat, bridles still secured to the livestock lines.

Aerax dismounted near the first corpse, giving Seri his reins. Tyzen drew up his mount beside them, followed by Ardyl and Kelir.

"These men must have been attacked immediately upon reaching this side," Tyzen said, "because the horses are still aboard."

So they were. But the horses *had* been led off the boat . . . and then were loaded onto it again. Perhaps by the woman waiting there now.

"Were they set upon by bandits?" the big Parsathean warrior asked, face grim.

"No," Aerax said, and crouched to examine the man's body. Four crossbow bolts jutted from his chest. His purse strings were newly cut, leaving only bits of leather string still attached to his belt. "These men *were* the bandits."

Ardyl huffed out a laugh. "These men? You are certain?"

Nodding, Aerax scanned the road. "This one approached her while the others unloaded the ferry." Perhaps appearing amiable, because she'd allowed him close. But the scuffle of prints told Aerax the man had not remained amiable. Jaw hard, he continued, "Then she used him as a shield when the others loosed their crossbows at her. The remainder were killed by her sword, except for the one who ran."

Silver glittered as Ardyl's brows rose and she glanced toward the woman at the dock. "Her?"

Aerax shook his head. "Another woman was here."

"Where is she now?"

So close. Lizzan must be, though he could not see where she'd gone.

From atop his horse, Seri said, "That boat is floating away."

Aerax pivoted back in that direction. Not floating away. But being steered away—as if someone concealed on the ferry had lowered the rudder.

Not just *someone*.

Aerax sprinted for the dock. Too late. She had already gotten so far that he couldn't make the jump. With a curse, he stopped at the dock's edge, gaze searching the crowded boat. Joy burst through him at the sight of her.

Ah, but Lizzan was not hiding now. Rising from the deck, she stood at the pilot's box, hand on the rudder. Not hiding. But still running.

And not looking back.

Pain constricted his chest. Lizzan would *always* look—to gauge how many people were behind her, to see what threat they might pose. That she didn't glance back said that she already knew he was there . . . and did not wish to see him.

He had known she would not. He had known. Yet it was still a knife to his heart, puncturing the joy.

Throat tight, he glanced down at Caeb, who lay despondently, watching the boat. Red stained his jowls and chest. A butchered goat haunch lay nearby—a treat from Lizzan, no doubt, yet he hadn't touched it.

Aerax could not ease his own pain, but he could the cat's. He crouched to scratch his neck. "Do you sulk because she left you behind or because she stopped you from playing with that bandit?"

The cat only gave a dejected sigh.

Aerax glanced over at the woman, who was baiting a fishing hook. "The woman who fought the bandits—was she hurt?"

The woman lowered her line into the water. "Quite badly."

His heart stopped, his gaze flying to the boat. Too far to jump. And a current too swift to cross without being carried far downstream.

"But that injury was done long before she arrived here,"

the woman continued. "And was not delivered by a bandit, but by a snow-haired prince she called a villain."

A full breath it took for Aerax to understand what she meant. That Lizzan was not injured now . . . but had been. By him.

Yet he would hear more, if this woman had more to say. So hungry he was for more of Lizzan. He would take what was given secondhand, even if it hurt. It was not a hurt undeserved.

He *was* a villain. And the time would come when Aerax would have to become a greater villain still.

"The bandits had nine horses," Kelir said from behind him, his gaze on the ferry. "She does not likely need so many mounts. Will she sell a few to us?"

Aerax knew not whether she would. But his heart still thundered from the moment he'd thought her injured. She might be well. But he had to see it for himself.

Gripping his heavy mail tunic, he dragged it over his head. "I'll ask her."

And hope she would not refuse to speak with him. If she did, or if she ran again, he would likely soon discover how many times a man's heart could be ripped from his chest.

But being with her again would be worth every one.

CHAPTER 9

LIZZAN

She would not look back. She would not look back.

Then she did, when cheers and laughter erupted from the riverside. Her gaze found Caeb . . . but no Aerax. Perhaps she had been mistaken, then, believing she'd heard the low rumble of his voice while concealed between the horses on the ferry's deck. If she hadn't heard him, Lizzan would have revealed herself. She had no reason to hide from Parsatheans. Only Aerax.

Yet he wasn't on the dock. Or in the water, a hasty scan of the river confirmed.

If he was, that wouldn't concern her much, because he was a strong swimmer. Though he'd also have to be a fool, because even a strong swimmer could not swim straight across a swift-flowing river.

Movement upstream caught her attention—as did the snow-white hair that didn't belong in the jungle. Rising out of the foliage at its base, Aerax climbed the statue of Nemek, which anchored the rope that crossed the river. So he would make his way along it, swinging arm over arm above the water, until he reached the line that tethered the boat to that rope. Just as she would have done to escape him if the ferry hadn't arrived.

So Lizzan would not escape him.

Quickly she glanced away, but he was still there in her mind. As he always was.

Even after closing her eyes, she could see him climbing the statue and swinging out onto the rope. He'd once told Lizzan that when he was very young, his mother shaved his hair every morning so that Aerax would not be so easy to identify . . . and so that strangers might treat him more kindly. But when he'd realized why, Acrax had never let her cut it again—because too many times, kindness had become cruelty after learning who he was. And he preferred that people show him who they truly were from the start.

When Lizzan had met him, his hair had been a snow-white tangle to his waist. Not long after, he'd cut it to a more manageable length that was just as visible and unmistakable. Recently he must have trimmed it again, for the ends only touched his broad shoulders—and he still carelessly tied back the strands that might fall into his eyes. Nothing of his face did he hide. *Never* did he hide it.

For even without that white hair, Aerax's features declared who he was. The statue of Varrin in the palace courtyard might have been Aerax, too—or his father, or his uncle, or any of Varrin's descendants. All possessed the same wide brow and sharp cheekbones, the same square jaw and full mouth, and looked out onto the world with a heavy-lidded stare. Nothing of Aerax's mother could Lizzan see in him, except for sometimes in a quick grin or wry response.

But although there was no mistaking who his father was, no one would have mistaken Aerax for one of the royals. Not before the red fever, when his underlinens had been rags too threadbare to be of further use at his mother's inn, and his winter clothing was made of furs that he'd pieced together by hand. Feral, they'd called him then—and so he nearly was. Almost always outside, and rarely in the company of other humans.

Until Lizzan. And he was dressed now much as he'd been when they'd met. In full summer, Aerax had emerged from the forest after a hunt with a boar's carcass slung over his shoulders, blood and dirt painting his skin, and wearing only a deerskin tied around his hips.

Now he wore an underlinen tied in the same fashion, leaving most of his legs and torso bare. But life at the palace had changed what wasn't covered. It had been ten summers since Lizzan had seen him without a tunic, and he'd always been tall, but he'd also run lean compared to the other royals. Now every muscle seemed heavier, his chest broader, his arms thicker . . . as his father's had been, and as his uncle's were. But she supposed that was what happened when a man did not have to forage or hunt his every meal, and could instead sit down to a palace feast.

Not all was different, though. His every movement was as fluid as it had always been—another lethal predator emerging from the jungle.

And there was nowhere for Lizzan to run.

The roar of the river covered the sound of his approach. She thought the horses might startle at his sudden appearance, but the bandits' mounts were apparently accustomed to crossing the river, and to violence and blood. They'd only been uneasy when Caeb had come near them. Now they were settled again and did not stir, even when the heavy thud of feet against the deck sounded.

She would not look back. Resolutely she stood at the rail, staring at the riverbank ahead, her grip tight on the rudder. They were not yet halfway across. So she was trapped here with him.

This was supposed to have ended.

Despite the noise of his landing, she didn't hear his approach. Could only feel it. So she was not startled by his nearness when his voice rumbled quietly so near her ear.

"Lizzan."

She closed her eyes. So badly she wanted to turn toward him. To see him. "You're not supposed to say my name."

"You said mine when no one else would. Never will I not say yours."

Warmth filled that quiet statement. Everything foolish within her responded to it, like morning dew steaming toward the sun. Oh, but so *much* of her inside was foolish.

"Then what do you wish of me, Your Highness?" She would not say his name now. "Does your seeking me out mean your duty to Koth is done?"

Oh, she had meant that to slice. To wound. But it was a blade that turned back on herself. She knew Aerax wasn't here for her. Yet she wanted so badly for him to say that he was.

"It is not." His voice roughened to a painful rasp, as if her words had wounded him, too. "I needed to see that you are well."

A bitter laugh ripped from her. "I am, Your Highness. Perfectly well. As you could see if I weren't covered in blood that is not mine."

"I am glad of it, Lizzan." That rasp of pain was still there.

No more should she speak to him. Yet she needed to know—"Have you seen my family? Are they well?"

"I see your brother Cernak often. He is my keeper."

Astonishment had her turning. A keeper was a member of the palace guard who was assigned to an individual royal—and they were always near that royal. Always.

Her hopeful gaze searched the dock. Only Parsatheans. "Is he here?"

"He stayed in Koth. Only a few soldiers were sent with us."

Of course. Because their numbers were so thin. Yet despite the pain of knowing why Cernak hadn't come, hope was intermingled with it. A keeper was a position of high rank—not a position given to someone buried under a sister's shame. "If Cernak is a keeper . . . then the rest of my family fares well?"

A hesitation returned her gaze to his face. Despair slipped through her. Aerax's every expression she knew. And the shadows in his eyes now told Lizzan that the burden of her shame was as heavy as she feared.

"I requested that he was made my keeper. To the rest of your family, I gave them my mother's inn and see that they have everything they need."

Bitterness filled her again. He meant food and clothing. But that was not all they would need. Lizzan's mother had been a well-respected magistrate, her younger brother a talented healer—both with purposes they loved. "You are a prince, Your Highness. Is there nothing you can do to restore their station?"

"I have no influence in the palace," he said quietly. "I only serve as a prop."

"Ah." She laughed, short and hard. "That is why you did not leave Koth with me? So you could be a prop?"

Again she had revealed too much. That she was still hurt. He should not be able to do this to her. The wound ought to have been healed over, as her face had been, with only a scar left. Yet it still dripped with blood.

Now Lizzan wished that she could not read him so well. Because there was agony in him, too. She steeled herself against it.

"If that is what you came to tell me, Your Highness, then you can go now."

"Go where?"

"What do I care?" She gestured to the river. "Jump in and see where it will take you."

His grin suddenly appeared, the one that immediately tried to pull its reflection from her lips. She steeled herself against that, too.

"I will wait aboard so that I can return the ferry to my companions," he said.

The Parsatheans. She glanced at the docks. "Interesting companions you have. And you have even begun to dress like them."

Wearing nothing except that linen tied around his waist . . . and her braid in the pouch hanging from his neck. Her heart she had put into that pouch, and he still carried it so close to his own. Yearning stole through her again, unwanted and unbidden. To spread her hands over that broad chest. To nestle in where that pouch was—and to always know the warmth of his skin, to feel the rise and fall of his breaths.

Such a fool she was. Why could she never harden herself against him? Instead silken heat tugged at the pit of her stomach, a sheer longing to touch him.

"I saw that you'd taken the bandits' crossbows. I didn't want to drown in a prince's heavy armor if you shot me off the line." His voice roughened with amusement. "Though I would not mind so much, if it turned out as the last time you sent me into the water."

When she had kicked him from their fishing boat for teasing her. Then he'd failed to surface, panic had taken her over, and she'd dived in after him. But it had all been a ruse to get her in the water, and she'd been so furious at him— and so relieved—that she'd kissed him.

It had been their first kiss. But far from their last.

Their last had been near the same boat, filled with provisions before he'd sent her off alone.

The memory finally hardened her heart. "This time I would not go in after you."

"No doubt my new friends would save me."

She snorted in disbelief. "Friends? You?"

He laughed softly, a sound that called to all the laughter that had once lived between them. "It is truth. There is a warrior girl, Seri, who is much like you. And a prince, Tyzen, who is everything I am not. And a young monk . . ." A frown creased his brow. "Whose name I can't recall."

Oh, she would not laugh. "I see you are very close to these friends."

"I would introduce you," he said, his gaze caressing her face. "They seek to form an alliance to stand against the Destroyer. I think that you would be eager to fight for such an alliance."

Because he knew her too well. Yet she needed no help from him. "I will find my own way toward it."

"So you will."

She would. Lifting her chin, she told him, "If you must

recruit, speak to the woman on the dock. She followed the Destroyer around the world in search of her son—and says she saw nothing but bodies and blood, but can likely tell the alliance more about the Destroyer than anyone else."

"And you listened to her story?" His voice deepened. "Little have you changed since leaving Koth."

She scoffed. "I have."

"Then little has my admiration for you changed. Always you would stop to listen to those who were alone, for you knew that is what they often needed the most—for someone to see them, to listen to them. And I have always loved that about you." Closer he came, until her heart thundered. His callused thumb skimmed the line of her jaw. "Just as I have always loved this stubborn jut of your chin."

Pain and pleasure swept through her. He said such to her now? When her only hope of surviving him was to finish this?

"Do you know what I have always loved about you?" she asked quietly, turning toward him, tilting her face up to his.

Such a fire lit his dark eyes as his gaze fell to her mouth. "Tell me."

Lizzan always preferred action to words. In a swift movement, she stepped back and kicked him square in the chest, sent him toppling unbalanced over the side.

She heard the splash. Saw him surface—sputtering with laughter, wearing the grin she loved so much. But though that grin drew her own, just as it always had, that was not the reason she gave.

"I have always loved how well you swim!" she called out instead. "So strike for the shore, Your Highness!"

He laughed again—and did as she'd told him, the water gleaming over his bare skin. Lizzan watched as the current carried him downstream, watched as he reached the riverbank at such a distance from the ferry docking that she would be gone long before he could walk his way back upstream. When he was safely out of the river, she stopped watching and turned away.

She did not look back again.

CHAPTER 10

AERAX

By the time Aerax reached the ferry boat and guided it back across the river, the caravan had caught up to them again. Kelir waited on the dock and caught the mooring rope Aerax tossed to him.

"She would not sell the horses?" the Parsathean asked, securing the boat.

Curse it all. "I forgot to ask."

The big man grunted with amusement. "No surprise that is. I saw what other important matters were on your mind. When she sent you into the water, you only needed to float on your back and you could have sailed across the river instead of swimming."

Aerax could not stop his laugh, for it was true. It mattered not that she'd been wearing bandits' blood, disheveled and stained from traveling and sleeping in the jungle. Lizzan would always be the most alluring of all women to him, and his cock had hardened to full mast the moment he'd stood near her.

"Ten years I have known our prince." Degg approached

the dock, regarding Aerax with sly amusement. "Never have I heard him laugh before. Or seen him smile."

Because the last full happiness Aerax had felt was before he'd gone to the palace. Afterward, only fleeting joy had he known—only with Caeb, or the few times Lizzan had visited him.

"And now his laugh has fled again, Degg," Lady Junica observed with a sharp smile. "Perhaps there is a common reason that you never see him laugh when you are near him."

Degg was not the reason. The councilor was nothing to Aerax. Only his purpose mattered. His purpose . . . and Lizzan.

His gaze fell on the fishing woman. And that was where his laughter had gone. Not because Lizzan had named him a villain, but because she had told her story to this woman . . . and had likely told it for the same reason that she listened to so many others.

Because she was alone. Because she needed someone to hear her.

But she did not want that person to be Aerax.

So he had a new purpose—to see that this alliance was as strong as it could be. Because Lizzan would find her way toward it, and among these warriors who resembled her so fiercely, she would not be alone. She would find friends.

Sweeping up his clothes and armor, he stepped down from the dock. Lizzan had laughed that he'd dressed as the Parsatheans did. In the north, the cold demanded layers of furs and skins—as did a Kothan prince's costume. Already he'd shed as many layers from that costume as he could, but if given his preference, he'd wear as little as the southern warriors. If his new purpose was to help see an alliance formed between the northern realms, however, then he would still dress as a prince.

A prince with minders. Degg hovered close behind as Aerax approached Tyzen.

"I am told this fisherwoman followed the Destroyer around the world in search of her son," Aerax said, and saw the High Daughter glance up from where she was examining the body of one of the bandits. "She might have heard more about his weaknesses, or learned what his purpose is."

Tyzen nodded. "I will ask two of our warriors to stay and see what she has to say, then catch up with us after they've learned all they can. Does that suit you, Kelir?"

"It does."

"And what of the horses?" Tyzen asked. "The bandit-slayer would not sell them?"

Aerax avoided that answer by pulling a tunic over his head.

Kelir laughed at him again. "Next time we will send Scri to ask. Nothing will distract my sister from securing a new mount. Unless it is your hope to see the bandit-slayer again?"

That would always be Aerax's hope.

By the time each wagon and cart in the caravan had been ferried across the river, it was nearing midday. No hope did Aerax have of catching Lizzan, but easily he could track her—until they reached Oana.

It was a village unlike any other he'd seen, with much of it built into the jungle canopy. Rope bridges served as paths between gargantuan trees fed by the same springs that filled the healing baths.

For much of his life, Aerax had hunted amid the giant pines of the northern forest, but the size of these trees dwarfed those by comparison. Yet his awe was nothing to Seri's, who told him that on the Burning Plains, there were so few trees that she hadn't seen one until she'd been nearly a dozen years of age.

"Many wondrous things I have seen on this journey now," she said, head tilted far back. "Never did I think one would be trees as tall as Syssia's towers."

"Not that tall, I think," Tyzen told her. "More of a height to Ephorn's tower."

The young monk riding behind Tyzen joined in, naming another tower, and all three argued until they reached the stables where the bandits' horses were kept—but Lizzan had already paid for the animals' board and left. Aerax tracked her to the wide wooden steps that spiraled up a tree trunk and into the village's higher levels, but no trace of her could he see on the stairs.

Nor could he go in search of her. No time did Riasa waste before securing a private dining hall at an inn, where they might discuss alliances with the High Daughter.

Seri volunteered to wait at the stables and to purchase the horses if Lizzan returned. Aerax bade Caeb to remain with the girl, so the cat would not go wandering in search of Lizzan and panicking those who would not expect to encounter a saber-toothed beast prowling through the canopy.

The inn was on one of the lower levels, with a fine view of the falls beyond the wooden railing that edged the dining hall. Aerax found himself seated near the head of the table, across from Tyzen and with the High Daughter at his right side. To his left was Riasa, and then Lady Junica, and he could not tell if the tightness of the councilor's expression was because she could not easily prevent him from offending the High Daughter from that distance—or if her back still pained her, even upon the cushioned chairs.

Beyond her sat Degg. Then Uland, the Kothan captain who served as the head of their guard, but who was not here in that capacity. Instead he might supplement any answers regarding the Kothan army if the Krimathean needed them. Kelir and Ardyl had likely joined them for the same reason. Easily they sat talking to Uland. Between Kelir and Tyzen was the young monk, who blushed fiercely and quivered like a yearling buck that had caught wind of a snow cat whenever Kelir or Ardyl spoke to him.

And whose name was Preter of Toleh, Aerax learned when introductions were made. So now he could tell Lizzan that he had made three friends. But more importantly, they might be hers—if this alliance could form and hold.

No time did the High Daughter waste there, either. Tankards of mead had only been set down when she pointed to her own eyes before gesturing to Tyzen's.

"You wonder if my moonstone eyes possess sight beyond what is seen?" At her nod, he shook his head. "Only my mother and foremothers had that gift."

She blew out a frustrated breath, which Tyzen apparently had no trouble interpreting.

"The Destroyer's spells made him invisible to that sight. They could only see the destruction he left in his wake."

Aerax frowned. "Do they see his trail now?"

Again Tyzen shook his head. "My mother's mother, Queen Venys, was slain by the Destroyer and reanimated as a demon. My mother killed her, and then she herself returned to Temra's arms five years past." A faint smile touched the boy's mouth. "It is full strange to be among people who know little of Nyset's heirs. In the south, the warrior-queens of Syssia have been feared and loved since ancient times, when Queen Nyset struck down the Galoghe demon. And before the Destroyer killed her, Venys was the only warrior to have ever made him bleed."

Faintly Aerax recalled hearing those tales—of how the goddess Vela had walked within the ancient warrior-queen for a thousand years, together chasing and battling the twelve-faced demon. And more recently, of another queen who had cut off the sorcerer's arm.

But few had believed the latter tale, dismissing it as a story that had grown larger in the telling—because when the Destroyer had marched north, he had two arms. "Are you certain the Destroyer comes? Many times I have heard that he returns. Never before has it been true."

"We are certain," Tyzen said. "Vela herself appeared before my sister and tasked her with building an alliance between the western realms."

The moon goddess had visited his sister and given her this message?

Aerax suspected that he was about to give offense. He'd heard of others who'd claimed to receive messages from the gods. Typically after they were found wandering in their nightclothes. Yet none of them truly had. No gods ever came to Koth. Not in dreams, not in temples. Not since

Varrin's blood had transformed the island into a prison for them.

Carefully he asked, "And this sister is Yvenne, your queen?"

"Queen of Syssia and of the Burning Plains," Tyzen confirmed before grinning. "She was not dreaming when Vela visited her. Nor was she alone. If you wish to hear an account of it, Kelir and Ardyl witnessed that meeting—and Vela also favored them with her attention. Would you hear from them?"

Looking to the two warriors, the Krimathean nodded.

At their seats, Kelir and Ardyl exchanged glances, eyebrows raised as if asking whether the other wished to start. The scarred Parsathean then drew a deep breath before reciting in a cantering rhythm, "On the banks of the river Lave, far south of the Burning Plains, a warrior who did not yet possess the heart of a king was grieved by the foulest treachery—"

"The short version," Tyzen interrupted. "She needs only hear what occurred in Drahm, not the entire tale."

"For the best, then, as Kelir has not memorized the full song—only the parts where he is most featured," Ardyl said with an amused glance at the other warrior. "I will tell you how it was, my lady, though it won't be as prettily said."

With a wave of her hand, the Krimathean urged her to go on.

"Kelir and I were serving with four other warriors as our king's Dragon guard when Vela appeared before us as one of her priestesses, but with her eyes shining bright as the moon. Her skin shone, too, and her voice and her touch were as ice and steel."

The Krimathean's lips parted on an indrawn breath and she nodded—not as if in surprise, but in recognition.

"You have seen the goddess, too?" Kelir asked.

She met his eyes and then tugged at the edge of her red cloak, as if to indicate that Vela herself had given her the quest, instead of merely receiving it from one of Vela's priestesses.

"Then you know how she appeared," Ardyl said. "She spoke first to each of the Dragon guard"—her voice thickened with emotion and her hand came up to touch her braided hair, as if in memory of another touch—"and then to Yvenne and Maddek she went. There she said that Anumith the Destroyer and his armies had landed on the sunset shore."

At the far end of the continent. Then Aerax would doubt no longer that the Destroyer came. Grimly he said, "How much time until he arrives?"

"Vela told this to my sister two summers past," said Tyzen. "If the Destroyer travels the same route as he did toward that shore, it will be three years more before he reaches the western realms. But we believe his return march will be faster. Two years, perhaps."

Because the sorcerer had already destroyed everything along that path a generation past; razing everything to the ground again would not take so long, and there were far fewer people to fight him.

"Not long to prepare," Aerax said.

"It is not," Kelir agreed, his expression grave. "Especially as Vela warned us that the Destroyer left seeds that would grow in his absence to weaken the western realms in advance of his return—and that we must root those seeds out where we can."

Aerax frowned. "Seeds?"

"Some hidden, some not," Tyzen answered him. "The demon of Blackmoor and the warlord who controlled him was one of those seeds." A bitter expression passed over his features. "As was my father, when he attempted to weaken the alliance between Syssia and the other realms west of the Boiling Sea. We called it the Great Alliance," he added wryly, "but Vela said six realms alone was not great enough."

"So she tasked Yvenne with uniting all the western realms," said Ardyl.

"And so she began," Kelir continued. "First our queen sent other ambassadors and warriors to the realms farther west—to those who will be the first in his path. Yvenne urges those realms not to fight but to march in this direction, so that we might all join against him, and so all the western realms have more time to gather together. But we do not know yet how successful those ambassadors have been or if the queens and kings will leave their lands. And if they will not . . . the warriors' priority is to help those citizens who wish to flee."

Already people were fleeing. Aerax asked, "You believe he will come to these northern realms first?"

Tyzen nodded. "The southern route from the sunset shore would force him to cross the Dragon Sands—and the Destroyer might survive that desert, but his armies would likely not. Unless he attempts to cross the flaming mountains instead of using Stranik's Passage, he will come by the northern route."

"Are you monitoring the western passes?"

"Three hundred alliance soldiers have been sent to the mountains."

Not to fight, Aerax understood. But so that if the Destroyer came that way, there was better chance of at least a few soldiers surviving to ride back to Parsathe and warn the alliance that the Destroyer was taking a southern route.

"My lady," Tyzen said, returning his gaze to the Krimathean, "to every western realm, we intend to offer our strength—at the heart of which is thirty thousand Parsathean riders. Whether he crosses the highlands west of Krimathe or the frozen plains west of Koth, we will be ready to meet him in force. And if we cannot hold him in the north, we will retreat south through Stranik's Passage—then make another stand in Blackmoor, and slaughter his armies as they emerge from the tunnel."

The Krimathean gave him a dour look.

"It will not be so easy," Tyzen admitted. "But his armies cannot attack in massive numbers if they are coming through the tunnel—and we hope that *our* numbers will stop them in the north. Yet whatever occurs, it is likely we will stand against him in Krimathe. And so it is your realm that would bear the weight of the alliance that gathers there, including the thirty thousand Parsathean warriors . . . and their horses."

The Krimathean stared at him in clear disbelief.

"We would bring what we can," Tyzen said, undaunted by that look. "If you join our alliance, then we will immediately begin sending supplies north to be stored in anticipation of our arrival. But we cannot yet know what the other realms will bring, especially if they must travel far or in haste."

Still the Krimathean stared at him.

"Initially we thought to gather in Blackmoor," he told her. "But your cousin said that Blackmoor is still recovering from the demon's blight, and cannot support all of those who flee south through the tunnel in addition to an alliance army."

Which would require not just feed for warriors and horses, but new storage built to hold it all, and fuel for cooking fires and fields for their camps. No matter how many of their own supplies the warriors brought, hosting such a large number might lay waste to the realm's resources—and in the battles against the Destroyer, perhaps more than Krimathe's forests and fields would be laid to waste.

"And if we are quartered in Krimathe," Tyzen continued, "we will have two opportunities to stop him: once in the north—and if that fails, again in the south."

The Krimathean closed her eyes, her expression torn. She looked up again as Kelir sat forward and spoke in a low, resonant tone.

"Many generations past, the demon Scourge left nothing but blood and ashes across the plains where my people lived, and only by uniting our tribes against the demon were we able to defeat him. But that alliance was only a beginning, my lady," he said quietly. "For we remained united, named a Ran to speak for us, and each tribe sent a warrior to serve on the Ran's Dragon guard. That is what we would build here: not merely an alliance, but Dragons made of warriors from every realm—with claws that will make the Destroyer's armies bleed, with deadly stings to pierce his defenses, with wings that we will stretch across the western realms, so that everywhere he goes, so too we will be. And all the while, our Dragons' armored scales will protect the people at the heart of every realm. As one we will gather, so many together that when the sparks fly from our swords, his armies will face a Dragon's raging fire—and as silver-fingered Rani rides her dragon to carry the dead into Temra's arms, so we will be the Dragons who send the Destroyer back into whatever foul pit he crawled from."

Each word kindled its own spark in Aerax's chest, so that a raging fire already seemed to burn there. As it did to the Krimathean, he saw. Her eyes were alight, as if seeing the warriors gathered and the Destroyer's end.

Tyzen did not wait for that flame to cool. "We know full well how much we ask of you and your people, my lady. In return, we would pledge to Krimathe our lives, our blood, and our steel—and a promise that after the Destroyer's defeat, we will help your people rebuild. Will Krimathe pledge itself to this alliance and join the gathering of Dragons?"

The Krimathean eyed him with a narrowed gaze as sharp as the smile she wore, as if to tell him that she was well aware of how neatly coordinated his and the warriors' persuasive maneuvers had been. Then her smile softened and she held out her hand.

With a relieved laugh, the prince grasped her forearm as she gripped his, sealing their agreement. More relieved grins appeared on the Parsatheans' faces, tension easing from their shoulders as if a softening wind blew through them all.

Seated beside Aerax, Riasa had been watching the exchange. Now she sought explicit confirmation. "Then our people will join the southern alliance, my lady?"

The Krimathean turned to the captain and nodded.

"I will tell your cousin upon our return," Riasa said, appearing pleased by the other woman's answer. "And will you also hear from the Kothans?"

Eyes narrowing on Aerax, the High Daughter inclined her head again.

Lady Junica leaned forward in her seat and said, "My lady, on behalf of all Kothans, let me first express my humble gratitude—"

The Krimathean silenced her with a glance, then looked to Aerax. Clearly he must be the one to speak.

His jaw tightened. She ought to hear this from Lady Junica. No fine stories of goddesses did he have, no rousing words to inspire with.

"We need Krimathe's help," he said bluntly. "Koth is besieged and has not enough soldiers to defend the island."

The Krimathean frowned and glanced at Riasa.

The captain asked what the other woman could not. "Besieged by whom?"

"Bandits in the outland forests." A great lake surrounded the island that formed the heart of the realm; only the King's Walk connected the island to the outlands. "Patrols found no camps—and some outlanders claimed they were not bandits but malevolent spirits."

A frown creased Riasa's brow. "We have heard rumors of terrors in the north."

"They were but illusions." Lady Junica broke in, exasperation filling her voice. "Created by a band of murderous thieves who knew that terror is more effective than any blade and makes cowards even of the brave."

Aerax's teeth gritted. So they had said of Lizzan, too— that she was a coward. Yet Aerax had seen for himself bloodied tracks that vanished to nowhere. Bandits left signs of their passing. What Lizzan had seen left a sign in the claw marks on her face. Still Aerax's uncle and the Kothan council claimed it was *only* bandits.

Yet Aerax needed no fine manners to know that if he said any of that now, Lady Junica or Degg would counter it all. Instead of presenting a request for help to the Krimathean, they would present a squabble.

And there *were* murderous thieves, too. "Two winters

past, the bandits attempted to take the King's Walk. Though they failed, the soldiers defending it were slaughtered."

Riasa's lips parted, her stunned gaze searching his face. None of Koth's enemies had ever come near to taking the land bridge before. "How many?"

"Nearly a thousand," he said grimly. Fully half of Koth's soldiers.

"A *thousand* bandits?"

"That was the number of soldiers killed." All but one. "There were fifty bandits."

Into the astonished silence came Lady Junica's heavy sigh. "We know not if that was the true number," she said. "It was only the number that our scouts reported before the battle. But no one who fought that day survived. We believe it must have been many more, for our soldiers would not have fallen so easily."

Again Aerax clamped his jaw to stop his reply. Lizzan had told them how the soldiers had fallen. Yet they had not believed a word she'd spoken.

Riasa frowned. "If all were killed, why did the bandits retreat?"

"They also must have sustained heavy losses—too many to continue their advance over the bridge," she said. "Fifty bodies we found. So you see, that cannot have been their full number, for they still plague the outlands. Though there are no outlanders left for them to murder."

"The bandits killed all the Kothans who lived off the island?"

Lady Junica shook her head. "We have brought the outlanders into Koth's heart for their protection. Now our remaining army guards the shores and the King's Walk . . . and we have not enough soldiers to patrol the forests and root out the marauders. That is why we seek Krimathe's help."

Riasa glanced at her future queen before looking again to the councilor. "What of the rumors that Koth has been abandoned?"

"Untrue," Lady Junica said. "Never would our king leave the island."

Never *could* he leave it. Not with Aerax away and his heir still unconfirmed—though Aerax wished for nothing more but an island empty of all its residents. As long as Kothan outlanders took refuge on the island, he could not destroy it.

But Aerax only said, "All were still on the island when we left." And if that was not still true, there would be no island to return to. "Will you send warriors north to help Koth?"

The Krimathean's dark gaze held his for a long moment, and dread hardened in like a solid weight in Aerax's chest before she slowly shook her head.

By the torrent of indrawn breaths around him, Aerax was the only one unsurprised by her response.

Riasa spoke, sounding baffled. "Your answer is that we are *not* assisting the Kothans, my lady?"

She confirmed the captain's words with a nod.

"Whyever not?" A strident note of fear in Lady Junica's voice was quickly smoothed as she continued, "My lady, if you fear the Destroyer will appear in Krimathe as suddenly as he did before and catch your realm unawares, surely that is not possible? None of us knew that he *could* come through Stranik's Passage instead of taking the mountain passes, but this time . . ."

She trailed off when the Krimathean fixed her with a look and shook her head. That was not the reason.

Lady Junica tried again. "Do you fear that Koth will not return the favor and send our soldiers to Krimathe when the Destroyer comes? That might have been true a generation past. None of our realms helped each other; we were only concerned with protecting our own. But now there is an alliance—" She broke off as the Krimathean denied that reason, as well. "If the alliance's plans fail, and the Destroyer secures the passage before our armies retreat south, Koth might be a valuable refuge for *all*. The Destroyer did not attempt to cross the King's Walk. But if these marauders take the island first, no refuge will there be for any of us."

With a sigh, again the Krimathean indicated that was not her reason for denying them.

Then they all looked to Tyzen as he said, "Could these bandits be one of the seeds left by the Destroyer, so that he might weaken Koth—and so there will be no refuge for those who flee from him?" He met Aerax's eyes. "You say the outlanders spoke of foul magics."

"They did," Aerax said. "Another claimed that it was wraiths who killed the soldiers."

Lady Junica sharply added, "That *cannot* be. Nothing of magic can exist on Koth's heart that is not Varrin's own." With a lift of her hand, she gestured to Aerax's hair, as if to remind them all of how his ancient forefather had become a god. "That was Varrin's gift to us—that we would be safe from magic that would do us harm."

Riasa's brow creased. "Perhaps there are no foul magics on the island, then, but you said these marauders were in the outlands—where there also might be magic."

"The marauders who killed the soldiers defending the King's Walk were not wraiths." Again Lady Junica appealed to the Krimathean. "My lady, Koth will also pledge to you our blood and our steel and help defend against the Destroyer when he arrives. But I fear that without your assistance, we will have no blood and steel to offer."

Around them again were baffled stares when she shook her head—and fear and frustration from the Kothans.

All of Aerax's control it took to swallow the hot bile of his own frustration. For he knew what had happened, and why they were being denied. At the river, the Krimathean had waited for the entire caravan to cross before following—all the while sitting on the dock with two Parsatheans left behind to hear what the fisherwoman had to tell them.

To the Krimathean, he said, "The woman at the ferry told you a story?"

"What story?" Lady Junica asked, puzzlement creasing her brow. "That she followed her son around the world?"

Not that story, but another—one that had named Aerax a villain. But he cared nothing of that, except that never could he complete his purpose if Koth received no help.

Her gaze on his, the Krimathean nodded.

"And now you would like to hear the truth of that battle?" he asked. When she nodded again, Aerax stood from his chair. "Then I will find her."

"Find who?" Lady Junica asked again.

Always Aerax would say her name. But he would not give them opportunity to prepare a false defense against her. So he only said, "Someone who you'd best pray still cares for all who live on the island."

Or Koth might soon reap what its lies had sown.

CHAPTER 11

LIZZAN

She had not known there would be so many stairs. Nor had she expected them to be so uneven.

But though she stumbled, Lizzan would not falter. The most splendid of all ideas had come to her as she'd ridden into Oana earlier that day—that she would take a quest from the goddess Vela.

She knew not why it hadn't occurred to her before. Perhaps because she'd not met Laina, or anyone else who had worn the red cloak. Perhaps because she'd not met the fisherwoman, who had spoken the truth of redemption.

Or perhaps because her thoughts had been so full of Aerax. But the ale in the bandits' barrels had taken care of that. So strong it had been. As had been the beer at the tavern she'd visited upon reaching the village. There she had looked for work but was told that in the past season, travelers coming from the north along this road had dwindled to almost none, and even fewer now arrived from the east. As if everyone who intended to flee had already fled.

But no worries did Lizzan have. Thanks to the bandits, her purse was full. So she had lingered at the tavern, and as promised she told the story of Ilris's mother—and told it again and again to those curious about a woman who was from Oana, and as they all tried to guess who it might be. And in every telling, Lizzan thought that the fisherwoman had been correct: soon they would all be dead.

But Lizzan might make something of her death. If she served Vela, so simple it would be to undo all the shame her family knew.

Simple, *after* she reached the temple. High into the canopy it was. As if she might soon climb to the moon and visit with Vela herself. She stumbled up the final stairs, thighs and lungs burning—then saw the counterweight lift that she might have used.

But the path was never easy, as they said.

The temple doors sprang wide at the slightest push. She had not known what to expect. In Koth there stood a moonstone temple that was Vela's, but the fires were cold and no priestesses tended it. The crystal palace was the realm's only true temple, built by a man who'd become a king, and then who'd become a god.

No crystal or moonstone was here. Only wood. It seemed a plain room, and at its center stood a petal-strewn altar and an offering bowl on a pedestal.

The only person inside was a small figure in black robes, her face veiled. As Lizzan staggered through the entrance, sweating and her chest still heaving, the priestess came forward. Nothing of her face could Lizzan see under the black veil, yet the concern in the priestess's voice could not be mistaken.

"Are you injured?"

Lizzan looked down at herself. Dried blood stained her armor and linens. Likely she ought to have taken a bath before coming. "It is a bandit's blood," she said, then corrected herself. "*Several* bandits' blood. Can you see through that veil?"

"Likely better than you see through your ale," said the priestess, voice warmed by amusement now. "You are very drunk."

"Only a little very," Lizzan said. "It helps me think clearly."

"I doubt that is so."

"It is true." Lizzan touched her hands to her head, fingertips pressing to her temples. "There is always . . . ice screeching in here, and the sun blinding me. But the drink makes it easier to think. And quiets the screeching. I am so cursed tired of the screeching."

"You may take your rest here, then." The priestess began to move deeper into the temple. "There is a sleeping chamber through this way."

"I need no rest." Lizzan stopped her. "I need a quest."

"When you are clear of mind, we will speak of one."

"I *am* clear of mind." Her throat tightened. So far she had come. She could not be turned away now. "I know exactly what I must do."

"Then you do not need Vela to tell you. Go to the healing baths, young one—" The priestess cut herself off, tilting her head as she regarded Lizzan through her veil. "Ah, no. Perhaps not in this state, or you will drown. Sleep, then go to the healing baths, and then return."

"Do not send me away. Please." Eyes burning, Lizzan moved toward the altar. "My family lives in shame. I would ask that Vela will help me clear my name."

"Not while you are—"

"I have an offering." With hitching chest and trembling fingers, she fumbled with the strings of her heavy purse, then dumped the contents into the silver bowl with a clatter of falling coins.

"A generous offering, indeed." The priestess reached in and unearthed a severed finger from the pile of gold. "It has been many ages since Vela has asked for offerings such as these."

One of the bandits' fingers. Heavy mortification spilled the tears that had gathered in Lizzan's eyes. She had been in such a hurry when cutting away their purses. Hurrying to escape Aerax.

Yet he'd found her anyway. And confirmed that her family bore the weight of her shame.

She reached for the finger. The priestess pulled it away from Lizzan's grasp, her voice changing to steel. Cold warning rang through every word. "*Never* take an offering from my bowl."

Then Lizzan would not. "I will bring you more, if you would but hear me."

"It is not this bloodied offering which has made me stop to listen, Lizzan." The priestess's hand seemed to shine as she tossed the finger back onto the pile of coins, and her glowing fingertips swept through the teardrops that had splashed onto the bowl's rim. "I will hear you for these."

If this priestess wanted her tears, then Lizzan had many to give. "I only need a quest. Please."

"You need no quest from me. You wish to lift the shame your family bears—but the path that I would put you on is no different from the one you will take on your own. It is not my help that you need."

Lizzan shook her head, wiping at her nose. "I *do* need your help. For there is only one way to know redemption."

The priestess's veil no longer concealed her face, and so bright her skin was. Her eyes glowed like the moon on snow. "What way is that?"

"By dying in glorious battle while saving many lives, or while helping to stop the Destroyer. No one in Koth will say my name, so I must sacrifice myself while performing a feat so incredible that my name will reach their ears, and no longer will my family bear my shame."

"*Must* you die?" The skeptical arch of the priestess's brow said not.

But Lizzan knew it was true. "To all of Koth, I am a villain. And no villain was ever redeemed, except in death."

"I know of many villains who were redeemed and lived."

Perhaps a priestess did. "But the people of Koth do not.

Those stories are never retold. I cannot think of one villain who is as reviled as I am, and who did not have to die. Not one."

"But you are no true villain. You did nothing wrong."

For all that it mattered. "That is not the story told. So I need a story that will be sung until it reaches every ear on Koth."

"And you think I will point you toward this glorious battle?"

"I hope you will, for I know not where to go."

"You know exactly where to go, if you intend to find your way to my alliance and to stand against the Destroyer."

"I do. But I am lost, and know not where to begin." Lizzan pushed the tears from her eyes with the heels of her hands. So dazzling the woman's gaze was now. "I know a quest will take me far away from all I know and love."

"I daresay you have already done that."

So she had. "I have also known pain at the edge of my enduring."

As all who quested for Vela must endure.

"Have you?"

Her throat clogged by emotion, Lizzan nodded.

"You have not yet," the priestess said.

Yet. "Then I will endure it."

"So you will." Her voice warmed, as if touched by a southern heartwind. "A quest is often for those who do not yet know their own strength. But there is little you can learn, Lizzan, for you have always known yours."

A pained laugh shook through her. "So I have. But no one else did."

"One did."

Aerax. Hurt gripped her chest, and she could only respond with silence.

The priestess gave a heavy sigh. "Then I will start you on this path. This is what you must do—leave this temple, and vow to protect with your life the first person you see. And on the day of the first snowfall, you will know honorable and glorious death, and your name will become legend."

Relief loosened the constriction on her heart. "I thank you."

"You thank me for nothing." Her cold fingers brushed Lizzan's cheek. "It gives me no pleasure that you ask this of me, and that you are brought to this. But I would help you on your journey, as I do those who quest for me—though you must promise me first that you will drink no more. For if you continue on *that* path, you might soon care more for your ale than your honor."

Lizzan would never do such a thing. Yet it was a promise she could easily make. Untying her flask, she placed it into the offering bowl. "No more."

The woman regarded her with shining eyes. "You are certain? Not even children's mead can you have."

Lizzan frowned. That weak mead barely warmed the gut, but there was little other option that she dared consume. "What am I to drink, then? If it is water, then it had best rain often, or I will always be shitting myself."

Behind her veil, the priestess's mouth curved. "I will help you in that, too, and purify all that passes between your lips."

Lizzan nodded, and then her breath caught like a knife in her throat when the priestess lifted her hands. From the woman's glowing fingers dangled a silver chain and a small medallion.

Her father's medallion—which Lizzan had tossed into the lake by the King's Walk, with the silver still slick with her blood and his. Where the waters were so deep, no hope was there of retrieving it.

Yet the priestess held that necklace now. "Lower your head to me."

Shaking, Lizzan did.

"This was always meant to be yours." Those frigid fingers brushed Lizzan's skin when she settled the chain around her neck. "Do not throw it away again."

"I will not," Lizzan whispered, clutching the medallion as it nestled between her breasts. "How was it meant to be mine?"

"That I cannot tell you," said the priestess, and her voice

was warmer and softer now, her face again concealed by the veil. "But as you start down this path Vela has set you on, perhaps you will learn."

This path. Which would begin outside this temple.

Heart pounding with anticipation, Lizzan strode to the doors, then out into the warm and humid air. A flash of white caught her eyes, drew her gaze. In a snowstorm she would see Aerax first. Now he was merely climbing the stairs toward the temple. Ahead of him walked Caeb and a Parsathean.

Pivoting too quickly, she stumbled back into the temple. "You must give to me a new quest."

"You are not on a quest," the priestess said mildly.

Had the woman *already* forgotten her? "I was set upon a path—"

"That you were."

"Now I need a new one."

"That I cannot give." The priestess cocked her head. "Did you expect your path would be easy?"

Lizzan had known it would not be. But she had not expected anything as difficult as this. Breathing deep, she tried to control her turmoiling emotions, to see beyond them. The path ahead was clear. She had asked Vela for victory in a glorious battle that would remove the stain on her name. Now she must protect a Kothan prince.

That must be what would lift her shame. She would save a Kothan's life—and it was a path no different from the one she would have chosen, had she never been exiled.

So a soldier she would be again.

But not a soldier for Koth. Instead she served another. "What of Vela's cloak?"

"Vela's cloak?" the priestess echoed.

"All those who quest for her wear red."

The priestess only sighed again.

No matter. Lizzan would find her own cloak and dye it as red as blood. With trembling fingers, she smoothed her hair back. Then hastily she dragged the long strands down, hiding her scars. Then defiantly she drew her hair back one more time.

Never again would she hide from him. Never again would she run away.

Oh, but it was not easy. To stand, exposed, as light spilled through the opening doors. To wipe her cheeks again, removing all traces of tears. To turn and face Aerax without stumbling, though she swayed as if the floor were uneven.

So quickly he moved, catching her arms, steadying her. With the sunlight behind him and stabbing into her eyes, she could not see his expression. But his disbelief and laughter she heard well enough.

"You are drunk?"

"Only a little," she said, for her senses were painfully clear. Everywhere Aerax touched seemed to burn, his words a delicious rumble across her skin. And she could smell the river upon him. Oh, and now this was clear, too—why he must be here. She had shoved him into the water, so a kiss must follow. "But I would have to be *very* drunk to let you kiss me."

His handsome features she could see better now, the sudden and sharp intensity of his gaze on her mouth. "Do you wish me to?"

"I *should* not."

His lips quirked. "What should you do instead?"

"Shove my boot up your ass."

"Would your foot be in it? Perhaps I would not mind so much."

Always he made her laugh. But she should not do that either. So although the laughter bubbled up, she pressed her lips tight to stop it.

"Shall I kiss you, then?" His thumbs caressed the curves of her shoulders. "I would give anything you wish, Lizzan. And a kiss would be the finest of all things."

So it would. But she shook her head. "I have already gotten what I wished for. That is why I am here. Now I only need my cloak."

Aerax went still, hands tightening on her arms. "You asked for a quest?" At her nod, he turned to the priestess and snarled, "You took her vow while she was drunk?"

From behind him, another snarl echoed his. Caeb.

Instantly the priestess bristled. Her body snapped taut, and she replied with her own snarling, "Do not forget where you are, feral princeling. I do not answer to you, and *never* would I—" With an audible click of her teeth, she fell silent. A breath passed. Lizzan could all but see the razor-sharp smile in her voice when she spoke again. "I will find that cloak for you."

With a sweep of her robes, she strode toward a back chamber. Caeb prowled past Lizzan and Aerax, slinking his body against their sides before continuing on toward the altar, where he sniffed at the offering bowl.

"Do not eat the finger," Lizzan warned him.

A disdainful glance Caeb sent in her direction, as if of course he knew better than to steal from a goddess. Lizzan's gaze fell upon the offering bowl again, and though moving her head made the world spin, she looked up at Aerax with a grin.

"If you toss a coin into that bowl, the priestess shines like the moon."

Aerax did not laugh as expected. Instead he frowned. "She glowed while talking to you?"

Lizzan nodded hugely. "So very bright."

"Were her hands as ice?"

A shudder ripped through her. "Not as ice." Ice was sharp, like knives. "They were as snow."

Still his troubled gaze did not leave hers. "What did you ask for?"

"To lift all shame from my family."

His expression softened. "Of course it would be that. What must you do—and how might I help you?"

Everything within her stilled. Aerax would *not* help her. Not if he learned how she meant to fulfill her quest. Instead he would fight every step she took on this path.

Yet this path was all that Lizzan had left.

So she gave him a half-truth. "I was to protect the first person I saw outside this temple. And I do not think she meant Caeb—so it must be the girl who was walking ahead of you."

"Seri?"

He turned, and Lizzan saw the young warrior standing outside the open temple doors, peering in curiously at them. Nodding, Lizzan said, "You are traveling with the Parsatheans?"

"Until we secure an alliance with the High Daughter of Krimathe." Frustration tightened his expression. "I always forget my purpose when I am with you. Securing that alliance is why I sought you out."

Of course it was. Not to be with her. Not for a kiss.

Careful not to stumble, she stiffly pulled away from him. "Why am I needed for that?"

"The High Daughter refuses to send her warriors north without first hearing the truth of what occurred on the King's Walk."

Lizzan laughed, hard and sharp. "And what is the point of my telling her? Who are the councilors with you? They will only say that I lie again."

"Lizzan." With his intense gaze locked to hers, he said, "Your name has been struck from the books. They must pretend that they do not hear you at all—and so *nothing* can they say in response to you."

Oh. Well.

That sounded very fine, indeed.

The priestess returned, shaking out a cloak that billowed dust from its threadbare length—and the cloth was so faded, it seemed more like the pink of a rash than the red of a quest. "This was the best that I could find."

Lizzan cared not at all. Gratefully she took the battered cloak, then staggered as she swung the thin cloth around her shoulders. Again Aerax steadied her, frowning, then looked to the priestess when that woman spoke again.

"Feral princeling," she said, "our goddess has a message for you, as well."

Eyes narrowing, he seemed to brace himself. "What is it?"

"That you must become who you truly are."

Lizzan snorted out a laugh and flapped her fingers. "Like a slimy worm into a beautiful butterfly."

Aerax's lips twitched before he frowned down at her again. "I will tell the High Daughter that you'll speak with her in the morning," he said. "You are full drunk."

Laughing, she shook her head. So little he knew her now. "I am not *near* full drunk." And she had very much to say. "All will be fine."

She patted his chest reassuringly, and then pushed him out of her way.

CHAPTER 12

LIZZAN

B y the time Lizzan made her way to the inn, her purse was full again—or would be, when the Parsathean girl paid her for all but one of the bandits' horses.

And she felt so very fine. Like a blade sharpened to a thin, brittle edge.

Perhaps Caeb sensed it. The snow cat walked at Lizzan's side as she climbed the stairs, his presence large and comforting. Or perhaps Aerax feared she would stagger drunkenly onto her face, and told the cat to remain close, so that she might hold on to his ruff for balance.

Or perhaps it was for her protection. Barely had she stepped into the room when a furious cry rang out and a Kothan soldier lunged at her, his chair clattering as it fell.

And truly, perhaps she'd drunk a little bit much, because her body was sluggish to react. Her understanding moved slowly, too. When she saw that it was Uland of Fairwind, a soldier she knew well from her early years within the Kothan army, Lizzan's first thought was not to defend herself but to look behind her for an enemy that they would fight together.

Yet Aerax must have expected what she had not. His hand shot out. A meaty *thwack* sounded as he blocked the man's swinging fist with his palm, and then he snatched Uland's mail tunic and dragged him close.

"Take care, Captain," he snarled into Uland's face, and Lizzan tightened her arm around Caeb's neck, willing him to stay in place. "My cat loves this woman more than he does me. If you hurt her, he will tear you apart—and I will not stop him."

"*You* would defend this coward? Then your hair might be white as snow, but your blood is yellow as piss." Disgust and rage filled Uland's expression as he jerked back out of Aerax's grasp, then looked to Lizzan again, voice rising. "Never should anyone defend a coward who ran away to hide while my friends were slaughtered!"

Lizzan hadn't run away. She hadn't hidden. If she had, she would not still see her father and soldiers torn apart before her eyes. She would not still feel the hot splash of their blood. She would not still hear their screaming and the wraiths' screeching blended into one.

And she had marched in here with her gut on fire, ready to loose arrows from her tongue. Now the burning in her throat made ash of every volley that she would have sent.

But she'd expected to find councilors, not soldiers. And Uland had been her friend once, too—but that friendship was another casualty of that horrifying night.

"Captain Uland, stand down." That firm warning came from Degg the Red. "She is nothing to you."

As if in response to that, Uland spat at Lizzan's feet. Caeb growled, showing not just his saberlike fangs but his sharp front teeth, and Lizzan buried her fingers more deeply in his ruff.

"Do that again, Captain," Aerax said quietly, "and I will feed you to him, limb by limb."

Uland was more of a fool than she knew. Instead of backing down, Uland turned his furious gaze to Aerax—as if he believed Aerax's words were a toothless threat. "It is said you helped her away that night."

"So I did."

"Captain Uland, recall the law," was Lady Junica's sharp reminder. "Her name is struck from the books. You are speaking of someone who does not exist."

Visible was the battle that raged through Uland then, as he stared at Lizzan with poisonous hatred—before turning it on the target who *did* exist before him.

"The feral prince has been defanged and declawed, but he is still led around by his cock," he hissed to Aerax. "So until he is depricked, he will never be a man of Koth."

Never a man of Koth? Aerax had been born one, as surely as Uland had been. And if Aerax were led by his cock, then two years now he would have been with her.

Lizzan shook her head, the frozen tension easing from her shoulders. She had been stunned by Uland's attack, but never would she let Aerax fight this battle for her.

"What good is a prince with no prick?" Lizzan asked Uland, and won a small victory when his wrathful gaze moved to her face and lingered on the scars—the evidence that she had *not* hidden away. "If a prince could not beget snow-haired heirs, he would only be as useful as a soldier without a brain. And yet Koth seems to have at least one of those, and given him the rank of captain."

A furious breath whistled through Uland's gritted teeth. He opened his mouth.

"Uland!" Lady Junica snapped. "You do not see her and do not hear her. Now take your seat."

Stiffly, he did. And so would Lizzan, it seemed—though not near Uland. After bidding Caeb to go with the Parsathean girl, Aerax led Lizzan farther down the table. She had been aware of the others in the room, how they had all surged to their feet when Uland had lunged for her and then tensely waited. Now she observed them more closely. During the confrontation, two Parsathean warriors had angled their bodies as if to shield the young men behind them from any violence that might erupt. One of the youths must be the nameless monk—though his chinless beard suggested that the monk was not as young as the pale-eyed boy beside him. No doubt that boy was the prince who was everything Aerax wasn't.

She supposed that meant the prince was courteous and well-mannered, for there was nothing else that Aerax wasn't. In all other ways, Aerax was everything. Koth claimed to produce the finest of all things; in Aerax, it had truly created the finest of all men. With the finest of all backsides. So tight it was as he prowled ahead of her, his muscles thick and supple.

Oh, and drunken lust would not do at all. She was here . . . for something else. To persuade the Krimathean.

But his ass was *so* very fine. She allowed herself another lingering glance while her sluggish brain churned through what Uland had said of pricks and claws and fangs. She could hardly fathom that the soldier had dared say it at all. Not only because of Aerax's rank, but because of Aerax himself. For he was the finest of all men, but also the strangest. As if he reserved all of his emotions for the very few people he loved, so much that he seemed to burst with them. Yet Aerax gave nothing to those he didn't care for, and didn't hide how little he felt. Upon meeting him and being subjected to his flat, unwavering gaze, often people were unsettled in the same way Lizzan and the fisherwoman had been unsettled when they'd first sensed that a predator approached through the jungle. Yet Uland had spoken as if he thought Aerax were truly defanged.

Perhaps because most of Koth's royals had always boasted and swaggered. They were like mammoths, trumpeting their strength and ancestry. In comparison to that, a fool might look at Aerax and believe quiet was the same as meek, instead of seeing a man who was as silently lethal as a snow cat.

And a man who had little care for Kothan law, when he introduced her to the Krimathean by name. "This is Lizzan of Lightgale, my lady."

Laina frowned at her. Though the frown was not at *her*,

Lizzan realized. Instead she frowned at Lizzan's cloak. Her brow rose in query.

"You wonder if I pretend to be a Nyrae warrior or if I have taken a quest?" Lizzan guessed before answering, "It is a quest."

Dismay filled the Krimathean's expression.

"It is what I need to do," Lizzan said quietly, "to restore honor to my family name—and to help stop the Destroyer."

With a sigh, Laina nodded before gesturing to an empty seat that had been placed between Aerax's and Riasa's. On the table was laid a hearty feast—and flagons of mead.

"Vela came to her in the temple," said Aerax, and Lizzan felt the gaze of the prince across the table sharpen upon her. "The priestess glowed like the moon and had skin like ice."

"Snow," Lizzan corrected, reaching for the mead. The priestess had said no more drink, but she was already a little drunk, so surely a sip to quench her thirst and to dull the edge of Uland's words made no difference. When Lizzan was sober again, then she would start anew. "And it was not the goddess, for her face was not full round as the moon is. Only her eyes were. And her voice."

Quiet fell as she sipped, but it was merely the quiet of the Parsatheans exchanging glances with the prince, then all looking to her, as if to weigh the meaning of what Aerax had said. And though she did not exist, the Kothans stared at her as if she were a gutworm crawling on the floor. Or a snake. A poisonous one.

Oh, but she had not a care what they thought, for the mead smelled so lovely and strong . . . but was the weakest she had ever tasted. As if mere water, it was.

It *was*.

Her laugh rose up even as she tried to swallow. The priestess had said she would purify all that Lizzan drank, but she had not expected that the mead would be purified to water. Coughing and laughing, she pounded on her chest—then drained the full mug before slamming it to the table.

She leaned forward to look past Riasa and aimed a bright grin at the other Kothans. "The last time I sat before a gathering of councilors and royals, it did not go so well for me. Though this time it might, for I have been introduced to the High Daughter before. But not properly, because I failed to tell her my name."

And why had she done that? Why? What fealty did she still owe to Koth, except that the people she loved most were there?

Except for the one who was here. But she looked past him to Laina. "I trust that they were not properly introduced, either, and failed to tell you much. No matter. I will remedy that. Here beside you is Aerax, a bastard prince whose name was not written in the books after his birth, who was treated as less than nothing by nearly all of her fine citizens, and who long despised everything about Koth—until the red fever put him near to the throne and made him a part of the courtly intrigues within the crystal palace. And then he would not leave it."

Aerax's narrowed gaze she felt upon her. With the fire burning in her gut again, she raised her brows, daring him to challenge her.

He did not. And just as well, for she was not done. "And there is also Degg the Red, who despises Aerax because the bastard prince did not earn his rank. For that is the promise of Koth—you must only work hard, and you might rise to be whatever you wish to be. So our royals labor to earn the ranking they are born with. All snow-hairs are taught royal lessons until they have the strongest of minds and are the sharpest of warriors. But instead of royal lessons, Aerax spent every day and night providing for his mother, because she could find no help or trade with the locals who shunned her for having a nameless bastard son. So when that feral prince was given a place in the crystal palace without having worked for it, Degg would not forgive him."

She looked to the councilor, who was exerting so much effort not to hear her that his face and ears had flushed to nearly match his hair. "Degg will tell you that he earned his place on the council by working so very hard, too. And likely he did. But what he will never say is that *everyone* works hard. From the mines to the palace, everyone labors. Yet they do not rise. He will say it is because they do not work hard enough, or fail to focus their efforts in the right way—but he will never admit that his place now is the result of opportunity that others who worked as hard never had, and merely because his father knew Lady Junica."

Who regarded Lizzan now with a calm, steady gaze. A woman who had voted for Lizzan's exile.

But Lizzan had no arrows for her. "I have nothing ill to say of you," she said, her throat tightening. "I have long admired your fight to reform the law so that the books serve as a record instead of as a judgment. And I can only imagine the depth of your grief when the red fever took all of your family." Parents, sisters and brothers, husband and children. And it must not only have been grief, but also guilt—for Lizzan knew too well the pain of being an only survivor. "But despite all that you endured and lost, still you have heart enough to care for all of Koth and her citizens. And I do not fault you for believing what was said of me. When I met with the council, you at least asked me what occurred and listened to my story. But you did not know me at all—and there was no one who would speak to my character—so you could not also know how everything I said was twisted into shameful cowardice."

She turned her gaze to Uland, who stared at her in silent fury. "But Uland might have known, if he'd but taken a moment to think. Never once while we served together did I run and hide. Not when we were all puking as we cleared the island of bodies taken by the fever. Not when we searched for marauders in the outland forests and encountered a family of ice walkers instead. Not when we were mired in a devourer's mudsink and certain we would never escape. Never once did I falter or set my own life ahead of other Kothan lives. Yet you accepted a story that I had deserted my soldiers and lied about the wraiths? You believed that I was a coward, despite the evidence of the years you have known me? It is as if your brain was scooped out and replaced with a rabbit's fart."

Uncertainty flickered through the rage Uland still leveled at her, but Lizzan cared not at all what he thought now. She reached for Aerax's mead and took a deep swallow to wet her parched tongue, then turned to Laina again. "So that might do for proper introductions. What did you wish to hear from me?"

Laina appeared bemused—and of course could not speak. Instead it was Riasa who said, "What was it that killed your soldiers? If our warriors are to head north, I wish to know what we will face."

A sensible request. "Wraiths," Lizzan said. In response to the sound of a disbelieving scoff, she shot an irritated glance in the Kothans' direction. "They will say there cannot be wraiths on the island—and perhaps it is true. Perhaps they were not truly ice wraiths, but some monster I had never heard of before. I confess that I took no time to sit one down, pour it an ale, and ask what it was or where it had come from."

"Then why claim they were wraiths?"

"Because they resembled everything I have heard of them—that they are the souls of the dead but do not know the mercy of Temra's embrace. Instead they are imprisoned in bodies corrupted by magic, and they are twisted by the pain of their undying torment until all they know is anger and hatred."

"Or hunger," said the male Parsathean warrior, and when all eyes turned to him, he gestured to the woman beside him. "Ardyl and I have encountered blood wraiths."

Which must not have given him the scar on his face, or he would be one of them now. A blood wraith's corruption began in its flesh and could spread to others, but the wraiths in Koth had possessed no flesh. Only ice.

"It is true what they say, yes?" Lizzan asked them now. "They raise the hairs on the back of your neck. And they *feel* foul."

"They do." Ardyl shuddered as if merely remembering

the sensation, reaching for her drink. "And never will I forget the sound they made."

"The screeching," Lizzan said—and unbidden tears blurred her vision. Here were two people who knew the horrors she spoke of. No longer was she alone in that. "As if they could not bear suffering alone in that twisted ice, and meant to make you join them in that torment."

"Though the blood wraiths were not of ice . . . it is as you describe," the scarred warrior said before turning to the monk beside him. "What do you say, Preter? Could it have been wraiths?"

"It should not be possible," Lady Junica said before the monk gave answer. "There is no magic on Varrin's island but his own. We are protected from every other god's power."

"Therein might lie the answer, my lady," the monk told her, in a voice more assured than Lizzan expected in one so young. "Most wraiths are born of a god's corrupted magic. Those in Parsa and around the monoliths—or the blood wraiths that Ardyl and Kelir encountered—are souls trapped by the Destroyer's foul magics, and his power comes from Enam. But natural magics might have been used instead, as when stone wraiths are created—and one stone wraith by itself might slaughter a thousand soldiers. How many of these ice wraiths were there?"

"I truly do not know." Lizzan's face warmed beyond the flush of her drunkenness. "I ought to have known. I ought to have been able to count. But it seemed that they came from nowhere behind us, then razed through our numbers before they raced across the bridge to cut through the bandits. And they were so very fast. But there were hundreds upon hundreds, it seemed."

The monk's eyes shadowed as if her answer troubled him, though he did not say why. Instead he frowned thoughtfully, rubbing his whiskerless chin with his forefinger. "Were you able to kill any?"

"I think not. Their limbs would shatter if hit with a bludgeon, but we were armed with swords and crossbows. We were there to fight bandits, not wraiths. By the time we realized how to . . ." Throat closing, she shook her head. "There were not enough of us left."

"So they crossed the King's Walk into the outlands?" Riasa asked. "Are these the terrors that we are sent to fight? We will take bludgeons, then, but if foul magics on that island are turning people to wraiths, better to abandon it— just as every other place infested by wraiths is abandoned."

"No one on the island has been turned into a wraith! And certainly not hundreds and hundreds of people." Lady Junica leaned forward to address Laina. "If there were wraiths, they are vanished."

Lizzan nodded, wiping her mouth with the back of her hand as she set down Aerax's tankard of water that smelled like mead. "Melted."

"Melted?"

The disbelieving echo came from at least three mouths, but it was to Laina that Lizzan said, "They had killed everyone. Do you think I did not follow them beyond the bridge? I would have smashed every one of them to pieces." A raw laugh escaped her. "But there was no need. The first freezes on Koth never last through the night. A heartwind blew from the south and all I smashed were puddles."

Before trudging back across the Walk, to the carnage that was all that remained of her father, her soldiers. And there Aerax had found her among them, cradling her father's body and wishing that she were dead, too.

"Do you see, then, why this is such a difficult tale to believe?" Degg the Red said. "These wraiths came from nowhere. They vanished to nowhere. And they left no trace."

"If the bodies of a thousand soldiers are not trace enough, you bum-birthed scut, then look to my face," Lizzan snapped.

"Or look to me," said Aerax, and her heart leapt into her throat. "All that she says is true. I was there near dawn, and not a sign of the wraiths did I see until I reached the bridge. From there, the ground was torn up with their tracks as they escaped across the Walk, but the sign ended not far into the forest. If you did not see the bits of melting ice nearby, it would seem as if they'd vanished."

Lips parted, Lizzan stared at him with a thousand emotions churning in her breast. Astonishment, for that speech was the longest she'd ever heard him say in the presence of other people. Joy, for he had finally spoken on her behalf. Anger, for it had taken him so long.

And bemusement. "You will help to clear my name *now*? This might be the fastest reward that anyone on a quest has ever received."

Though her task was not done. Nor would it be, until the first snow fell. She was still on a path to die in glorious battle . . . because her reward would not truly come so soon, no matter what Aerax said on her behalf. Not if the mutter she heard from Uland about a prince hoping to wet his cock was any indication. Koth would not believe their feral prince, either—the council would make sure no one believed it. Aerax had been right when he'd said they'd already made up their minds. Yet still. It would have meant everything if he'd spoken for her before.

Faintly she heard Riasa ask, "Were there any other attacks this past winter?"

"There were not," Aerax said, still holding Lizzan's gaze as all the emotions within her settled into a familiar pair—hurt and frustration.

"If these wraiths are a concern to Krimathe, then I daresay we are meeting at the right time," Lady Junica said. "Your warriors could arrive in Koth before the end of summer—"

"Why did you not say this in front of the court?" Lizzan demanded of Aerax, and the table fell silent. She had not meant to interrupt. But she was a little drunk, and that had been a little loud, and she had little care. "Why wait until now?"

His expression darkened as it did when he recalled a memory that still angered him. "Because you are no longer in Koth," he said. "So you are safe."

"Safe? From what?"

His jaw hardened. "My uncle."

King Icaro? Bewildered, she stared at him. "What would he have done to me?"

"Executed you. I told him what I had seen. He knew you spoke the truth. But he feared that talk of wraiths would stir a panic, and would have sacrificed you to prevent it. So I traded my silence for your life." His gaze searched her face, his eyebrows drawn. Abruptly he leaned toward her, voice fierce and low. "You truly believed that I held my tongue because the council had already made up their minds? With all the evidence of the years you have known me, did you not realize that only the promise of saving you could have compelled me to remain silent?"

Her throat closed. Aerax threw her words to Uland back at her—and perhaps he was right. All the years she had known him said that he would have spoken for her. But there were many years she had not known him.

"After you went to the palace," she told him in a hoarse voice, "you did not let me know you at all. You gave me little to believe in."

Something bleak moved across his expression, dimming the fierce light in his eyes. He nodded and sat back. "That is true."

And it was a truth that hurt him. Because unlike the words of people he cared nothing for, Lizzan's words could run him through.

Yet she could not reach out to him, her own shredded emotions pieced together with disbelief and confusion. The king had known the truth and still meant to name her a coward and a liar and execute her? Had the council known, too? But the pain and pressure in her chest was so great that she could not even give voice to those questions.

Riasa did. Frowning, she looked to Lady Junica. "Did you know of this?" Dimly, Lizzan was aware of the councilor shaking her head. Then to Aerax, Riasa said, "What did your king fear?"

"That Koth would no longer trust in Varrin's protection," Aerax said flatly.

"That is true," Lady Junica stated. "Rumors of the Destroyer's return had been spreading across the realms. We'd heard of families abandoning their homes and that the roads were in chaos. I did not believe in this tale of wraiths, but the court was concerned then—and has been since— that the panic infecting the other realms would come to Koth. So we make great effort to reassure the people of their safety. The Destroyer did not come to Koth before. He will not again."

"Are you certain of that?" asked the moonstone-eyed prince. "Or is it merely hope?"

"It is faith." Lady Junica gave him a slight smile. "Just as you trust in Vela, I trust that Varrin will protect our island from the Destroyer's magic and his armies."

At his thigh, Aerax's fist clenched and unclenched before he indicated Laina with a jerk of his chin. "But at issue is whether *she* will trust him."

By her troubled frown, the Krimathean did not appear as if she would. And Lizzan could hardly blame her. To send her warriors into a forest that might be infested with wraiths?

A shiver raced over Lizzan's skin, and she reached for another flagon. "Perhaps Koth *ought* to abandon the island."

"The best of all ideas," Aerax muttered.

Lady Junica did not think so. "Abandon all that we have built and accomplished? Even if this story of wraiths is true, it has happened but *once*. Never before, never since."

That was truth, too. And no matter what the king and council had done, to Lizzan the realm was still worth saving. For her mother, for her brothers—and to everyone else who lived there.

On a heavy sigh, she looked to Aerax. *The best of all ideas*, he'd said in answer to her suggestion of abandoning the island. As if he still had no love for Koth, despite staying there. And abandoning the island might come to pass if the Krimatheans did not offer their aid. Yet he had come here seeking that aid?

Because he put Kothan lives ahead of his hatred for the realm. Just as he had after the red fever, when he'd accepted his position at the palace. Though Lizzan did not know him as well as she once had, of that she was certain—if people were in danger, then Aerax would help them. Even if he hated them.

So she trusted him to speak the truth when she murmured, "*Have* there been more wraiths? Do you think there might be?"

Easily he could destroy Koth now. To simply say *yes*, and the Krimatheans would tell them to abandon the island, instead.

But he shook his head—jaw clenched, as if he resented the answer even as he gave it. "There should not be."

Should not. As if he knew more than he had said. But Lizzan would not question that now. Always her purpose had been to protect the people of her realm. Despite her exile, that had not changed.

She looked to Laina. "I am full glad that I will never be a queen. I suspect your heart urges you to send the help Koth asks for. Yet you also must weigh the danger to your own realm if the Destroyer comes while your warriors are fighting in the north. You must weigh that these councilors have come to you with no intention of lying, but also blinded themselves to the truth that their realm—and your warriors— might face greater danger than they will admit to. And you must weigh the words of a disgraced and drunken soldier, and whether to risk your warriors or to tell these Kothans to flee south along with everyone else. I do not envy the burden you bear."

Laina huffed out a laugh and rapped her knuckles on the table as if to emphasize her agreement.

"I will never be a queen, but wearing these cloaks, we are sisters of a sort." Lizzan reached forward past Aerax and covered the woman's fist with her hand. "And you *will* send your warriors north—but not wholly for Koth's sake, I think. For there was something else I told the court that they took for a delusion. In truth, I was not certain of it myself until I began escorting Lithans fleeing from the east, and heard the stories they told of their realm . . . and of King Goranik."

The Krimathean went utterly still, her gaze boring into Lizzan's.

"I asked if finding him was your quest, do you recall?" Without waiting for the woman to confirm that she remembered, Lizzan said, "If it had been, I would have told you then how the bandits were slaughtered on the Walk, and that when I followed the wraiths into the forest, I saw that not all of them had been killed. The bandit's leader still stood, and the charging wraiths parted around him as if he were a boulder in a river. My soldiers and I had only glimpsed him before, but that night, I saw the mark of Enam around his eye, and the gray skin that betrays Hanan's silver blood flowing through his veins. I felt his sheer strength when he knocked me aside as if I were a doll."

Strength not unlike this woman's, as her hand turned beneath Lizzan's and her fingers squeezed to the point of pain. Despite a similar blessed ancestry, her skin was not gray, so her blood must run red instead of silver.

"Then he was gone—and afterward, I was not truly certain that he'd been there. I was not myself as I chased the wraiths into the forest. Battle-madness had come upon me, and in that frenzy, I might have seen anything. As it was, he seemed to me not a man at all, but a creature so foul that even the thought of him now makes my skin crawl. And who has not grown up hearing the horrid tales of the sorcerer-king of Lith? What realm does not fear that he would do to them what he did to Krimathe? So I thought the battle-madness had given the bandit his face and built him into a monster even more terrible than the wraiths." She drew a shuddering breath. "But the Lithans who fled from that realm described him exactly as I saw, so I knew that I had not imagined it. And in all of their tales, Goranik is dead. Yet nobody is certain of how he died or who killed him—whether his son returned to take his crown, or if it was another warlord who did it. They only know that the throne was suddenly empty. So I believe Goranik did not die, but that he abandoned Lith . . . and that he is now in the north, in the forests surrounding Koth."

The woman's fiery gaze shot past Lizzan. Harsh steel scraped through Riasa's voice as she spoke for her. "It is the sorcerer alone? Is he not with his army?"

"I know not how many bandits still live, but their numbers cannot be many. He could not have hidden an army in those forests."

Teeth gritted, an expression almost of agony contorted the Krimathean's features while her gaze pleaded with the captain.

"You cannot abandon your quest, my lady," Riasa said softly. "Too much depends on it. But I will bring you the head of the king who killed your mother. I will bring you the head of the prince who held you down and—"

Laina gave a sharp shake of her head and tugged at the edge of her cloak.

"That is your quest?" Lizzan asked. "The son? That is why Vela told you to go east?"

The woman nodded, her dark eyes afire with hate unlike Lizzan had ever seen.

"Then I hope you find him quickly, and join your warriors in the north." Steadily Lizzan held that burning gaze. "You *will* send them to Koth?"

"She could not stop us," said Riasa. "Laina is not the only warrior whose mother was killed when Goranik betrayed Krimathe. With or without your approval, my lady, I will lead north any warrior who wishes to go. But I would rather have your approval."

A tight nod gave that approval. Lizzan sensed the relief that swept through the other Kothans, saw it mixed with admiration when her eyes met Aerax's.

And he was now under her protection . . . as they all traveled north to find a sorcerer-king who'd already torn Lizzan's life apart. She suspected that she'd just put them all on the path toward a glorious battle, a battle that would clear her name. *That* victory she would celebrate.

But Lizzan had also just orchestrated her own death. She would not change that fate, not with her family's honor at stake. And yet . . . the way Aerax *looked* at her now. The way he spoke her name, his voice so deep and warm. As if everything were not finished between them. It had to be, though.

It had to be.

Throat aching, she shoved her chair back. "I need a drink."

CHAPTER 13

AERAX

Lizzan had told him that she would find her own way to the alliance. And so she had. Already the southerners and Krimatheans seemed to welcome her as they all celebrated in the public room at the inn. They listened with full attention as she stood on a table to recite the tale of Ilris's mother—and then they shouted encouragement after Kelir asked her to tell them how she had defeated the bandits at the river.

From a bench at the edge of the room, with nearby seats shoved aside to make space for Caeb's huge body lounging beside him, Aerax laughed with the others as she made the bandits out to be bumbling fools who had shot crossbow bolts into their own leader before practically impaling themselves on her sword . . . though not one word of it did he truly believe. Bumbling thieves would not have plagued the road for as long as these had. Only the most ruthless and dangerous of thieves could have, and her victory had not been mere luck.

Caeb sat up when his part in the story came. Again there

was laughter as Lizzan described something akin to a curious kitten playing with a rolling stinkbug, instead of a savage beast slowly ripping apart a man who'd meant to kill the woman he loved.

"It was well done," Aerax told him quietly, scratching the cat's ears. Caeb yawned before resting his big head on Aerax's lap and purring contentedly.

So Aerax was content, too. That contentment could not last, he knew. Soon he would have to turn again to his purpose. Soon he would fulfill the destiny that the goddess had given him. *You must become who you truly are.* He might pretend that was a huntsman, as he preferred to be, or the feral prince that Koth had made him. Yet those were what he'd been and what he was—and a villain was what he must become.

But not yet. This night, he would sit content with his eyes and ears and heart full of Lizzan.

At a table nearby, Uland, Degg, and Lady Junica were embroiled in a quiet argument that Aerax paid little attention to. The other Kothans would not acknowledge Lizzan's presence, let alone fill themselves with her, yet that was not the reason for their discontent. Instead Aerax was likely the reason, after he had told them that he intended to continue north with the southern alliance, instead of first returning south to Krimathe and then traveling with Riasa and her warriors north along the plains road.

Little could they say against his intentions. The alliance with Krimathe was made, the councilors no longer required a snow-haired prop, and a Kothan prince should never be gone from the island longer than necessary. The northern road they were on now was the fastest route back to Koth. There was also no need for him to return to Krimathe with Riasa and wait for her to gather her warriors—Uland and the councilors could lead them north on the plains road.

The only argument they'd made was that they had not enough guards to split into two parties. There Aerax had pointed out that he would have enough protection traveling with the Parsatheans.

He had not said that Lizzan alone would be protection enough.

For she was the true reason he intended to travel north with the alliance. The councilors had known, as well, though they could not refer to her.

Yet even they could not know the full reason . . . that where Aerax would go, Lizzan would also come. For Aerax knew that she'd seen him first coming out of the temple. Just as he'd only seen her before she'd run back inside.

That she'd lied and said it was Seri only meant that she was not done running from him. She'd needed to hide the truth—and Aerax would let her.

But he would not force her to travel with Kothans who spit on her. Better that she travel with the southern alliance and make friends among them.

For they were so like she was. Kelir was the next to stand and tell a tale, though he did not climb up onto a table. It was the song he'd begun before, of a warrior betrayed when his parents were murdered . . . and was the story of how the southern alliance had formed, Aerax realized as it went on, and other Parsathean warriors picked up where the last left off.

No fools were these Parsatheans, or the queen who'd sent them with a song already prepared for these occasions. They held their audience in silent, rapt attention—and the story of this alliance would likely spread farther and faster than Tyzen or the other ambassadors ever could travel.

Lizzan's face was flushed as she listened, and through the tale Aerax had seen her eyes glisten with tears and sparkle with laughter. Even his heart thundered as it neared the finish, as they sang of thousands of mounted warriors charging toward a walled city. Yet as victory was finally had, and the Parsathean king raced to claim his bride, Lizzan's gaze met his and little of the ending did Aerax hear.

And no longer was he content. For he had never claimed his bride, though she'd pledged herself to him. He had known the taste of her skin and the fierceness of her kiss. He had known the meaning of her every smile, her every frown. He had known the rhythm of her heart and the warmth of her breath.

When they'd been young, it had been enough, because there had always been the promise of more to come. But he should not have been so content then, for now he would never be content again. Not without Lizzan beside him.

And across the room she remained.

When the song was finished, toward him instead came Lady Junica, her expression tightening with every step. "Will you escort me down to the baths? I am told that if I soak long enough, tomorrow I might ride a horse instead of a periwag."

That would not be the only reason for the escort. But Lady Junica's obvious discomfort did not allow her to speak much as they headed to the pools under the inn, with Caeb prowling down the stairs behind them.

Made from natural rings of yellow stone, the baths steamed a thick mist into the air, making every breath seem heavy and wet. A slow current ran through, spilling from pool to pool—some deep and some shallow, some warm and some hot. As the attendant approached them to take their clothes, and Lady Junica still had not spoken, Aerax realized he was also in for a soaking. His second of the day, though for this one he would be full naked.

He stripped off his armor and saw the wary glance the attendant gave to Caeb. "He will bathe, too," he said, unbuckling the cat's harness. Despite the rinse Aerax had given him at the river, the bandits' blood still stained his fur.

Near empty the baths were, for most of the inn's guests were still upstairs. A few other figures Aerax could see, but the thick mist offered privacy and they appeared indistinct at even a small distance.

They were led to a pool deep enough for Caeb to swim in, and with ledges for sitting on. Dropping the robe the attendant had given him at the edge, Aerax stepped in before Lady Junica, then helped her down. Sitting, she was submerged to her shoulders while the water only came to Aerax's chest—until Caeb jumped in, and then the water rose to her chin and the splashing wave interrupted her blissful sigh.

"So you are not the only one who likes to swim," she said with a laugh, before giving him a sidelong glance. "Tell me, Aerax—do you wish to take Koth's throne?"

She could not have surprised him more. "I do not."

"Are you certain? I would help you."

And he was wrong, for *that* surprised him more. "I am certain."

"It is a shame. Do you truly despise everything that Koth is?"

After seeing his mother shunned? After knowing how Kothans treated those whose names were struck from the books? After learning what lay beneath the crystal palace?

"I have made a few exceptions." And all of them were related to Lizzan.

"Then why did you stay?" Her gaze searched his face. "That is what I cannot understand. Why did you not go with her?"

His eyes narrowed. "Who?"

She laughed. "That is not a game I will play. You know full well that if I had my way, names would only be recorded in the books for the purpose of tax collection." But she did not pursue the question again, instead tilting her head back against the edge of the pool and closing her eyes. "Degg and Uland are persuaded that you lied on her behalf so that she might spread her thighs in gratitude. But was it truth what you said about seeing the wraiths' tracks?"

"It was."

"You also said the wraiths 'escaped' across the King's Walk."

Curse his tongue, then. "Did I?"

"You did. Though everyone else said they charged across to attack the bandits. But you did not say 'charged' or 'attacked.' So what did you mean by 'escaped'?"

"I meant they attacked."

"My dear boy, even if you do not become a king, you must better learn how to lie."

Aerax said nothing to that. A warning would only make her more curious, and the truth would be a death sentence. To protect Koth, his uncle would have executed Lizzan merely for insisting there were wraiths. And because no one had believed her . . . no one had asked where the wraiths had come from.

But that was the only path where these questions led. Only death waited for anyone who asked them. And on Koth, death was not the end of a punishment.

It was when torment began.

Lady Junica sighed. "But since you did not lie about the wraiths, tell me—how did she survive, except by running and hiding?"

Aerax stiffened. "Lizzan is no coward."

"I believe it." Without lifting her head, Lady Junica looked up at him. "And when she spoke before the court, I found her credible. Except she had no answer to that. How did she survive, when no one else did?"

"She is a fine warrior—"

"As were many others. And there were other soldiers with more experience. Most of the high command was there to observe her, and each of them earned their rank by being the finest of Koth's warriors. Yet she alone survived. So the others on the court argued that the only possible answer was that she hid until the fighting was over . . . and I saw no other answer, either. Now I ask you if there was another answer—because if there is, I should very much like to give that answer to our soldiers and to the Krimathean warriors before they face Goranik."

Aerax shook his head. "She did not say."

"Then you should persuade her to. And if she does not easily give up the answer, persuade her harder."

His muscles tensed. "Harder?"

With threats or violence? If that was what Lady Junica meant, she had sorely misjudged him—and sorely misjudged saying this to him. He liked this woman, but he would kill her here before he allowed her to harm Lizzan.

But it was Aerax who had misjudged, as he realized

when she said, "Given how you look at her, I think that you will not have any trouble managing that—and you'll have many nights upon the road to persuade her with." Wearing a slight smile, Lady Junica closed her eyes again. "Ahh, these waters truly work wonders on my back. I thank you for the escort and the company while I soak and ramble on."

Her rambles were schemes that might depose a king and save an army. Snorting out a laugh, Aerax abandoned the ledge and swam to Caeb. The cat was in a playful mood, and as these waters were much warmer than those they usually swam in—and because leaving the pool would expose how his mind was filled with thoughts of persuading Lizzan—Aerax lingered with him.

Lady Junica didn't linger as long as they did, and she waved away his offer to help her climb out. Wonder slid across her face as she bent easily for her robe and covered skin pinkened from the heat of the pool.

"Truly, I might be able to ride in the morning," she said with a note of awe, rolling her shoulders. "I feel as if my bones have been oiled—and I am not fatigued at all. Even the mosquito bite that I've been itching all day is gone. Imagine if during the red fever . . . If we had . . ." Voice thickening, she closed her eyes. "If my family had come here. But the fever took them too quickly. We could not have traveled so far. And there were wandering healers from outside Koth who claimed to have Nemek's potions, but they were all exposed as charlatans. Yet this water must be truly blessed. Why do you not sell bottles of this water?" she asked the attendant who came to assist her with the robe.

"Nemek's blessing cannot be sold," the girl told her solemnly.

"What if I do not buy it? May I simply fill a bottle to take with me?"

"Nemek's blessing cannot be stolen."

Lady Junica tilted her head, eyes narrowing. "What if I pray to them and ask for more of their blessing before I fill the bottle?"

The girl smiled. "Nemek are generous and will give it. But I suggest you also fill your heart with gratitude and humility before you fill your bottle, for if it is done with a heart full of entitlement and greed, you might find that water is nothing but water."

"I will be both grateful and humble."

"Come, then. We have bottles that seal tightly and will not leak during your travels—and though you cannot buy the water, you can buy the bottle."

The councilor arched a brow. "I suppose the bottles are expensive?"

"Only if you are rich," the girl said, and continued down the path. "Or if you travel with a prince."

Lady Junica laughed and began to follow her before pausing and glancing back at Aerax. "Do you think there will be anything left of its healing magic after we reach Koth? No god but Varrin has power on the island . . . but what if a blessing is captured in water and brought in from outside?"

Did she think he would know? Aerax did not, and said so.

"I suppose we will find out," she said, then frowned. "But how could we not already know that answer? These healing baths have stood as long as our island has, and I cannot be the first who brought water from these pools."

That was truth. "Perhaps that knowledge was also struck from the books," Aerax said flatly. "If a bottle of water made Kothans doubt Varrin's protection or if they looked to other gods when they were sick and frightened, surely whoever brought that bottle would be called a charlatan and exiled, too. Or executed."

For a long moment, she stared at him. Then slowly, she nodded. "Perhaps."

He looked to Caeb after she was gone. "You had best hope we've been in the water long enough to drown your fleas, or else you will be covered in the healthiest fleas that ever lived."

Sheer disdain curled the cat's upper lip. Aerax laughed at him and began to swim toward the edge of the pool—

then halted at the ledge as a figure resolved out of the heavy mist. Wrapped in her red cloak, Lizzan followed behind an attendant. Abruptly she stopped when her eyes met his, uncertainty flickering over her expression.

Heart pounding, Aerax did not move even as Caeb surged out of the pool to greet her, a cascade of water raining from his fur. Her gaze followed the cat before swinging back to Aerax.

And Lizzan must have been done with running or hiding. Lifting her chin, she said something to the attendant, who nodded and turned back toward the entrance. Without hesitation, Lizzan continued toward them, lips curving as Caeb padded to meet her.

"You resemble a giant drowned rat," she told him, then laughed and covered her face when his response was to shake the water out of his coat. "Now you are merely a giant rat."

Affectionately she rubbed her face against Caeb's, and then he settled down to begin licking his fur dry. She continued to the edge of the pool, biting her lip when she met Aerax's eyes again.

Her own eyes seemed shadowed and tired. "You looked to be leaving."

"Not if you are joining me," he said in a low voice. "But what of Seri? Do you not have to protect her?"

Perhaps Lizzan was not full done with hiding, for she stood by that lie. "She is surrounded by Parsathean warriors. I daresay she is safe enough for now," she said with a shrug, before hesitating. "In the morning, you go south to Krimathe with Riasa?"

He shook his head. "The others do. I go north with the alliance."

Surprise and relief flittered through her expression before her eyes shadowed again. "There are things that need to be said before we travel together. But . . . for a little while, can we be as we were before? Before my exile, before you went to the palace, before the red fever—when we were the finest of friends."

"I would always be that for you," he told her. "Not only for a little while."

"But a little while is all we have."

That truth speared through his heart. Hoarsely he said, "Then I will gladly take what time we have."

"As will I." Her voice was thick and her gaze averted from his as she slipped the red cloak from her shoulders. She wore only her father's medallion around her neck, and it was if she shoved Aerax's head underwater into the healing heat, stealing the breath from his lungs and the sense from his brain.

Nudity was nothing. Regularly Kothans shared public bathhouses and sweat huts. Yet *Lizzan's* nudity was everything. No other woman had Aerax ever looked at and imagined touching her bare flesh or suckling her soft nipples to hardness. Yet with Lizzan, he saw all the places where she might be pleasured. And there were so many. So many that he'd already touched and kissed. So many that he already knew would make her sigh and moan and beg.

There, there . . . and *there*.

As she stepped into the bath, his eyes worshiped every span of her skin, every lean muscle, every soft curve. She had changed in the ten years since he'd last seen her so fully exposed. More pale scars knitted her flesh, more curls grew between her thighs, more generous were her hips.

And from head to toe, she was still perfection.

Though she must not feel so. She settled into the water with a pained groan, then sank deeper and tipped her head back, until only her face was above the surface. Her eyes squeezed shut. "My skull feels as if it is about to crack."

Frowning his concern, Aerax moved nearer. "Did you fall?"

She slitted open an eye. "Do I seem so drunk?"

"As much mead as you've had, you shouldn't be able to walk." And he had watched her closely enough to know. "Instead you seemed more sober with every sip."

"I am paying for that sobriety now." She laughed, and the water rippled around her face. "I will tell you a secret, but you cannot tell the Parsatheans. One day I might challenge them to a drinking contest and I prefer to win."

He preferred that she won, too. "Tell me."

"I was nearly full drunk at the temple. But the priestess said she would purify everything that passed between my lips . . . and so all that mead became water."

Aerax grinned. "Truly?"

"Truly." Lizzan laughed again, then groaned as if it hurt her. Tenderly Aerax cupped the back of her head, began massaging her temples with his fingertips, and she sighed. "This feels so fine."

Better than fine. Touching her felt like more than he deserved. His chest tight with emotion, Aerax told her, "Then lie still until your head no longer hurts."

"I will." Though she apparently did not intend to lie quietly. "You have been making use of the battle masters at the palace."

The tutors who taught the royals a warrior's skill and were always available to give lessons or to train with them. "Why do you say that?"

"You blocked Uland's fist. But that sort of combat is not something we practiced together." An impish smile curved her lips and she peeked up at him. "And the size of you. You have always been strong, but thick arms and a broad chest do not merely come from palace feasts. You must practice with them often."

"There is little else to do." And hot pleasure rushed through his veins, knowing that she had looked his body over as closely as Aerax had hers. "If you like, I will let you examine all of me so you might measure what is bigger than it used to be. There is one part in particular that swells every time you are near."

She snickered. "I would suggest the part that swells the most is your head. But as your skull does not grow, we know your brains cannot be bigger."

"It is not my brains," he agreed, his heart light within his chest and his cock heavy between his thighs. "After years of palace lessons, they are smaller than before."

"I would not say so."

"No? What would you say, then? Tell me at length how clever I am."

Her brow arched. "I also would not call you 'clever.'"

A fair point, which he acknowledged with a soft grunt.

Smiling, she closed her eyes again. "And your other royal lessons?"

"I fail them all."

"Do you put in any effort?"

"I put in effort to avoid them. They would teach me how to dance and chew and smile, so that I might be a prettier prop. They teach me nothing worth knowing."

She hummed in agreement. "You are pretty enough without any lessons."

"First you admire my warrior's chest and arms, and now you flatter my face—though earlier, you would hardly even look at me. Is it because you cannot resist how strong and handsome I am?"

"Indeed," she laughed, flicking water at him. "I do not pretend to be blind. I will leave that to those in the crystal palace."

As she should, yet Aerax would like to hear more. "What do you mean by that?"

"I would leave blindness to those like Degg who think that because you do not take your lessons, you learn nothing. Or those like Uland who think you are declawed, as if they cannot see the difference between claws that have been removed and claws that are sheathed." The shake of her head tangled her floating hair in his fingers. "I knew they called you feral—but until this day, I didn't realize they only meant you have no sweet manners. I thought they understood what they'd brought into the palace. But if they are more afraid of Caeb than they are of you, they cannot know."

Because he never showed them. "Caeb has bigger fangs, so that is what they see."

"Caeb also wears a harness so they believe he is tamed, when in truth he would kill any one of them without a moment's thought. Is that what your princely clothes are—a harness so they can pretend you are tamed?"

"Those are for the prop," Aerax told her. "I wear a leash."

"But who holds that leash? It is not King Icaro. It is not Koth." Her voice tightened. "And it is not me."

He could only give her the truth. "It is me."

She bit her lower lip and seemed to contemplate that, eyes closed and floating quietly. Finally she asked, "There is something you must do?"

"There is."

"And you've had this purpose since you went to the crystal palace? This is what put distance between us?"

"It is," he admitted bleakly. A distance that had formed while Aerax had struggled with all he had learned beneath the crystal palace. First denying that it was his responsibility, then rejecting as impossible the only solution he saw, before finally accepting that it must be done and that he was the only one who would do it.

"Why did you never let me help?"

There were many reasons, but he gave her the simplest ones. "Because it must fall to one of Varrin's bloodline. And I could not put this burden on you."

"Is it so heavy?"

It was only the weight of thousands upon thousands of souls. It was only the weight of an entire island.

But Aerax would not burden her by answering that, either.

At his silence, she sighed. "What can I give that will help you?"

Emotion filled his throat. Even now, she offered this. "Already you helped by convincing the Krimathean to send her warriors. I had no words to persuade her, but you did." A short laugh escaped him. "Perhaps I should have paid more attention to Degg's lessons."

"And learn to have a silky tongue? You don't need one." Abruptly she twisted around to face him, with Aerax's hands still caught in her hair. Water dripped from her nose and chin as she met his eyes.

He didn't want to let her go. "Your head—"

"No longer aches."

Aerax did. His cock ached at her nearness and his heart ached when he released her. Then he stiffened as she moved closer, straddling his thighs with her knees braced on the ledge at either side. Short his breath became, fire raging through his blood.

"Lizzan . . ." He groaned her name. Hands shaking with the urge to touch her, his fists clenched and unclenched at his sides. His body burned volcanic. The only cool relief was in the lake blue of her eyes as her gaze locked with his, and he would drown in the answering need he saw there.

Her breath quickened. "This is also as before."

"Worse," he gritted out. Though that was not true. "Better."

"Both," she agreed, and her eyes closed. "Can you still restrain yourself?"

He could. And always for her, he would. Unless she gave him leave, never would he let loose the feral beast within.

At his abrupt nod, she slid closer, until his turgid cock-stand rose tall against her belly and she linked her arms around his neck. His surging arousal demanded to devour her, to claim her, yet Aerax restrained every movement but the unclenching of his fists, so that he could grip her hips and hold her against him. So many times before, they'd sat in this intimate way to talk, to kiss.

And it seemed that talking was what she intended now. "I think you have learned very well the games royals play," she said. "You are simply not willing to play them."

With a rough laugh, he told her, "There is one I'd like to play now. Lady Junica asked me to find out how you survived the wraiths."

Lizzan went still. Uncertainty crossed her expression. "Why does she wish to know?"

"So she can tell the Krimatheans. She says you evaded the answer before."

She gave a troubled sigh. "So I did."

"Now she wants me to seduce the answer from you."

A sputtering laugh cleared the shadows from her face. "Truly?"

"Truly."

"And how would you do it?" Grinning, she leaned closer until her mouth was but a breath away from his. "With delicate kisses and poetry? Were there lessons in seduction given to the palace, too? Did you avoid them or attend?"

"No lessons," he rasped against her lips. "I know what to do with you."

"Once upon a time, you did." She brought her hand forward to cup his jaw, her thumb slipping over his bottom lip, drawn back tight over gritted teeth as he bore the onslaught of his need. "What would you do with me now?"

"All that I have dreamed these many years with my cock in my fist," he told her, his voice as harsh as her breathing suddenly became. Always it had been thus, that Lizzan responded to his words and his need as if they were another touch. "I would lick at your throat until you were begging for my mouth on yours."

"That has always been a good start with us," she said huskily, the pulse racing beneath her skin. "But if you kissed me, you could not tell me what you would do next."

"Over and over, I would taste your mouth until we were both dizzy, until your eyes could not longer see and you could only cling to me."

"I am not so weak."

"I would make you so, Lizzan."

She did not argue that. Breathlessly she asked, "And then?"

"Then you would most likely complain how you needed and ached here." His palms slid up her sides to cup the softness of her breasts, half covered but unconcealed by the water. She arched her back, gasping as his thumbs swept over the hardened peaks, and her reaction sent hot pulses of lust the length of his shaft. "These baths are supposed to heal every pain. Yet I think only my mouth could ease yours."

Her laugh jiggled the softness filling his hands. "I think you are right."

"So I would worship your tits with my tongue and teeth." He bent his head so that she could feel the warmth of each word against the wetness of her skin, jealously watching the water lap at her nipples with her every panting breath. Despite the heat, the tips of her breasts had tightened into rosy buds, and the evidence of her arousal pushed his own toward agony. "Let me, Lizzan."

"Once," she breathed.

Only once. With his gaze on hers, Aerax lifted her breast and lightly closed his teeth over her nipple, his tongue teasing the trapped flesh as he gently tugged. By her moan, the pinch of his teeth was all pleasure and no pain.

"That I would do," he told her gruffly, aching for another taste but she had said *once*. "Until you could bear it no more."

"Aerax." His name became a needy whine and her hips began a helpless rocking. "I cannot bear it now."

"But you would. For so long." Gripping her rounded ass and stopping those torturous movements, he pulled her closer, burying his face in her throat. "As you did when we hunted the falt."

Whose white pelt they would lay beneath them on their moon night. But it had still been a midsummer day when they'd hunted the falt, and they had not even completely hauled the enormous tusked beast onto the lakeshore before they were upon each other. Barely restrained he'd been then, too, as he'd kissed her until she'd clung to him. Then he'd worshiped her breasts, sucking at her nipples until she'd been nearly sobbing with the pleasure of it.

"More seed have I spilled over that memory than any other," he told her now, his mouth skimming the curve of her neck. "How you grabbed hold of my hair and shoved me to my knees, then pushed my mouth to your cunt and told me to feast."

She whimpered. Her fingers slipped between them, but he was there first, his right hand letting go of her ass to delve between her widespread thighs. His thumb brushed her clitoris and she stiffened before moaning, winding her arms around his shoulders again and fists tangling in his hair.

"Never will I forget the taste of you, as hot and bright as the sun. Or the sounds you made each time I stopped licking long enough to suckle your clit." Sounds so near to those she made when his thumb swept back and forth over that slippery bud as his tongue had. She panted into his ear, rolling her hips as if seeking a firmer touch—and Aerax gave it. Always he would give what she needed. "I remember how you began to shake, and I had to hold you up to my mouth lest you fall. And when you came, how I thought you might crack the sky with your scream."

And tear out his hair. As her fingers threatened to now, as she shook through an orgasm and muffled her cry against his shoulder. Yet that pain was always the sweetest of all agonies, knowing that he'd given her so much pleasure.

But Lizzan had always been generous in return. As she was now, her mouth hot against his throat when she panted, "And then?"

Never had they gone much further. But that he had dreamed, too. "Would I be unrestrained?"

"You would."

"So mad I am for you, Lizzan. Unleashed, I would feast upon you again and again, until you begged for more than my tongue in your cunt," he rasped, and then his breath hissed out in agonized pleasure when she canted her hips forward until the thickness of his cock nestled into the lush furrow between her thighs. "You are so wet for me."

He felt her smile against his skin. "We are in a bath, Aerax."

"No bath is as hot and as slick as your need." Then his head fell back, another groan escaping through his gritted teeth as she began to glide up and down the base of his shaft. Still a virgin was he, but Aerax had known the clench of her sheath around his finger. "So many times I have imagined the hot grip of you clutching my cock. Imagined it over and over again, yet not one imagining was as sweet as this."

"Is imagining all you would do?"

He growled. "I would spread your thighs and fuck full deep."

Her breath shuddered into his ear and she rode his length again. "And all of this would be inside me. Would I be under you?"

"Above me. So little control would I have." So little he did now. His fingers dug into her ass, his breaths coming in ragged heaves as he dragged her cunt up and down his pulsating flesh. "If you were not on top, I might fuck you through the ground."

"And if on my knees?"

Bent over and his for the taking. Fiery sparks began to flash behind his eyes. "I would mount you so hard, you would feel me in your throat."

"There are easier ways to choke me," she murmured, and the laugh that shook through him rattled the chains of his restraint, and then the stroke of her hand down his erection was a furnace that threatened to destroy all control. "Are you near to coming?"

A harsh grunt was his only answer. No more could he do. His cock was embraced by her strong fingers and her slick cunt. Every other part of his body was focused on restraint, that he did not lift her onto the edge of the bath and bury his head between her thighs. That he did not cover her and push deep, so deep into the sultry wetness that tortured him so sweetly.

She nipped below his ear, a pinprick of ecstasy that shot across his skin to crash into the frantic ache of his cock. Her hand tightened and harder she stroked. "Are you near?"

His body gave the reply that he could not, the muscles of his stomach crunching tight, jaw grinding. Abruptly she shoved back off the ledge. His hands skimmed up her back as she flattened out, head diving beneath the surface. Scorching suction surrounded the crown of his erection just as the orgasm slammed through him, and the sensation was nothing he could have dreamed. All that Aerax was seemed to surge through his turgid flesh and empty out into her mouth. There was nothing of him left when she was done, lifting her head to find him slumped back against the edge of the bath and trying to breathe again, to see again.

But always he would see Lizzan's smile. She straddled his thighs, wound her arms around his neck, and brought her face so close to his.

"Your seed did not become water, but I believe Vela just purified your prick," she said, and as his spent lungs huffed out a laugh, she caught his mouth in a kiss.

This, the goddess must have purified, too—for never had Aerax known anything so sweet or so fine as Lizzan's smiling lips upon his. The kiss ended too quickly, her hands framing his face as she drew back.

"This is not what I intended to do when I next saw you," she said on a sigh. "Being near you makes me forget all else."

An affliction he suffered, too. "I am not sorry."

"Nor am I." Her fingers twined into the hair at his nape. "You are fair good at seduction."

"I forgot that began this," he admitted, and watched her smile return. "And I'm fortunate you are easily pleased. I couldn't have seduced you in full."

New light touched Lizzan's face. "You still haven't had your moon night?"

"I am pledged to you." He frowned. "Do you think I would ever touch another?"

Her shrug seemed careless, but the searching depths of her gaze were not. "I was exiled and my name struck from the books."

And she had pledged herself to Aerax while *his* name was still unwritten. No difference at all did it make to him. Had she thought it would?

"What of it?"

"Nothing at all." Blithely she walked two fingers from his chest to his throat. "Except that I bedded hundreds of men and women after leaving Koth."

His eyes narrowed. "All at once?"

She snorted out a laugh, but a rare vulnerability he saw in her prevented him from teasing more. Not for a moment did Aerax believe it. She was still as virgin as he. But Aerax had not left Koth with her at the same moment she'd been rejected by her people. If she needed him to think that hundreds of lovers had desired her . . . in truth, that was easy for Aerax to believe. Harder to believe was that she'd allowed someone close enough to warm her bed.

In Koth, taking casual lovers was often frowned upon, for legend said the god Varrin had not. There was always a pledge of love first, followed by marriage that bound them together, and so they remained until death.

Aerax knew that the story of the devoted god was as false as Koth itself. Yet in that aspect alone, he was truly of the realm.

There was only Lizzan. There would only *ever* be Lizzan.

After a moment, she sighed and glanced up at him. "I thought it might be the purpose that only someone of Varrin's bloodline could do—to fill the palace again with snow-haired babies."

"My uncle has done that well enough with his new wives."

Again her shoulders rose in that not-truly-careless shrug.

He caught her stubborn chin and made her look at him. "Even if we were not pledged, do you think I'd touch a woman who would never have spoken my name before a scrawl of ink gave me worth? Who would never have even seen me?"

"I thought it might be a prince's duty."

"They've tried to tell me so." But he shook his head. "My only duty to Koth is to make certain it does not sink while people still live there. Never would I allow a child of mine to be born on that island. If I could, Lizzan, I would exile *everyone* I love from it. I am glad you are not there— and if your brothers and mother were not so stubbornly devoted to preserving all that Koth pretends that it is, I would have sent them away to find you."

Her chin quivered against his thumb. "You are glad I am exiled?"

"I am not," he said, his throat thick because his heart could not bear the gleam of tears he saw. "I miss you fiercely. I hate that you bear a shame you should not. But I am glad you are away from Koth."

"And I would rather be nameless there instead of cursed and shunned here." Blinking rapidly, she tilted her head back, drew a shuddering breath. "Why did you not tell me the true reason you remained silent? Did you think I wouldn't understand that you wanted to save my life? Do you think I wouldn't have done the same for you?"

"I knew you would." His chest ached. "But you always put Koth first, Lizzan. I feared you would agree with my uncle, and sacrifice yourself to prevent a panic."

Her glistening gaze met his again. "You thought I would sacrifice myself?"

"You would."

"Only if there was no other choice!" A watery laugh shook through her, and disbelief hardened into flat resignation as she continued, "And there apparently *was* another choice, and it was exile. But now, when I might finally decide the path for myself, there is no other choice at all."

Her bleak declaration slashed at his heart. "Lizzan—"

"Aerax." She stopped him, fire returning to her gaze. "I would have also chosen exile, but the choice would have been *mine*. Instead you finally join the list of those who decide what is best for me without a care for what I want."

Hurt ripped through his chest. Those were her family who had not wanted her to become a soldier, so they had not even allowed her fencing lessons. The family who had tried to turn her gaze from Aerax, so that she would pledge herself to another. Always he had supported every wish that she'd made, even if it meant staying in a realm he hated. Even if it would have taken her away from him.

And it *had*. That pain fired his response now. "As you did the High Daughter?"

She frowned at him. "What?"

"Not telling her about Goranik until it suited you, to spare her the hurt of knowing he lived yet being unable to pursue him while on her quest. Did you not decide what was best for her? And you do not even love her, Lizzan."

Her lips parted and she stared at him, as if in new realization.

But he was not done. "You follow the path that you decide is best for you. That I will always support. But you *only* do what is best for you, Lizzan. All else is nothing. Before the red fever, how often did we speak of changing the law of the books? Yet after the red fever, how often did you think of it?"

Shame flickered through her eyes. "Almost never," she whispered.

"Because my name was finally added to the pages. You got what you'd wanted and so you abandoned the fight. It became something you hoped someone else would do . . . someday. Though there are other bastards on Koth still nameless and unseen. But it no longer affected you."

Her chest hitched, her gaze wildly searching his before she abruptly closed her eyes and averted her face. Her throat worked before she said thickly, "When I saw you, I intended to say that it is best for us both to forget all that we were before the red fever, and stay away from each other as we travel north. Perhaps these failures will make it easier. We became such a disappointment to each other."

A disappointment? Never could Lizzan be. Yet he had made her feel so.

"You are no—" Aerax broke off, and panic clutched his heart when she began to rise out of the water. "Not like this," he said hoarsely, catching her hips before she could step out. Once before he'd let her leave with hurt and misunderstanding burning between them. Never could he again. "Please. You are no disappointment. After the red fever, I know you had barely a moment away from your duties, let alone time to petition the crown. Please, Lizzan. Do not go when we are like this."

Her body trembled. Tears spilled down her cheeks but even as denial coursed through him, she sank down again, hiding her face in his neck. So tight he held her, near sick with relief.

"Forgive me." His hand stroked down her wet hair. "I

learned more from my royal lessons than I thought. I was hurt, so I used words as weapons to aim at your soft heart."

"That is not the result of royal lessons," she said on a tremulous little laugh. "That is you, being exactly like your cat."

Lashing out. "So it was."

"And I know you saved my life by trading your silence," she told him, her voice muffled against his neck. "I *am* grateful. Even if I do not seem it. This is all easier if I am angry."

He did not fear her anger. "You have never liked anyone making your choices for you."

"True. But I suspect that exile was not a choice for me until you made it one. So I am grateful." She drew back, offered a wavering smile. "And I have chosen the path I take now."

"Your quest to restore your family's honor?"

Silently she nodded.

"So perfect you are, Lizzan." He did not deserve to even touch her.

Sadness softened her smile, and she raised her hand to trace the scars that raked down her face. "Am I?"

"You are. And more beautiful than you have ever been. Never before did you wear your courage and your strength so nakedly as you do now."

"Most people only see a curse."

"Most people are fools."

"As I am," she said with a sigh. "Such a fool, to be here with you as if nothing between us has changed—as if we are not strangers to each other now."

Her words caught Aerax by the throat. "We are not," he said hoarsely.

"We *are*, Aerax. We hardly know each other. For ten years, we have barely even spoken." Her breath shuddered, eyes squeezing tight as if to stop tears from falling again. "Do you recall when I took you to meet my family?"

"I could hardly forget." One of the most extraordinary events of Aerax's life. Six years had passed since he'd found her hacking at a tree. Every free moment afterward, they'd spent together, and then a single kiss had ripped away the veneer of simple friendship to reveal the need growing beneath—and six years was suddenly not enough for either of them. A lifetime would be barely enough.

Since the law would not recognize a pledge between them, Aerax had wanted to leave Koth with her then. But Lizzan wanted to at least attempt to secure her family's approval. So she'd invited him to her home—not the first invitation she'd given, but the first he'd accepted.

Never had he been to her home before. Never had he been to *anyone's* home. But he knew what to expect, so he'd been ready for a battle. For years, her family had hurt her with their refusal to support their softhearted daughter's intention of becoming a soldier. And her father was a high commander and her mother a magistrate—one a defender of Kothan law, and the other an executor of it. He'd expected to enter a cold and strict household, to remain unseen and unheard. He'd expected it would be a fight merely to make them acknowledge his presence.

Instead he was given a kind welcome—the only welcome he'd *ever* been given in Koth—because they loved Lizzan as much as he did. They had not approved of the match, for they believed it was not in her best interest. Yet they had listened to both Aerax and Lizzan.

For the first time, he'd understood how her family's love had made her path to being a soldier all the harder. Easy it would have been to rebel against cold tyranny. It was much more painful for her to push back against warm affection and good intentions.

It was also the first time anyone other than his mother or Lizzan had spoken to Aerax as if he were someone worthy of respect. And it was the first time he'd been spoken to not as a son, not as a friend, not as a snow-haired bastard—but as a man.

So he had listened to Lizzan's parents in turn, as they'd argued that his unwritten name was only a minor obstacle compared to what lay ahead. Aerax's hopes for the future looked nothing like Lizzan's. He wanted to leave Koth; she wanted to stay. They had pointed out that no matter which path he and Lizzan took, one would come to resent the other—because either Aerax would be trapped in a realm where he was treated as nothing or Lizzan would have to abandon a long-held dream—and that resentment would only lead to pain and separation.

All they'd said had seemed sensible to both Aerax and Lizzan. So they had agreed to remain friends, resolved to endure a little pain and frustration so they could spare each other heartbreak later.

That resolution only lasted until separation was nearly upon them. Yet they *had* tried.

Now she asked quietly, "Do you believe that you would have come to resent me?"

After he'd stayed in Koth for her? "Never."

"Nor I you, if we had left. Such adventures we might have had—and there are always people to protect and defend. I would have fought as hard for our happiness as I did to become a soldier. But what they said made so much sense."

"It did." But a heart was not ruled by sense. "Perhaps that was why they believed I would learn to resent you. They did not understand how much I love you, Lizzan."

"You mean, how much you love the girl you knew."

His heart twisted. "Lizzan—"

"Ten *years*, Aerax." She cupped his face, her unhappy gaze searching his. "Are you still the same boy you were then?"

After all that had happened? After all that he knew now? "I am not," he admitted hoarsely.

"And I am not the same girl."

"The heart of you is the same," he argued. "Do not say that has changed."

"Perhaps my heart has not. As yours has not, either." Her chin trembled before firming again. "But we are strangers to each other. And if we do not remain strangers, there are two ways forward for us—either what we learn of each other now will bring disappointment and taint the precious memory of all we were before . . . or we will learn to love each other again. But, Aerax"—with two fingers over his lips, she stopped him when he would have spoken—"the end will be the same. We will separate. You *must* return to Koth, true?"

Throat aching, he nodded.

"And I cannot," she said thickly. "So this time, we must be sensible. My parents were wrong then. We would not have resented each other and eventually separated. But *now* there is no other end. We will part either now or later. Now is painful enough. But if I learn to love you again, and have to leave you again . . ." Her voice broke. "I cannot, Aerax. I cannot. So we must be strangers to each other now."

It was sensible. Yet they'd had another option before. "Can we not be friends?"

She gave a teary-eyed laugh. "That is all I meant to do in this bath. Yet my fingers had not even pruned before I was riding your cock. You and I can never be only friends, Aerax."

That was truth. Yet he could never be a stranger to her, either. "I will do my best to disappoint you." It would not take much effort. "Then you will not be hurt, but glad to see the back of me when we reach Koth."

Another laugh broke from her, and she rested her forehead against his. "If there is disappointment, it will be me disappointing you. On my part, I suspect that I will love you more than I ever have."

"As I will you."

"Then there is only more pain ahead."

"I would bear that pain, Lizzan."

"But I cannot." She drew a broken breath. "I cannot. This quest is supposed to bring me pain to the edge of my enduring. But *already*, Aerax . . . Since leaving Koth, I've been so lost. And hurt. I cannot bear much more."

And he could not bear hurting her. With agony clawing at his chest, he told her, "Then strangers we will be."

She nodded, crying softly now with her hands still cradling his face, her forehead pressed to his. "It's the only sensible path."

"It is," he agreed gruffly, and she kissed him, a sweet and salty press of her trembling lips. "But what of another seduction?"

A laugh shuddered through her breaths. Tears streaked her cheeks when she pulled back to wipe her eyes, and then she reached down to clasp the medallion between her breasts. "I'll tell the Krimatheans how I survived the wraiths . . . but do not tell anyone else from Koth."

At that moment, Aerax cared nothing of Krimathe or Koth. But always he would care for Lizzan. "It protected you?"

"One wraith had already . . ." Voice wavering, she touched her scars. "I could barely see through the blood in my eyes. Then my father was with me, his armor shredded—but he was unharmed. Until he gave this to me and then . . . he was . . ."

Torn apart. "He saved you."

She swallowed hard before nodding. "As long as I can remember, he'd worn this. If the Kothan court had discovered that he'd carried some sort of magic with him . . . they would have said he'd never truly earned his rank. That his status would have been unfairly earned. But he *had* earned it. And I would not let him be dishonored. So I threw it into the lake alongside the Walk."

Then the necklace should have been forever gone. And she had not been wearing it on the ferry boat. "Where did you find it?"

"Vela gave it to me. And said it was always meant to be mine."

"What does that mean?"

A small shake of her head said she didn't know.

"Does it protect you now?"

"I have not yet stabbed myself to find out. But I suspect it does. Vela also said that she would give to me protection on this quest."

So that Lizzan could protect *him*. That did not sit easy within Aerax, yet he was glad to know she wore that medallion. "When does the quest end?"

"On the day of the first snowfall, after a glorious battle." She offered a wavering smile that faded as her gaze searched his. "Why do you go to the battle masters? You say there is nothing else to do, but you could find something to occupy you. Instead you make yourself into a warrior. Do you intend to kill your uncle?"

"Only if I must." For if Aerax's intentions were discovered, King Icaro and all the palace guard would try to kill him. "Would you stop me?"

Slowly she shook her head. "Whatever your purpose, I still know your heart. You have no wish to rule. And you despise Koth but wouldn't stay there out of hate. Which means you stay to help someone you love." She bit her lip. "Is it my family? Because I can think of no one else you care for."

Her belief in him clogged his throat with emotion. Gruffly he said, "Some are your family."

Her father. Her mother's parents. But Aerax could not explain to her without adding more to the pain she already bore. This was his burden alone.

"Then I will not stop you. Instead I will thank you." She caught his face in her hands. "Will your name be struck from the books again?"

"When I am done, there will be no books."

Surprise flared through her gaze, followed by concern. "You will be reviled by all of Koth."

A true villain. "I am used to it."

As if that did not reassure her, she shook her head and her gaze filled with determination. "You must do something for me. On this journey, you must make friends among the southern alliance. True friends."

A laugh shook through him. That was what he wanted for *her*.

"Listen to me, Aerax," she urged fiercely. "I know you well. In your life, you have cared about very few people. You have loved even fewer—your mother, though she is gone. Caeb. Me. Is there anyone else?"

"Your family."

"But you love them *through* me. After you met them, you liked them well enough—just as they liked you—but only a few times did you ever speak with them. You love them because they are a part of me. They have your loyalty because I am hurt if they are hurt. So you would always help them as you would me. Is that not true?"

Aerax could not say. He could not see a difference.

"No matter." Her hands smoothed down to rest on his shoulders. "You said the girl Seri was much like me?"

"The Parsatheans are all much like you."

"You enjoy their company?"

"I do."

"Then I want you to see them as part of me, too. It will make me happy to know that when you are finished with your purpose in Koth, you'll have somewhere to go and won't be alone. Caeb is not enough."

It would also make Aerax happy, for the alliance was exactly where he hoped she would be, too. Not so pleased by Lizzan's speech, Caeb padded forward to butt his head against her shoulder.

She scoffed and flicked water at him. "Do not take offense, you fool. You are a fine friend. But Aerax would do well to have more human ones."

The cat gave answer to that by flicking water back, though the size of his paw aimed a deluge at her head. Water dripping down her face, Lizzan leveled a dour stare at him until Caeb settled down again to lick the damp from his fur.

Ignored now by the cat, she looked to Aerax. "Your flea-bitten dustrag has no say in this."

Grinning, he said, "So I'll find friends on two legs instead of four. Should I also find a wife? Must she also have two legs instead of four?"

Her lips twitched, but solemnly she shook her head. "You must pine for me always."

"I would." Except her faith in Aerax gave him hope that he would never be a villain to her. To all of Koth, yes. But not to her. "But I think instead that I'll find you, and see if you will learn to love me again."

As if his words were knives, she made a wounded noise. Abruptly her eyes filled again and she threw her arms around his neck, holding tight.

Tension gripped his muscles. "Lizzan?"

"Aerax." Her voice was a ragged whisper in his ear. "To the end of my days, I will love you. I promise you that."

No sweeter promise could she have made. But pain filled his chest, because Aerax heard what else it was.

A farewell.

"Not yet," he said, voice raw. Tomorrow they would be strangers. But not yet. "Stay a little longer."

With her cheek pressed to his, she nodded, her arms tightening before she drew back to kiss him.

Aerax had wondered how many times a man's heart could be ripped from his chest. Now Lizzan did with every kiss, each one sweet and hot and quick, as if she meant to fill up a lifetime of kisses, as if she knew each one might be their last, as if it were too painful to stop because that meant she would go.

Until it became too painful for her to stay. With a sobbing breath, she pulled out of his arms—and it took all of Aerax's strength to let her leave. She kissed Caeb, and then, slinging her red cloak around her shoulders, she vanished through the steam.

Aerax closed burning eyes, jaw clenched against the howl of agony building in his chest. Not even an eternity spent soaking in these healing baths could repair a heart in shreds. The only remedy was being with her again.

Voice hoarse, he told Caeb, "Recall to me again why we do not go after her?"

The cat only rubbed his head against Aerax's, so it was he who had to remember the thousands in torment, whose pain was the foundation of all that Koth pretended to be, and who must be freed.

But there was hope. She had given it to him.

"This may end in separation now, but when it is done, we will find her," he vowed to Caeb. "There is nowhere she can go that we will not follow. To the ends of the world, we will hunt her."

With a rumbling purr and a rough lick to Aerax's cheek, the cat agreed.

CHAPTER 14

LIZZAN

After her exile, Lizzan's first destination had been Oana. She'd had no true desire to go. Heartbroken, she'd had no true desire to do *anything*. So when a fellow traveler had said the baths might heal the wounds on her face, Lizzan had not cared—but Oana had seemed as fair a place as any other.

The journey south by the mountain road had taken two full turns of the moon. By then the scabs had cleared, leaving behind livid and painful scars. By then the marks had been mistaken for Vela's curse often enough that she'd wanted them gone.

But the baths had not healed her wounds. The journey had taken too long for that. Instead the baths had healed the scars, and Lizzan had emerged from the water with the white marks she still bore.

It seemed that everything she'd ever done had taken too long. She had waited too long to pledge herself to Aerax, and so the red fever had separated them. She'd spent too long serving Koth and believing that their future together would sort itself out. And she had spent too long running from him, because his betrayal had still been an open wound, and she hadn't known he could heal it.

Now there was no time left. And only scars remained, still livid and painful, in ragged slashes across her heart.

Once, Lizzan might have dulled them with ale. No more could she. Still, she spent the hours before dawn in a dark corner of the inn's public room with the comfort of a drink in her hands—and except for the ache in her chest that kept clogging up her throat, she felt finer than she had since leaving Koth. As if the baths had erased from her body the years she'd spent on the road and sleeping in whatever spot she could find.

She could have done without the clarity of mind that came with it. Especially now, in the quiet and the dark while everyone else slept. Never did Lizzan like to be left to her own thoughts. Too quickly they became jagged knives trapped within her skull, sawing away at everything inside her.

Relief and distraction came near sunrise. The innkeeper began flitting between the tables, where the guests who had not taken a room—or had not made it to their beds—snored away the night's revelry. They awoke with groans and complaints of pounding heads, and at the innkeeper's suggestion, most abandoned the public room for the baths.

When Riasa came down the stairs, Lizzan stood—then sat again when the captain indicated that she would join her there. And so she did, picking up the young monk along the way, who had been sitting alone at his own table.

"Preter, is it?" Riasa asked as she took a seat beside Lizzan.

"It is," the monk confirmed through a yawn. His rumpled hair and bleary gaze added that he wasn't fully ready for conversation yet.

Riasa called to the innkeeper for a pot of tea and a breakfast before looking to Lizzan with a rakish glint in her eyes. "You ought to have joined us last eve."

With a laugh, Lizzan shook her head. After leaving Aerax, she'd wanted only solitude and drink, and sought out the private dining hall where they had met earlier in hope of finding both. There had still been pitchers of mead laid out with the feast—but also Riasa, laid out between the two Parsatheans who'd attended that meeting. So Lizzan had politely apologized for the interruption. Though in truth, it seemed there was no interruption at all as she spent a few moments combining the shallow remains of each pitcher into one container, then left them to it.

"We were all impressed by how steadily you poured while the table was jolting. Kelir said afterward that he'd never seen such fierce concentration." Riasa sat back as the innkeeper placed in front of them a platter of smoked fish in cream, alongside a slab of bread. "I told him that we might have shocked you terribly."

"Why is that?"

"You are from Koth." Riasa dabbed a bite of bread into the cream, eyebrows raised. "Are not such things frowned upon?"

"They are. But people still do them." The sight of food churned her stomach, so Lizzan refilled her mug. "No one from the nearby villages would ever be seen at the inn that Aerax's mother kept—so anyone who didn't want to be seen often went there. And her rooms were always full."

Now Lizzan's own mother and brother likely had the same business, since Aerax had given them the inn. They would be shunned even as people used them to conceal their own shameful hypocrisy.

She sipped to ease the sudden burning in her throat before continuing, "When there was a snowstorm or it was too bitterly cold to be outside, Aerax and I would sometimes spend time at the inn." Though hidden out of sight—and there they had received an education in all the things people did in their beds. "You can imagine how we passed that time."

"I would have sneaked into the rafters to watch," Riasa said.

It had been through a hole in the wall . . . but it was the same. "I think that Kothan and Krimathean children are not too different, then."

"Children?" Riasa scoffed. "I would watch from the rafters *now*. Particularly if it were Kelir and Ardyl below me. You ought to have at least taken a chair."

Lizzan snorted into her mug but got no chance to reply when Riasa's attention moved across the table, where the young monk's cheeks had burnished a deep red.

The captain clicked her tongue against her teeth. "Now I have made you blush. Have we shocked you, instead?"

Preter shook his head, his blush spreading beyond his beard and down his throat. "I would only say that Tolehi children are no different, either. And that even as adults, sometimes we watch what we cannot have."

"I see," Riasa said, and all at once her expression altered from teasing to sympathetic. "Did I tread upon your toes last eve?"

"Not at all," he said ruefully. "Ardyl and Kelir pay me no attention, because I keep my toes well covered. It would do no good for them to know. Especially as a bedding is only sport to them." All at once his face blazed brighter. "I do not mean to step on *your* toes, Captain."

Riasa shrugged. "It is only sport to me, too. Is it because you are too young?"

Irritation flashed across his features. "I am two years short of a queen's age."

Lizzan's eyebrows shot high. That made him twenty and eight years of age . . . a year older even than she was. "You do not look it."

His wry glance said he was well aware. A sigh followed. "They prefer to have their sport and move on, with everyone happily satisfied. But we travel together, so there would be no moving on. There would only be awkwardness after."

"Perhaps at the end of your journey, then," Riasa suggested.

"Let us hope so." Preter laughed, then grimaced, rubbing his head.

Lizzan knew well the pain he was feeling. "The baths would take care of your headache. That is where everyone else has gone."

His blush appeared again. "And all without their clothes."

"So they are," Lizzan agreed, eyeing his. Beneath the sleeves of a loose brown robe, strips of linen wrapped his wrists—and as far as she could tell, they wrapped his limbs completely. Aside from his head and hands, no skin was visible. "You don't like to see people naked?"

"I have become accustomed to that. I am not so accustomed to being seen."

"Request a private bath, then."

Anticipation lit his face. "They would accommodate me?"

"If they are not already full. But before you go—do you have knowledge of magic?"

Though he didn't draw away or move, it was as if a veil suddenly dropped over his eyes. "Some. Why?"

"I wonder if you recognize this." She drew her father's medallion from beneath her tunic and held it out as far as the silver chain around her neck allowed. "My father gave it to me on the King's Walk."

Rising from his chair, the monk bent for a closer look. "A charm? May I?" At her nod, Preter took hold of the medallion, rubbing it between his fingers as if to better make out the faded markings. "What does it do?"

Easier to show than tell. Lizzan tugged a dagger from her boot and drew the blade across her forearm.

"Not even a scrape," Riasa breathed, then her eyes narrowed. "Though it shaved off a few hairs. What if there is force behind it? Your skin does not break, but does it bruise?"

"It bruises—though perhaps not as easily."

After she'd chased the wraiths into the forest, Goranik had knocked her aside so hard that she'd shot through the air like an arrow and slammed into a tree. Her mind had been spinning dizzily as she'd gotten to her feet again. And for days afterward, she'd been sore, with a lump at the back of her head.

But the tree had cracked. Afterward, she recalled that it had—but barely did she see it then. Not with the wraiths charging around her. Not while their screeching filled the forest.

She forced those memories away. Still her hand trembled as she tried to sheathe the dagger, missing its mouth so many times that the blade would have cut up her leg if not for the necklace she wore.

Riasa sat back with a low whistle. "So this charm is why you did not die when you should have."

"It is."

"Do the Kothans know?"

"Only Aerax. The others might question my father's honor. Never would I let them taint his memory. But if more can be made, perhaps you can use them against Goranik."

Riasa nodded, looking to Preter.

"There is some faint embossing, but it appears to be nothing more than a coin hammered flat," said the monk, sounding baffled as he turned the medallion to examine the other side. "Where did your father come by it?"

Lizzan shook her head. "Perhaps he told the story when I was very young, because it seems as if there is *something* at the back of my mind. But I cannot remember. My mother might know."

"She is in Koth?"

"She is." Lizzan reached for her mug. "More recently, I came by it through Vela."

Preter glanced at her sharply. "What do you mean?"

"After the Walk, I threw it into the lake. But Vela gave it to me at her temple here and said it was always meant to be mine—and not to throw it away again."

"I would heed that warning," Preter said dryly, sitting.

So would Lizzan. "What do you make of it?"

"Not much. But I am no master of charms."

Riasa said, "I will take an imprint and show the priestesses in Krimathe."

Preter nodded. "Also we might consult the monks in Radreh."

The monastery that was the southern alliance's next destination. A troubled look passed over Riasa's expression at that suggestion, then cleared into a wide grin.

"There is our Queen Layabed!" she called to Laina, who

was coming toward them in her red cloak. "While you have been dozing, my lady, I have been cementing our new alliance and taking the Parsatheans' measure. I found them dedicated to their task, flexible of mind and body, and quite tireless . . . though not the equal of a Krimathean, as it was two against one, and I am not the one soaking in a healing bath this morn."

Silently laughing, the Krimathean took the seat beside Lizzan's. She inclined her head in greeting to Preter, whose face was blazing again as he poured tea into her mug.

"You continue east today?" Lizzan asked.

With a shadow passing over her features, the Krimathean nodded.

"You leave us in good hands, my lady," her captain said quietly. "All will be well."

On a heavy sigh, Laina nodded again and sipped from her mug.

Then they would not likely see each other again. Mead-scented water roiled in Lizzan's stomach as she said, "I must apologize to you. I have no liking for people who make decisions in my best interest instead of letting me choose for myself. Yet I did the same to you, when I did not say that Goranik might be alive. It was arrogant—and also selfish, because I prefer not to think or speak of that night on the Walk, so I grasped for any reason not to. And I am sorry for it."

Laina and Riasa exchanged a glance before the captain said, "We knew he was still alive. We did not know *where*. But we guessed he must be."

Lizzan's brows rose. "How did you guess?"

"As you did. Our spies in Lith reported that he was dead. But they could not uncover a credible account of who had killed him or how he had died." Riasa shook her head. "But we also expected that he would have an army with him— not a handful of bandits."

That handful of bandits had done as much damage as an army. But Lizzan only said, "Still, I regret that I did not tell you when I should have."

The gentle squeeze of the woman's hand on hers felt like

forgiveness that made Lizzan's chest ache. Then Laina's gaze narrowed on Lizzan's cloak and she pinched the edge of the thin cloth between her fingers, frowning.

Most likely comparing the threadbare cloak to her own, which was thick and looked as plush as velvet. "I think the priestess did not expect someone to come asking for a quest," Lizzan told her, which only deepened Laina's frown.

Preter's forehead creased. "Does not Vela herself bless the cloak of everyone who quests for her?"

"Against wind and rain, cold and sun." Or so the legends said. And indeed, despite the heaviness of Laina's cloak, she had not seemed affected by the jungle's heat. "But my quest will end on the day of the first snowfall. So I do not need the protection."

"Especially as Vela gave you the other," Riasa said, and when Laina glanced at her askance, she explained, "The goddess gave her a charm that protects her from blades."

Or from a wraith's icy claws. Yet that did not seem enough for Laina. As when Lizzan had asked why the goddess didn't simply help them defeat the Destroyer, anger flashed across the Krimathean's face. Her fingers went to the ties at her throat.

As if she intended to exchange cloaks, and give to Lizzan the blessed one. Lizzan stopped her, shaking her head.

"This one suits me." Threadbare and frayed, just as she was. "I only wish it were not so faded. But while on this quest, I intend to redden it with the blood of my enemies."

Or the blood of Aerax's enemies, as she protected him. But she supposed there was no difference. His enemies would always be hers.

"That seems a fine plan," Riasa said with a laugh.

A smile curved Laina's mouth, yet it seemed with reluctance that she tied the strings of her cloak again.

"Since you are traveling with the alliance, I hope you do not encounter too many enemies," Preter said wryly. "But I will be glad to have with us a charmed warrior who is also one of Vela's Chosen. After today, the number of Parsathean warriors in our party will be near half of what we began with."

Lizzan frowned. "Have you lost so many?"

"Not killed. Sent home." He looked to Laina. "This morning, two warriors begin the journey back, so that Queen Yvenne will know of our progress—and so that she can begin sending supplies for the Parsathean army north to Krimathe. Otherwise she would receive no word until we all returned from the far north, and a full year of preparations would be lost. Also there are two warriors still at the river with the old woman, and when they are done, they will catch up to the caravan and join the two other warriors we have tasked to protect them."

"Mevida's caravan?" Lizzan asked in surprise. "The caravan we traveled with?"

With a nod, Preter said, "The innkeeper mentioned how few travelers he'd seen of late. The bandits might be to blame for how few came from the south. But there have also been few travelers from the north, and an empty road usually points to some danger upon it."

"That is truth," Riasa said.

"So Kelir and Ardyl tasked two warriors to stay with the caravan. We cannot all ride at that slow pace, but if we are ahead of them, we will likely encounter whatever preys that route before they do. But if we don't, they will still have protection."

News that lightened a weight on Lizzan's heart. She had rejected Mevida's offer of a job because she'd not wanted to travel as far north as Koth. Now her path took her in that direction, yet she could still not travel with them. But perhaps she would help protect them from a distance.

And she was apparently not the only one who'd felt some guilt for abandoning them. Lizzan glanced at Laina, saw the same relief in the other woman's expression. With a short laugh, she tapped her mead to Laina's tea so they might drink to their mutual ease.

When she set down her mug, Preter watched her with

narrowed eyes. "Are you always drinking on the road, too? Or only in villages?"

"Used to be both," Lizzan told him, as it was a fair question to ask of someone whose sword might protect him. "But no longer. At least while I am on this quest."

He raised a skeptical brow and glanced at her mug.

Ruefully she admitted, "As soon as the mead passes my lips, Vela changes it to water."

Laina snorted and quickly slapped a hand over her mouth.

Riasa's laugh echoed around the empty room. "So Vela forbids my lady from speaking and she takes away your drink. Never will I ask for a quest. She would turn me into a celibate who cannot even use her hand."

"I have been on that quest for far too long," Preter sighed mournfully, and Lizzan choked on her drink while Laina buried her face in her hands, shoulders quaking.

"Do you wish me to go upstairs with you?" Riasa said when she was able, wiping tears of laughter from her eyes. "We will end your quest now."

"I thank you for the offer, Captain, but I suspect the bath will be all the nakedness I can survive in one day."

Grinning, Riasa shook her head before rising from her seat. "I will walk down with you, then," she said before turning to Lizzan. "They likely have quick-drying clay that we can use to make an imprint of that medallion. My lady, after you finish your meal, I will meet you in the stables and see you off along the road. My first farewell to you was difficult enough. I doubt I will bawl more quietly during the second."

Laina nodded, then inclined her head when Preter bowed his farewell to her.

With a soft ache in her chest, Lizzan lingered a moment longer. "I also wish you a safe journey and happy fulfillment of your quest. And I must thank you for demanding to know what happened on the King's Walk. Speaking my truth to those who wanted to hear it—and finally learning the true reason for my exile—meant everything."

Laina gripped her hand. The wealth of emotion in her

eyes was easily read, wishing her also a safe journey . . . though they were both on quests that would bring them pain to the edge of their enduring. No safe journey would be had, no matter how they wished. But here, for at least a moment, it was a shared journey.

Throat tight, Lizzan took her leave.

The baths were livelier this morning than they had been last eve, when she'd been with Aerax. The tightness in her throat moved down to her chest. So sweet he'd been—and never had she loved him more. It had taken all her strength to walk away.

Yet it was the most sensible route. Pain would come for them both. But perhaps she could spare him a little of it.

Riasa waited for her near the entrance. "The attendant said there is a skin clay that will serve our purpose. We only wait for her return."

As did Degg and Uland, who seemed to have given up searching for their own clothes among the red cascade of Parsathean linens in the changing room. Wearing robes and with faces flushed from the heat of the baths, they eyed Lizzan with quiet hostility. She saw none of the uncertainty of the previous eve, as if they had talked themselves again into thinking of her as a lying coward.

Very well. She cared not at all if they comforted themselves with lies. When they so willfully disregarded the truth, their opinion could have no weight on her.

"Are you here to round us up, Captain?" Uland asked of Riasa.

"Soon. From here, I will see my lady off," she told him. "Then I hope to be on the road as quickly as possible."

"I will be ready."

The smiling attendant returned to show the way to the storeroom, then left again to help the Kothans locate their belongings.

"Have you heard that the prince and the councilors now travel north with all the Kothan guard but their captain?" Riasa asked as she smeared the clay the attendant had given them into a thick layer across the blade of her axe.

All but Uland. Lizzan looked at her in dismay. "I knew the prince did. I thought the others would go with you."

"That was the original intention." She watched as Lizzan pressed the face of the medallion into the clay, then turned it over and pressed into another spot. "But the councilors decided very late to join the prince. Though they did not say so, I gathered there was worry that if you and the prince were the only ones to speak of Koth on that journey, the reputation of the realm and her king would be so sullied that the southerners might not ask Koth to join the alliance."

That characterization sliced at Lizzan's throat. "I did not mean to damage Koth's chances with the alliance. Only to tell the truth."

"If there was damage done, it was not you who did it," said Riasa. "Perhaps your king thought he did what was right. And perhaps it *was* right. Queens and kings must consider what is best for an entire realm, while mere warriors such as ourselves only confront whatever dangers lie in front of us. So it is not for me to say whether painting you as a coward was best for Koth."

Lizzan did not know, either. It had not been best for *her*. But if it had prevented a panic in Koth? If instead of fleeing the island and not trusting in Varrin's protection, the thousands who stayed were saved when the Destroyer returned? Surely that was worth her life. But she simply didn't know what was right. Her gut screamed that the truth ought to have been said . . . but her gut might merely be screaming her own self-interest.

When she made no reply, Riasa continued, "It *is* for me to say that your king is responsible for the choices he makes. So if there is any damage to Koth's reputation, then it is his alone to fix. As I suspect he will have to do when the southerners reach Koth, no matter what your Lady Junica and Lord Degg have to say along the way." She examined the clay on her blade. "This has set well enough for now. Once we have ridden beyond these giant trees, I will keep it in the sun until the clay fully hardens, and then it should slide from the blade without cracking. And if it does not, you will know when one of my warriors comes chasing after you with more clay."

"If the monks at Radreh can identify the medallion, I'll ask them to send a message to you," Lizzan said as they left the storeroom.

Riasa gave her a quick look and seemed about to speak before the scene ahead distracted them both.

The captain grinned. "This must be what poor Preter had to become accustomed to."

The Parsatheans, who hadn't bothered with the robes while waiting for the attendant to hand out their clothes—a process in which the attendant held up identical-looking linens and belts and a warrior called out ownership of them. Beside the attendant was Seri, who seemed to be looking through the pile for a lost item, helped along by Tyzen—in a robe, clutching his clothes to his chest. The prince held up a leather pouch that looked to Lizzan like all the other pouches, but Seri shook her head and claimed it belonged to a warrior named Ferek.

Trailed by Riasa, Lizzan threaded her way through the forest of wet skin and thick muscle, exiting the baths and the hot steaming air into a cool, shaded morning. And as always, her gaze found Aerax before she saw anything else.

Upon the road south, he walked with Caeb beside him. They were still an arrow's flight away, yet Lizzan could see that a sloth's neck was clamped between the cat's jaws, the heavy carcass dragging along the ground between his powerful legs.

Her gaze returned to Aerax, her heart filling her throat. Strangers they should be. Yet it had been so long since she'd seen him this way—returning from a hunt, wearing nothing but a cloth tied around his hips, with blood and dirt streaking his skin. Hardly could she tear her eyes from him.

"Do you think Caeb intends to carry that all day?" Riasa asked, sounding amused.

"He will eat it while Aerax makes ready." Which was likely why he'd hunted a young sloth. Given a choice, Caeb would have killed an adult and spent several days consuming it, napping between each enormous meal. But even a cat of his size and strength could not drag around a fully grown sloth. "Did they not do the same when you traveled with him from Krimathe?"

"Never did I see them hunt together before. Always the cat hunted alone and the prince bathed him after."

A chill scraped down Lizzan's spine. Aerax had said that everyone in the crystal palace believed he was defanged because he never showed his teeth. But only a fool would look at him prowling alongside the cat now, and mistake him for what he was. Although Aerax had no claws or fangs, the only difference between him and Caeb was their number of feet.

Riasa was no fool. "On this journey, I do not think you will worry overmuch that the Parsatheans' numbers are halved."

She would not. Instead she had a new worry, because people often tried to kill what they feared. And Vela had tasked her to protect Aerax. So there must be something to protect him *from*.

"Take care when you are at Radreh," Riasa said.

Lizzan tore her gaze from Aerax. "Why?"

"Have you been there before?"

"To Radrana." The city at the base of the mountain. "Not to the monastery."

"Nor have I. But I do not like what I hear coming out of that realm." She cast a glance toward the baths, where a number of Parsatheans milled near the entrance. "The young monk and Prince Tyzen seem careful when they practice their magic. The monks of Radreh are not known to take the same care—and now you bring them a powerful charm that might be valuable to anyone who hopes to fight the Destroyer."

Frowning, Lizzan said, "You think they will try to steal it and risk Vela's wrath?"

And Lizzan's.

"I cannot know. I only think you should take care. And

as the monks know magic, too, do not fully rely on that charm to protect you."

"I have my sword," Lizzan reminded her, and when Riasa nodded, she returned to the part the other woman had skipped blithely past. "The prince and the monk practice magic?"

"I assume that Preter gives the prince lessons. Always, they are together—and what other reason is there to spend time with a monk?" Riasa's mouth pursed with sudden amusement. "Though I rather liked that one."

"As did I."

"Then perhaps I will end Preter's quest when we meet again in the north. But now I must go and see my lady off—no farewells!" Suddenly Riasa backed away a step, as if to escape the weight of Lizzan's heavy sigh. "No farewells, Lizzan of Lightgale. My warriors and I will be in Koth before the first snow falls, so we will meet again."

Chest tight, Lizzan nodded. "Then we will. And a safe journey to you."

"And to you . . . though I do not know how safe you will be. Already you are marked as prey."

With a grin, Riasa took her leave—and there was no mistaking her meaning. Heart pounding, Lizzan turned to face Aerax and Caeb as the cat veered off, dropping his sloth a few paces away before continuing on. Aerax came straight toward Lizzan, his gaze locked with hers, yet she was aware of Caeb closing in from behind.

So many times she'd seen them move as one being before. Most long-toothed snow cats were solitary, but some brothers remained together—and stalked their prey in this way. Separating, one captured their target's attention with a direct approach while the other circled around.

Different paths, but a singular goal. And the scrape of Aerax's teeth over his bottom lip, the hot path his gaze took from Lizzan's head to her toes, told her that both man and cat were hungry this morn.

Purring, Caeb prowled past her, rubbing against her back with enough of his weight behind it that Lizzan was forced to step forward—closer to Aerax, who stood before her now an arm's length away.

Less than an arm's length, as Caeb lithely turned and paced behind her again, shoving her forward another step.

Aerax's voice was lower and more intimate than any stranger's could have been as he touched his fingers to his bloodied chest. "Will you look after him while I am in the bath?"

Look after Caeb while he ate the sloth. Which was not for the cat's protection as much as it was to reassure anyone who came across him that they would not be next. It was the same reason Aerax bathed him so often. Though he was no less deadly when clean, people were more likely to believe him tamed when he wasn't covered in dirt and blood.

Caeb pushed her forward again, as if demanding an answer. Pulse racing, Lizzan nodded, and then her gaze fell to Aerax's broad chest and her heart stilled. Three shallow furrows gouged his flesh.

"That is not the sloth's blood?" Instead it looked like a wound from the sloth's claws.

A flush darkened his cheeks. "I am out of practice."

And Lizzan had *already* failed to properly protect him. Nor could she, if he disappeared into the jungle. "You are out of your senses to be hunting now at all! This is not the northern forest. You do not know this jungle or the beasts that live here. Even I rarely venture off the road."

His brows rose. "You decide what is best for me now?"

"No, I—" Her teeth snapped together. Her face burned. "I only mean that you should take care."

His expression softened. But as Caeb paced past her again, pushing her so near that only a breath of space separated them, Lizzan knew that softness did not mean Aerax was less dangerous to her.

Head tilting back to meet his gaze again, she reminded him, "We must be strangers on this journey."

"Then before we leave, I will introduce myself to you, Lizzan of Lightgale." His thumb lightly swept the sensitive skin beneath her uptilted chin. "I am a bastard prince with a purpose that has put distance between me and everyone I love . . . including my cat. He only wants to hunt and to be with the woman who holds our hearts. For years, I denied him both. But last eve, he and I came to an agreement— that we will hunt together again."

Heart swollen, she said, "I am glad of it."

"And when my purpose is done, we will find you."

Pain punctured her swollen heart. "Aerax . . ."

"But we will be strangers now," he said gruffly. "If that is what you need."

She needed more time. Another season. Another year. Another life.

But she had chosen her path. Throat aching, she said thickly, "It is."

Caeb snarled and shoved her into Aerax's chest. Instinctively she braced herself, hands flattening over his ragged wound. Aerax didn't flinch but Lizzan hissed out a breath, preparing to snap at the cat, then froze when Aerax caught her chin.

Suddenly there was only him, and his mouth hovering near hers, the roughness of his voice. "The eve before last was the full moon. Instead of letting you run, I should have hunted you down and taken you then."

Hot yearning tugged at her core. But a moon night with Aerax was something else that she'd waited too long for. "You should have."

At her response, heat flared through his eyes. His voice deepened. "We will still be on the road when the moon rises full again."

"But we are as strangers." Even to her ears, the protest sounded weak.

"And what of it? Strangers fuck." He moved his mouth to her ear and softly growled, "They fuck at inns, in the private rooms and shadowed corners. They fuck beneath the stars, atop the pelt of a northern falt, with your thighs spread wide and your cunt wet from my tongue. Every night, we could be strangers. So dark it would be when I covered your body with mine, you would not see my face. You would only feel me deep inside."

Lust twisted in her belly and threatened to buckle her knees. Only sheer will kept her upright. "We will not be that kind of stranger."

His reply was a hum from deep in his throat. "No?"

"We can't," she whispered painfully, even as Caeb pushed her closer.

"Why?"

Because she would soon die. But she could not tell him. Instead she could only think of the ale in the barrels at the stable, the ale that would do nothing to dull this agony or this need, but still she thirsted for it so mightily. Thirsted for anything that could ease this terrible pain.

Pain that overwhelmed her, so a sobbing little breath shuddered from her parted lips. Immediately she felt Aerax withdraw, though he did not move much. His mouth gently pressed to the side of her jaw. "You have nearly a full turn to think on it, Lizzan."

She did not want to think at all. But she would probably think of nothing else.

Eyes closed, she nodded, and Aerax took all the warmth in the world when he left her. Some returned with the affectionate rub of Caeb's face against her cheek.

A shaky laugh broke from her. "You are as bad as he."

Purring again, he butted his head into her shoulder before padding back to his breakfast.

And never so badly had she wanted a drink. All would be easier. So much easier.

But the path was never easy.

Pulling out her knife, she went to help Caeb. His saber teeth were deadly at the kill and his incisors sharp, but he couldn't easily tear away flesh from bone without turning his head and gnawing with his side teeth. A full meal he could eat that way, but it was faster to butcher the meat for him.

She was elbow-deep in search of the organs that Caeb

liked best when his soft growl alerted her to someone's approach.

Lizzan glanced back. It was the scarred Parsathean warrior, Kelir. Riasa had said that he'd admired Lizzan's fierce concentration the previous eve, yet now the fierce intensity was his.

"What did the goddess say to you?" he demanded, crouching beside her, his gaze as heavy and sharp as the axe he carried at his belt. "Tell me exactly what was said."

Taken aback, she stared at him. "Regarding what?"

"Regarding the one you protect." Worry flared through the command in his voice. "Seri is my sister."

"Oh." Her stomach sank. "Aerax told you that she was the one I saw first?"

Aerax rarely spoke to anyone—and it had not been his quest to share. So she had never imagined he would.

Kelir shook his head. "Seri overheard."

Because Lizzan had been a little drunk, and a little loud. Curse it all. "I didn't know she would hear. But she was not the first I saw."

The warrior blinked before his brows pulled together in a dark frown. "You lied?"

"To Aerax," she said. "For it was he who I saw first. But our past was . . . painful to me. So I was not prepared to tell him."

"So you lied," he said flatly.

"I did."

A muscle in his jaw worked as he stared at her. "To save yourself pain?"

"And him." Not only with a lie, but what she could not bear to tell him.

Abruptly he nodded. "I will not expose your lie, but I will also not assist it. If the truth is asked of me, I will speak it. And you must confess to my sister as soon as you are able."

"I will. I thank you." Lizzan sighed. So many apologies she'd had to offer this day. "And I am sorry. I did not intend for her to overhear or to bring you worry."

"It is relieved now. To hear that Vela believed my sister needed protection . . . a horde of dangers I imagined coming for her."

She gave him a wry look. "They come for Aerax, instead." And when Caeb growled softly, she tossed him the sloth's heart. "So you'll also help me protect him, especially if he continues hunting."

Caeb's disdainful glare as he licked the heart said that she need not even tell him.

"As will we," said Kelir. "What did Vela say?"

"That I must protect the first person I saw. She didn't say what I protected him from—only that my quest will end on the day of the first snowfall, in a battle that will clear my name. So I protect him until then."

Expression thoughtful, Kelir nodded. "Vela speaks no lies, but her meanings are not always clear. And sometimes they are exactly as she says."

Lizzan could not imagine another meaning to an honorable and glorious death. But that she would not say in front of Caeb, so she only nodded.

Kelir's gaze sharpened. "You have traveled this road before?"

"A few times I have been hired as escort between Krimathe and Radrana."

"The warrior who was familiar with these northern realms is now guarding the caravan. Can we depend on you to guide us? We would hire you."

"You can depend on me," Lizzan said. "But I am on a quest. I can take no coin . . . though I will take a supper every night and feed for my horse."

"You will get them." His gaze hardened. "But do not lie again. Unless you wish to make enemies of us."

Lizzan very sincerely did not.

CHAPTER 15

AERAX

It seems the delay is at an end," Lady Junica said as a group of Parsatheans rode toward them from the stables, with Lizzan near their head. "Will you help me into my saddle? I should probably avoid any attempt to pull myself up, lest I find myself on a periwag again."

While one of the Kothan soldiers held the bridle, Aerax hefted her astride, then mounted his own horse. The sun peeked through the tall trees from on high, and already Riasa and her Krimathean warriors had taken their leave of Oana—as had the caravan. The alliance party was the last to head out.

Degg nudged his horse alongside Aerax's, gesturing with his chin at the Parsatheans. "What were they looking for at the baths?"

"Seri's claws."

In a leather pouch, which was thought to have been accidentally dropped into the water and carried by the current from bath to bath. In the time it had taken for the wound on Aerax's chest to close, the Parsatheans had searched each of the pools. They'd not yet found the claws when Aerax had left the baths and donned his prince's costume again.

"The girl warrior?" Degg asked. "It appears she located them."

To Aerax, Seri appeared near tears. And the Syssian prince who rode at her side seemed to be consoling her. "I think not."

"They are around her neck."

"It was not those claws." All of the Parsatheans wore varying numbers of drepa talons as trophies, but they hadn't taken off the necklaces before bathing. "It was the silver claws they wear into battle."

"Silver?" Degg clicked his tongue against his teeth, shaking his head. "There is the answer, then. When I was a boy, we used to make a game of waiting for the bathhouse attendant to leave so that we could take coins from the purses in the changing rooms. No doubt the children in Oana do the same."

Lady Junica huffed out a laugh. "What a little scoundrel you were, Degg."

"Unlike some, I did not have to labor at a young age to provide for my mother, so I had plenty of time for mischief."

Aerax eyed him silently. That had clearly been a reference to Aerax's childhood, yet he heard no smug insult in Degg's tone.

The councilor flushed. He slanted a glance at Lady Junica before lowering his voice and confiding to Aerax, "I could not sleep for thinking of what was said of me last eve, of how I resented you unfairly . . . and there was a truth in those words that did not sit comfortably. So I hope that we might start anew."

What was said of me. As if the words had been birthed from the air, and Lizzan still didn't exist to him. So Aerax cared not at all what Degg did. But he could start anew, by not caring all over again.

He grunted his assent.

Degg looked pleased, and when Caeb prowled out from between the trees and onto the road, the councilor added,

"When I've made amends to you, perhaps your cat will let me near him without snarling."

Doubtful. But Aerax said nothing, eyes narrowing on the cat as Caeb came closer. Lizzan had not bathed him, yet his jowls were hardly bloodied.

"Lizzan cut up your meat?" Aerax shook his head at the cat. "She spoils you."

Which the cat likely believed was his due—and that Aerax did not spoil him enough. That would not change. Aerax had spent enough time nursing and mincing meals for this fool beast.

"Did she also discard of the carcass for you?" When Caeb responded by drawing back his lips to show his front teeth in a self-satisfied grin, Aerax said in disgust, "You are the laziest of all cats."

Unconcerned, Caeb yawned and stretched his long body from his raised hindquarters to flexing forepaws, unsheathing claws that gouged deep into the packed dirt of the road.

Breaking ahead of the other group, Lizzan and Ardyl approached the Kothans at a trot. From behind Aerax came the mutters of the four soldiers who had remained to guard the councilors. Before Uland left with the Krimatheans, he'd sharply reminded the soldiers that anyone whose name was not written in the books should not even be seen. And perhaps they did not see Lizzan, but they saw her shining Kothan armor and took offense to it being worn by a coward.

They fell silent so quickly that Aerax suspected Lady Junica had given them one of the razored glances that she used to slice people to shreds.

Lizzan's gaze was on the soldiers, her expression tight. Aerax knew not if any had been her friends while she served in the Kothan army . . . yet by the set of her jaw, he suspected at least one of them must have been.

The shunning had to be so much harder for Lizzan than it had ever been for him. Born nameless, he'd never had friends to lose. At least outside Koth, she didn't have to bear seeing those whom she'd once fought beside shun and insult her.

Nor would she now. If they wished to learn what a feral prince truly was, they only needed to insult her again.

"At last we are ready," Ardyl said to Aerax. "Your party is set to leave?"

Watching Lizzan, Aerax grunted an affirmative.

"Who is the lead guard?"

"That is I," said Sen, a brown-haired woman whom Aerax had thought well of until the mutters had begun.

"We have asked Vela's Chosen to serve as our escort through this unfamiliar territory," Ardyl told them. "I understand that your people will not see or hear her. But take care what you ignore—if she gives us warning and you pretend not to hear it, and by doing so bring more danger upon us, I will slice your ears from your head. If you have issue with that, say so now."

Her gaze swept the councilors and guards, who all remained silent—either because they had no issue with it, or because they could not even acknowledge Ardyl's warning by Kothan law, since it regarded Lizzan. Aerax knew not what the reason was and cared less.

As if satisfied by their response, Ardyl nodded. "Kelir and I ride at the head, while Ferek and Raceni ride at the tail. Between us, arrange yourselves in any order you wish. We only ask that you do not speed ahead of us or fall behind—and do exactly as we say if any threat appears."

"They will," Aerax said.

"Let us ride, then." Ardyl reined her horse around and set off.

Aerax nudged his horse forward. Angling toward him, Lizzan's gray gelding trotted beside his. She held out the sloth's bladder, washed and bulging with the meat she'd stuffed into it.

"If Caeb is hungry later, this is what remains of his breakfast."

"You treat him as if still a kitten," Aerax grumbled, and glared at the cat, who looked full pleased with himself again. "Leave that for some other weak and starving animal. If Caeb is hungry later, he can catch a squirrel."

"There are no squirrels in this jungle." Her eyes laughed at him. "Stop poking at our helpless kitten and take it."

Obediently, Aerax took the heavy bladder. "Your heart is too soft for him. You'd best pray he doesn't step on a thorn, or by the time we reach Koth, he will be riding your horse while you walk beside it."

Though that would not happen. Because then Aerax would give to Lizzan his mount, and he would be the one walking.

Her grin said that she knew it, as well. "You are merely jealous."

That she had fed Caeb small bites that had been lovingly cut up by her knife? "I am," Aerax admitted, even as he watched her smile vanish—as if she realized that only friends might tease each other as she'd just teased him. "For I must be a stranger to you, but he will not be."

For a long breath, Lizzan searched his gaze, the lake blue of her eyes full of shadowed depths. With a short nod, she finally urged her gelding to a faster pace and caught up with Ardyl, riding ahead.

This time the mutters were about him. A resentful "someone believes he doesn't have to obey the law" reached his ears, and Aerax would have paid it no mind but for the surprising response.

"Because he does not," Degg snapped, turning in his saddle. "His name is written in Varrin's own book, and that is set above the Book of Law. So mind your tongues."

Lady Junica's brows arched high and she gave to Aerax a questioning look. He shrugged in response. A profound effect Lizzan's words must have had on Degg, for he seemed not to be starting anew but leaping straight to Aerax's defense.

Degg glanced at the bladder balanced on Aerax's thigh. "I would take that and offer it to Caeb when he is hungry. Will your cat like me more for giving him a treat?"

"He will not like you less." Aerax handed over the bundle, glad to be rid of it. Despite the washing Lizzan had given the organ, flies would likely swarm it by midday—

and no doubt, that was why she had passed it off to *him*. "Don't expect to feed him. When Caeb wants it, he will come and take it."

Degg nodded and busied himself tying one end of the bladder to his saddle so that it hung near his knee.

"Do not take his leg with it," Aerax said under his breath, and Caeb gave him a disdainful look before loping ahead to catch up with Lizzan.

An ache threatened to fill his chest until he breathed past it. Already the heart she'd shredded had healed, because what Lizzan had torn apart was the man she hadn't recognized—a man that Aerax hardly recognized, either. The man who'd been without her for so long, who'd had a purpose but no path forward, who'd lost everyone he'd loved except a cat. But it had not been the baths that had healed him. Instead it was the hunt he'd begun. The hunt that would bring her back to him.

And now Aerax was no longer a stranger to himself. He was not without her, though she rode ahead. His purpose and his path were clear. He would have her again.

But until then, she wished for Aerax to be a stranger to her, and so he would. She wanted to ease the pain of their coming separation, and Aerax only wanted to give her pleasure enough to last until they were together again. For that, however, he could be patient. The journey to Koth would take at least two full turns of the moon—and even when they'd tried, Lizzan and he had never been able to stay away from each other for long.

And this time, he would not try.

Despite Ardyl's statement that she and Kelir would ride at the head, instead it was she and Lizzan who led the procession. Kelir rode a few paces behind, followed by Seri, Tyzen, and Preter.

With Lizzan's task of making friends with the southerners in mind, Aerax brought his horse alongside Kelir's. There he had little to say—but as his minders quickly followed and created a cluster of councilors, warriors, and princes, a conversation was struck up around him. Aerax paid no attention to any of it. Not with Lizzan so near. He would rather hear the sound of her laugh as she talked with Ardyl, would rather watch the play of dappled sunlight over the liquid black of her hair, would rather feel the full warmth in his chest when Caeb butted his head against her leg, seeking attention, and she bent in the saddle to rub her face against his.

His body tensed when both she and Ardyl suddenly glanced back—though not because of any danger. Instead a quiet argument had arisen behind him that he'd ignored until it drew Lizzan's attention.

Abruptly it ended, with Seri's sharp "It matters not if the same silversmith makes them, they will not be the same!"

A moment later, Tyzen rode up between Kelir and Aerax. The boy's jaw was set and his face flushed.

After exchanging a glance, Lizzan and Ardyl faced forward again.

Kelir said quietly to Tyzen, "If you wish to help, make no offer to replace them. At least not so quickly. Instead give her time to grieve for what was lost."

"How long will that be?" the boy asked tightly.

The warrior shrugged. "As long as she needs."

"It will be forever," Tyzen muttered. "She is more stubborn than a lump-headed bison."

Kelir huffed out a laugh. "So she is."

Still upset over the loss of her claws, Aerax gathered. He glanced behind, where Seri was glaring at Tyzen's back, yet there was a wobble in her chin when Lady Junica gently asked her, "They were precious to you?"

The wobble firmed before she said thickly, "Ran Maddek had them made for me in thanks for serving as a Dragon to his bride."

"So they are not just a weapon, then," Lady Junica said, and Seri shook her head. "Kelir told us what it means to be a Dragon. You must be proud to have served your queen in that way."

Determination lit Seri's eyes. "And I will again, if Yvenne is ever named Ran."

"But she is your queen?"

The girl nodded.

Lady Junica frowned. "Then what is the difference between a queen and a Ran?"

Seri seemed to struggle with the answer, so it was Kelir who said, "In Parsathe, when we speak of queens and kings, it does not carry the same meaning as it does in other realms. Our queen is married to the Ran, and so is the Ran's closest advisor and a powerful influence throughout the Burning Plains. But only the Ran is chosen to speak for all Parsatheans—and we might call Maddek our king, but never would we call him King Maddek."

"Maddek is your only Ran?" The councilor arched an inquiring brow that was aimed at Kelir now, too. "Do you and Ardyl still serve on his Dragon?"

"They do," answered Seri proudly.

"Yet you are here?"

"Because of me," said Tyzen, seeming in good humor again. "Maddek is the heart of the Dragon . . . and my sister holds *his* heart. Any wound that Yvenne feels is agony to him—and if I were killed, a deep wound it would be. So by protecting me, they look after Maddek's heart from afar."

Head cocked, Kelir frowned at the boy, as if intending to argue—and then he met Ardyl's eyes when the other warrior glanced back. They both shrugged.

"I might have said that we came because Ran Maddek asked it of us," Kelir said. "But Tyzen speaks the truth of why we agreed."

"So a Dragon is not merely a palace guard," Lady Junica mused, "but more similar to a keeper, whose loyalty is bound to one particular member of the Kothan royal family."

Tyzen looked to Aerax. "Where is yours?"

"Cernak also protects my heart. So I bade him to stay and look after his family," Aerax said, and watched Lizzan's back stiffen, as she was reminded of the stigma they suffered under. And though Aerax wished that Cernak had joined them so Lizzan could reunite with her brother on this journey, better that he was in Koth protecting her mother and younger brother.

"From what does he protect them?" Tyzen asked. "Do you fear the bandits or the Destroyer?"

"Neither." It was Koth that Lizzan's family had to fear.

As Lizzan knew, too. The look that she cast over her shoulder said so much. There was gratitude, that he'd made certain her family were cared for. But it was the depth of her despair that sliced Aerax open, filled him with the shame that nothing he'd done had truly helped them. The only remedy was leaving the island . . . and her family would not go.

"For what reason do you think the Destroyer left your realm alone before?" Seri asked curiously.

Riding beside her, Degg answered more quickly than Aerax could. "His magic is from Enam, and that god has no power on Koth."

"But given the size of his army, he did not always need magic," the young monk pointed out. "His warlords took Rugus's mountain stronghold, which can only be reached by a bridge similar to the King's Walk, and not a sorcerer was among them."

"There was the Smiling Giant," Tyzen countered.

"But he had no magic of his own. Only the beastly strength the Destroyer gave to him. And he was stopped by an axe, not a spell."

"So he was." The prince's face clouded and he looked to Aerax before saying, "It was my father who smote the Smiling Giant—and became a hero to all of the alliance that formed in the Destroyer's wake. Except it was not long afterward that he began planting seeds for the Destroyer's return."

Aerax nodded. "A proper villain, full of ambition. My father only bedded my mother and then left her and his bastard child to starve during the Bitter Years."

Lady Junica sucked in a sharp breath. "Our king would never have—"

"I was there. That *is* what happened." Aerax cut her off

before adding, "Prince Tyzen has just said his father was the Destroyer's tool. These southerners do not expect perfection of their allies. Only honesty."

Kelir nodded. "That is truth."

Lady Junica threw Aerax an exasperated look. "Then try not to be so very honest. Unless, of course, it is regarding why Koth was left untouched by the Destroyer."

"Because the island is the perfect trap," Lizzan tossed back, her gaze meeting Aerax's in a brief, shared memory. Years ago, they'd spoken of this—and of all the reasons why the usual explanations made no sense. That Anumith the Destroyer feared Varrin's power, that the sun god's magic was weakened by the cold and ice, that the King's Walk was too well defended. So Aerax had pointed out the simplest of explanations: that Koth's own legends had made its conquest not worth the risk.

"A trap?" Kelir echoed, appearing fiercely interested. "How so?"

"Best that our prince explain," she said. "It was Aerax who thought of it—and because our councilors can add their own thoughts if he is the one to tell you."

All looked to him.

Aerax shrugged. "The island will sink if none of Varrin's snow-haired descendants stand upon it. If the Destroyer and his army had crossed the King's Walk, the snow-hairs would only need to abandon the island to kill him."

A fire lit in Kelir's gaze. "What of the people on the island?"

"If even half evacuated the island when we heard of his approach, those who remained could escape by boat under cover of night. The Destroyer could not know that no one was left except one of the royals—for one must remain."

His eyes narrowed. "Would you?"

"I would."

"Hold, hold!" Lady Junica broke in, her expression filled with horror. "You speak as if this plan is a true option."

Brows raised, Kelir glanced back. "Is it not?"

"Of course it is not! You speak of destroying Koth!" Her

disbelieving gaze moved to Aerax. "How could you even conceive of such a thing?"

"Easily." And gladly, for Aerax could fulfill his purpose even as he killed the Destroyer.

She seemed taken utterly aback. "Full glad I am now that you do not wish to be king. I knew you despised our home, but never did I think you could speak so casually of sinking it."

One day, Aerax would do more than speak of sinking the island. But not yet. "Then take your ease. Already I have spoken to my uncle of practicing evacuations," Aerax said flatly. For the only way he would fulfill his purpose was if Koth was emptied. Yet his hope to clear the island during those practices had been denied. "He claimed that such plans were unnecessary, because Varrin's power would protect the island from the Destroyer once again."

"So he will," said Lady Junica fiercely. "And I will not see all that our people have accomplished sink into the basin. Why bother to fight the Destroyer, when we will destroy our home ourselves?"

Was that a true question? For it made no sense to him. "You would trade the lives of thousands of soldiers and warriors and Kothans, so that you can save a rock?"

"The island is not only a rock," Degg said, frowning at both Aerax and Lady Junica. "And these arguments matter not at all. A trap is useless if the Destroyer knows it is there."

"Unless the trap contains a lure that the Destroyer cannot resist. But what even is it that he wants?" Tyzen shook his head. "He only destroys before continuing on. Is that what he enjoys—the pain, the horror? What does he search for, or does he even search for anything? I have never heard that anyone knows what his purpose is. He conquers realms but doesn't stay to rule them. Though now that he has been around the world, perhaps he finally returns to take a crown. He tasked my father to find a bride for him."

Aerax frowned. That had been a full generation past. "He intended to return to the western realms even then?"

"Who can know?" Tyzen lifted his hands. "Perhaps he has tasked a thousand men to find him a thousand brides, and his next march around the world will be one marriage after another as he fathers a thousand children. Who knows anything of his true intentions?"

"I care nothing of what his intentions are," said Ardyl, who was not so many paces ahead now, as she and Lizzan had slowed their horses as if better to listen to the argument behind them. "All that matters is that we kill him."

"How can that be all that matters?" said Lady Junica. "If we destroy all that we are while fighting him, then how is what we do any different?"

Ardyl frowned at her, and seemed about to answer before her gaze shifted to Kelir. Mouth tightening, she faced forward again.

"Every realm that joins the alliance will make sacrifices," Kelir said to Lady Junica.

"So they will," she agreed. "As would Koth. But even if you lay waste to all of Krimathe, the forests can regrow. Buildings can be restored. But how can you unsink an island?"

"Perhaps Varrin would," Aerax said dryly.

Lady Junica threw him another angry, baffled glance— as if she could not understand how he might speak of it all so easily. Once, Lizzan had looked at him the same way, and fighting with her had tied painful knots in his heart. It had been one of the few arguments they'd ever had, though her stance had been that a Kothan soldier's duty and honor was to protect both her people and her home. With her life, if necessary. So he'd asked her how many soldiers and people the Destroyer would have to kill before sinking the island became an option. There she'd finally conceded, but said that it should be the last option—and not the first option, as Aerax had believed.

He didn't believe it anymore. Now, destroying Koth was the *only* option. And his heart twisted into knots again, because although Lizzan claimed to have faith in him and his purpose, he hadn't told her the extent of it. She might still think him a villain when he was done.

But now, it was difficult to tell what she thought. Her eyes were fixed on the road ahead, as if ignoring all that was said behind her.

As Aerax would have liked to do, when Seri asked Lady Junica, "How does Varrin protect the island? I have not heard his story."

For the best, Aerax thought, as it was mostly lies. Yet no happier topic could Seri have struck for most Kothans—especially Lady Junica, who likely thought Aerax also needed the reminder of where he'd come from. Or a lesson.

Yet it was Tyzen who responded first, his moonstone eyes casting an unreadable glance in Aerax's direction. "In the story I have heard, Varrin is a monster."

"A monster?" Lady Junica laughed, as if the idea was too preposterous to even offend. "It was he who saved all the world when he exposed Enam's eye."

Kelir frowned and shook his head. "That was silver-fingered Rani and Nemek."

"It was they who performed that task," Lady Junica said. "But it was at Varrin's request that they did it." She looked to Seri again. "Varrin was born in the truly ancient times—when the sun god still ruled unchecked, scorching the earth with his fiery light and scouring the skies with his unending storms. To escape Enam's fury, all living things hid in caves by day, and the only relief they knew was during the night and under his sister Vela's silver light—for even in the mountains and in the far north, there was no ice or snow or cold. And Varrin was still a child when Enam forced himself on Vela and filled the heavens with her screams. So when her twins, Justice and Law, were born—"

"We have seen where she gave birth to them," Seri broke in, wide eyed. "We have been through the labyrinth dug out by her fingernails as she labored."

"Near Blackmoor?" Lady Junica sounded no less impressed than Seri. "Was it a wondrous place?"

The girl nodded. "Though lonesome and bleak, with the bones of those who could not find their way through strewn over the ground. And I was nearly killed by a leatherwing with a beak as long as a spear. They nest in the cliffs and then dive for their prey."

Kelir grunted. "It did not even come near to you."

"I'm fairly certain it did," said Preter. "I felt the wind it made as it passed over her head."

"It came near enough that I saw the vile gleam in its reptilian eye," Tyzen agreed, "which was close enough to skewer her. And now we must apologize to Lady Junica for interrupting her tale."

"No need for apologies," she said, laughing. "I had the brief thought of seeing the labyrinth for myself, but if there are leatherwings that dive at my head, I will be content with descriptions of it."

Seri nodded solemnly. "Painful her labor must have been to scratch such deep furrows in the earth."

"As every birth is painful," said Lady Junica with a faint, melancholy smile. "And it is said the bloodied waters of her womb were still streaming down her legs when Vela flew with Justice and Law into the heavens, and together they imprisoned Enam within the sun, using Nemek's hair to bind him. So fully did they wrap him in those unbreakable braids that not even a sliver of his burning light escaped, and all the world rejoiced that the scorching of the earth had ended. Beneath Vela's gentle silver gaze they came out of their caves and began to build their cities—and Koth was the finest of all."

Seri shook her head. "The finest was Parsa."

The monk scoffed. "It is well known that Toleh was the finest."

"Syssia was indisputably the finest," said Tyzen with a wry glance over his shoulder. "But do continue, my lady."

Eyes snapping with amusement, she did. "In those days, Koth was not an island, but a shining city atop the peak of a mountain. It was there that a boy came to the city gates, nameless and naked. No one knew which cave he'd lived in or who his family were—but he came to Koth's shining city hoping for a better life than he'd found in the forests and wilds. He named himself Varrin, and first he labored in the stables, then labored in the mines, before earning a position sweeping floors in the Great Hall where all the world's finest minds gathered to write their poetry, practice their magic, and share their knowledge. There he listened and learned, even as the discussions became more fearful, and terrified eyes turned to the northern peaks, which were turning white."

"Because the world was freezing," Seri breathed.

"It was, for Vela's gentle light was not always upon us. Enraged by his imprisonment, Enam never stopped struggling against his bonds. And though Nemek's braids would not break, one day the knots might loosen and he might slip free. Regularly Vela looked to make certain the knots were still tight, turning her face away from the earth—and with each full turn she made, the colder it became. But this time, no refuge could be found in the caves. Herds were slaughtered for their furs, but no number of blankets were warm enough. Forests were burned for their heat, but the trees never regrew fast enough. Only with their magic could sorcerers keep their fires lit, but there was nothing to eat except snow, so all the fires were growing dim. By that time, Varrin had learned a little of magic, and warmed by his own small fire, he trudged out into the freezing stillness in search of help. Weakened and gaunt, he was so very close to death—and it is said that was how he found silver-fingered Rani."

"Though she was not silver-fingered yet," Seri said, reaching for her belt—for the pouch that contained her claws, Aerax realized. Sheer grief moved across her face even as Lady Junica nodded.

"He found her sitting atop the Fanged Mountains, her eyes spitting lightning and sobbing tears that fell like boulders of ice—for she and her dragon had no rest, flying the souls of those who had starved and frozen into Temra's arms, and all the world was near to dead."

"She is the most softhearted of all the gods," Seri said quietly. "It seems almost a punishment that she must be death."

"But her soft heart is a gift to us," Lady Junica said. "For when Varrin told her what must be done, she didn't hesitate before mounting her dragon and flying to the sun. She knew Vela might kill her for what she intended, but Rani wasted no time to consult with the moon, for more lives were lost to the cold with every passing moment. There she grabbed hold of Nemek's braids, though Enam's heat burned through the silver and scorched her flesh. But only Nemek can break their hair or untangle a knot—and try as she might, Rani could not force apart the windings of the braid to allow even the smallest bit of Enam's power to shine through, because the bindings had been wound too tight. Still, Rani tried until her fingers were cooked to the bone, then flew to find Nemek to heal her so she might try again. But Nemek could not heal her injury, for it was their own hair that had burned her—yet they would also risk Vela's wrath, and flew with Rani again to the sun, where Nemek untied a single braid."

Seri nodded. "The knot that covered his eye."

"That was what Varrin had suggested they do. Enam should never be freed, but if even a portion of his power could peek through, that magic would be enough to warm the world without scorching it. And with her task done, Rani returned to him, and he wept to see what had happened to her hands. So he led her to Koth, and cared for her dragon using the knowledge he'd learned in the stables. And he forged her new fingers, using knowledge he'd learned in the mines. And he spoke with her, talking of all he'd learned while sweeping floors, and so as time passed, they pledged their love to each other—though they could never kiss and never touch."

Seri gave a wistful sigh. "Because she was death."

Lady Junica nodded.

Kelir gave her a skeptical look. "Rani took a lover? I have never heard this part of the tale before."

"That is because of what happened next," she said. "For the gods don't like it when the stories about them do not flatter, and try to silence the voices that tell them."

That was true enough, especially for men who called themselves gods. But Aerax gritted his teeth, and also remained silent.

"In time, Varrin earned Koth's crown and became a great sorcerer, whose only fealty was to the realm and her people—and to silver-fingered Rani. He cared not that he grew old, for he knew that when his life was done, finally she would be able to hold him in her arms. And although his advisors begged him to take a queen, his loyalty remained with Rani, so he used his magics to strengthen his seed and beget his heirs directly from his loins . . . and is also why his descendants still resemble him so strongly," she said, which drew every eye to Aerax. "The seed of his line is so strong, little of their mothers are in them."

"And a little of her is the best of me," muttered Aerax, earning a quiet chuckle from Tyzen, who also had a monster for a father but had at least inherited his mother's eyes.

"But Vela had not forgotten what Rani had done, for although the world was saved, the goddess was angered that she'd not been consulted. But her wrath was aimed at Varrin. She knew it was he who'd made the suggestion to uncover the sun god's eye, and she began to whisper into the ears of the other gods that Varrin hoped to completely free Enam, stirring their rage and fear. Rani, hearing the rumblings that were echoing through the heavens, raced to him carrying the length of Nemek's braid that had been untied from Enam's binds, and knotted it into a belt around Varrin's waist—so that if the gods tried to harm him, instantly he would be healed."

"Healed?" Seri echoed, her eyebrows arching. "Could she kiss him then?"

Expression sorrowful, Lady Junica shook her head. "Far worse it would have been if she did, for Rani's touch is not an injury that can be healed but death itself, and the braid was still a binding. So if Varrin died, the belt would have trapped his soul within his deceased flesh, and she couldn't have carried him into Temra's arms."

Preter's eyes narrowed. "He would have become a wraith—but in an unmoving and rotting body, not one that is magically animated."

"I believe so. Varrin did not wish to wear the belt, because it meant he would not die—and so never would Varrin be in Rani's arms. But he could not remove the belt or untie the knot she'd made."

"So he would live forever?" Seri asked. "Is that how he became a god?"

"An immortal man is not a god," Lady Junica said. "But as a thousand generations passed, Varrin's knowledge and power became equal to a god's. For he never stopped improving himself, until he was the keenest of all warriors, the strongest of all sorcerers, the greatest of all kings. From the stone of the highest peak of the Fanged Mountains, he built the crystal palace, which gleamed as a jewel beneath the sky, and through the years he guided Koth to become the finest of all realms. But all he truly wanted was for silver-fingered Rani to hold him in her arms at last—and he prayed to Nemek the Healer to come and untie the knot, so he might finally grow old and die."

"Did Nemek answer?"

"They did. But even a thousand generations is only a blink to a god. Vela had not forgotten her anger toward Varrin, and the other gods had not forgotten their fear. So Vela sent war to the eastern realms, that silver-fingered Rani would be so busy on the battlefields, she could not come to Varrin's aid. And when he looked out from his crystal palace and saw Nemek approaching from across the frozen plains wearing their withered face, Varrin knew that he had been betrayed."

Lizzan glanced over her shoulder, frowning. "Their withered face?"

Lady Junica nodded before abruptly pausing, as if remembering she wasn't supposed to have heard Lizzan's voice.

Scoffing, Lizzan shook her head and looked forward again. Yet why had Nemek's face surprised her now? Aerax knew she'd heard this tale many times.

But as a stranger to her, he could not ask.

Smoothly recovering from her misstep, Lady Junica continued, "Instead of help and healing, harm and disease were coming to Koth—but Varrin was no longer a weak and powerless boy. As Nemek approached, Varrin did not eat, until his body was so gaunt that he could wriggle free of the belt without untying the knot. Then he went to the Kothan silver mines and forged a false belt, so finely wrought that even a god could not tell the difference. So when Nemek came before him, Varrin untied the knot himself. In their astonishment, Nemek stumbled back, and in the moment they were unbalanced, Varrin bound their wrists with the true braid, so their fingers could not reach the knot to untie it."

"I would use my teeth," Seri said, and brought her wrists to her mouth to demonstrate when Lady Junica looked at her in confusion. "They did not?"

"I . . ." The councilor blinked. "Nemek are not a warrior, so they must not have thought of that."

"You say Varrin was a warrior, so he would have," Kelir said, and turned to Seri. "They could not use their teeth if their wrists were bound behind their back. If you must tie an enemy instead of killing them, do it in that way—not only looping around the wrists, but winding the rope in between so they cannot work their hands free as easily."

"I will," the girl told him before looking to Lady Junica again. "So that must be how Varrin tied them."

"It must be," she agreed. "For they did not escape. Instead he gave them warning that no gods except for Rani would ever be welcome in Koth, and tossed Nemek away from the mountain, sending them back to the frozen plains."

"He had grown so strong?"

Nodding, Lady Junica said, "Which only enraged the gods all the more, not only that he would defy them, but that he *could* stand against them. Vela could not send her oceans to drown such tall mountains, but she sent wolves and warriors—and all of them, Varrin struck down. Law reached into the molten heart of the mountains, but Varrin capped Koth's peak so it would not erupt, and Justice cracked Koth's stone foundation, but Varrin mortared it again with his own blood. Then came Stranik, who wound his coils around the realm and began to squeeze, hoping to bring famine and fear as he always does. But Varrin tricked the snake god into eating his own tail, and when Stranik had consumed himself until only his head remained, Varrin kicked the god far into the southern realms."

"And we in Toleh thank him for that," Preter said dryly. "For then Stranik slithered into the caves of the Fallen Mountains, scraping through narrow tunnels so that he might turn inside out and unconsume himself, and forced the Farian savages who still hid there to emerge from the stony depths and onto our lands."

Eyes sparking with amusement, Lady Junica said, "For the sake of our alliance, perhaps Koth will extend its apologies. But I assure you that Kothans were not sorry then. Though they soon would be," she continued, her smile fading. "For even Varrin had barely the strength to defend against what came next."

Seri's brow creased with concern. "What was it?"

"Vela became so enraged that she threw a piece of herself down from the heavens. Varrin saw the moonstone fall from the sky, ablaze with white light, and used all of his power to shield Koth when it struck." Mournfully, Lady Junica shook her head. "When the dust and fires cleared, his hair had turned white as snow, and no longer did Koth stand atop a mountain peak. Instead it was at the bottom of a vast crater, for the moonstone had obliterated everything that surrounded Koth. And now Vela could send her oceans against the realm, for beneath the northern ice are frigid waters—and in rivers, those waters began to stream toward the crater in which Koth sat, and as the basin filled, would surely drown all those who had survived the moonstone."

"But Varrin cast a spell to make it float?"

"He had not enough strength left," she said. "Shielding the realm had taken nearly all of his power—and recall that he no longer wore Nemek's braid as a belt. His body had been battered as Koth fell, so he was finally near to dying, which was all he'd wanted. Yet now his people might also perish, and he was too weak to save them . . . unless he became as the gods were, for they do not inhabit frail bodies but are the essence of sheer will and magic. So with his last breath, he did not attempt to cast a complicated spell that would lift Koth, but instead cast a simple spell that dissolved his mortal form and bound his essence to the island—even though it meant that he would be undying, and never know the warmth of Rani's touch."

Seri gave a heavy sigh. "He sacrificed his heart to save his people?"

"He did," said Lady Junica. "For when his mortal form dissolved, only sheer power remained. That he used to lift the island above the rising waters, and to create the King's Walk from the shattered remnants of the mountain so that his people would not be trapped at the center of the lake that was forming. He warned the other gods that always he would protect Koth from their magics, and that if ever his descendants no longer stood upon the island, Varrin would know the gods were to blame and he would fly into the heavens to destroy them. So the gods only had to leave the island alone—and out of fear of Varrin's wrath, that is what they do."

"Even silver-fingered Rani?"

Lady Junica shook her head. "She alone can come to Koth. As she must, to carry the dead into Temra's merciful embrace."

So many lies. Aerax's jaw clenched. There was no mercy for the dead on Koth. And silver-fingered Rani would never come again to an island that would be her prison. Yet saying so would do nothing but endanger anyone who heard it—whether they believed it or not.

And they would not believe it. All of Aerax's ancestors had made certain of that.

"But some of the other gods' magic must touch the island," said Preter. "For it is warmed by Enam."

Lady Junica nodded. "And we can also see Vela's light, and our gardens still carry some of Hanan's blessing. Those

Varrin allows, for it is not harmful magic—and he does not wish to separate Koth from the rest of the world. Only to protect it."

Kelir gave a sideways glance at Tyzen. "That does not sound like a monster."

The young prince shrugged. "That is the story I was told."

"By whom?" Lady Junica asked sharply. "Who would tell such vile slander?"

"My mother," Tyzen said wryly, then added when the councilor began to stammer and blush, "though she was only repeating the story to my sister and me as she heard it from another—for this was ten years past, when we were locked in our tower, and all that we knew of the outside world was what she saw with Vela's sight . . . which also reached to Koth, as the moonlight does."

"Someone in Koth said Varrin was a monster?"

"Those were not the words used; that was what my mother called Varrin after the story was told. For in that version, he slaughtered his own people and used their undying souls as a lure for silver-fingered Rani—and it was those trapped souls that Varrin used to keep the island afloat after Vela attempted to free them by flinging the moonstone from the heavens."

Heart thundering, Aerax stared at the prince. *Ten years.* Even as Lady Junica and Degg sputtered of slander again, Aerax knew which version Tyzen's mother had heard—the truth that his uncle had told to him beneath the crystal palace. A truth that Aerax believed only two people in the world knew.

Yet when those moonstone eyes met his, they seemed to pierce Aerax through, for here was another who knew. And his queen did, too.

But Aerax made no answer. By Varrin's rule, acknowledging what the boy had learned meant that Tyzen must die. And Aerax already carried too many of the dead on his shoulders.

"Is that why Yvenne has forbidden us from crossing the King's Walk?" asked Kelir.

Tyzen nodded, eyes still on Aerax, but still nothing could Aerax say as icy chains pulled tight around his lungs. If King Icaro heard of this, no alliance would he ever make with them. Not if they might expose the truth. Instead he would call the southerners liars and discredit their names to every Kothan.

As he had Lizzan.

"Your queen forbade you from coming to the island?" Lady Junica's perplexed gaze moved from Kelir to Tyzen. "Then how will you speak with our king to make this alliance? For he cannot leave the island—and I promise you that tale of Varrin is all slanderous lies."

The prince gave her a reassuring smile. "Then it is fortunate we travel together now. By the time we reach Koth, surely we will find a solution."

Aerax had already found a solution—and that was sinking the whole cursed place, which would be easily done. The difficulty was not killing anyone who lived there while doing it. For then he would become not merely a villain, but a monster.

But so would Aerax be, by not doing anything. And Aerax had no wish to kill his uncle. Had no wish to take the king's place.

Yet more and more, that seemed the only option left.

CHAPTER 16

LIZZAN

"Y ou do not look well," Ardyl said.

Lizzan laughed, slitting open an eye as the Parsathean settled down beside her. They had caught up to the caravan just as that group was beginning their midday meal. Despite an invitation to join them, Kelir and Ardyl had decided only to stop long enough to rest the horses.

After seeing to her gelding, Lizzan hadn't wasted time finding shade beneath a tree and taking her own rest, for she felt as well as she apparently looked. Throbbing pain had settled between her temples not long after they'd left Oana. She knew what was coming next. Trembling hands. A churning stomach. A racing heart even when nothing threatened her, and feeling as if she couldn't catch her breath even when she was sitting still. She had experienced it all before when she'd gone for too long without a drink.

She'd hoped the baths would have cured her of it, as they had cured the pain that followed a deep drunk. Yet that seemed not the case, and the next few days would not be the finest ones she'd ever known.

But she had no wish to confess that she had a drunkard's illness. So she told Ardyl, "I am only tired."

"As I am. I've not had much sleep of late."

She certainly hadn't last eve. Without opening her eyes, Lizzan snorted, and Ardyl gave a short laugh.

"The Krimathean was worth the lost sleep." A heavy sigh followed. "But every other night . . . never have I been anywhere so loud as this jungle. And I thought I would become accustomed to the noise, but I have not."

Nor did many who traveled this road. "There is a vine that will help you sleep."

"A vine?"

Nodding, Lizzan glanced over and found Ardyl lying on her back, with one arm pillowed behind her head and chewing a strip of dried meat. "It is called the corpse vine, but it is safe as long as you are not tangled in it."

"You have used it?"

"Many times."

"Is it so potent that we cannot be roused? We have sleeping draughts but only use them when we take the half-moon milk."

So the female warriors could sleep through the stomach cramps that came while shedding their menstrual blood in one night. But on the road, sleeping so soundly was rarely safe. "It can be weak, so that it merely helps you fall asleep, or so strong that nothing will wake you until dawn. I can show you how to find it when we stop for camp."

"There will be many of us grateful for it."

If all the Parsatheans were tired, they did not look it. Whereas the Kothans seemed to be wilting in the heat—except for Aerax, who never appeared anything but comfortable in his skin. Even in the prince's armor he wore now, he seemed at complete ease while watching Degg mince toward a lounging Caeb with the sloth-stuffed bladder in his hands.

As if Degg meant to make friends. She didn't think Aerax was making the same effort in return—though he had today with Kelir, by riding alongside the warrior and not always letting his grunts and scowls serve as answers.

Just as Lizzan had asked him to. And though she'd called herself foolish, the sweet warmth of Aerax's effort was the only thing to make the pain in her head bearable this day.

But *Degg*. Lizzan couldn't fathom what the councilor was up to. Though perhaps it was an attempt to persuade the southern alliance that Koth's bastard prince and councilors were not fully at odds, as they tried to repair the damage they believed Lizzan had done.

Though she didn't think any part of this morning's ride had persuaded them that Aerax was not at odds with much of Koth.

She looked to Ardyl, who was using one of the claws around her neck to pick at her teeth, as if a piece of dried meat had gotten stuck between. "What would you have said to Lady Junica?"

"Hmm?"

"When you said that only killing the Destroyer mattered, and she replied that if we destroyed Koth to stop him, no different would we be. It seemed you would say something, and then did not."

"Ah." With a sigh, Ardyl let the claw fall against her neck and gestured to the wineskin near Lizzan's leg, which she'd filled that morning with the ale from the bandits' barrels before leaving the remainder behind. As Lizzan passed it over, Ardyl sat up and said, "I would have told her that if she ever had to trade between the lives of her family and the home that she lived in, she would choose the family. But then I recalled what you said last eve. All of her family was lost to the fever?"

Gravely, Lizzan nodded.

"Then I can have nothing to tell her that she does not already know."

"That is not what it seemed."

"But it is true, I think." She gazed across the busy clearing, to where the councilor sat with Tyzen and Preter and Seri. "What age would her children have been now?"

A pang struck Lizzan's heart. "She had a daughter near Seri's age. And a son the same age as Aerax."

Nodding as if that confirmed something she had suspected, Ardyl said, "I was a babe when the Destroyer's armies came to the Burning Plains. My entire clan was slaughtered, except for me, because I was hidden away in a granary. All that I have of them are these." She touched the silver piercings on her face, then showed Lizzan the silver ring around her thumb. "Each of them wore a ring marked with their name and their parents' names—but the Destroyer's men piled their bodies and all of their belongings into a giant pyre, and all their names were melted away. But a babe does not wear a ring. So I know not who my parents were. I know not if I had sisters and brothers, or what my true name is. I have been told stories about my clan by people who knew them, but I have no memory of them at all, no knowledge of the stories they told of each other and that an outsider could not know, and no connection to the territory where they lived. I know not even the place where I was born. Do you?"

Chest tight, Lizzan nodded. "In the back of a cart on the road outside Lightgale, because my mother believed I would not come for a few more days, so she traveled to Fairwind to hear a dispute."

"Have you ever passed that spot without thinking of that story, even though you cannot remember it yourself?"

Lizzan shook her head.

"Just as it must be for her," Ardyl said, looking to Lady Junica again. "I envy that she has so much more than a few bits of silver to remind her of what was lost. There must be so many places on that island that hold the memory of those she loved, it surprises me not at all how fiercely she protects them. But she is clearly a woman of sense, and knows those memories are truly held here"—she tapped the side of her head—"instead of in those places. And then there is her admiration of Varrin."

With a sudden laugh, Lizzan asked, "Which version? For never have I heard the one where he is a monster before."

"And I am inclined to believe it, merely because it came from Tyzen's mother."

"Truly?"

A strange expression moved over Ardyl's face. "You need never ask that of a Parsathean."

As well she knew. Lizzan repeated dryly, "Truly?"

"Ah. You assumed it was a jest?"

Surely it must be. "Was it?"

Ardyl shook her head. "A warrior-queen of Syssia would not spread idle lies, so she must have had good reason to believe what she saw. But what I believe of Varrin matters not at all. I only mention it because Lady Junica so clearly admires him—and when he sacrificed himself, it wasn't to save the island, but to save the people on it. That is the god she has faith in and would hear no slander against. So I would wager that if she faced the decision, she would choose to save lives rather than to save the island. Just as I would kill anyone who tried to take these piercings from me. But if I had to decide between saving Kelir or Seri and these piercings, I would rip them out myself, though they are all I have left of my family and my clan, because I do not even have memories of them. But until that moment came, I would fight to keep both. Just as she was, when arguing against sinking the island."

Nodding, Lizzan sipped from the wineskin.

Ardyl gave her a sideways glance. "Your prince seemed rather eager to sink it."

Huffing out a laugh, Lizzan said, "He has no love for Koth."

"And seems to have no love for your king."

"Aerax has no love for anyone." At Ardyl's narrow look, Lizzan amended, "Except for a few. But do not judge him by that—or the king. In truth, Aerax thinks well of him. Or used to."

A threat to execute her would have changed that forever.

"What sort of man is your king?"

"Sad," said Lizzan, though that was not the full truth. "All of the royals I have ever seen are . . . large and bright and strong. King Icaro is no exception. But there is a gentleness to him. His brother—Aerax's father—seemed harder, more selfish. And Aerax hated him. He spoke well of Icaro, though. He told me that his uncle truly grieved his first wife when she died of the red fever, and that he dotes on his surviving daughter, but also truly loves his new wives and their children. And I do believe that Icaro cares for all of Koth and wants the best for all his people."

"So he lies to them, as he did when you were exiled?" Wearing a disgusted sneer, Ardyl shook her head. "Never would my people be so forgiving. How can you trust a king who would lie to you?"

At a loss for an answer, Lizzan lifted her hands. "I suppose most people want comfort, not truth."

"So he treats them as we do children? But that is not even the same, for though we might soften a truth, we do not lie to our children. What of you? What would you prefer to hear?"

"I would rather hear truth," said Lizzan, and the same truth forced her to add, "Though when I speak, I often give comfort, instead."

"Well, do not give any comfort to me," Ardyl said wryly. "I am no babe, though you saw me sucking a teat."

So she had. With a snort, Lizzan tilted her head back against the tree again and closed her eyes. By the gods, after all the times that Aerax had kissed her breasts, she was fair glad that a little tit-sucking did not turn anyone into a child. And neither did giving comfort. She would save Aerax pain, but that did not mean she was treating him as a child. Truly, it didn't.

Truly.

A rdyl had spoken truth about the noise. By the time they made camp, every sound from the jungle seemed to be rattling around inside Lizzan's skull and trying to bludgeon its way through her skin.

At supper, the scent of roasting meat turned her stomach. She sat sipping from her wineskin, aware of Aerax's steady gaze on her though she wouldn't meet his eyes, while the conversation around the fire seemed to amplify every other sound. When Lady Junica implored the Parsatheans to tell them of their favorite legend, as she had told them of Varrin, Lizzan could bear no more. Though she wanted to hear the tale of the demon Scourge that had ravaged the Burning Plains, the hoofbeat rhythm of the song began to sway in her stomach until she feared she might vomit.

At the edge of the clearing, she laid out her bedroll but knew better than to hope for sleep. Shivering in her cloak despite the heat of the evening, she turned away from the fire and closed her eyes against the dizzying dance of light and shadow on the canopy overhead.

Tension gripped her when she felt someone approach. Then solid, muscular warmth stretched along her back, and she turned toward Caeb to bury her face against his chest. Tears of relief trickled from beneath her lashes when his rumbling purr didn't add to the cacophony of noises, but instead drowned all the others out.

She must have dozed. She woke with her head pillowed on Caeb's right foreleg and with his ruff tickling her nose. No more firelight danced against the ferns and leaves; instead only a soft glow touched the canopy. No voices could she hear beneath the unending chorus of the jungle, as if everyone had gone to bed.

Until Seri's faint whisper came. "Is she already asleep?"

A little spike of pain shot through Lizzan's head when she sat up, but at least her shivers had eased. She rubbed the sleep from her face and as always, her gaze went first to Aerax, who was drawing his mail armor over his head. With him were Ardyl and Seri . . . who had asked him to accompany them so that they could draw near to Caeb, Lizzan realized. She didn't know if he'd already snarled at them or if they had simply known to take precaution.

Ardyl grimaced. "We did not mean to wake you."

Eyeing Aerax, who next removed his linen tunic, Lizzan

shook her head. "I would have woken, anyway, when Caeb left on his hunt. You need the corpse vine?"

"Is it too dark to find any?"

"Not with Caeb's nose to help us. That will be your first hunt this eve," Lizzan told him. "We will pretend you are a hound."

Gracefully the cat rose, lashing his tail into her face. With a grin, she swatted it away, then gripped handfuls of his ruff to haul herself onto her feet. From her bedroll, she collected her boots and dragged them on.

"We will return with torches," said Ardyl, before leading Seri back to the campfire.

"You come with us?" she asked Aerax when he drew nearer, wearing only his fine brocs and boots, and the leather braces on his forearms that sheathed his short knives.

He nodded, his gaze searching her face. "I would ask that you join Caeb and me on our hunt, but you do not look full well."

"Then I look as I feel," she said with a sigh. "But I am only tired."

"And you've had nothing to eat this day."

As if he had watched her to know. "Tomorrow I will."

Though she might puke it up. But she could eat nothing now . . . or go on this hunt and protect him, as she'd been tasked.

Throat tight, she told him, "Lower your head to me."

Brows drawing together, he did—then began to shake his head and argue when she lifted her father's medallion from her neck.

"Quiet yourself," she told him. "Only this morn, I demanded that you take care while you hunt this unfamiliar land. This is how you will."

A muscle worked in his jaw. "You also said that you will be a stranger to me. Do you give your father's medallion to all strangers?"

"Only the ones who foolishly run into the jungle," she said, ignoring the ache in her heart. "Because it is Vela's law of the road that strangers should help each other."

His hand caught her wrist with the chain dangling from her fingers. "You will have no protection."

"I have my sword. This camp is full of Parsathean warriors. And I can run faster than any of the Kothans, so if we are attacked by ravening beasts, they would be eaten first while I get away."

His lips twitched. "Is that also the law of the road?"

"That is the law of the bitter, exiled soldier."

Amusement gleamed in his dark gaze, but still he shook his head. "Caeb will be with me."

"And if you are hurt, who will protect him?" Eyes narrowed, she lifted her chin. "Do not deny me this."

Though his jaw clenched and his gaze demanded that she relent, after a moment he bent his head. Moving close enough to feel his breath on her cheek, she looped the necklace over his head and ran her fingers along the chain, her skin brushing over his as she searched for kinks and twists that might weaken the links. But there was only smooth silver from his nape to where the medallion hung just above the pouch that held her braid.

She looked up, and his intent stare stole her breath. It was in a whisper that she said, "Return it to me when you are done?"

Eyes burning into hers, he nodded.

Heart pounding, she stepped back. Her racing pulse made the drumming in her head beat all the harder, but barely she noticed it past the throbbing that overtook every span of her skin.

On a shuddering breath, she looked past him, to where Ardyl and Seri waited a short distance away. "Ready, then?"

CHAPTER 17

LIZZAN

Ardyl's long glaive with its curved blade served better than Lizzan's sword at hacking through the foliage from their path, so she and Seri forged ahead with Caeb. Lizzan took Ardyl's torch and followed behind them with Aerax at her side. The giant ferns of the jungle south of Oana had given way to more trees, though smaller than near the baths, and their broad trunks looked as if a dense clusters of ropes had been twisted together and drawn up toward the canopy. In the flickering torchlight, their exposed roots and the shadowed burrows beneath resembled enormous hands digging gnarled fingers into the soil, desperately anchoring themselves to the ground.

"What made these tracks?" Aerax asked.

Distractedly, Lizzan paused to lower the torch nearer to the ground. Two-toed hooves, short stride.

"A dappled roe, I think," she said. A small deer that didn't live farther north, so he would not recognize their prints.

"Good eating for Caeb?"

"And better hunting. I have only seen them dart across the road. It will be a chase for him."

He crouched to study the hoofprints for a moment, and desperately Lizzan tried to see him as a stranger—not easy to do, when there was so much of him to see. After she'd given him the medallion, he'd removed his brocs and boots, since nothing could cut his feet. Only an underlinen was tied around his waist.

She could not deny how practical it was to wear little on the hunt. Blood and dirt could be easier cleaned from skin and linen than from leather and fur. Yet not for a moment did she believe that was Aerax's only purpose. Curse him, he must know how her gaze roamed over his body now, lingering on the broad mountains of his shoulders, then traveling helplessly down the rugged plains of his back on a trail that led to the tightest of all asses.

But no good would this do her—or him.

Abruptly averting her eyes, she started off again. "We fall behind."

Not that it mattered. The trail ahead was easy to follow. But an ache took up residence in her heart to match the ache in her head, and Lizzan didn't trust herself alone with him. Didn't trust that she wouldn't turn to him and dull every serrated thought in her brain with the hot pleasure of his kiss. Did not trust that those jagged thoughts wouldn't lead to a full and painful confession—but she was *not* treating him as a babe. Vela had charged her with his protection. And Lizzan knew all too well how hearts needed protection, too. So she must continue in this way. As strangers.

They caught up to Seri and Ardyl, who'd stopped to wait . . . because Caeb had, turning to face the trail and impatiently flicking his tail as if they were two wayward children. With a grin, Aerax scratched beneath the cat's chin before sending him forward again.

Swinging her glaive, Ardyl sliced through a tangle of vines that Caeb had slinked his way under. "How did you come to befriend a long-toothed cat?"

Instantly Lizzan and Aerax were no longer strangers, but united as one. So many times they had told this story.

Never would they tell all of it.

"The eastern outlands of Koth rise up into the base of the Fallen Mountains," Lizzan told them. "There we went hunting and came across Caeb's mother already dead."

Aerax nodded, and as Seri and Ardyl were walking ahead, they did not see how his face darkened. "She had been caught in a hunter's snare."

"And we could see that she had been nursing, so Aerax followed her tracks to the den. There we found Caeb," Lizzan said. "His eyes had not even opened."

"I would have left him to die, for it would be one less snow cat to fear while I hunted." Aerax's gaze caught hers, the torchlight revealing the softening in his expression. "But Lizzan shed a lake of tears and demanded that I take the kitten home and care for him. So I spent two full years as his nursemaid, until he could hunt alongside me."

Lizzan playfully narrowed her eyes at him. "You say that as if I did not help you. I did."

"You would come to pet him and kiss him, and fly away when it came time for a bath."

"Because *I* did not like baths." She had not liked them until she'd discovered how lovely it was to share a bath with Aerax. As he well knew. Heat curled through her lower belly as his gaze continued to hold hers.

"I do not like baths, either," said Seri, and blithely ignored Ardyl's laughing reply that everyone who came too near her was well aware. "I'd rather be a cat and lick myself clean."

"You stepped in horse shit while making camp," Ardyl reminded her.

"I did not say that I would lick my boots," scoffed the girl before looking back at Aerax. "What age is Caeb now?"

"Near five and ten."

"That is as old as I am." Seri regarded the cat again with new appreciation in her expression. "No wonder, then, that he seems to understand you. I have seen wolves and horses so well trained, but never imagined a cat could be. But he's been with you a long time."

"So he has," Aerax said, and added nothing more.

Because anything more would be a lie. Caeb's understanding had naught to do with his age. At two years, the cat had understood them just as well.

That was the part she and Aerax would not tell—and it was a memory Lizzan hated to recall, though it had begun as a day full of excitement, as she'd accompanied Aerax on her first hunt. For nearly a year, they'd practiced swords together—and he'd promised her that when the snows melted, he would take her with him into the outlands.

It was not even midday when they'd come across a small band of hunters skinning the carcass of a huge snow cat, which had been unremarkable in itself. Snow cats were rarely hunted except by fools with no care for their own lives—and when they were, it was almost always for their fur, or because they'd developed a taste for human flesh, or had been slaughtering a village's livestock.

And if she and Aerax had remained undetected, they would have probably continued on without ever thinking of it again. But they were seen.

Lizzan hadn't feared the hunters at all. Aerax had been wary of the four men, as he was of everyone, yet she didn't think even he had expected the hunters' angry reaction to their presence . . . or the shouts not to let them escape.

Completely unreal it had all seemed when the hunters had charged at them with swords drawn, as if a girl and a boy who were barely older than children posed a dangerous threat. Immediately Lizzan had reached for her own sword, though it was short and dull, but Aerax hadn't brought the weapon they practiced with. He'd only been armed with the short knives he used to clean and dress his prey. So she'd stepped in front of him, prepared to protect them both.

And there she had learned what became of a young boy who'd survived on his own for much of his life, who'd taught himself to hunt by watching the predators in the forest.

Like a beast unleashed, he'd sprung for the nearest hunter, a savage whirlwind made of furs and blades that tore through the man's neck before he launched himself at the next, feinting past the man's panicked swing of a sword and slicing through the back of his knee. As the hunter had screamed, Aerax opened him from gut to gullet—and barely a moment had passed before he vaulted over the dying man and slammed full-bodied into the next man's chest, snarling as he ripped out the hunter's throat with his teeth. Then he'd spit blood and throatflesh to the ground, looked to the last hunter, and growled.

The man had fled, and Aerax followed—while Lizzan had stood trembling, disbelieving what she'd just seen. Near a full year she'd known him, nearly a full year they'd practiced together. Never had she'd seen him move like that before. She hadn't known anyone *could* move like that. He'd not been like a boy at all, but a vicious animal.

A few moments had passed while she stood frozen, then she'd shaken herself and began to follow—until the screams she heard in the distance told her that Aerax had already caught up with the man.

Then she'd discovered why the hunters had reacted as they did.

No true law was there against killing a Hanani beast. Nor would a person usually succeed. With the god Hanan's blood in their veins, those animals were not only bigger and stronger than others of their species but far more clever. As clever as any human, it was often said. But most kept their distance from humans. And although killing one of the Hanani broke no law, it was because most people would only kill the animal while defending themselves. To *hunt* one seemed as unimaginable a horror to Lizzan as hunting a child would be.

Yet that was clearly what the four men had done, and then drained the snow cat's silver blood into casks—as if they intended selling it—which had been horror upon horror to Lizzan.

As it would have been to anyone, had she and Aerax

spoken of what they'd seen. So the hunters had meant to silence them and leave them for dead.

By the time Aerax had returned to her, his face and furs covered in the hunters' blood, she'd been weeping uncontrollably while cutting the snow cat down from the tree where she'd been strung. Lizzan had flung herself into his arms, hugging him tight, and together they'd sought out the den. There they'd found Caeb, a small ball of fluff that didn't even yet have fangs.

Later that same night, as she'd nursed Caeb from a small bladder of milk, his tiny paws kneading her neck and pricking her with needlelike claws, Aerax had confessed that he'd feared she would never again look at him without terror.

But he hadn't frightened Lizzan. Instead she'd been afraid *for* him. No one pretended to see him in Koth . . . but they would see him if he ever again tore out a man's throat. They would be fearful—and people hurt what they feared. Even at that young age, Lizzan had known it.

And after she'd casually asked her mother's mother, a healer, what use someone might have for Hanani blood—and was told not to speak of such foul things—Lizzan feared for Caeb, too. But she had not known why to be afraid until Cernak told her of a rumor that corrupt monks and dark sorcerers would pay fortunes for the blood.

She had told Aerax, and he had agreed—never would they say what Caeb truly was. And after Caeb had grown old enough to explain the danger to him, he had made the same decision.

Lizzan had never known if there was truth in the rumor. And Shim, the Hanani stallion, seemed not afraid of people knowing what he was.

But neither she nor Aerax would take the risk with Caeb, and the cat did not seem to want to, either. Perhaps not even out of fear, but so that he would be more likely left alone, instead of people always trying to talk to him.

Now he paused ahead, nostrils fluttering as he sniffed the air, before turning in a new direction. Lizzan also caught a scent, the sweetly fetid stench of rot.

"We will see if that is something caught in the vine, or just something dead," she said, taking the lead alongside the cat, until the smell led her to where a monkey the size of a rabbit was entangled in a green vine that wound around the base of a tree. Lizzan scratched her fingers through Caeb's ruff. "You have found it for us. I thank you. Go and take your own supper now."

She glanced back at Aerax, who silently asked with a lift of his brows whether she wanted him to stay. With a shake of her head, she bade him to go, and watched as he and Caeb swiftly disappeared into the shadows.

"I know that vine," said Ardyl as they drew nearer. "It also grows in the southern jungle, where the river Lave meets the Boiling Sea—but there the vine is bigger. Much bigger. I have seen a young trap jaw caught in its coils while the rotting juices fed the roots. We call it a constrictor vine."

"So the corpse vine does, too." Lizzan touched the tip of her dagger to the vine's hairy surface. Like a baby gripping a mother's finger, the vine gently curled toward it. "But unless you are of that monkey's size, you only need take care when one of these thorns pierces your skin. That much venom will put you into heavy sleep, though not immediately. You could still walk back to camp. The only danger is if you fall asleep near the vine and it grips a naked limb, so you do not awaken. Also the venom will make you say truths."

"That is no danger," said Seri. "Parsatheans only speak truth."

"It's a danger if there are truths you don't intend to say. I once told a merchant who'd hired me to escort her wagon that every time she opened her mouth to offer her lump-weeded opinion, it was like watching someone burst a pimple, full well knowing what spilled out would turn a stomach but it was still impossible to look away."

Ardyl laughed. "How long did that job last?"

"She put her boot in my ass that day." With her blade, Lizzan sliced through a length of the corpse vine, and used her cloak to protect her bare hands as she rolled it up. So badly she wanted to use it. So very badly. But she could hardly protect Aerax if the venom rendered her unconscious until morning, and she knew from many attempts that the weaker remedy no longer had any effect on her. "If you only wish for help falling asleep, rub these hairs on your skin. This is enough to share with all of your warriors. It will keep for a full turn in a moistened jute sack . . . which we ought to have brought with us."

Seri held out her hand to take the coil. "I care not at all if I stick myself with one of the thorns. I intend to sleep as the dead for a full night."

"Then you are the fortunate one," said Ardyl as they returned to the path they'd made. "I am on first watch this eve. A half night I will spend guarding the camp with my fingers plugging my ears."

For Lizzan, that would only keep the worst of the noise in. And the ache, too.

"I do not mind the noise so much." Seri ducked low beneath a hanging fern so her torch would not catch on the leaves. "Instead it is feeling as if I am about to be swallowed. Or as if all these trees will soon fall over and crush me."

"You are sky-starved," Ardyl told her, then looked to Lizzan and explained, "The same happened to many of our warriors when they joined the alliance army at the river Lave, especially those who first came to the jungles or forests. On the Burning Plains, the sky is open. Every rising and setting of the sun and the moon are there to see. But here . . ." She glanced up. "It seems there are no stars at all. I know the moon is three days past full, but it is hidden behind these leaves. Even on the road or in a clearing, the sky is but a narrow view. Tracking time is near impossible. And it is all so—"

"Dreadful," said Seri.

Ardyl nodded. "I do not like it much, either."

"Sky-starved." Wearing an irritated pout, Seri kicked at a root. "Do not tell my brother. He will coddle me. And say nothing to Tyzen, or he might begin cutting down trees."

"I will say nothing." The corners of Ardyl's lips twitched.

"But I might not have to. Did you already pierce yourself with that thorn?"

The girl groaned in realization.

"You came through Stranik's Passage," Lizzan said. "You did not feel sky-starved then?"

Seri shook her head. "That is different."

"But you are beneath a mountain. And it is full dark."

"The darkest dark you have ever seen," the girl agreed.

And only a few years past, that tunnel had been a mere legend—a story from the beginning of time, when the goddess Temra had broken through vault of the sky and began reshaping the world with the pounding of her fists. It was said the snake god, Stranik, had fallen asleep with his body stretching the length of the western realms, and as Temra's pounding fists forced the Astal mountains to rise, they covered the sleeping god. When he awakened and slithered away, the shape of his body left a passageway under the mountains.

But in ancient times, that tunnel had been used to imprison a demon and sealed off . . . until a generation past, when the Destroyer had opened the passage and marched his army through. Freed from its prison, the demon had plagued Blackmoor, and the passageway had been filled with revenants. Only after the demon was slain had a safe route opened from Blackmoor in the south to Krimathe in the north. But that was a route Lizzan had never taken—and if Temra was merciful, it was a route she would never take.

Ardyl's wry look told Lizzan that she had not completely suppressed the horror from her voice as she'd spoken of the tunnel. "You would not like to pass through it?"

Lizzan would rather fling herself into a snake pit. "Did you like it?"

"It is not as terrifying as all the wagon drivers make it out to be," Seri told her earnestly, clearly delighted by the terrors that *had* been there. "The bones scattered about *can* appear to move if you stare at them for too long by the torchlight. But the revenants have been cleared. And I sensed no demon's foul magic lingering to raise the hairs on my neck."

The hairs at the back of Lizzan's neck rose *now*. "You are braver than I."

"The shape of Stranik's scales was still etched into the stone walls, and you could clearly see them from beginning to end." Awe filled the girl's voice as with her hands she drew an arc over her head, as if even now envisioning the walls of the tunnel around her. "The span of his body even longer than we could travel in a half turn."

A fortnight spent in a lightless cavern that resembled a snakeskin. Shuddering, Lizzan shook her head to rid herself of the horrid image.

"Some of us enjoyed that journey more than others," Ardyl said with an amused glance at the other warrior. "I would not trade the jungle for the tunnel again, no matter how loud it is."

"I would," the girl said.

"Soon you will not have a jungle to trade," Lizzan told them. "In two more days, the road climbs into the vales of Cleastan and leaves this forest behind. And if you are very lucky, you will also miss the rains that come this time of year."

Seri shot her a baffled glance. "It pours every day."

"It merely sprinkles for a short time. What comes soon is the spring deluge from Temra's Heart." Heavy rains were carried north on a wet ocean wind between the Astal range and the Fanged Mountains—though by the time it reached Koth, the heartwind was but a warm breeze that melted the last of the snows and heralded the first blooms . . . and was Lizzan's favorite time of year. Pushing past the ache in her throat, she continued, "But we'll avoid the worst of the rains if we are far enough into the hills . . . though it will not be near so warm. Have you enough furs?"

For none of the Parsatheans wore tunics. Aside from a few female warriors who bound their breasts, as Ardyl did, all above the waist was bare skin.

"We are well supplied," Ardyl told her.

Perhaps for a Kothan summer. But if they stayed longer, they could find what they needed in the north.

"Do you think we will meet a great many dangers on the way?" Seri asked, with a faint slowing and slur to her words. "For we have not on this journey yet—and I need to prove that I will be worthy as the head of Yvenne's Dragon."

Ardyl grinned. "I do not think you need worry of that as yet."

"So many wondrous feats I thought we would accomplish already," the girl lamented. "But only one leatherwing has dived at me. And I did not even kill it."

"Be patient." Ardyl consoled her while tossing an amused glance to Lizzan. "A sorcerer-king lies ahead."

"But if there is a battle, Kelir will make me stay away from him."

Some of the other warrior's amusement faded. "And if Kelir does not, I will."

Sudden tears gleamed in Seri's eyes. "I am the youngest of warriors here, but I am still a warrior in full."

"So you are," was Ardyl's gentle reply. "But Kelir and I wish to see you become an old warrior—as do Maddek and Yvenne."

"As does Vela." Wiping her cheeks, Seri looked to Lizzan. "You will see that I am protected . . . but what do you think I must be protected from?"

Lizzan's heart sank into her stomach. *Mother Temra, have mercy on her now.* She had full forgotten what the girl had heard.

She came to a stop and the ache in her head suddenly seemed more like a spike. The other two women turned to face her, Seri's gaze imploring and Ardyl's slightly narrowed—as if Kelir had already told her what Seri believed, and waited for Lizzan to clear the girl's misunderstanding.

"I . . ." Had no true idea of what to say. Grimacing, she plowed forward. "What you heard me say was not the truth. It was Aerax that I saw first, but I was drunk and hurt—and feared that I would be hurt even more. So I told him that I was protecting you, instead."

Seri's lips rounded, a small furrow of confusion forming between her brows. Her gaze darted to Ardyl before returning to meet Lizzan's. "Vela did not tell you to protect me?"

"She did not. Though of course I would, if you should ever need it. But that was not Vela's demand."

The girl seemed to struggle with that a bit longer before nodding. "That is fine news, then, is it not? The goddess knows I need no protection, for I can well protect myself. Clearly your prince needs it more. He does not even carry a sword." Abruptly her brows drew together again. "Though you lied to him to save yourself? So he is your enemy? But you seem as friends. Why would Vela ask you to protect an enemy?"

Throat tight, Lizzan shook her head. "He is no enemy."

"And you are no friend, if you lie to him," scoffed Seri before looking to Ardyl. "No hope do I have that this great alliance can ever stand against the Destroyer. Not when these realms are full of people who treat their friends as enemies by always lying to them. Not when they live in fear that the people who are closest to them will be the ones who harm them. If they cannot even believe that the people they love will not hurt them, how can they possibly believe that the warrior they have just met will fight beside them? What trust could there be in such an alliance? And without trust, how can it hold strong?"

"Perhaps fear will be enough," said Ardyl quietly.

"Only until they fear something more. Then the alliance will fall apart. So while they are ruled by their fear, there can be no hope." The girl's despairing and angry gaze settled on Lizzan again. "And you are a drunk and a liar."

With a sharp stone lodged in her chest, Lizzan nodded. "That is true."

Seri huffed out a disgusted breath and stalked ahead.

Following more slowly, Lizzan said to Ardyl, "Perhaps I shouldn't have given her the vine to hold."

"Perhaps." Both steel and sympathy lay in the other woman's gaze. "And perhaps you should drink less, so you need never fear what truth is said."

The short laugh that burst from Lizzan rattled in her aching head. All day she'd been drinking from her wineskin. For all the good it had done. "So I have been told by Vela, too. But I do not recommend it. It only makes you hurt more."

"Only because it makes you care more."

"I could not care more. Already I care too much."

Ardyl nodded, but her gaze was distant, head cocked. "Do you hear . . . ?"

Lizzan rushed with Ardyl to the edge of the clearing, where they stopped. With dismay, Ardyl said, "Perhaps we shouldn't have let her hold the vine."

For Seri was already back at the camp . . . and yelling to her brother that Lizzan was a drunk and a liar. If anyone had fallen asleep before, they were not then, and Lizzan saw her lie settle in stone on some of the Parsathean warriors' faces when they looked to her—and heard the outright laughter from the Kothan soldiers.

But at least Aerax was not there to witness it, so Lizzan did not care what was said of her, or what anyone thought.

She did not care at all.

CHAPTER 18

AERAX

By the time Aerax returned from the hunt, the camp-fires were burned to coals that were only kept alive for ease in making the morning meal. The waning moon was still near full, and high enough to flood the clearing with silver light. All was as quiet as the jungle ever seemed to be, as if the entire camp had made use of Lizzan's vine, though he could feel the gazes of the two Parsatheans on watch as he walked to where Lizzan had made her bed earlier. Behind him came Caeb, dragging a minstrel boar's haunch that was so large it would keep him busy chewing until dawn.

Only the faintest glow of moonlight reached the shadows beneath the trees at the edge of the clearing. There Lizzan's bedroll was gone. But no trouble did he have finding her, following Caeb a few paces to where she sat wrapped in her cloak, her back braced against a tree trunk.

He dropped the minstrel boar's snout and jaw near Liz-zan's feet, with the long and bloodied tusks still attached. The entire head had been so big that he couldn't easily carry it, but Aerax thought she would be amused by the gift.

"It was not a dappled roe," he said, crouching before her with a grin. "And it also had a mother. So I was fortunate you gave me this."

He lifted her father's medallion over his head and ignored her reaching hand, moving nearer until she let him place it back around her neck.

"A minstrel boar?" Shadows shifted over her face as she looked up at him. "Were you hurt?"

Frowning, he studied her through the dark. Her voice sounded nearly as hoarse as it had many winters past, when for seven full days she'd lain in bed, fighting a cough. "I was not. You're not sleeping?"

"I did for a short time." Her breath shuddered. "Then I could not."

Now she sounded exhausted. And as his gaze adjusted to the dark, she seemed so frail to him . . . and so near tears.

An ache took hold of his heart. "You didn't use the vine?"

Her short laugh sounded nothing like amusement, and nearer to despair. "How could I complete my task if I cannot awaken when danger comes? So instead I sit here, while my every thought tears my head apart."

Her eyes closed, and the tears that spilled beneath her lashes all but destroyed him. Throat raw, he cupped her face in his hands.

"Lizzan," he said thickly. "What are these thoughts that are hurting you? I will chase them away."

Another painful laugh shook through her. "We do not do well as strangers."

"I'm not sorry for it."

"No." Her lashes were wet spikes as she looked up at him again. "I would not have you be my enemy, either."

"Never would I be."

"Yet that is what I have made you. I have lied to you since the temple."

"This I know," he said gently, sweeping her cheeks with his thumbs. "I see you before anything else, Lizzan. So I saw you emerge from the temple doors and look to me first. I know that I am under your protection."

"You knew? Of course you knew." She answered herself on a trembling breath before reaching up to lay her hand against his. "But I meant to protect you from more than that. For I did not tell the full truth of my quest."

He cared not how many times she lied to him. "What truth?"

"That on the day of the first snowfall, there will be a glorious battle in which my name will become legend and the shame lifted from my family . . . but I will die in that battle."

"No," he said softly. "You will not."

"Aerax." Her fingers squeezed his as if to impress each word upon him. "That is what Vela said would happen."

"So you will abandon the quest."

"And wear her mark on my face? Be truly forsaken and shunned?" Her eyes closed tight, spilling more tears. "Never could I bear it."

"Then we will visit the next temple along this road and make an appeal to the priestess. You were drunk," he reminded her. "Vela should never have taken your vow when you could not have full understanding of what she asked of you—"

"It is what I asked her for," Lizzan whispered, and it was as if a glacial wind blasted through Aerax, freezing everything within him, stopping his heart and halting his breath. "It is my reward."

Her *reward*.

All inside Aerax seemed as snow, heavy and muffled and frozen. Dimly he was aware that Caeb had abandoned his supper and of the cat's snarling approach. Dimly he heard the echo of the speech Lizzan gave to him now, as if her explanation about villains and redemption were not sinking into his head but instead careening around the empty hollow of his chest so that each word could batter his unbeating heart.

But never could Aerax be frozen for long when he was

with her, and Lizzan's hot tears against his hands began to melt him again. Began to spark a fire. He was burning full bright when she said in an agonized voice, "I only wanted to spare you pain."

No pain did Aerax feel. For she was *not* going to die.

Never would he allow it. Not even if it meant ripping Vela from the sky.

"You believe this hurts me?" he asked, and Caeb's quiet growl underscored his voice. "You think pain is what I feel now? Because it is not pain, Lizzan."

She went still, her gaze searching his face. "You're . . . angry?"

Angry. Did she not know he would destroy anyone who would take her from this earth? Yet *she* was the one who threatened it now. What he felt was not anger. Nothing so tepid described the fury rampaging through his heart, the rage that he fought with all his strength to suppress, because *never* would he touch her in anger, and he still held her face in his hands.

Behind him, Caeb paced back and forth as if in a cage, snarling low and his unsheathed claws ripping the ground with every turn.

Lizzan's gaze flicked to the cat before meeting Aerax's again as he asked softly, "Is this what you think is best for you?"

Her throat worked before she answered. "It is the best of what I have left."

"You could think of no other way to lift their shame?"

"What other way is there?" Her tortured gaze searched his. "By speaking the truth of what happened on the King's Walk? No one believes it when we do."

"And so you think this is best for your family?"

Lips trembling, she nodded into his hands.

His jaw clenched. "Did you think to ask them what they thought was best? They *chose* to stay in Koth, knowing what they would bear. Do you think for one moment that they would ever choose to trade their shame for your life? No. They would choose to bear *worse* if it kept you alive."

Her chest hitched. "Aerax—"

No longer could he touch her. Dropping his hands from her face, he surged to his feet. "You will tear their hearts out."

"Please, do not make this harder—"

"And you will destroy *mine*!"

His fury echoed through the trees and was joined by Caeb's, as the cat roared a resounding denial into her face. With a cry, Lizzan covered her ears. Shouts came from the camp but Aerax did not turn to look. Nothing were they to him. Nothing was anything else to him now.

"You think I will *ever* let you do this? Abandon your quest," he commanded.

Though tears streamed down her cheeks, her chin came up. "I cannot."

"Then at the next temple, I will take my own quest." Aerax stepped back into the moonlight, where Vela might see and hear him. If the goddess didn't like what he had to say, then she could send a moonstone to crush him . . . yet still that would not stop him. "My reward will be saving your life, as I seem to treasure it more than you do."

Another furious snarl from Caeb, and Lizzan's face crumpled as if the cat's anger destroyed her heart as she would destroy theirs.

"Please, Caeb—"

"And if Vela denies me a quest, I will tie you hand and foot," Aerax promised her. "I'll carry you to where it never snows and pass the rest of our lives there."

A painful laugh ripped from her. "You would abandon your purpose and Koth now, when you would not come with me before?"

"Never before did I believe you would toss away your life! There is nothing I would not do to save you. I would return with you to Koth, for Vela's power has no reach there. I would kill my uncle, make myself king, and rescind your exile. I would burn the books to remove all stain from your names. And if soldiers still called you a coward to cause you pain, I would tear out their tongues if they even whispered the word."

She stared up at him in horror. "You would be everything you hate."

Aerax laughed harshly and crouched before her again, cupping her nape in a firm grip, making her gaze meet his. "If I have to become a monster to save you, that is what I will do."

"No," she whispered.

"I will. Though strangers it would truly make us—but you already have done that." Fury still surging hot through his veins, he told her, "All I have known of you is softhearted, generous, and strong. But to ask for this quest and name your death as a reward means you are also cruel and selfish and weak."

Her expression shattered. "Aerax—"

"And cowardly, too," he said, and she sucked in a sharp breath, fist flying to her stomach and pressing there, as if to stanch a wound. "You would take the easy path. But I will not let you."

Tears welled up again but she denied them. Eyes closing, she averted her face, her features a mask of desolation. "Go away from me, Aerax."

As strangers again. Pain shot through the rage that had gripped him, but he would not succumb to it. With a look to Caeb, who dragged the boar's haunch closer to Lizzan and settled in, Aerax turned and stalked back into camp.

They had built the fire up again. Hair mussed from sleep, Lady Junica and Degg sat near to it, along with a few Parsatheans, Tyzen, and the monk. No doubt Caeb's roar had woken everyone—or Aerax's shouting had.

He took a seat near Kelir. At the warrior's other side, Seri snored away in her bedroll.

Nothing did anyone say, until Degg ventured to comment, "It does not snow here in the jungle."

Lady Junica shook her head. "It did during the Bitter Years."

The years when all had seemed lost for Aerax's mother, too. But he would not allow Lizzan to come anywhere near as close to death as his mother had.

"It never snows by the Boiling Sea," said Kelir. "Though if Vela wished it to, perhaps it would."

"Or you could just let the coward do it," came a mutter from the group of Kothan soldiers, still lying in their bed-rolls.

Aerax was aware of the tension pulling tight around the fire as he rose to his feet, but he would not become a monster yet. Instead he waited, until the soldiers turned in their beds and saw who he was, still covered in the dirt and blood of his hunt.

"Recall this moment if ever you need saving. *Never* would Lizzan stand by while you died," he said softly, dangerously. "And if you wish to test it, I'll come to you now to rip out your throats—for although you have pissed on her name, though she is tired and hurting, she would fly over here to stop me. The only doubt is whether she'd be fast enough. Do you wish to test it?"

Mutely, the soldiers shook their heads.

"I thought not," Aerax said.

CHAPTER 19

LIZZAN

The rains came the next morning.

Wind thrashed the jungle canopy, sending broken branches hurtling to the ground while torn leaves swirled as in a blizzard. Beneath the gray light, the jewel-like tones of the jungle were dulled, and Lizzan could not remember a more miserable journey. Not even her first trip along this road, with her face still scabbed and painful, and when tears had soaked her furs nearly every morning.

Now she had no tears. And no sleep. The pelt of the northern falt shed the rain but couldn't keep away the nightmares that chased her while she lay beneath it. So she only waited until dawn, with head pounding and stomach churning.

On the road, she was glad of the rain. The jungle was as quiet as it had ever been, as everything within it waited out the storm. Those who rode behind her were no different. No one spoke, riding with heads down. Lizzan traveled with her hood up and a dozen paces ahead of the rest of the party, where no one would see the shakes that racked her body or know how fever burned her skin. So much worse the drunkard's sickness was this time than it had ever been.

She rode alone. Caeb kept pace beside her but offered no affectionate rubs. Instead he watched Lizzan as if to make certain she did not abandon the others and speed ahead to complete her quest.

She might have, if not for that same quest. But she could not protect Aerax if she was running away from him.

And he was truly a stranger to her now. So she didn't know why he cared to save her. He didn't speak to her and she saw only hardness in him when his gaze met hers. Only anger. Because he thought her selfish and weak.

. . . and she was. Never before had Lizzan seen it so clearly. Yet as his accusation added to the knives that were her thoughts, all she saw now was the empty road ahead and she only felt the weight of his judgment behind her.

And she only wanted this journey to end.

The road slowly climbed higher, the jungle thinning out into rolling hills. But they did not escape the rain. Mud soon covered her horse's legs, her boots, the hem of her cloak. The only conversation she had was when asked how far away the next inn stood.

On the fifth day, they reached a village nestled in a green valley. Happy memories Lizzan had of the last time she'd been here, a summer past. Under the sullen gray clouds and dripping with rain, little did the village resemble that warm and welcoming one, yet to Lizzan, there seemed no better place. Her tremors had subsided and her headache had retreated, leaving only fatigue. All she wanted was sleep, but couldn't bear what awaited her in dreams. There, a coward she truly was. She had faced the wraiths at the King's Walk, but she'd been running from them ever since.

Though the rain still fell, conversation started up again behind her as they rode toward the inn. She heard talk of warm beds and bread that wasn't sodden—and she, too, looked forward to the first full meal that her stomach would allow since Vela had begun turning all her drink into water.

Not so lively was the village. All seemed quiet and grim,

as were the villagers who came to their doors to watch them pass. Lizzan felt their wintry gazes on her face and pulled her hood forward, a knot tightening in her chest.

At the inn's stables, good cheer fully returned to the others as the Parsatheans and Kothans cared for their horses. Lizzan lingered with her mount before making her way to the inn alone. Too early it was for proper supper, so no villagers patronized the place yet. Hood up, she claimed a table in a shadowed corner. The others were gathered together in clusters at the center of the inn, mead already in hand and a barmaid bringing more, their easy laughter echoing through the room.

Aerax was not among them. Likely he'd gone to either buy or hunt Caeb's supper before he took his own.

The innkeeper came toward Lizzan, and the throbbing in her head returned. She had seen other innkeepers wear that hostile expression before. Always the cause was the same. Always it ended the same.

But she didn't want to fight. She only wanted a meal and then to sleep.

Stopping beside Lizzan's seat, the innkeeper bent low and hissed, "I will not serve you here."

Lizzan was already preparing to go. "Then I will take my meal to the stables—"

"You will take nothing—and you will not stay in the stables. This village knows full well what Vela does to anyone who offers shelter and aid to those who wear her mark."

Her scars. "I am not cursed—"

"So you said before. And this village has paid the price of believing you."

Lizzan closed her eyes. So it always was. "What has happened?"

"Livestock slaughtered. Vanishings as we have never seen before. Seven gone. *Seven*, and two of them children. Do you recall sitting in this inn with the blacksmith and bouncing her son on your knee? She has not forgotten or forgiven herself for trusting what you said." The innkeeper's voice thickened with rage and grief, and her scalding gaze swept over Lizzan. "Now you come here in a red cloak, as if you are Vela's Chosen? We are not fooled. Your cloak is soaked through, and you are not her Chosen but forsaken and cursed. If you wish to see morning, run from this place and never let your shadow darken our village again."

Her throat a burning ache, Lizzan stood. "Were the vanishings north or south of the village?"

"North." The innkeeper gave a hard laugh. "If that is the direction you go, then perhaps you will pay for what you've done here."

Lizzan had done nothing. But never would they believe it. They never did.

To Ardyl she went, bending her head near to the other woman's so that she might be heard over the boisterous conversation around them, and forcing every word past the hot jagged stone in her throat. "There is a bridge a half day's ride north. I will meet you all there in the morning."

Ardyl frowned. "Why do you go?"

Lizzan gave no answer to that. Most likely Ardyl would hear the reason later, from a villager who warned them against associating with a forsaken woman. But Lizzan had her own story she was supposed to share. "Will you tell them of Ilris's mother?"

Though still frowning, Ardyl nodded. Lizzan thanked her and hurried toward the stables, giving apology to her gelding for the brevity of his rest as she saddled him in haste. But she could not linger now. That she knew well.

Yet she still was too late. As she rode into the stableyard, four villagers approached on the path to the road, led by the blacksmith whom Lizzan had shared a meal with the previous year. The woman's face was a mask of fury and vengeance. No doubt the heavy axe she carried was how she intended to dispense it.

Lizzan dismounted. Once before she'd tried to ride quickly past a mob that had come for her, and a hurled stone had blinded her horse in one eye.

"I am leaving," Lizzan called to them, though she knew

nothing would change. But at least there were only four . . . for now. "You will not see me again."

"As I will not see my Brin? No." The blacksmith shook her head. "Before you leave here, I'll take the knee you bounced him on."

Her heart ached. She recalled full well the curly haired, laughing boy. But she would not pay for what she hadn't done. Nor would she hurt the blacksmith and the villagers, if she could help it—and with her father's medallion around her neck, Lizzan should be able to hold fast.

She only needed to defend until they tired themselves out. "Back away," she told the blacksmith. "Back away now."

Then her stomach lurched, for always she saw Aerax. And always he saw her, though he was still distant enough that this might not become a slaughter. If she could get away before the blacksmith's attack came. For if he saw that, no hope would there be for these villagers.

Instantly her plan changed to escape. Pivoting, she sprang toward her gelding, intending to swing into the saddle and set him immediately to a gallop. Instead a furious cry rang out. A hard blow between her shoulders slammed Lizzan forward, sending her sprawling into the stableyard muck.

Stunned, she stared down at her hands, wrist-deep in the mud. The heavy plop of the axe into the nearby muck told her what had happened—the blacksmith had thrown the weapon. And hit her. If not for her father's medallion, she would have been dead.

Caeb's deafening roar split her ears. *Oh no, no.* Temra have mercy on them all. Scrambling to her feet, Lizzan raced toward the blacksmith and flung herself in front of the woman even as the giant cat lunged into the air. She saw how desperately Caeb suddenly twisted, trying to change his direction midleap, sheathing his claws and tucking his head down so his fangs wouldn't slash her. Still he slammed broadside into her chest, the weight of his massive body knocking her back to the mud.

No breath did she have then to even cry out. Wheezing, she curled up onto her side, her cheek cushioned by mud or horse shit and it didn't matter, because Aerax had his knives in hand but seemed not to see the villagers as he knelt beside her, hoarsely calling her name, and Caeb was nudging her shoulder, mewling in helpless apology.

But she still had to go. Though the confusion and shock of Caeb's sudden attack had frozen the blacksmith and her companions into immobility, their anger would thaw them again soon enough. And there were only four villagers now, but soon there would be more.

There were always more. And if they came for her, Aerax would kill them all.

Barely able to draw breath into her aching chest, Lizzan crawled to her feet. Aerax cupped her muddied cheeks, his skin bloodbare as his gaze searched her face. But death sparked deep in his dark eyes as he looked beyond her to the villagers.

"No," she wheezed, gripping his tunic and bringing his attention back to her face. "They are afraid and grieving. So let them be. This will be over with as soon as I leave."

His jaw clenched and his lethal gaze shot past her again. "Why must you leave?"

"Because it is easier for me to go than it is to fight." And she was so, so very tired; so tired that her voice broke at the next. "Even if that makes me a coward."

Abruptly he looked down at her again. His expression grew tight, his throat working. "Lizzan—"

"It doesn't matter." She pushed away from him and turned toward her horse. All of her seemed so heavy, sodden boots trudging through the muck, her red cloak blackened with mud, and her heart mired in the shit her life had become. "None of it matters anymore."

CHAPTER 20

AERAX

Lizzan's gelding was tethered on the side of the road. Aerax drew his own mount to a halt, his gaze searching the ground. Even as she'd ridden out of the stable-yard, Caeb had followed her. Aerax had, too, as soon as he'd saddled his own horse. Their tracks told him that for much of the way, the cat had remained behind her—but here they were side-by-side, headed into the wooded forest that blanketed this hillside. As if she'd asked Caeb to accompany her.

It would not only be Caeb who did.

Swiftly Aerax followed their trail. The careful placement of their steps, moving while making as little noise as possible, told him their purpose—they were on the hunt. For Lizzan had missed her supper and Caeb had abandoned his.

Because she'd been driven away from a village by the edge of an axe. Over and over again, he saw the weapon flying toward her back. Saw her fall to the ground. All else was lost in a haze of grief and rage. He'd heard some explanation, for Caeb's roar had drawn everyone from the inn, and the Parsatheans had demanded an answer. He'd heard them speak of Vela's Mark and a curse and dead children, that she was forsaken and unwelcome even at an inn. Yet *none* of it made any sense. That Lizzan would be shunned here, not just Koth—and not merely ignored and nameless.

And had she not told him? In the healing baths, Lizzan had said that she'd rather be nameless in Koth than cursed here. But Aerax hadn't understood what she'd meant, because he couldn't understand how all the world did not see the shining jewel she was. But even here, she'd been tossed in the mud.

Chest tight and aching, he paused where she and Caeb had stopped to study a set of tracks. His heart slammed into his throat. As they'd traveled north, the woods and creatures in them had become more familiar to Aerax than those in the jungle. This one, too. The shape was similar to that of a man who walked on the balls of his feet, but three times the size and with curved claws that gouged the earth with every step.

A woodstalker. As a boy, Aerax had seen one of the massive apes. The howls and screams of battle had drawn him to a snowy canyon where a woodstalker and a sun raptor had fought over the remains of a mammoth that the reptile had brought down. With fangs that rivaled Caeb's, scythelike claws on its feet and hands, and long-armed strength, the woodstalker had torn the giant raptor apart. Aerax had taken care never to come across one again.

Yet now Lizzan and Caeb hunted *two.*

Heart thundering, he raced after them. From ahead, a primal scream sliced jagged ice down his spine and was answered by Caeb's roar. Not far distant from him now. He vaulted over a stream and Caeb charged out from between the trees ahead before turning and roaring again. A woodstalker burst into view, matted fur as pale as birch bark, fangs gleaming in the poor light.

Barely did Aerax see Lizzan before she was on the beast, leaping from the tall branch of a tree and onto its shoulder, her sword stabbing deep into its neck. The wood-stalker screamed, reaching back with talons that shredded the hood of her cloak but skated over her skin. Its grasping hand caught her around the shoulders and yanked her off even as Aerax rushed forward, knives in hands.

His blade sliced through the beast's ankle, and then he gripped a handful of the ragged fur and climbed the thick leg to stab the back of its knee. Howling, the woodstalker crashed forward, leg buckling. Caeb lunged for its exposed throat, his fangs stabbing deep into muscle and tearing through veins that spurted crimson across his chest. Weakly the wood-stalker reached for the cat . . . with Lizzan still caught on its hand, choking and thrashing.

Shouting for Caeb, Aerax surged across the woodstalker's convulsing form. Lizzan's hands were at her neck, fingers desperately dragging at the thin silver chain at her throat. Terror razed his heart. When the woodstalker had raked his talons through her cloak, the claws had caught beneath the necklace, pulling it tight enough to choke. Only the charm that prevented the silver chain from slicing through her skin had saved her from beheading, yet wouldn't save her if she couldn't breathe.

Aerax couldn't break the silver links without yanking the chain tighter. Snatching her sword, he carefully wedged it between the claw and the necklace before bearing down with all his strength. Barely did the blade scratch the talon's enameled surface.

With a growl, Caeb shoved him aside, caught the claw between his bloodied jaws and snapped the talon in half.

With the tension on the chain released, Lizzan rolled free, gulping air before coughing uncontrollably. Aerax caught her up in his arms, holding her tight as she wheezed into another coughing fit.

Yet Aerax could not hold her as long as he needed to. "Did you kill the other?"

Still coughing, face red, Lizzan shook her head—and mimed firing a crossbow.

"Injured?"

She nodded, stabbing her fingers into her chest.

Wounded, then. So he would finish it. Taking her sword, he bade Caeb to stay with her. He found the female lying still—though not dead, as Lizzan had said. The crossbow bolt had barely penetrated the dense muscle over her heart. Instead she was sleeping.

Drugged with the corpse vine on the arrowhead, most likely. And this had not been a hunt, but a perfectly executed ambush that used Caeb as a distraction and a lure.

With the second woodstalker dead, he returned to the first. Lizzan had not moved from where she'd been half lying against the woodstalker's corpse, though Caeb had pushed in close to her and her arm was around his neck. No longer coughing, she stared up at the sky, rain pattering her muddied face.

Chest aching, Aerax crouched at her side. "You risked your life to slay the monsters that threaten a village, though all who live there would spit on you," he said gently. "But what is it you do now?"

"I'm wishing it would snow," she whispered, and Caeb made a wounded noise that Aerax felt through to his soul. "And I don't mean to hurt you by saying so. Or to make you angry. You are right. I am selfish. I *would* do what's best for myself now, Aerax. But this is all that I have left."

Heart torn in two, he shook his head. "I am not angry." And was ashamed he had been. What he'd thought was selfishness was Lizzan's pain, and he'd raged at her for suffering. "And this quest cannot be all you have left."

"It is," she replied brokenly. "Everything I wanted to be, everything I wanted to do . . . it is all gone. There are no jobs for me along the plains road anymore. I tell them that my scars aren't Vela's curse, but still—whatever grief or pain befalls them while I am away, they blame me on my return. And now the same here. I have no other path ahead."

Throat raw, he cupped her cheeks in his hands. "You have the alliance left. Tell me you do not wish to defeat the Destroyer."

"I do. But I have been a soldier all my life. I know what

fate awaits me there. I am a body that will be thrown at the Destroyer's front lines—and that would be a fine and honorable death—but not a whisper in Koth would be said of it. I asked for the quest so that my death will be something *more*. So that I will not merely fall on a battlefield, but will help my family, too. And I'm just . . . so tired." Her eyes squeezed shut and tears slipped over her lashes to join the rain on her cheeks. "I'm so tired, Aerax. Barely can I shut my eyes before the wraiths wake me again. I used to quiet them with ale or the corpse vine—or anything that would dull the knives in my head. But I can no longer. And I cannot sleep. So I am ready for all of this to be done."

"I see you are," he said thickly, and brushed his lips over her trembling mouth. "But I still will not let you."

She gave a sobbing little laugh.

Pressing his face into her wet hair, Aerax gathered her against his chest and turned, so that she leaned against him and not the woodstalker's filthy corpse. Cradling her in his arms, he tucked her tear-streaked face against his neck. "I never said to you why I became a hunter."

"You did," she said, her voice muffled against his skin. "To provide for your mother after your neighbors ravaged her garden during the Bitter Years."

The two years without a summer. Only four years of age he'd been during the first year—and Lizzan had been three—yet they had not known each other then. And would not have. After Aerax had been born, no one would sell or trade with his mother. Yet she'd always had Hanan's own touch in the garden, and she'd kept dally birds for eggs and goats for cheese long after others in the village had eaten their livestock.

Had those hungry people ever come to her inn, she would have fed them. Instead they stole everything she had and left her and Aerax with nothing. So Aerax had begun hunting for their meals . . . as he had told Lizzan.

"But I didn't tell all of it." He swallowed past the constriction in his throat. "After the snows came, we found nothing even when foraging all day. Already she'd taken me to the crystal palace, but my father wouldn't acknowledge me and sent us away. I remember nights when it seemed all we had was warm water to drink—and when we did find something, always she gave me most of it."

"You told me this," she said softly.

So he had. "But not of the evening she put out the fire, though it was the bitterest night of the winter. Because she was so weak, she'd not even been able to forage that day. So she said she would hold me until I fell asleep—and that in the morning we would both wake, warm and comforted in our mother's arms."

She sucked in a breath. "Mother Temra?"

He nodded against her hair. "Though I didn't understand then. I thought she was speaking truth when she told me that when dawn came, we would go out in search of something to eat, and there would be so much to find, never would wc be hungry again. But I did not want to wait until morning. So I went. And the rabbit I came across must have been as starved and as weak as we were—but even if it was nothing but fur and bones, we would have eaten it. So I took it home and woke her."

"What did she do?"

"Sobbed until she was sick from it. Kissed me and asked me to forgive her for being so silly. Said I was the finest of all boys—and told me my name." He felt new tears against his throat and clutched her closer. "So proud I was to hunt every day after that, though I had little skill, and a few times we were almost near to starving again. But never again did she lose faith that the next day might be better. And it was years later when I finally understood what she'd almost done."

Another sobbing breath. "Were you angry with her?"

"No." He saved his anger for those who'd stolen from her and refused to help her. Who'd taken her every hope.

"I am. I wouldn't have known you *or* her," she said, and Caeb gave a soft snarl of agreement. "Did she ever speak of it?"

"Once." And she'd been so painfully ashamed, it still

hurt his heart to remember. "She said that it had seemed her only choice was to watch me starve slowly or for us both to go peacefully in our sleep. Then she told me that more options had been easier to see when morning had come and there was food in her belly."

Lizzan gave a heavy sigh. "Perhaps I am not so angry at her. And I know very well why you told me this story. But it is not the same."

"It is not. You are not starved of food—you are starved of sleep. So I will provide that for you, Lizzan." Gently he tilted her face up. "Whatever you need to keep this world from battering you into the mud, I will provide it. This night, I will protect you as you sleep. And the next, if you still need it. I will shield you from those who call you a curse, and who have taken your every hope. Until the morning comes when your heart is full again, and you see that there are so many more options left."

Tears coursed down her cheeks as she pressed her forehead to his. "I love you, Aerax."

"That I know. As I love you." He stroked his hand down her muddied back before surging to his feet, carrying her up with him. "But for now, you need more than that. Beginning with sleep and food . . . and a bath."

And it was his heart that filled again when she laughed a little at that.

CHAPTER 21

LIZZAN

Lizzan woke to the soft pattering of rain on the white pelt overhead, with the heat of Caeb's big body stretched out along her back and her front cuddled up against Aerax's side, her head pillowed on his chest.

"You are well?" His murmur was a quiet rumble beneath her ear.

With emotion filling her chest, she nodded before raising her head. The falt's pelt was draped over Caeb's massive bulk to form a low tent, and little could she see but darkness and shadows. But she knew Aerax's face better than her own, so her aim was true when she pressed her mouth to his. The deep hum of pleasure in his throat seemed to echo beneath her skin, and when his hand came up to grip her nape, she opened to that wordless command.

But her body made other commands, urgent and undeniable. She paused, waiting for it to pass—but it didn't.

Aerax went still. "Lizzan?"

She cursed softly, thumping her forehead twice against

his shoulder, before scrambling out of the furs. His laugh followed her out of the tent.

She knew not how long she'd been sleeping, but as soon as she stumbled away from the camp, forever did she seem to piss. Rain fell in heavy drops from the branches overhead, splattering her hair and shoulders, which were near bare. She was only dressed in her linen undertunic. Following the slaying of the woodstalker and Aerax's sweet vow, she had a vague memory of bathing in a freezing stream, then washing every piece of her clothing from her boots to her cloak. Little beyond that could she recall, though much must have been happening around her.

She and Aerax were not the only ones in the camp. All the Parsatheans seemed to be, and Lady Junica's tent. She quickly washed and returned to the clearing—which seemed nowhere near where she'd left her horse, though she had no memory of riding.

Out of the shadows came one of the Parsatheans on watch. Seri, who'd spoken little to Lizzan since the night she'd taken the corpse vine. Now she carried a small clay pot that had been kept warm by the fire but not too hot to hold, and the meaty scent wafting from it made Lizzan's stomach roar its neglect.

"Ardyl saved this for you," the girl whispered.

"I thank you." She glanced at the sky, found the faint glow of the moon through the clouds. Near dawn. "You are on second watch?"

Seri nodded.

Then she had slept a half day. "You did not stay at the inn?"

In the faint glow from the fire, she saw the girl's fierce frown. "After they chased one of our number away? Never would we."

A hot lump filled Lizzan's throat. She had not thought that they considered her one of their number.

"And we took the heads of the woodstalkers back to the village, and told them who killed those monsters."

Not much difference would it make. Still they would

believe Lizzan was the reason the woodstalkers had come to their forest. Yet sweet pressure built in her chest that the attempt had been made.

The girl hesitated slightly before adding, "It is said you leapt in front of the woman who threw an axe at your back."

"I did."

"Why?"

"She'd lost her child. And she was afraid. So many people are," Lizzan said. "And they need someone to blame so they don't feel so helpless. So you may be right when you say that this will be an alliance born of fear. But when all those who are terrified come to understand that something is truly being done, and that they aren't helpless anymore . . . perhaps the fear will turn to hope."

For a long moment, Seri said nothing. Then, "You should not have fought the woodstalkers alone. We would have helped you."

Lizzan hadn't been alone. Caeb had come—and then Aerax. But she understood that this was something near to an apology. "Next time I will ask you to fight with me."

"I would like that," the girl said, then drew a line from her throat down to the center of her chest. "The beast's talons would have hung down to here."

"A fine trophy," Lizzan agreed dryly, eyeing the shorter claws on her necklace and the girl's bare chest. "Until it stabs your tit."

Seri grinned, then broke into a laugh as Lizzan's stomach roared again, and handed over the clay pot. Carrying her supper, Lizzan headed for the tent, ducking to crawl inside where the heat generated by Aerax and Caeb warmed the air. There Lizzan sat hunched over beneath the falt pelt, slowly spooning up the thick stew.

Aerax's voice was a low rumble through the dark. "When you have eaten your fill, then I will eat mine."

Sudden heat unfurled through her belly. A flush spread across her skin, leaving her hot and shaking as she took another bite.

Swallowing hard, she whispered, "So we are not strangers again?"

"Does it matter?"

Not when she recalled his voice in her ear, telling her of all the things strangers did in the dark. *When I covered your body with mine, you would not see my face. You would only feel me deep inside.*

He would not be inside her this night. Not in the way she craved.

Yet she would take all that he gave.

His big hand curved over her knee, gently squeezing. "I will be whatever you wish me to be, Lizzan. But know this—I will never let you fulfill your quest."

Heavily she sighed. "I do not truly know if I *have* a quest."

He came up onto his elbow, the shadows of his face deepening into a frown. "What do you mean by that?"

"Exactly as I say." She scraped the spoon around the bottom of the pot. "When I went to the temple, the priestess refused to speak to me about a quest. Because I was drunk."

He shook his head, his voice perplexed. "But she gave to you the cloak."

A cloak that was not deep red and was soaked through, and so could not be a cloak worn by Vela's Chosen. Of all the things the innkeeper had believed of Lizzan, only that had struck her as true—though she had not been trying to fool anyone else by wearing it.

Instead she'd been fooling herself. "The priestess only gave the cloak to spite you, I think. After you snarled at her. And because I kept pestering her for one, even though she said I was not on a quest. And Vela, too, said she would not give me a quest. But then she relented and gave to me a task, so I *thought* it was the same. Now I am not so certain."

"Then you will not die in battle?" Fierce satisfaction hardened his voice. "As it should be."

Her chest tightened. "I am not certain of that, either. Vela said that the path she would put me on was the very same path that I would choose. So whatever battle lies ahead—

and whatever happens to me—is nothing that Vela will or will not do. All that she truly did was make certain that I would be near to you."

"To protect me," he said flatly. As if rejecting that path, too.

"Perhaps. Or perhaps it is a gift." Lizzan was glad to have finished her supper, for now her throat felt so swollen that she could not swallow. "I would have kept running from you, Aerax. You'd sent me away from Koth alone, and when you appeared again, you hadn't come for me. And I didn't know then the truth of my exile, or the purpose that kept you on Koth, or that you would find me again when it was done. So it was as if the very last hope I carried with me had been destroyed, and all that I had left was lifting my family's shame."

Gripping her thigh, he pressed his forehead to her knee. His voice roughened in sheer agony. "Always I would have come for you—"

"I know." She pushed her hands into his hair, urging him away from that supplicant's pose. Nothing did he have to apologize for. "*Now* I know. But that is what I mean—if not for Vela's task, I would have stayed far from you, terrified that I would be hurt worse. As it was, *still* I tried to stay away. Yet if this path takes me toward a battle that I will not survive . . . I want nothing more than to be with you until that day comes. After all the time we have waited and wasted, Aerax—if we only have until the first snowfall, I will take it, and be glad of every moment."

He raised his head, and even through the dark she saw the fierce gleam in his eyes. "As will I. Have you finished your meal?"

"I have." She set aside the pot, her blood seeming to pulse hotter and slower, her every word breathless. "Are you restrained?"

"Until our moon night," he growled softly, his head bending to her knee again. "Spread your thighs so that I can see your need."

"I do not know how you can see anything," she whispered, but did as he said and let her legs fall wide.

"I see how eager you are by how quickly you open to me." His open mouth scorched a path up her thigh. "I feel how you tremble when I touch you, and that fires my blood hotter than anything my eyes might see. Do you think you will scream?"

Breathing ragged, Lizzan shook her head. "We do not want to wake the kitten."

His lips curved against her skin. For Caeb was already awake, purring rough and loud—but no attention did he pay to them now. He never had, as if human matings were nothing more remarkable than a fly buzzing around his head.

"It is not the kitten who will hear," Acrax said gruffly before nipping the taut tendon of her inner thigh. "They will look to our tent as we looked through the wall at the inn. Which one would you have them see if it were you and me?"

Lust poured through her veins, hot and thick. "The brute and the boatbuilder's wife."

He growled softly in approval, moving higher. "It is always the brute and the boatbuilder's wife. Tell me why, Lizzan."

So many reasons. And it had been raining that day, too—but by then, she and Aerax had found the cave on the windward side, and no longer took shelter as often at the inn. So it had been nearly two years since they'd looked through the wall, and so much had changed since. They'd just had their first kiss. And never before had there been so much tension between them in the small secluded room where they'd hidden away.

But the boatbuilder and her wife had seemed no different than before. Regularly they would come in, and always it was the same: the boatbuilder would tie a cloth over her wife's eyes and have her lie on the bed with legs spread. Then the boatbuilder would lead someone else into the room—also blindfolded—then watch as that person fucked her wife. Sometimes strangers were brought in, but many times she and Aerax had seen people from nearby villages with familiar faces behind the cloth.

That time, it had for certain been a stranger brought in—a big man, shaggy haired and wearing a tunic of mammoth hide, his face decorated by the tattoos of the broken clans of the northlands.

Lizzan didn't know what had affected her most. The size of him as his body had covered hers or the depth of his grunts. The plumpness of her thighs when she'd wrapped her legs around his waist to receive every heavy thrust. The explicit coarseness of everything he'd said, or the way the boatbuilder had rubbed herself to climax while watching them.

Or that it had been the very first time Lizzan had imagined that it was herself on that bed, with Aerax pumping deep inside her.

With his breath wafting through her damp curls, Aerax lightly rubbed the point of her clit with the side of his thumb. "What do you think of most often?"

"The sound she made when his cock sank into her sheath." Panting, Lizzan squirmed beneath that teasing touch. "What do you think of?"

"The sound *you* made when his cock sank into her sheath," Aerax said, and no longer could Lizzan bear it. Fisting her fingers in his hair, she guided his mouth where she so desperately needed it, then muffled her cry between clenched teeth at the first hot slick of his tongue.

And that had been the very first time, too. The first time she'd touched herself while watching—and had been overwhelmed with surprise and embarrassment that she'd been so wet. But Aerax had caught her hand, and just as they'd watched the brute do with the boatbuilder's wife moments before, he'd tasted the arousal on her skin. And it had been the first time she'd come, when Aerax had kissed his way down between her legs before settling in to lick all that wetness away, and the hungry sounds of pleasure he'd made had driven her wilder than any noise that had come from the bed. In desperation she'd writhed against his mouth, until he'd made her come again, and then she'd begged to have him inside her.

Only when he'd begun to sink between her thighs and she'd cried out in pain had they come to their senses—for it had not been the full moon, and Vela always demanded a virgin's blood as her due. So they'd pulled away from each other, but Aerax had seemed in agony to her, his erection so thick and swollen. There she'd tried to ease him with her mouth, but he'd lost himself to his lust so quickly, mindlessly thrusting past her lips until she'd choked, that they'd realized the danger they were in. For she had not cared how rough he'd been, so exciting was his need for her. She'd loved how he'd lost all control. But their blood boiled so hot together that, until their moon night, at least one of them would have to practice restraint.

Lizzan had not been sorry that it was Aerax who'd volunteered.

Not sorry then, not sorry now. In full abandon she sought the pleasure of his mouth, back arched and thighs widespread, with her hands cupping her breasts. Her legs began an uncontrollable shaking when he swirled his tongue around her clit, again and again, before settling in for a long, suckling kiss that seemed to slowly tug her every nerve to the breaking point before setting them afire. The orgasm raged beneath her skin, blazing through her senses before reducing her to ash that drifted softly back to the furs.

Slowly Aerax kissed his way from her belly, to her breasts, to her neck, before finally taking her lips, and she gasped into his mouth when his thick shaft parted the drenched furrow between her thighs.

His hips rocked, gliding his erection over her sensitized clit. In a low voice, he asked, "Are you still pledged to me?"

Breathlessly she nodded. "I am."

"Will you take my cock this full moon?"

She would take it now. "Please."

He parted her lips in a sultry kiss, every thrust of his tongue rekindling the fire below as he slowly, relentlessly fucked the seam of her cunt. Desperate for more pressure, she begged, "Let me ride you."

"Not this night." His voice roughened as he surged

harder against her. "Soon I will have you in this way, but feeling the stretch of your sheath around my cock as I fuck into you again and again, unrestrained, and use your cunt as I was meant to."

So badly she needed that. Wrapping her legs around his waist, she arched beneath him, meeting his thrusts, though each one was too much, his erection sliding and rubbing over her clit until the world flared bright again and she came, crying out as her inner muscles squeezed and squeezed on nothing.

With a guttural moan, Aerax buried his face in her throat and his big body shook above hers, and between them she felt the pulsing of his shaft and the hot splash of his seed.

Then his weight settled over her, his forearms braced alongside her shoulders, and he lowered his head for a leisurely kiss that curled her toes all over again.

She held him tight, fingers threading through his hair. On ragged breaths she told him, "I want every day ahead to move so slowly. Unless they are between us and the full moon. Those, I want to hurry past."

Except they would also hurry the day of the first snow.

Her heart ached softly when he said, "It matters not how quick or slow the days are. No matter what happens in the battle ahead, and even if every day afterward is spent with you, never will there be enough of them."

"So no more time will we waste," she whispered.

Not even a moment.

CHAPTER 22

AERAX

"We should probably speak of our intentions for when we reach the monastery later this day."

"Intentions?" Aerax glanced over at Lady Junica, who had ridden up alongside him, with Degg just behind. A morning chill still clouded their breaths, for it seemed that in the past days as the road had climbed higher into the mountains, they'd also been chasing the last of winter. "This night is the full moon. I have but one intention this evening, and no part of it includes monks."

Her brow furrowed. "The full moon? What has that to do with . . ." Her gaze moved to Lizzan, who rode at Aerax's other side, and her mouth rounded in realization.

Riding only a pace behind Lizzan, Kelir abruptly urged his mount forward, looking to Aerax in disbelief. "A moon night?" He shook his head. "Which of you is the virgin?"

Lizzan grinned and guided her horse slightly to the side as Kelir settled in between them, though a half stride behind. "Both."

The warrior looked to both of them in astonishment before his expression firmed and he nodded decisively. "You will need an inn," he declared.

"And if we cannot find one," said Lizzan, "the stable will do."

Aerax nodded. "Or the center of the market square."

"Or any wall that will support our weight."

"Or atop this horse."

Lizzan gave him such a look that, if the moon had been high, he would have dragged her into the saddle that instant. Though nearly a full turn had passed since they'd decided not to waste another moment—and they had not—it mattered not at all how many times they'd fallen asleep together, satisfied. Each morning Aerax woke hungrier for her than ever before.

Though it was not always morning when he awoke. Every night, Aerax and Caeb slept with her between them, yet Lizzan still jerked out of sleep, skin slick with cold sweat and her breath racing. Many times, comforted in Aerax's arms and with Caeb's purr at her back, she slipped into sleep again. Other times, she kissed Aerax so desperately that he knew it was not only more pleasure that she sought, but also for him to help chase away what haunted her in dreams.

He cared not at all that she sometimes used him in the same way she'd used her ale. He would be anything for her—and at least it was a remedy that would not make her as sick as the drink had.

Despite the amusement that curved her mouth, Lady Junica solemnly pointed out, "If the prince does not announce himself upon his arrival, it might be seen as an insult to the monks."

"Then we will remain outside the city gates," said Aerax.

"Do you hear this?" Kelir demanded of Ardyl, who still rode slightly behind. "It will be their moon night!"

Ardyl shrugged. "Lizzan said as much to me some handful of days after we met."

"And you said nothing to me?" Kelir turned a wounded gaze to Aerax. "I would have given you the advice every warrior should hear before they take a woman to the furs the first time."

From behind Aerax, Degg huffed out a laugh. "I daresay that from all we have heard, they don't need that advice."

Kelir acknowledged that with a nod but said, "I still would like to give it. Many a warrior has benefited from all that I know."

Ardyl snorted. "Is that so?"

"I would hear it!" called Tyzen before riding closer with Seri and Preter at his sides, so that they all now formed a tight cluster on the road. Abruptly the prince paused, glancing to Seri with a flush under his skin. "Though this will not be my moon night. But if it is regarding how to please a . . . that is, if you could tell me what would most . . . Ah, perhaps at another time."

Face fully red, he fell silent with all eyes upon him.

"At this time, you wish to discuss our plan upon reaching the monastery," suggested Lady Junica.

Tyzen gave to her a grateful look. "That is precisely so."

Nodding, she turned to Preter. "Will the monks take offense if a royal prince from a realm that seeks their assistance does not announce himself to them?"

Aerax's teeth gritted in irritation. "I am hardly a royal prince."

"You have snow-white hair," said Degg. "And you were sent to Krimathe and played a part of those negotiations. If you do not attend those at Radreh, they might take it as a signal that Koth believes they are less worthy than Krimathe. And already we have a generations-old rift to overcome."

Jaw clenched, Aerax looked to Preter. "What say you?"

The monk gave a light shrug. "In Toleh, any visiting royal would not seek us out first, but our king—for *he* would take offense if they did not. That royal would then secure his permission to visit us. But Radreh has no king or queen; they are ruled by their monastery council. And monks are taught not to take offense easily, but still we sometimes do."

With a sigh, Lizzan told Aerax, "Then it seems you are not done playing the prop."

"You think yourself a prop?" Degg asked disbelievingly, for after all these days together upon the road, he and Lady Junica still did not directly acknowledge Lizzan or speak to her—but neither did they pretend not to hear her. A wry expression crossed his face as he continued, "Did you not say that you would kill your uncle and make yourself a king?"

"You know very well that he has no wish to rule," Lady Junica said to Degg in exasperation. "And no wish to kill our king."

"I will if it saves Lizzan," said Aerax, and Lady Junica closed her eyes and shook her head.

"You do not have to be so very honest," she said to him.

"But as you are being honest," Degg said, "do you truly believe you will have to?"

Aerax looked to Lizzan, who appeared nearly as exasperated with him as Lady Junica was, though with more amusement mixed in—and who had become near certain that she was not truly on a quest. She still wore her cloak, though it had faded more with each passing day until it was now a pale pink. But she'd told him that she believed whatever lay ahead was not a fate given to her by Vela, and instead her fate was one that already lay in her path.

Aerax would *not* allow her to die. He knew not what might change that fate, but if Vela's magic had no part in it, then taking Koth's throne and hiding Lizzan away on the island would not help her.

"Likely not," he said.

"Well, then," said Lady Junica. "Perhaps we should move away from discussions of royal assassinations and talk instead of what we hope to accomplish in Radreh?"

Aerax gave to her a narrowed look. "Do you wish me to tell you in detail, as I have told Lizzan in our furs? For I only care to accomplish one thing."

"Look how he no longer grunts and growls as he makes his argument," Degg said to the other councilor with a grin. "My lessons have finally sunk in, and he can speak quite well when something is important to him."

"This should be important to him," Lady Junica snapped.

Smoothly Preter broke in, "Never would any monk interfere with a sacrifice to Vela. More likely, they will offer to throw your prince a feast before the . . . festivities begin."

"The festivities?" Lizzan laughed at him. "Are monks so in need of entertainment?"

"Sometimes," Preter admitted while blushing.

Perhaps taking pity on him, Lizzan abandoned her teasing and looked to Tyzen. "What will be the alliance's approach?"

"We will appeal to them as we did to Krimathe," the young prince told her. "For they might be critical to our purpose if we hope to defeat the Destroyer. Their monks might provide defense against his spells and use to their magic to assist our warriors."

"As those from Toleh will," said Preter. "But above all else, we hope they might help teach others in the north to do the same."

"Teach people to use *magic*?" Lizzan stared at him as if he'd gone mad. "In so short a time? Do not monks study their entire lives?"

Preter nodded. "Most do. But there are those with an affinity for natural magics who learn more easily."

"An affinity?"

"You have likely heard of some who are. Those who always know when the weather will turn. Or they know where it is best to dig a water well. Or their gardens always grow even if they are tended less."

Lizzan's eyebrows shot upward and she met Aerax's eyes. "Like your mother did."

Arching a brow, Preter looked to him. "Did she?"

Aerax grunted an assent.

"Then it is people such as your mother whom we will try to find. For their magic is not dependent on a god's whim and is not bound by the same limitations."

Degg frowned at him. "What limitations?"

"That a god's power must be invited in." He gestured to Lizzan. "That is the purpose of Vela's quests. The goddess cannot merely change whatever she wishes; she must perform her magic through others. Vela does not transform your ale to water before it touches your lips. Instead you have agreed to let Vela work her magic *through* you, and so the ale changes to water as it flows over your tongue. The same it is for her priestesses and oracles, and also for most monks—many of us in Toleh invite Vela to work through us, others invite Nemek. But in truth, nobody needs a god to work through them to perform magic. It is simply much easier to learn if that conduit is already open, and a spell that might take years to master will only take a fortnight for others. Such as when a god has already touched them . . . or their ancestors."

He paused, looking to Tyzen, who sighed and lifted his hand, palm up. Lips pursing, the prince blew softly across his skin as if encouraging a spark to life. Aerax shot a glance over his shoulder as an answering wind blew heated air against the back of his neck.

A murmur rose up from the others as a ball of flame suddenly danced in the prince's palm—though both Preter and Tyzen were looking to *him*.

"As I told you," said the monk to Tyzen, sounding pleased, before he told Aerax, "You are sensitive to magics, too. You felt the spell Tyzen cast?"

Aerax scowled and shook his head. "I only felt a breeze."

"There was no breeze," Lizzan said, eyes bright. "So you are as your mother was."

"Or as your father was," Lady Junica said, and Aerax's scowl deepened, but the councilor was not looking at him. Instead wonder lit her face. "King Icaro and his children likely are, too. For they are all descendants of Varrin, and though he was not yet a god when he had children, still he was a powerful sorcerer . . . and his magic did not come from the gods. So he must have had an affinity for natural magics, too. A strong affinity, for his power rivaled the gods' power."

Preter nodded. "Very likely he did."

"If Varrin had lived only a generation past, he would

have defeated the Destroyer before so much harm was done." She sighed before turning to Aerax. "You should take these lessons."

As if he'd waited for such an opening, Tyzen spoke up. "Preter will teach you the fire spell."

Aerax already knew one spell. He did not wish to know more.

For Lady Junica had it wrong. Varrin might have defeated the Destroyer, true—but in his own time, Varrin had also been a destroyer. And Aerax would never let himself become what Varrin had been.

When he made no response, Lady Junica aimed a small frown at Preter. "We have heard the monks of Radreh are courting dark magics again, but I know not if it is only rumor. Do you know?"

The monk gave her a wry smile. "That is something I am here to find out. They purged the viswan from their numbers many generations ago. But have they invited them back? We would like to know, as well."

Degg frowned at them both. "The viswan?"

"As I said, everyone can learn to wield natural magics," the monk told him. "But without a conduit or an affinity, it takes acute focus and years of study . . . and the result is often lacking in power. So there are those who took easier paths."

"They killed a snow-haired princess," Lady Junica told Degg. "And drained her of blood."

Realization swept over the councilor's face. "I knew that a murder was the reason for the rift between our realms. But I did not know that was the reason for the murder."

Preter nodded gravely. "They hunt the Hanani, too, and use the blood as a conduit for their magic."

Aerax's gaze flew to Caeb, who prowled a few paces ahead of their group, before meeting Lizzan's eyes and seeing his alarm reflected in hers.

"And now we bring a snow-haired prince to their realm? And a moonstone-eyed prince, too?" Degg shook his head before turning to Lady Junica. "Is that a risk we take?"

"Aerax is not without protection," Lizzan reminded them. "Vela herself tasked me to remain at his side."

"Tyzen is not unprotected, either," Kelir said.

Lady Junica sighed heavily. "If the Radrehi monks have truly purged the viswan, then Prince Aerax's presence could heal the rift between our realms . . . which may be necessary if any alliance is to be formed."

"The monks may be of more use than against the Destroyer," Preter pointed out. "If Goranik is in truth the leader of the bandits who are attacking Koth, the monks would be a valuable ally against a sorcerer . . . and I may also have time on that journey to take their measure and to determine whether we can trust the magics they use."

"So our approach is to be hopeful, but not foolish," Lady Junica said.

With a faint smile, Tyzen nodded. "Though in truth, that has been our approach this entire journey."

Though that drew a laugh of agreement from the Parsatheans, Aerax saw the worry that settled into Lizzan's expression. "What is it?"

"I wonder if we have been fools since we have left Oana," she said on a sigh. "For I have just recalled what Riasa told me—that she did not like what she had heard coming out of Radreh."

"Those are the same rumors we have all heard," Lady Junica said. "That they are practicing dark magics again."

Lizzan shook her head. "What strikes me is not that there are rumors, but that they *came out of Radreh.* We have been on this road for nearly a full turn, and what has come out of Radreh? Nothing at all. The only travelers we have met were from the villages between Radreh and Oana—and none who came from farther north. Has no one at all from Koth or the broken clans traveled south in this time?"

"Perhaps everyone is done fleeing the Destroyer and now they are settling in and shoring up their defenses."

"So I thought, too. But the plains road is still choked with travelers fleeing toward Krimathe and Stranik's passageway," Lizzan said.

"And an empty road points to some danger upon it," Preter said quietly.

Lizzan nodded. "I thought the woodstalkers must be to blame. But we have been upon this road for so much longer now . . . and it is still near empty."

Aerax saw her worry reflected in all other faces now. "Is there another route?"

"No route but the way we came."

"What do you suggest?" he asked her.

She shrugged, looking to Kelir and then to Ardyl, who also shrugged. "I suppose that it is too late to turn back," she said. "So let us be hopeful . . . but not foolish."

CHAPTER 23

LIZZAN

The sheer cliffs that formed the haggard face of the Radreh monastery loomed into view long before Lizzan could see the city at its base. The chambers inside were said to have been carved into the heart of the mountain during ancient times, when Enam's power still scorched the earth, yet nothing of those rooms could be seen from outside. Instead it looked as every other mountain did.

But they didn't need to reach the city to know that all was not right, for the road was not all that was empty. On their approach, so were the fields and crofters' huts, as if abandoned. Cold and heavy dread filled Lizzan's belly and became a solid stone as they neared the city walls.

The city gate stood ajar. City gates were *never* ajar. They were open, or they were closed. Not caught in between.

They rode through the gates into the silence of a deserted city. While the Parsatheans stood guard, the Kothan soldiers quickly searched through the gate's guardhouse and nearby homes. They returned to report that it seemed those who'd lived there had left in haste.

"What of livestock?" Kelir asked, frowning.

"Also gone."

Expression grim, Aerax returned from his own search with Caeb at his side. "I'd wager that three full turns have passed since they have gone. There is no recent sign."

"Either they sought shelter in the monastery," said Preter, "or the monks invited them in."

Lizzan looked to him in disbelief. "An entire city? And for so long?"

The monk nodded. "After the Destroyer came, we opened the ancient chambers that once housed cities many times greater than this one—so that if we failed again to protect our people, at least they might have a place to hide."

"What would these people take shelter from?" Ardyl's gaze rose to the monastery's face.

There seemed a more pertinent question to Lizzan. "And is that threat still here?"

"Do you sense foul magic?" Kelir asked Tyzen, and the prince glanced to both Preter and Aerax before shaking his head.

"Only unease."

"As we all feel," said Ardyl before turning to Kelir. "Let us be hopeful, but not foolish."

He nodded and looked to Lady Junica. "You wish to announce yourselves to the monks, but first let us be certain that no danger awaits you there. If your soldiers will escort you outside these gates, two of my warriors will remain with your party."

Expression taut, Lady Junica nodded. "That seems prudent."

Kelir looked next to Tyzen, who was already shaking his head. "I go with you," the prince said. "I am no monk and only just learning, but it also seems prudent to have two magic users with you."

"And I will be his guard," said Seri earnestly. "If you

have to fall behind so that Tyzen can escape, I will stay with him."

Kelir's jaw clenched and a war seemed to take place across his expression before he glanced at Ardyl. The other warrior tilted her head slightly, gave a light shrug, and finally he relented. "You must do everything I say."

The girl beamed. "As if you were Ran Maddek himself."

Kelir then looked to Lizzan.

"We go," she said, meeting Aerax's eyes. "Though Caeb will stay."

The cat snarled and she reached down to grip his ruff, bending her head toward his. Quietly she said, "You must protect our horses . . . and the Kothans, too. But more importantly, we know not if the threat is out here or in there. If out here, we will need you to race to the monastery and warn us, so that we do not leave there and face an unexpected trap."

Though he gave a frustrated growl, Caeb rubbed his face to hers in agreement.

She glanced up at Aerax, who nodded his agreement, as well. Under no circumstances did they want Caeb in that monastery, where someone might recognize him for what he was.

The Kothan soldiers were by now most familiar with Ferek and Raceni, whom they'd ridden beside for near a full turn now, so those two Parsatheans would remain with them. When all was settled for staying and going, Kelir led them on foot through the silent streets.

A great chasm lay between the city and the monastery, crossed only by a wide crystal bridge. If the chasm had a story, Lizzan did not know it—and Preter did not tell it, only warning them not to look down as they crossed, for the bottomless void often made visitors dizzy. She knew that Seri looked when the girl abruptly sucked in a breath and scooted farther from the edge, though they were already a safe distance from it.

"That does not seem a secure door," Kelir said grimly,

eyeing the entrance ahead. "It is but painted wood that would only need an axe to open it."

"You are welcome to take your axe to it," Preter responded with humor. "And we will wait outside forever while you try to chop through."

"I will only wait until moonrise," Aerax said. "Then I take Lizzan back to an inn."

That drew a grin from Kelir, but he eyed the door anew. "It is spelled?"

"It is." With his robes swaying around his ankles, Preter trotted up the steps to the doors. Lizzan didn't hear the spell that he cast to open them, but she saw Aerax's sudden tension in the set of his shoulders, the way he shook himself—as if ridding his skin of an unwanted sensation—and the scowl that darkened his face.

"You are well?" she asked him softly.

"I am." His eyes caught hers and his gaze softened, heated. "But we'd best be out by sunset."

When the full moon would rise. She grinned her agreement.

No sound came from inside. With a fluid ease and silent communication that spoke of the many dangers they'd faced together, Ardyl and Kelir went through first before gesturing for the others to follow. Lizzan stepped into a great hall that near took her breath at its size and height. Stone columns carved into statues paraded its immense length and breadth. Murals decorated the stone walls—even at a glance, she recognized a dozen legends depicted there—with passageways leading in all directions.

And all of it she could see . . . though the torches on the walls and columns were unlit.

"Where does the light come from?" she whispered as the Parsatheans fanned out, spreading toward the distant sides of the hall as if to determine whether it was as empty as it appeared.

"From a sun chamber," said Preter. "It is open to the sky, and spelled to spread the light through all the chambers— or else we would be as pale as Farian savages fresh from their caves. At night, the chamber gathers the moonlight, too."

Fortunate for them, but the moon did not always shine full and bright, or through the night. "No small task would it be to light every torch."

"It *is* a small task," Preter said, reminding her of how easily Tyzen had created a flame. "But over time, the smoke becomes an irritation. So they are not often lighted."

She nodded and looked to Kelir as the Parsatheans returned.

"I see no one," he said. "And no sign of battle or panic, or whatever led them to spell that door."

Preter gestured along the hall. "These chambers are not arranged the same as they are in Toleh, but there should be a place nearby to greet visitors."

Ardyl's brow arched. "Though the doors are locked?"

"I do not expect anyone there. But a message might have been left, or some indication of where they've gone . . . and a map. Every monastery is a maze of chambers so that if ever they are under attack, an invading army will become lost—and every chamber has at least two exits, so no one fleeing from them can be trapped. But although I will never become lost, it helps to know which direction to go."

Ardyl appeared bemused by that. "If you know not where you are going, how are you never lost?"

"I will not forget the route back to these doors. And if you always know a way out, you are never trapped." He gave them a wry look. "Stay close to me. More than one visitor to a monastery has taken a wrong turn and never been seen again."

"I would feel better with chalk to mark our way," muttered Kelir as they followed the young monk toward one of the passageways.

"Could you lead us back?" Lizzan asked Aerax.

He nodded. "There is enough trace dust to mark our trail. But if we are gone too long, Caeb would come looking for us."

And could find his way to them by their scent—which would also lead the way out.

"This way," Preter said. "There is the offering bowl. Any visitor who wants something from the monks must sacrifice an item that is precious to them."

As the young monk paused to dig through the bowl, Lizzan could only recall the finger in Vela's temple, and the goddess's cold command to never steal an offering from her. "You would take something?"

Preter shook his head. "I look to see what sort of people have come and what they believed was precious to . . ." He trailed off, picking a necklace from the bowl and turning to Kelir. "There is this."

A leather lace decorated with the same raptor claws that each of the Parsatheans wore—though the number of claws was many more. At least a dozen, it seemed.

"That is Toric's," Seri breathed. "He was here?"

Lizzan glanced at the others. All seemed affected by the sight of the necklace. "Who is Toric?"

Ardyl took the offering from Preter, her thumb gliding over the curve of a claw. "He is one of our Dragon guard—"

"And the greatest hunter in the firebloom tribe," Seri broke in.

"But he was infected with the sun god's magic. He feared the Destroyer would be able to see through his eyes as Vela sees through our queen's—so he left the Burning Plains rather than be made into the Destroyer's spy."

"He intended to search for a way to purge Enam's poison." Kelir took the necklace next, his voice thick. "He must have come here . . . but he has not returned home, so they did not find a cure."

"It would not be so easy," Ardyl said softly, then looked to Lizzan and Aerax before explaining, "Vela called him our Dragon's wings, and said that Toric would fly so far from home that he would not be himself when he returned. This monastery is not far from home."

Jaw tight, Kelir nodded and returned the necklace to Preter. "If a threat came while he was here, Toric would not abandon this city or these monks."

"We will ask what became of him, or if he is still here,"

said Preter, and then he held up what looked to Lizzan a thick and fleshy worm until she understood that it was a penis. "I see nothing else of note, aside from this. This man must have wanted something from these monks very, very badly."

"Or his lover did," Kelir said dryly, before grimacing. "It does not rot?"

"Not in the bowl." Where it was dropped back in again. "Come. The welcome chamber looks to be this . . . one. . . ."

He slowed to a halt and Lizzan glanced to see what had stopped him before pivoting away again, watching the passageway. Deep gouges had slashed the door, and the wood had splintered as if battered until it broke. Aerax crouched beside her, his body tense, his gaze sweeping the floor.

Gripping his axe, Kelir urged the monk aside. The shattered door no longer latched and swung open easily.

Lizzan took the barest second to glance over her shoulder and into the chamber. Dried blood. Splashed across the floor, the far wall. Her stomach tightened as she resumed watching either end of the passageway.

"Bodies?" she asked as the others followed Kelir in.

"None," Aerax said, and she backed with him toward the chamber entrance, where she stopped while still keeping an eye on the corridor. One end of the long passageway continued past more chambers. The other led back to the great hall.

"What kind of claws make these?" Tyzen asked Aerax, and she looked to see them examining the gouges in the door before Aerax moved deeper into the chamber and knelt by a bloodied track.

Heart thundering, she almost didn't hear the sound echoing faintly down the passageway. Instantly she hushed the others and they all fell silent.

Click-click-click-click. So quick. But not light, but more like a rapid tapping of a sharp stone against another rock, and coming from the direction of the great hall. Ardyl joined her at the chamber entrance and they both tilted their heads. *Click-click-click-click.*

"What is that?" she whispered.

"A wraith," Aerax said grimly.

Lizzan's pounding heart jolted to a halt. "You are certain?"

"These tracks are almost the same as from the King's Walk."

"Then we leave now," commanded Kelir, ushering Tyzen and Seri toward the door.

Preter looked torn. "But what of the people from the city?"

"If they are still locked away and safe, they will stay that way. If not . . ." Kelir shook his head. "We'll return with help—"

"Shh," hissed Ardyl, swinging her glaive forward, gaze fixed down the passageway, where the *click-click-click-click* came ever faster now, louder as it neared. "Back into the chamber. Preter, where is the second exit?"

"This way."

Ardyl and Lizzan backed into the chamber, silently swinging the door closed—though Lizzan could not make herself go further, standing at the edge of the door and peering through one of the shattered panels at an angle that gave her a view of the corridor where it joined the great hall.

Aerax's strong forearm came around her waist as if to drag her away with him. "Lizzan—"

"I have to see," she whispered. "I have to see."

"But then we run."

She nodded.

He waited with her, his strong body at her back, jaw against her temple as they both watched. A shadow moved at the end of the passageway and Aerax hauled her away from the door. Oh, and she'd been a fool to look. Better not to know what came after them, what was screeching now as it charged down the corridor, a body that had once been human but was twisted and emaciated and made of stone, with the *click-click-click-click* that was the sound its claws made, which were not of ice but still like knives.

They sprinted after the others, passing through a second blood-splashed chamber and into another long corridor. A crash behind them was followed by an echoing screech as the wraith followed through the welcome chamber.

Terror grabbed Lizzan by the throat, made every breath a tortured wheeze until she fought back the fear. She raced with Aerax to the next chamber where Kelir waited at the door, gesturing them in—perhaps hoping the wraith would not know what path they'd taken but not waiting to see if it did. Preter passed through another chamber, another, always turning through a maze of blood-splattered stone.

At the end of a long corridor they paused, gasping for breath.

"Stone wraith," Lizzan told them, chest heaving. "I go last."

Aerax began to shake his head.

"I go last," she said again, reaching up to clasp her father's medallion. "I have Vela's protection. It cannot harm me with its claws."

"It is *stone*," Aerax snarled. "What if it crushes you with a heavy blow?"

"I hope not to find out. But if any of you can think of a way to kill a stone, I will gladly hear it, because I do not think my sword will do much or that this wraith will melt."

If any idea they had, no one had time to tell it. A *click-click-click-click* faintly echoed down the corridor and they were off again, Preter at the lead and Seri and Tyzen behind him. Kelir and Ardyl guarded their backs, and Aerax didn't let her come last but stayed at her side. It seemed forever before they stopped, with sweat dripping from their faces and breathing labored.

"It is quiet when it hunts us," Aerax told them. "Then screeches as it chases. If it is screeching, do not stop running."

"But how does it know each turn we take?" Preter held a hand to his side, pain etched on his face. "Does it smell us? Hear us? Is it because we are surrounded by stone and it senses us another way?"

"Does it matter?" Lizzan managed a breathy laugh. "It knows. It follows. And we are trapped, because we cannot go back the way we came without running straight to it."

"Is there also a second way out of the monastery?" Aerax asked.

Preter nodded. "The sun chamber."

"Which way is it?" Tyzen asked.

"Up, I should think." The monk laughed and lifted his hands. "I will take every path that leads upward, and pray to Nemek that we find it."

The wraith's screech tore through the corridor and no more did they talk, racing, turning. Her every nightmare it was to Lizzan, and every time it seemed they'd passed into a part of the monastery where the wraith had never been, soon more blood they would see, more signs of terror, of doors barricaded and broken, the lingering stink of a siege, walls painted the red of a slaughter.

Running down a corridor with all her senses tuned behind for a click or a screech, Lizzan nearly plowed into Kelir, who had nearly plowed into Tyzen when he and the young monk faltered and slowed.

Her gaze snapped to Aerax, who wiped sweat from his face with a swipe of his hand while scowling at a door.

Fearfully Lizzan glanced behind. No wraith yet. No *click*.

"Why are we stopped?" Ardyl whispered.

Out of breath, Tyzen didn't attempt to speak. Only pointed at the door. The stone all around it was scored with claw marks . . . but the door itself was untouched.

"Spelled?" Kelir said.

Nodding, Preter moved closer.

"Why did they not spell *all* the doors?" Seri said between gasps. "Can you lock one in this way?"

"It needs a special wood," Preter told her, slowly regaining his breath. "And time to cast."

"We have not much time now," Lizzan told him. "Can you open it? If it can be locked again and we escape through the other exit, the wraith could not follow our path."

Relief passed over their faces at her suggestion. They still could not go back the way they'd come, but perhaps the wraith would not be so close behind.

Preter opened the door and the metallic scent of old

blood spilled out, yet Lizzan didn't see the slaughter she expected. She had hoped—perhaps foolishly—that some survivors they might find.

And so they did.

Closing the door after they all had gone in, Preter immediately began murmuring and drawing symbols on the wood. Kelir circled the room, and with Aerax at her side, Lizzan moved to the bed where a man had been chained naked, his brown skin webbed with scars old and new.

"What is this?" Seri whispered in horror. "Is he alive?"

Barely. Every rib showed through his skin, and his lips were cracked and dry. She looked to Aerax. "Is there water left?"

They had sipped from Ardyl's wineskin at every stop for breath. Now she trickled some between the man's lips, despairing as it spilled out over his jaw—then heartened as his throat worked and he swallowed.

"Hold," said Kelir, and Lizzan thought at first that he meant for her to stop tending to the man, but the warrior spoke to Preter, instead. "There is no exit. That wall is bricked up with heavy stones. I do not think even my axe could break through."

Alarm shot through Lizzan's heart. Preter might lock the door with his spell, but they would be trapped—with no food, barely any water, and with evidence of the wraith's patience at every bloodstained chamber they'd raced through. They could not hope for the wraith to grow bored and leave them be.

"I'll carry him," Aerax said in the same moment that Lizzan scrambled for the chains. Heavy iron manacles bound the man's wrists, the chain links thicker than she had ever seen used for a prisoner. A chain such as this might hold a mammoth in place—and would maybe even hold Caeb.

"Do you see keys?" she asked, tugging the sheet around his still form. Kelir came to help with the manacles as the others searched.

"No keys," said Ardyl.

And they could not waste more time looking. "Forgive

me," she whispered before gripping the man's thumb and snapping the joint. Kelir did the same to the other hand, and they dragged off the manacles, scraping away skin but not as badly as the wraith would. Grunting, Aerax heaved the man's weight over his shoulder—and even starved, he seemed huge and heavy.

"Got him?" Kelir asked.

Teeth gritted, Aerax nodded.

"I'll take him at the next rest. Go ahead of us."

Ahead of Lizzan, Kelir, and Ardyl. No slower did they seem to run but the delay at the door and searching for keys had brought the wraith closer, and when the screeching began, the echoing shriek down the stone passageway was louder than before. Then Preter turned at the end of a corridor, and she heard Aerax's laughing groan when they saw the steep stairs spiraling upward.

The stairwell was narrow, only wide enough to climb in a single line, and this time Lizzan went last. Still they did not slow much, until the stairs continued higher and higher without end, and she could barely hear the others' heaving breaths over her own, could barely feel anything but the shaking furnace that her leg muscles had become.

Until a screech carried up the stairwell, and the wraith's clacking stone tread on the steps. The others picked up the pace and shouted encouragement, but the wraith was right behind her; she could feel its presence as if her fluttering cloak had become an extension of her skin, raising hairs even through the sweat pouring down her neck, her pounding heart trembling with terror.

Then Preter shouted, "Flatten down and hold on!" and she knew not what he meant, until ahead of her Ardyl seemed to fall to the stairs, but she hadn't tripped. Lizzan lurched up half a step and nearly sprawled atop her, gripping Ardyl's hand as a gale wind howled down the stairwell, carrying the sound of Preter screaming in effort.

Hair whipping into her face, Lizzan looked back. Three steps below, the wraith battled against the gale, its screeching maw gaping to reveal rows of serrated teeth, its eyes glowing the orange-red of volcanic rock. Knifelike fingers reached for her, and they couldn't slice her, she knew they couldn't slice her, yet still she could only picture the hot splash of blood and the screams, so many screams as everyone was torn to shreds around her.

Rage boiled through her veins and the wraith slowly gained another step . . . on feet that were like spikes and knives. Scooting down, she gripped Ardyl's thigh even as the warrior shouted her name and reached for her.

Lizzan snapped her foot into its stone chest. Its hand slashed down, claws shredding her brocs but gliding over her skin. Unbalanced, it tipped back. With a triumphant snarl, Lizzan slammed her heel into its chin.

It tumbled, clattering as it hit the wall and bounced, carried by the gale, skidding and falling out of sight around the spiral. The wind howled on and on, then suddenly failed—and still she could hear the distant clatter and crash continue down the stairs.

"We will not have long," Preter said, panting.

Her legs trembled like leaves in a storm when she climbed to her feet again. They were almost at the top, she saw, but even a half-dozen steps seemed impossible until Ardyl gripped the back of Lizzan's hood and began dragging her along.

Aerax transferred the unconscious man over to Kelir, then turned just as Lizzan flung her arms around him. His mouth found hers, hot and hard—and then they could wait no longer. Their boots pounded the floor as they raced through a great dining hall with long rows of tables carved from the same stone as the walls. The light overhead had warmed to a soft orange.

Oh, Temra be merciful.

"Find torches!" Lizzan called out. "The sun is setting!"

A new nightmare it became then, running through darkening corridors and chambers, shadows deepening on every side as night set in. So dark it became that they could only see within the glowing circle of their torches, for although Preter had said lighting them was a simple thing, it would mean he had to stop in each corridor and chamber long enough for him to focus and cast the spell, and no time did they have for that.

"Where is the moonlight?" Tyzen panted as they stopped again. "Vela rises full this night."

"A cloud . . . perhaps," Preter gasped.

That rest was almost no rest at all as a screech echoed through the dark corridor, and they could not see if it was near or far—and could only run again. Over and over they ran, stopping more frequently but never long enough. Another set of stairs felt to Lizzan twice as steep as the first, and though there were not near as many steps, each one seemed its own mountain.

They ran down another passageway and abruptly into a larger chamber that—for the barest, most joyful moment— Lizzan thought was the great hall.

Abruptly Preter swung back. "Help me with these doors!" he cried, moving to the enormous wooden door beside the corridor's opening.

Together they all pushed. Wood groaned and finally closed. A stout beam swung into brackets to brace the doors even as the wraith's muffled shriek sounded on the other side, and the terrifying scrape of claws that meant the creature would soon be tearing its way through as it had every other door they'd thrown into its path.

But to her surprise, Preter laughed breathlessly and leaned back against the door, sliding slowly to the ground.

"Is it spelled?" she asked him, hope swelling through her heart.

He shook his head. His hands lifted but he seemed too breathless now to explain.

Instead it was Ardyl, who collapsed beside him. "It is made of blackwood. It will get through, but not quickly."

The siege wood that many fortresses in the south used. Never had Lizzan seen it before, but she was glad to see it here. She looked to Aerax, who with Kelir was carefully laying the scarred man on the floor. He caught her in his arms then, and together they sat with Lizzan braced against his chest and his back to the stone wall. For the longest of times, not a word passed between them, and even the muffled scrape of the wraith's claws seemed so very far away.

Then from her position lying flat on the floor, Ardyl turned her head to look up at Preter. "Never have I seen anything such as that wind. It was extraordinary."

Even in the orange glow of the torchlight, his blush was fierce. "It is thanks to the narrowness of the stairwell. If I had done the same spell in this chamber, barely would the wraith have felt it at all."

"It is not thanks to a stairwell," Aerax said gruffly, tightening his hold on Lizzan. "It is thanks to you."

Nods of agreement came from the others and Preter was forced to take his credit due.

They fell quiet at a screech and a battering of stone against blackwood.

Kelir sighed and rubbed his face. "The sooner we go again, the farther ahead of it we will be."

Preter shook his head and swept his hand to indicate the darkness ahead. "If this is the wheel chamber, we do not want to hurry."

Lizzan closed her eyes on a groan. "The wheel chamber? I can imagine what that is. Do we now have to dodge giant stone wheels that will crush us if we step off the right path? I must confess, Preter, I do not like the festivities that these monks have left for us on our moon night."

He grinned, shaking his head. "It is a chamber that is the hub of all passageways. There should be a corridor that leads directly to the sun chamber—so we will want to take the time to find that one instead of rushing down another."

"I will begin." Seri bounced to her feet easily, as if they had not recently spent an endless time running for their lives. Grabbing up a torch, she looked to her brother. "Do you come with me?"

Kelir groaned and rolled over onto his back, arms widespread. "Not for the world will I move again."

"I will come." Tyzen pushed to his feet, tugging at the robes that had twisted around his legs at the quick movement.

"There will likely be a draft of fresh air coming from the sun chamber," Preter told them.

Seri nodded and struck out away from the door, torchlight casting a glow onto an enormous stone column ahead. The light did not reach the ceiling.

"Seri." The young monk stopped her with a word. "The chamber is a circle. So you will need to go in this direction or that"—he gestured along the walls where they rested—"for if you head straight forward, you will be walking for a very long time before you reach the other side."

A circle . . . though the wall seemed near straight, and barely any curve could Lizzan detect as Seri and Tyzen walked its length. They paused at a corridor, peering down it before moving to another. Then another, and still barely a curve did there seem to be, and though she tried to extend that curve in her mind, Lizzan could not fathom the size of this chamber.

"Preter." By the wary note in her voice, Ardyl must have been watching them, too. "How many passageways are there?"

"Hundreds. Perhaps even a thousand."

Lizzan laughed before tilting her head back against Aerax's shoulder again. "We should soon begin to help search," she said against his neck.

"Soon," he rumbled in agreement. "But first, take more rest."

As he no doubt needed, too, as he'd not only been carrying his own weight for half of the night. She closed her eyes, with his scent filling her every breath.

Despite the muffled screeching, she must have slept. For she startled awake as Tyzen suddenly spoke into her ear.

"Do you still love him?"

"Who?" said Seri, as close to Lizzan as Aerax, whose body had stiffened against hers.

"Toric." Again Tyzen sounded as if he sat beside Lizzan. *"You said you would only ever marry him, for he was your tribe's best warrior."*

Seri scoffed. *"It was a jest."*

Yet Seri was not here. Nor was Tyzen. Ardyl and Kelir looked to each other, as baffled as Lizzan was.

Preter, with his head tilted back and his eyes closed, said with a slight grin, "They must have found the echo chamber. If there is something that all the monastery needs to hear, it is said there."

"It sounded like truth," said Tyzen. *"And I imagine that you would only marry a warrior as skilled as yourself."*

A snort of laughter drew Lizzan's gaze to Kelir, who was shaking on the floor.

"Then I will be always alone," said Seri, *"for when I am my brother's age, never will there be a warrior as skilled as I will be. So when I marry, I only wish to be loved, as fiercely as our Ran loves his queen."*

Pinching the bridge of her nose, Ardyl shook with silent amusement that became a muffled howl behind her hands when Tyzen spoke next.

"There is something I have left unsaid."

"Oh no," came Seri's dismayed response. *"Do not—"*

"I love you. With all my heart, I love you."

Seri groaned. *"You confess that as if we will die."* Irritation filled her voice. *"We will not die here."*

"I would die for one kiss," Tyzen said earnestly, and Kelir covered his face with his hands, sputtering.

Lizzan looked up at Aerax in amazement as there was a silence that was not quite silence, but instead filled with a wet and breathy sound so familiar to their first kisses. Yet although there was amusement in his dark gaze, there was concern, too.

"Did you get enough rest?" he asked softly.

There would never be quite enough after this night. But she nodded.

"There," said Seri, slightly breathless. *"I have kissed you. But are you dead?"*

"I think I have just begun to live," Tyzen said in awe.

Kelir, who'd been wiping tears from his cheeks, lost himself all over again.

"But we cannot do this," Seri told him, exasperation

clear in her voice. *"I hope to serve on Yvenne's Dragon. You are Yvenne's brother and serve her. Will you not always?"*

"I will. And so we will always be near to each other."

"Too *near,"* Seri said. *"If I serve on Yvenne's Dragon, I must take a vow to always protect her first. Yet if I marry, I must vow to protect that person first. If my duty takes me away from a spouse, no conflict is there—but if we are always close, because they also serve the Ran? The day may come when I have to break a vow to the Ran or break a marriage vow, and I become an oathbreaker either way. Do you never wonder why my brother and Ardyl always keep someone between them? It is because that person is always Ran Maddek."*

"He has been between them?" Tyzen sounded taken aback.

"Not in that *way . . . or if he ever was, not since they were all young. But they always knew he would be Ran, and that they would serve as his Dragon. So it is their duty that lies between them, for they love each other and will never love another in that same way. Yet even their moon night, they shared someone between them. Despite all the strangers that they have taken to their bed, never have they been with anyone but each other—yet never have they really touched each other, only the person between them. And they are content and happy that way. It suits them. It would not suit me. I could not share you with anyone."*

"Then I will only be yours."

"And if one day I must decide between saving you and saving your sister? It would tear my heart apart. So do not ask this of me."

Laughter over, Kelir sighed, staring up into the darkness above. Ardyl nudged his shoulder with her foot, and he smiled slightly, hand sliding companionably up her leg to grip her knee.

Stubbornly Tyzen said, *"If I can tear your heart apart, you must feel something."*

"That I love you? You are a fool if you do not already

know. But we cannot be more than we are now. Not with Yvenne between us."

"Then you will be more with another?" Tyzen gave a bitter laugh. *"And I shall be as Preter, secretly in love and heartstricken every time Kelir and Ardyl take another to their bed?"*

Groaning, the monk buried his red face in his hands.

"I am taking no one to my bed!" Seri shouted. *"But the Destroyer is coming and I'm asking you not to make me choose between you and Yvenne. After he's been defeated . . ."*

"After?" Tyzen's voice rang with hope.

"Would you wait for me?" Sudden uncertainty filled the girl's reply. *"Even if it is years?"*

"I will wait forever for you."

The breathless wet sounds came again. With another heavy sigh, Kelir said, "I ought to have ordered her to stay with the Kothans."

"You did as you should," Ardyl told him. "She *will* be a great warrior, but not if she is never allowed to test her nerves or push herself to the edge. And this night will merely be a story that she tells when she is old."

Silently he nodded, though his expression was still weighed with guilt and worry.

Ardyl looked to Preter, who stared straight ahead, obviously wishing for the wraith to come through the door at that moment.

"Kelir and I will tear you apart," she said quietly to him.

He cast her a wry glance. "That is what I hope."

She grinned, though it slowly faded. "We are generous with our hearts, and so we might come to love you. But Seri spoke truth. Our duty is always to Maddek, and when we no longer protect Tyzen, to Maddek we will return."

"As I will return to Toleh and to my studies—and one day, marry quite happily. But I am not averse to adventure. And I would like to have the memory to revisit."

"So you shall." Her eyes narrowed. "You have had your moon night?"

His blush flared again. "I have."

From the floor, Kelir grunted his approval. "Good, or we would have to fuck you now, and this is neither the time nor the place for it. First you must get us out of this maze."

Preter grinned. "As I'll be certain to, now that I have even more to live for."

As they all did. With a sigh, Lizzan looked up at Aerax. "Should we begin a search for that passageway?"

He nodded, helping push her to her feet when the movement pulled at aching muscles and she groaned. A few paces away, Ardyl did the same for Kelir, grasping his hand and hauling him up from the floor.

"If you will go in that direction," Aerax told them, "we will take the other. Keep eyes on your torch at each passageway. A draft from the sun chamber might be most easily detected that way."

Kelir nodded and looked to Preter. "You will be all right looking after him?"

He gestured to the man on the ground, who had stirred a little each time they'd given him water, but had not yet awakened . . . if he ever did.

"I will be well," Preter said. "If the wraith is nearer to breaking through than we think, I'll flare the torch so bright you cannot mistake it."

And Preter's torch would also serve as their guide back, Lizzan realized after she and Aerax had moved past a few dozen passageways. In the other direction, Kelir and Ardyl's torch already looked no bigger than a candle flame, but in all the dark was still easy to find. Soon they would be as stars in a moonless sky.

"This is not the night I envisioned," said Aerax quietly.

"It seems to me near what we planned. We are exhausted, sore, and my brocs are ripped to shreds."

She meant to make him smile but his face darkened, reminded of how the wraith had slashed at her. Stopping, he cupped her nape in his big hand to draw her close and bend his forehead to hers.

"I cannot lose you," he said hoarsely. "Never can I lose you."

Throat tight, she rose up for a kiss and so sweetly he complied. With a sigh, she drew back.

"How long do you suppose until dawn?" By the soreness that had settled into her muscles, she must have slept for a while.

"Not long."

Eyes squeezing tight, she nodded. "And this is neither the time nor place for a fucking."

"It is not."

"I have been well pleasured these past nights. We do not truly need a moon night."

"We do not," he said gruffly.

Her heart ached. "But if we only have until the first snowfall—"

"We will have longer."

"Even if that is true . . . no more time do I wish to waste, Aerax. We do not even have to fuck in full. You only need to breach me, and tomorrow will be the night we envisioned."

Lifting his forehead from hers, he cupped her jaw, tilting back her head to meet his dark eyes. "If you believe you must persuade me into fucking you, Lizzan, know that I care nothing for proper time and place. If you wish my cock inside you, whether a shallow thrust to breach your virgin cunt or to ride me full deep for years, you only need say so."

She breathed a shaky laugh. "I think here and now . . . only enough that we do not have to wait another full turn."

"So we will." Linking his fingers with hers, Aerax strode to the next passageway and set the handle of the torch into the wall sconce before drawing her back into the wheel chamber. He continued only a small distance beyond the torch's glow before they came to one of the massive stone columns, and there he backed her against it.

In the far distance was the tiny spot of flame from Preter's torch.

"Watch for a flare," Aerax rasped softly into her ear, unlacing her brocs and letting them fall around her ankles, where she kicked them away.

She nodded, breath shuddering when he lifted her against the column, wrapping her legs around his hips as she watched the pinprick of light over his shoulder.

He bent his head, teeth pinching her earlobe before he murmured, "You are not yet wet enough to take my cock into your sheath."

He only needed to say that again and she might be near to drenched. Yet she had no fear that he would not find the remedy. Palming her ass in one hand, he pushed his other between them, and his callused fingers found her clit and began a slow tease.

Sparks fired through her veins with each light touch. Soon she would be *so* wet. And Aerax would be hungry.

"Are you restrained?" she whispered, and he groaned a denial, burying his face in her neck. "You *must* be. Or the wraith will be upon us and we will not even know. Tomorrow you will be unrestrained."

She felt his nod and then his openmouthed kiss against her throat. The stone was hard and cool at her back, his strong hand gripping one side of her ass, his fingers creating magic between her thighs, drawing wetness and heat from a body spent by exhaustion and fear.

"Aerax," she breathed, hitching her hips into his light touch.

"So hot you are, Lizzan," he groaned into her skin. "So slick with your need."

His fingers left her, and into the silence of her panting breath and thundering heart came the faint jingle of his armor and the whisper of linen as he freed his cock. She felt him as she had so many times before, drawing the broad head of his erection through her folds of aroused flesh. Her arms tightened around his shoulders, her body pushing closer, seeking the moment she waited for so desperately.

"Inside me," she urged him, kissing his jaw, his neck. "Be inside me."

Then all below began to burn and stretch. She went still, gasping into his throat as his thick cock pushed deeper and deeper until it seemed there was no end to him.

"Hold," she whispered, and Aerax did, his big body rigid and shaking. "There seems more of you than there is room in me. Let us stay in this way for a moment."

"We need not do more." His voice was pure gravel. "You are breached. We might stop."

She could not. Because finally he was inside her, though the sensation was not all that she had envisioned. Yet Aerax was. The way he held for her now, though his body shook with strain. His hot heaving breaths that said his arousal knew no pain or discomfort as hers did and his desire had not ebbed. And the steel length wedged so tight and deep inside her that she could feel the pulsing of his flesh. His unyielding, unceasing need for her was the most incredible, wonderful thing she'd ever known . . . and *always* he put hers first.

Her fingers twisted into his hair, and she brought his face to hers.

"Three times," she demanded softly. "Fuck into me three times, as hard as you wish. And then we will stop for this night."

A growl rumbled through his chest. "Are you still hurting?"

"I was never hurting. I said your cock did not fit." Yet that had changed, too. Deeper he was even now, her body yielding to his, and no discomfort did she feel. Only fullness. "But it seems to have shrunk within me."

A tortured laugh escaped him. "It has not."

"Then fuck me. Three times. With full restraint."

That was likely asking too much. And it seemed he only had the barest restraint as he held her ass in both hands now, strong fingers digging into her flesh, and the sweet roughness of his grip vanished into the sweet roughness of his heavy flesh withdrawing from hers until only the thick crown stretched her entrance.

Sparks flew behind her eyes when he shoved back in, deep, full deep. Her cry made him still again, as if fearing he'd hurt her, but she shook her head, her lips trembling against his.

"One," she said breathlessly. "And it was so fine, Aerax. It was so fine to take you inside me again."

His ragged groan was matched by the roughness of his hands on her ass, rhythmically squeezing and kneading her cheeks as if in desperate substitution for the rough rhythm he wanted to pound out inside her. Yet even that caused no pain, for each pull and push seemed to carry forward to the sensitive flesh stretched around his shaft, little tugs that tightened her sheath around him.

Those he must have felt, too, adding to them with a sudden grind between her thighs, as if they were still virgins in their tent and rubbing together. But now he was deep inside her and instead of sliding through her folds, he stirred his cock the full depth of her cunt, and it seemed there was nothing sensitive that he did not touch—not even her clit, when he tilted her ass and began to rub against that, too.

"Aerax." She knew not what she begged for, except more. "Aerax."

Gritting his teeth, he withdrew again but *so* slowly, she would die of it. Her thighs tightened around his waist as she attempted to draw him in, but he held her back with that unyielding grip on her ass until only the very tip of him touched her, not even inside her cunt but nestled between her folds.

Near sobbing, she yanked at his hair. *"Please."*

And there was no burning with this breaching, only the delicious stretch of her body accepting his slow possession. Deeper and deeper he pushed, and there was no end to him, and no end to her, only the fierce pleasure that curled her toes and arched her back against the stone.

"Two," Aerax gritted out, and began another incredible grind, then cheating, cheating, he shoved her back flat against the column and began pumping against her, never withdrawing but using the give of her own flesh to remain so deep inside her while fucking, fucking, pressing against her clit with each thrust and building the pressure within her sheath to near unbearable tightness.

"Are you near?" he growled against her lips as his cock ruthlessly pumped faster, and her desperate whine served as her reply.

He stopped pumping to grind again, and she cried out, jerking her hips when he hit just right.

"There, Aerax. There," she told him, and he gave her *there* over and over and over, until the sparks streaming through her blood began to burn bright across her every nerve, her entire body pulling tight. With a snarl, Aerax fucked full into her on a hard thrust and the fire exploded within, blazing through her senses as they ground together again. His mouth found hers in the dark, a groan tearing from his throat as he pumped his release into her quivering sheath.

Never would she stop kissing him. Never. So it seemed for as long as he held her, but in the distance was still the pinprick of torchlight.

"Three," she finally whispered against his lips, sighing as she let her legs fall from his hips.

It seemed that everything after should be a disappointment. As he withdrew from her and his seed dripped between her thighs. As she found her brocs on the floor and used them to clean herself. As there was no bed to stay in together, reveling in their new intimacy, and instead they had to continue the task of standing in front of passageways and watching the torch for evidence of a draft.

Yet there was no disappointment. All of it seemed as wonderful as Aerax inside her. To be with him in this comfortable way, even when it was not the time and not the place. Always would be the time to love him. Everywhere would be the place.

The quick pace of someone approaching at a run made both Aerax and Lizzan peer into the dark.

"We found it!" Ardyl called out. "We left our torch by the passageway."

Relief lifted through Lizzan's chest. Together they headed back to Preter, who had already been joined by Kelir, Seri, and Tyzen—and the scarred man, who sat with his back braced against the wall and with the bedsheet wrapped around his waist.

Seri tossed a yellow sunfruit to Lizzan, who automatically caught it, then another to Ardyl and Aerax. "We found a garden chamber."

Growing sunfruit that was a rare treat in Koth. Eagerly she peeled the rind, which was yellow as the sun but lumpy and pebbled like lizard skin. Her mouth was already watering when she bit in and the sweet juice burst across her tongue, and this was the finest of all days. Despite the wraith. Simply the finest.

She looked to the scarred man, who had a small collection of discarded rinds and pits beside him. "So you are awake. I am sorry for your hands. It was the only way to remove the manacles."

From beneath shaggy black hair, he merely looked at her with wary and distrusting eyes—and he had no trouble holding an apple, she saw. As if she'd never broken the joint of his thumb.

"He doesn't talk," Seri said, smiling as she turned to him. "Anything more to eat?"

He shook his head.

"Can you walk?" Kelir asked him.

A nod, which Lizzan doubted until the man stood. For though he swayed for a brief moment, steadying himself against the stone wall, his first step seemed more sure.

"Perhaps take a moment to find your feet again," Preter suggested. "It might not be long before we are running."

Ardyl looked to him sharply. "Is the wraith nearly through the door?"

"Almost."

"Then you'd best find your feet while we're walking toward that torch." Kelir pointed into the distance. "And I know not what sort of man you are, but I am friend to the most stubborn of fools who would not ask for help until his heart was rent from his chest. Do not be as he was. If you are too weak to run, we will carry you."

The man nodded from beneath that tangled fall of hair, and Lizzan was abruptly reminded of Aerax as a young boy, emerging from the forest with his knotted, dirty hair and his body streaked with blood. Though unlike Aerax, he did not seem a man who'd grown up feral . . . but perhaps he had become that way.

They started out, Preter walking past Lizzan and discreetly coughing into his fist before saying, "I see the festivities have taken place."

Laughing, she nudged him aside a step. Apparently he'd noted that she wore no brocs now. It hardly mattered; her tunic was long enough to preserve even a monk's modesty.

Aerax returned from a visit to Seri with handfuls of more fruit. Happily she ate with him as they walked, and it was so wonderfully familiar. So many times they'd walked in this way together after foraging through the forest. Though here, the forest was the stone columns that vanished into the darkness overhead.

They were not far from the passageway when a snap of cracking wood echoed through the vast chamber. Lizzan's stomach dropped and then shriveled when the screech reached them across the distance. Immediately they picked up the pace, and with Aerax beside her, she kept a careful watch on the scarred man. To her eyes, he seemed to be learning to run as he went—or remembering how to.

Kelir grabbed up the torch when they reached the corridor, and nothing was there to see beyond the glow of firelight. No indication of how far they might run. Only darkness, ahead and behind.

Until the sound of the stone wraith's steps joined them as it entered the corridor. Not screeching yet. Only the *click-click-click-click* that their labored breaths and racing footsteps made near impossible to hear or to know how far behind it was.

"Here!" Preter shouted joyously, and new energy surged through her limbs.

The quality of the darkness changed, not pure black but the dark of a clouded night sky that shrouded the moon and stars. Cool air hit Lizzan's overheated face, and she followed the others through an archway into another immense chamber, too dark to know the full size but everything within her was directed upward, where the darkness was not a ceiling but the open sky.

"There will be a stair carved into the side," Preter told them between hard breaths, "though I know not *which* side."

"It will follow us out," Ardyl said, panting. "We are not done running."

"We are not," Aerax said grimly. "But if we must face it, I prefer to face it out there."

As did Lizzan. "Let us find that stair," she said, taking Aerax's hand and striking out toward the far wall—then pausing, for directly ahead was an obstacle that seemed darker than all else . . . and of enormous size. A statue? She did not wish to run at full speed into that.

Lizzan called to Seri to bring a torch as she moved forward, feeling for where the statue began. Her fingers encountered smooth stone carved with rounded grooves . . . scales, she made out even as the light fell over them.

Baffled, she called to Preter, "Do these monks invoke Stranik in their magic?"

"If they do, then no ally should we make of them," said Kelir.

Abruptly Aerax wrapped his arm around Lizzan's waist and hauled her back. "Away from it, Seri," he barked at the girl.

She stumbled back, and in the flickering light from her torch the scaly hide slithered past. Lizzan's heart stopped in her chest. For the thing was not a legless crawling snake, and as it shifted position, she could not see it turn but she could *feel* it turn, as if nothing so large could move without affecting everything near to it.

"There's a *dragon* in here," Seri breathed.

Into the silence that fell came a *click-click-click-click*. Lizzan turned with Aerax toward the corridor, and on the others' faces she saw the shock and indecision that had rendered them speechless.

"I will take my chances with the dragon," said Lizzan.

They must have all agreed, for as a group they raced along the scaly hide, and from the shadows and shapes she glimpsed—the edge of a wing, the curve of a talon—she gained the sense that they were running toward its head. Then she was certain of it, as they sky above them grew faintly brighter, and more she could see than just what fell in the torch's glow.

"There is the stair." Aerax pointed ahead, and Lizzan gave a breathless laugh, for there was nothing else to do.

To reach the stair, they only had to race past the dragon's snout, with its massive jaws and teeth. They only had to run straight into its view.

A screech split the air, seemed to tear open the difference between night and dawn, for Lizzan could see full well as the dragon lifted its enormous head and turned its gaze toward them.

The entire world seemed to move, but it was just that massive body shifting its position alongside them, a sinuous wall of black scales and wings.

"To the stair!" Kelir shouted over the screeching that was growing ever louder. "As fast as you can! Do not stop!"

Though Ardyl and Kelir were going to, Lizzan realized, faltering. She stole a glance back and saw that they'd come to a halt, weapons drawn as they faced the oncoming wraith. As if intending to slow it so everyone else could escape. Yet the wraith would tear right through them . . . and she could not let it.

"Do not stop, Aerax!" she shouted at him before spinning back, knowing that he'd follow but hoping to race faster. She passed the others and they, too, looked back, and her heart thundered as they fell in behind.

"Let me!" Lizzan shouted at the warriors ahead. "I'll slow it!"

Ardyl and Kelir gave no indication that they'd heard her even as she planted herself between them, her sword drawn. The wraith stalked toward them, fingers clicking, reddened eyes sweeping over them in a hungry stare that lifted every hair on her skin.

"Go," she snarled at the Parsathcans. Then Aerax was at her side and determination gripped her throat, for she was here to protect him.

So she would.

On a deep breath, she stepped forward—and the dragon flicked a wing. In stunned silence, she watched the wraith's twisted body shoot through the air and slam into the chamber wall, falling to the stone floor with a clatter.

Then get to its feet again.

"To the stair," Kelir said quietly, backing up. "Let them fight it out, but we will not stay here to be crushed."

Nodding, Lizzan backed with him—unable to turn, unable to look away as the wraith charged toward them, screeching. The dragon could flick the wraith away a hundred times, yet still it would come again. So she would not turn away until—

Aerax threw her to the ground, covering her body with his even as the world turned to fire overhead. The dragon's blast caught the wraith full on, and still it came; Lizzan's eyes watered as she watched the wraith continue forward through the engulfing flames but slower . . . slower, dripping bits of molten rock from its fingers, its feet softening and spreading until the screeching stopped, and there was only a thick, bubbling mass slowly spreading across the chamber floor.

"Melted," Lizzan whispered in awe.

Aerax huffed a quiet laugh in her ear before his weight

disappeared from her back. He helped her up, and she held him tight for a precious moment before turning toward the others.

"The stairs now?" Kelir asked. "Or do we go back the way we came?"

"First we free it," Aerax said.

Lizzan looked to the dragon and saw what Aerax already had—the thin silver chain around its long neck. "Do you think it will let us?"

"More importantly," Ardyl said, "will it eat us?"

Aerax shook his head. "If it meant to kill us, it would have already."

"It could have cooked us," Seri agreed.

Lizzan nodded, yet even accepting that the dragon had no interest in killing them, it was with trepidation that she approached its head. Eyes of liquid black watched her and Aerax as they stopped at a small distance to study the chain. No locks could she see—and the chain itself was fastened around its neck on a slipknot that would tighten if the dragon pulled against it. The other end of the chain was not attached to an iron loop bolted to the floor, as she expected, but instead disappeared into the chamber's stone wall, as if anchored by the mountain itself.

"The links must be spelled," Lizzan said to Preter. "Look at how thin the chain is. That could not hold a dragon."

"I sense no magic from it," he said.

"It should not be difficult to loosen the knot at its throat," said Aerax. "But we will have to draw the chain over its head."

Lizzan nodded. "I will do that. If it will let me."

Unknowing whether the dragon understood what they were doing, Lizzan put aside her sword before approaching the head, which the dragon had laid on the floor again, as if taking a nap. But its liquid black eyes were open, following Lizzan and Aerax as they walked past.

With his fingers lightly on the chain, Aerax followed its length toward the knot, which he would not have to untie but simply work slack through from the anchored end. She heard him murmuring to the dragon, and knew not if the creature recognized their intent—but it did not move or pull away as Aerax tugged on the chain, loosening the loop that circled its neck.

She more clearly heard Aerax tell the dragon that if it pulled, the chain would tighten again—and then Aerax looked to her.

"Slowly," he said.

Slowly she did, climbing the chain hand-over-hand to the top of the dragon's neck, where the scales hardened into triangular plates, as if a mountain range lined its body from the back of its skull to its tail. The chain had to be lifted over each peak, and Lizzan began dragging the silver loop forward toward the head.

When the press of its neck against the floor stopped the chain from moving, it became clear the dragon understood their intent, lifting its head to clear space between its scales and the floor.

It moved only a scant distance, yet Lizzan's heart thundered and the entire world seemed to shift beneath her. How strange and wonderful her life was, that she was helping Aerax free a dragon after everything else this night had brought.

Lizzan reached the horns that arched back from above its eyes, and there had to pause. She could draw the chain over one horn at a time. Not both.

"I'll help!" Seri called, and scampered forward. Lizzan saw Kelir's face go bloodbare as his sister quickly climbed the chain, gritting his teeth and pulling at his hair as if to stop himself from saying anything.

After the horns, there were only the protrusions on its face that the chain might catch upon. Lizzan went down between the eyes first, more quickly now, aware of the nostrils steaming farther below. She pulled the chain over a spike above its snout and the silver abruptly slithered the rest of the way down the slippery scales, dropping to the floor.

Free.

"Leap down!" Aerax held out his hands, and Lizzan reached for Seri as the dragon abruptly lifted its head, carrying them up, its wings unfurling. Temra have mercy. Staggering for balance, Lizzan gripped the girl's hand and they jumped. She nearly slammed into Aerax but caught herself, cushioning the impact with a forward roll that brought her straight back to her feet—then was flattened by a gust of wind from a flap of the dragon's wings. She turned onto her back, watching as it lifted up and up into the lightening sky.

Beside her, Aerax clasped her hand, and they watched the dragon until it was gone.

She glanced over. Kelir clutched Seri to his chest, holding her tight as she sobbed against him.

"I rode a dragon," she cried softly. "I rode a dragon."

So she had. Lizzan felt her throat burn and she looked to Aerax, who pulled her closer into a kiss.

Lying nearby, Ardyl said, "I am full ready to climb those stairs and leave this place."

Peter gave a heavy sigh. "If we go by the stairs, next we'll likely have to scale a cliff."

They went back the way they came, though not as quickly. Caeb found them midmorning, and everything within Lizzan rejoiced that he hadn't come before the wraith had been melted into a lump. So light her heart seemed with the cat and Aerax walking alongside her, enjoying a breakfast picked from the garden chamber. Preter had stopped at the echo chamber to tell anyone remaining in the monastery that the wraith had been killed, but had warned any citizens of the city not to attempt to navigate the maze unless a monk was with them—but already Preter believed that he would have to search for them and lead them out.

So they would likely stay in this abandoned city a few days . . . which seemed no hardship at all to Lizzan. They finally came to the great hall, and she was only thinking of a bath, and a bed, and Aerax as they stepped through the monastery doors and onto the crystal walk.

Where all around them, pale flakes fluttered from the sky.

CHAPTER 24

AERAX

S now.

 Despair ripped holes through Aerax's chest, and sheer determination filled them again. *He would not lose her.* And even as everything within him rejected what the snow meant, his senses rejected that it was there at all.

The day was too warm. And he could not smell the snow. Always it lent a distinctive taste to the air.

Beside him, Lizzan gave a desolated cry. "I'm not done." Tears swam in the lake of her eyes. "My heart is so full—and I am *not* done."

"You are not." Throat shredded by the emotions tearing through him, Aerax caught her against his chest, buried his face in her hair. "It is ash, Lizzan. It is only ash."

Muffled against his tunic, she shook her head as if believing he only meant to comfort her. And so he did, but not with a lie.

"Look and see," he urged her. "Perhaps the dragon set a nearby forest afire."

"I do not think so," said Kelir, stopping beside them. All

were still on the bridge, their eyes searching the sky. "That dark cloud has an unnatural shape and comes from farther south, over the flaming mountains."

"Perhaps it is Snagtooth Peak again." Ardyl brushed away ash that had fallen onto her hair. "I recall the last time it erupted. The ash did not fall south, but I remember how red the moon became each night as the smoke cast a veil across the sky. That was near the same time the firebloom tribe took me in—and I wondered for days if, in that territory, they used the firebloom's petals to dye the moon as they did our linens."

Kelir gave a short laugh. "That would have been a fine trick."

"The ash fell north of the flaming mountains then, too—even as far north as Koth," Aerax said grimly. "And was the beginning of the Bitter Years."

Two years without a summer, and the first snow had fallen a full turn before the harvest usually began. Expression clouded, Lizzan raised her face from his chest and looked up at him, and Aerax swept the remaining tears from her cheeks with his thumbs before gently kissing her mouth.

They were *not* done. Taking her hand, he caught up to Preter.

"Do you intend to immediately begin the search?"

The monk shook his head. "First I will find an inn, food, and sleep."

"After those, will you marry us together?"

Lizzan's fingers clutched tight on his. He glanced at her face, looking for any objection, and saw only happiness.

"I can," said Preter, looking pleased. "And that will also call for festivities."

Lizzan huffed out a soft laugh. "I do not care for festivities. But I would like a bath."

And so she would have one.

Familiar with the workings of an inn, Aerax quickly found the bath in the washing chamber beyond the kitchen, though Lizzan told him not to bother with carrying it up the steps to a bedchamber. They set the cistern to heating over a fire and Lizzan took his hand, yet she did not lead him to where he expected.

Already Preter, Seri, and Tyzen had taken to a bed, and Kelir and Ardyl were on their way to bring the Kothans and the Parsathean warriors into the city with them.

With Caeb padding beside them, she led Aerax to the public room, where the scarred man sat near the open shutters of a window, watching the ash fall outside. After they had freed the dragon, his gaze had not seemed so wary—yet as Lizzan and Aerax approached him, Aerax saw that it was again.

On a heavy sigh, Lizzan sat across from him and said, "Goranik is in the northern forest. He seeks to invade Koth."

The man's jaw tightened and he turned to look through the window again. When he spoke, his voice was as a rusty hinge.

"How did you know?"

"I saw him in the Kothan outlands," Lizzan said, drawing Aerax down to the bench beside her and bringing Caeb closer to scratch beneath his chin. "There is not a full resemblance between you, but if you were locked alone in that room as long as I suspect, you ought to be dead of thirst or hunger. You heal too quickly. Though you don't have silver blood, the monks were bleeding you . . . and judging by those scars, bleeding you for a very long time. And all the stories that I have heard from the people who flee Lith say that Prince Saxen vanished fifteen years past."

"Only fifteen years?" Surprise deepened the rasp of his voice. "It felt longer."

Lizzan seemed not to know what to say to that, though Aerax saw the softness of her heart in her expression. But though softhearted, she was not a fool—which meant she did not fully know what to think of the man or whether to trust him. So she'd brought Aerax with her . . . and she'd also brought Caeb. Who might be the only one among them strong enough to truly face this man, though his ribs showed through his skin.

"What do you intend now?" His wary gaze swept from Aerax to Lizzan to Caeb. "Whatever reason you have come to me, know that I cannot let you kill me. My death belongs to another."

"I have no wish to kill you. I need to know how to kill your father."

His burst of a laugh sounded like a barking cough. "If I knew, I would. But he is no longer fully my father. A demon inhabits his body."

Lizzan's fingers squeezed tight on Aerax's, and in their shared glance he saw her worry and fear that it was not merely a sorcerer-king, but a demon threatening Koth . . . and her family.

A demon who might be what she faced in glorious battle when the snow fell.

His chest tight, Aerax told her, "We will find a way."

Swallowing hard, she looked to Saxen of Lith. "Will you tell the others all that you know of your father? You don't have to say what Goranik is to you or reveal who you truly are."

Jaw tight, he nodded.

"Also, if you have been chained these fifteen years, you do not know that Anumith the Destroyer comes again." When the man's eyes closed, as if in dismay or pain, Lizzan asked, "Do you still serve him?"

His eyes flared open. "*Never* will I again."

"These warriors we travel with are building an alliance against him. I suspect they would include Lith in that alliance, if your realm would stand against the Destroyer, too."

Another rough bark of a laugh. "You think we only have to reject the Destroyer and all will be forgiven? The Krimatheans will laugh in our faces and then slit our throats. What other redemption is there for us?"

"I do not know," Lizzan said, and the emotional catch in her voice speared through Aerax's chest. "But I *have* to believe that death is not the only answer."

"If the Destroyer is coming, then so is death," Saxen said grimly. "So any other answer will not matter much."

"It will. This is an alliance of *all* the western realms. And even if you will not join, you can help. Did you and your father not travel with the Destroyer for a time?"

The man's face hardened. "We did."

"What does he want? Does he search for something?"

"Never did the Destroyer say what he wanted. Of course he would not. He is no fool." He looked to Aerax. "You love this woman? I would only have to take her away to have absolute power over you. What would you do to see her safe?"

Tension gripped his throat. "There is nothing I would not do."

"So you see. Any man who reveals what he wants is exposing what might give others power over him. The Destroyer never spoke of what he wanted."

Lizzan nodded. "If he searched for something, then we would look for it, too. And if we found it, we could destroy it. But what of his purpose? Why do so many follow him?"

The man gave a thin smile. "He is saving the world."

Sheer disbelief parted her lips. "From what? Himself?"

"He did not say what threat it was. Only that everything he did would save us all in the end—and that he was the only one who could bear the burden of what must be done."

Unease coiled through Aerax's chest. Too familiar that seemed.

"But you no longer believe it?" Lizzan asked.

"I was born into believing it. But I do not believe in much of anything now." His gaze swept over Lizzan's face before moving to Aerax. "Though perhaps I believe in kindness a little more than I did while chained to a bed. I owe you all a great debt."

"Kindness needs no repayment, but if you feel a debt, perhaps pay it by telling us all you can of Goranik and of the Destroyer," said Lizzan softly. "Though it need not be today. That discussion can wait until we are not all so very tired. And even if you do not join the alliance, you are welcome to join us when we marry. There will be a small feast if Caeb will hunt for us something worth roasting."

She addressed the last part to the cat. In answer, Caeb rubbed his cheek to hers.

The man smiled faintly. "If there is food, then I will not miss it."

Back in the washing room, Lizzan's heavy sigh made Aerax pause while removing his underlinen. He glanced over his shoulder at her, where she reclined in the bath with her lake-blue eyes upon him.

"What troubles you?"

"That I do not know which is my favorite view." Biting her lip, she swept her gaze from his head to his toes. "The finest of all asses, or the thickest of all cocks. When we are married, I might ask you to spend every night spinning round and round."

Why wait until marriage? She laughed when he spun for her now, and Aerax thought she liked the front view full well when he approached the tub. Her heated gaze remained fixed upon the heavy hang of his shaft, which thickened all the more the nearer he came to her.

"Sit before me," she told him, "and I will wash your shoulders and hair."

Heart full, he sank into the bath and into the cradle of her thighs, leaning back against her. Her knees were bent at his sides. Her arms came around his torso as he braced his feet at the edge of the tin tub, and she pressed her cheek to his.

"Now tell me what it is that troubles you," she said quietly, her hands slowly soaping his chest. "Is it the ashfall?"

His throat tightened and he shook his head. "It changes nothing. Whether winter comes early or never does, I will not let you die."

"And I will try very hard to stay alive. So it is not that, then. Is it this sensitivity to magics that you have? For you scowl so fiercely whenever it occurs . . ." Her wet fingers came up to trace the scowl he wore now and a thread of laughter came to her voice. "Or whenever it is mentioned.

Why does it bother you so? Usually you would either take full interest or have no care at all. So why does it trouble you?"

He caught her hand, the hollow of his chest aching. "I never wish to be as Varrin was."

"Why? Would it be so terrible?"

For a long moment Aerax could not answer. Yet he'd not answered her before, when the red fever had come through Koth and he'd taken his place in the palace. There, she'd also asked what had troubled him . . . and unable to tell her, *unwilling* to tell her, he'd pushed her away.

Never could he again. Voice thick, he asked her, "What do you hope our marriage to be?"

"Little different than what we have now," she said quietly. "Never could we be only friends, Aerax, yet the finest of friends we are still—though we would have that without marriage. There will be time spent in the bed, but we would also have that without marriage. There will be helping each other, as you helped me when all seemed so lost. But we would have that without marriage, too. And always I will love you, with or without marriage. So if there is any difference, it is only that we are no longer Aerax and Lizzan, two people who have come together. Instead we are Aerax *and* Lizzan, two people who *are* together, a joining and a sharing in full." A smile came to her voice. "Though I think we have that without marriage, too."

A sharing in full. "I think you have given that to me. But I have not given that to you."

"Do you speak of your purpose?"

"I should tell you what it is before we marry," he said hoarsely. "But I fear you might not wish to marry me if I do."

"Never fear that."

"Even though I might be Koth's destroyer?" Gritting his teeth, he shook his head. "The Destroyer said that only he could bear the burden of what must be done. I recognize myself in that. And I am certain that what I must do is right, but uncertain that you will forgive me for it. So perhaps I am not so right after all."

"It is *not* the same," said Lizzan fiercely. "You will sink Koth, but you will not slaughter the people who live there. That is *all* the difference."

Tension gripped his every muscle. "You know what I must do?"

"I do. Though I don't know why. But Aerax"—she flicked a bit of water into his face—"you suggested to your uncle an evacuation? *Pfft.* You, who do not care for anything that happens in the royal court, involve yourself enough to suggest that to him? Obviously you only hoped to move people off the island so they would not be killed when you sink it."

Never had his heart seemed so near to bursting with emotion. Already she had guessed. And still she loved him. "You would not stop me? For only you could."

"I trust your heart and your reason. But as you have eased my burden, so I would always share yours."

Aerax was silent but only because he could not immediately speak. So this was to be their marriage. Always she had accepted him. Had spoken his name, had seen him. And *still* she saw him. *Still* she accepted him and trusted him. Even though he'd kept so much from her and it had hurt her so badly.

"You are the finest of all things, Lizzan," he told her in a raw voice.

"That is you," she said, pressing a kiss to the side of his neck. "But I will let you believe it is me."

He breathed out a laugh, sliding down the length of the tub until his head rested against her shoulder and he could better see her face. "Do you want to hear the truth of Varrin and Koth? You may not wish to. For when you know, it will burden your heart."

"Do I choose truth or comfort?" Indecision warred over her expression before she presented to him that stubborn jut of her chin. "I will hear it. Is all of the legend a lie?"

"Not all. Varrin labored in the stables and the mines and

the great hall, and learned to use magic. And as the world froze, he found Rani and spoke to her about uncovering Enam's eye. He forged her new fingers and loved her—but there the difference begins, because that love was either not returned or not accepted. Her duty stood between them, so Rani told him she must leave. But Varrin wouldn't let her go."

Lizzan frowned. "How did he stop her?"

"In gratitude for saving the world, she'd given to him Nemek's braid, and he used it to tie her dragon to the mountain."

Her chest lifted on a sharp breath. "The same way that the dragon in the monastery was tied? Was that chain also made of Nemek's hair?"

"I expect so."

"That is why you said we must free the dragon?"

"And because it ought to be freed."

"Is it the same braid as Varrin's?"

He shook his head. "Though perhaps Varrin took the idea from those who built the monastery, or the Radrehi took the idea from him. They both lived in the same ancient times."

Nodding, Lizzan held him ever tighter. "And then?"

"Silver-fingered Rani begged of him to release her dragon, because all the while she was on Koth, people were dying—but they were not flown into the comfort of Temra's arms. And finally Varrin did, but only because she promised to return to him."

"But she didn't return," Lizzan said with certainty. "She wouldn't have. He'd shown to her who he was."

"She didn't," Aerax confirmed. "Varrin vowed that one day she would return to him, and tied the braid as a belt so that he would not age or die. He spent a thousand generations learning magic, ruling Koth, and building the crystal palace. And he was not true to Rani, as is said, and didn't beget heirs directly from his loins. He took many women to his bed and they bore his children."

Lizzan nodded. "No one of sense believed that part, anyway."

Then most of Koth had no sense. But Aerax only said, "All the while, Rani only returned to Koth to collect the souls of the dead, and his jealousy grew that she never returned for him."

"He sounds a true maggoty measle."

So he was. "Finally he prayed to Nemek to come and unbind his belt so that he could die, and Nemek came to him—but as in the legend, it was a trick. He bound their wrists and then stole all their hair from their head."

Lizzan frowned. "How did he cut it?"

"He did not cut it." Aerax's jaw clenched before he continued. "He peeled away their full scalp and then plucked the hairs from it."

She sucked in a breath, shaking her head in wordless horror before managing to say, "Why?"

"To finish the crystal palace, which he'd built for one purpose—as a trap for Rani. He knew the hair was strong enough to bind her, for it had bound the sun god. But after what he'd done to her dragon and to Nemek, he knew she would never trust him or come on her own. So to lure her, he slaughtered everyone in Koth except for his heirs, and imprisoned their souls beneath the crystal palace. Yet she knew it was a trap, and still she didn't come—though all their names he'd written into a book and shouted each night into the wind, so as to taunt her with all the souls she left in torment."

"That is why the other gods attacked Koth," Lizzan breathed. "And why Vela threw the moonstone."

Aerax nodded. "Hoping to destroy the crystal palace—or to kill Varrin, because he no longer wore the belt that had protected him. And it is true that he was near death as the waters began to fill the crater. But he did not bind his essence to the island so that it would rise, Lizzan. He instead bound the souls of the dead to the island."

For a few breaths she was silent, as if taking that in. "Then what happened to him?"

Aerax shrugged. "He did not become a god. I suspect he only lived long enough to tell the story he wanted everyone to believe—and to tell his heirs what must be done to keep the island afloat."

"Then silver-fingered Rani finally kept her promise and returned for him," Lizzan said with vicious glee. "I hope that reunion did not go as he thought it would."

As did Aerax. "We cannot know that part."

"I suppose not." She leaned her head against his. "So you would free all of those souls still trapped there in torment. How could I not also believe that is the right thing?"

She still did not fully understand. "Lizzan," he said hoarsely. "That island has been a trap for thousands of generations, and the same spell that imprisoned their souls in the crystal palace still imprisons every Kothan who dies there."

Her body stiffened behind his, her breath trembling. "Still?"

Clasping her hand, he nodded. "In a chamber beneath the crystal palace, you can hear them scream. They are trapped in the crystal. As wraiths are trapped in their corrupted forms."

"All of them?" Her voice broke. "My father?"

"And my mother," he said thickly.

She pressed her face into his shoulder and began to cry. Throat aching, he waited for the storm to pass, and knew what would follow.

Sheer determination. She lifted her head and said, "So this is my purpose, too. As Vela must have seen. She knew full well that this was a path I would have taken anyway."

He frowned. "What do you mean by that?"

"Oh, Aerax—do you not see? Vela threw a moonstone to free those souls, but she failed. Now I am tasked to protect you while you finish what she started. And so I will." She threaded her fingers through his, their hands clasped over his heart. "You should also tell this story to the others. All of Koth should know the truth."

"Even if they believed it, telling would mean their deaths."

"You told me."

"And no harm would I ever let come to you." Sighing,

Aerax said, "Not all of Varrin's descendants accepted what Koth is. There are some who would have destroyed the prison, and still other heirs who have told the truth after they learned what was beneath the crystal palace. They were executed by their kings, as were all the people whom they told, whether those people believed it or not. Those stories are written for the heirs as a warning—and I would have risked myself, Lizzan, but I would not have risked you. But now you are away from Koth."

"As are Lady Junica and Degg."

But they would not always be. "Let me think on it."

She nodded and held him tighter. "That is a true burden. It hurts to know that you were not only thrust into a prince's role after the red fever but had to bear so much more. So young you were, Aerax. It is no wonder that second heirs are always of at least a queen's age. We are both near that age now, and I still do not feel full prepared for what I have learned."

A new ache opened up in his heart, for what she'd learned was not all he had to tell her. "There is more."

She gave a short laugh and then drew a shaky breath. "How much more?"

"This, I will never tell anyone else. I hope that you do not either, for just as you were blamed for what you shouldn't have been, so this might also put blame where it does not belong—and it is regarding what happened on the King's Walk."

Her fingers tightened on his, her body growing tense. "Of that night?"

He nodded. "Varrin could not tie and untie a knot made of Nemek's hair, so he instead used a spell to bind the braids that make the prison. The spell is a lock, and the blood used to cast it is a key that must be turned each day. Only the snow-haired ruler and the heir are ever to know the spell, and I was taught it when my uncle told me the truth about Varrin."

"So you already know a little magic," she said softly.

"But it is not magic that I would wish to know." How to

keep all those souls imprisoned. "And although I am not truly in line for the throne, Icaro wished for his daughter to be the heir in all ways. But he taught to her the spell without fully telling her the truth of Varrin. So when she cast it, no strength did the spell have . . . and some of the souls escaped before Icaro cast it again with his own blood."

She was utterly still behind him. "They were the wraiths?"

"I believe so. I did not know then," he told her. "I did not learn until after you were exiled, when the princess asked me what she might have done wrong that her father no longer let her cast the spell. The fault is Icaro's, not hers—but she might blame herself. And certainly Koth would."

Lizzan's throat worked as she nodded. "So they would. Now sit up and I will wash your hair."

So he would. In a moment. Gently he asked, "Are you well?"

Tears gleamed in her eyes but she nodded again. "Though I wish I had a drink. Instead I must think on all of this for a while."

"Do you wish me to go?"

She shook her head. "But give to me a few moments."

As she washed him. So she would not be alone. Only alone with her thoughts. Obediently he sat up, with all his being focused behind him as she began to lather his shoulders. Full aware he was of every silent tear that fell, of the shift within her from grief to rage to hurt before turning toward acceptance.

Then turning toward him, as she pressed hot and open-mouthed kisses to the side of his neck. "Will you be unrestrained?"

Finally. Need hardened his shaft to steel. "I will," he said gruffly.

He felt her smile against his skin. "Here in the bath?"

"Not this time." After years of waiting, Aerax had no patience to deal with interruptions. He slid forward to give her more room to move. "Go to the bed and wait for me in the manner you wish to be fucked. All else will be as I want."

Her breath shuddered. Water sloshed as she rose behind

him, and he turned as she bent for a drying cloth sitting on a nearby bench, offering a teasing glimpse of the lush cleft between her thighs. With a hungry growl, he caught her hips, steadying her when his movement in the bath might have made her slip.

She went utterly still, her muscles quivering beneath his grip in the moment before he licked through the seam of her cunt. Her moan filled the air, and then she gave a cry that was as hot and sweet as the taste of her when he suckled hard upon her clit.

When her thighs began to shake, he drew back. "To the bed."

No argument did she give. Swiftly she left the bath and wrapped the cloth around her hips, concealing what was truly the finest of all asses, no matter what Lizzan said of his. Slowly Aerax followed the trail of her wet footprints, the sultry flavor of her need on his tongue.

Never would he forget how she waited for him, on her knees at the edge of the bed, braced on her elbows and ass upraised, as if the pleasure her cunt would give was an offering to him. Yet it was Aerax who would worship her on this altar of a bed, and he knew not what Vela had meant when she'd told him to become what he truly was—but his own meaning he found in Lizzan. He was the man who would do anything to see her safe. He was the man who would protect her with his very life. He was the man who would love her until the sky burned Temra to ash.

He was Lizzan's. Fully and truly Lizzan's.

Nothing else Aerax ever became would mean more than that.

And if there was pleasure to offer, it would be his to give. He'd told her to wait in the manner that she wished to be fucked, so no time did he waste before sinking full deep into the hot grip of her cunt. The sound she made was half gasp and half scream, her spine arching until her breasts pressed into the bed. Bending over her with his weight braced on his left hand, with his right hand Aerax played with her clit and his hips began a slow thrust.

"In this way, Lizzan?" he grunted against her ear. "Is this how you wish to be fucked? Mounted by your feral prince until your tight cunt teases the seed from his cock?"

Her sheath clenched as if his every word were a lick to her clit. An urgent cry muffled against the sheets was her response, its silent echo the slippery wetness against his fingers.

"So hot and slick you are, it will not take long." Already pressure built at the base of his spine as he stroked deep, over and over, until her breaths were coming in sobbing gasps and her ass was grinding back against him. "Then I will kiss every span of your skin before having you on your back, legs widespread as I fuck into you again."

"And again and again," she demanded breathlessly, for it was Aerax who'd been restrained but only because one of them needed to be, and Lizzan had always been as hungry as he. "But harder now, Aerax. *Please.*"

Always he would give what she needed. Gritting his teeth, he surged deep, fingers working her clit to the same brutal rhythm, fighting the nearing of his own release though her need gleamed slick on his shaft, though the tight clutch of her sheath on the length of his arousal drove him full mad, though the slap of wet flesh and her breathy cries were sweeter than all of his dreams. Then she stiffened, gripping the sheets as if to pull away from the ecstasy bearing down on her and he dragged her back onto his cock as her cunt began seizing upon him. No longer did he hold back then, fucking in short savage thrusts until the force of his own need emptied his seed deep into her quivering flesh.

Lizzan lay beneath him, shuddering and then smiling when he pressed his lips to the nape of her neck, then began kissing his way down her spine.

Slowly he fulfilled his promise, kissing every span of her skin before spreading her thighs and sinking into her again.

And again and again, until even her mouth would barely stir his spent flesh, and the softest brush of his tongue on her oversensitized clit made her push him away. There they lay together, all quiet but for their breaths, until Lizzan made a sound of amusement.

He swept his fingers through her hair. "What is it?"

"It is no different," she said softly, lifting her head from his shoulder to look down at him. "Restrained and unrestrained. Always at the end, I feel in this same way."

That was truth. For although there was no greater physical pleasure than being inside her as she came on his cock, lying together with her now was the same as it had always been. All sweetness, all contentment.

"But I know the reason," she continued, fingers drifting through the hair on his chest and resting her palm over his heart. "Never have you been restrained in the pleasure you give to me, and never have you held back your heart. So always I end here in this way, so utterly satisfied and fully loved, the most blessed of all women."

As he was the most blessed of all men.

But so he would have also been, if all he'd ever known of Lizzan was a girl hacking at a tree, and if she'd only ever said his name the once. In that moment, he would have done anything for her. And so he still would.

Anything but let her go.

LIZZAN

Three days after she and Aerax were married, Lizzan awoke to a commotion from outside the inn. Feeling deliciously sore and well-fucked, she slipped out of bed and went to the shutters. Below, a parade of people and carts were coming from the direction of the monastery, their feet stirring up the ash blanketing the ground.

"Preter must have found them," she said as Aerax came up behind her.

And they were settling back in to the homes they'd left behind, as if the city were a winter boot that had gone unused for a few seasons. Lizzan and Aerax finally came down from their bedchamber, and she stopped on a sudden laugh when in the public room she saw Degg cutting a red elk's haunch into small pieces for Caeb, while the cat lounged lazily beside him.

Aerax snorted. "Did he make you hunt that, too?"

The councilor seemed too pleased by Caeb's acceptance to be affected by any teasing.

Around midday, the innkeeper returned to the inn, a jovial man glad of the coins their stay had earned in his absence and who promised them all a celebratory feast to welcome himself home.

Indeed, all around them seemed in a celebratory mood—but not so the alliance. It seemed to Lizzan that the low spirits at the table could not wholly be ascribed to the slaughter within the monastery. During their wedding feast, the mood had seemed lighter than now, though on this day thousands of people had been restored to their homes.

But listening to the conversation, she realized that everything the alliance hoped to accomplish here was no longer possible.

"Are there no monks left at all?" Lizzan asked Preter.

"Perhaps a few who have not yet made their way out of the maze," he said. "But there is no council with whom to make the alliance, and now no monastery in the north that can teach magic to those with an affinity for it."

With a heavy sigh, she looked to Kelir. "Was your friend among the people in the city—the one whose necklace was in the offering bowl?"

Face grim, the warrior shook his head. "There are some who recall seeing a Parsathean ride toward the monastery a full turn before the wraith came. But no one recalls seeing him leave."

Which meant little. He might have left. Or he might not have. "Do they know how a stone wraith came to be in the monastery? Did the monks create it and it escaped their control?"

"They only know that the monks warned them that a wraith threatened the city and brought them all into the monastery for their protection," said Preter. "All thought the wraith was locked outside. But it was already in with them."

"It was Goranik who created the wraith, after the monks taught to him the spell," said Saxcn in his rusty voice, drawing all eyes to him though he hardly looked up from his roast. "It is no surprise to me that after he got what he needed from them, my father then used it to destroy them. That is what he always does."

All around the table fell quiet. Then Tyzen asked, "You are Saxen of Lith?"

A nod confirmed it, and Saxen watched them now—not warily, Lizzan thought, but with a sort of resigned expectation that she'd likely worn on her own face every time she'd been driven from a village.

Unease deepened the silence from the others.

Except for Seri, who frowned and looked to each of their expressions. "Why does everyone look at him in that way?"

"Because I am a monster, dragon-rider," said Saxen. "And also a monster's son."

She eyed him, gaze lingering on his scars. "You seem more like a monster's meal that has been chewed up and spit out."

He gave a short, rough laugh. "I am that, too."

Tyzen asked, "But what truly happened to you?"

His gaze returned to the moonstone-eyed prince. "Fifteen years past, my father traded me to the viswan monks in exchange for yet another spell—one that allowed a demon to possess his flesh."

Dismay and confusion passed over Preter's expression. "Did he intend to die? Or did the viswan betray him?"

"It was not a reanimation. He invited the demon to walk within him so that his magic would be strengthened by its power."

The monk's mouth dropped open and he passed a hand over his face, as if in disbelief. "He and the demon share his *living* flesh?"

Saxen nodded.

Kelir's eyes narrowed. "The viswan resided at this monastery?"

Shaking his head, Saxen said, "I was traded again to Radreh."

"What did the monks want with you?" Preter asked.

He gave a thin smile. "There was a promise of freeing me . . . after they got from me all the blood they needed."

"To strengthen their own magics," Preter said with a look of disgust.

"Were they doing the same with the dragon?" Seri asked.

"That I cannot say," the monk said. "I don't see how they would take anything from that dragon without it allowing them to."

Though she would be happy to speak of the dragon all day, Lizzan had been listening with an increasing dread weighing her heart. For it was not enough that Goranik was a demon. An even greater danger he posed now. "After leaving here, Goranik must have returned north, for we know he did not go south. Which suggests that after the slaughter at the King's Walk, he went to the viswan. Perhaps seeking the wraith spell there? But the viswan must not have known it, for they came to this monastery instead . . . and then returned to Koth with the spell in hand. For he had *seen* that there were ice wraiths on the island."

"And realized that Koth would have no protection against stone wraiths," Aerax finished grimly.

Face bloodbare, Lady Junica looked to Saxen. "Does your father still serve the Destroyer?"

"Always he will. Whatever he does now is most likely in anticipation of the Destroyer's return."

Then whatever was planned, they could not allow. Lizzan looked to Preter. "How do we kill a demon?"

"It is not known for certain."

"But demons *have* been killed." To Ardyl, she said, "I did not fully hear the tale of your Scourge. How did your people stop it?"

Ardyl grimaced faintly. "By uniting our tribes."

"But what method? What weapon?"

"It is unknown," Kelir said, looking abashed. "The songs only say that the Scourge was defeated by uniting the tribes."

But that was not the only story told of demons. Lizzan knew of one recently slain, the tale not yet warped by legend and time. "It is said that in Blackmoor, that demon was trapped in Stranik's tunnel until the Destroyer reanimated it as a tusker—and that Queen Mala used its own ivory tusk to stab through its eye."

"My mother used a blade," Tyzen said. "When the Destroyer reanimated her mother, she struck the demon-queen down with her sword."

Hope rose. "Was the sword of a special material or design?"

Tyzen shook his head and hope deflated. There was nothing similar between any of the stories.

"What of using the island as a trap?" Kelir said.

"Does a demon drown?" Lady Junica challenged him.

The warrior shrugged. "Perhaps one who inhabits living flesh would."

"Then would stone wraiths drown?" Degg asked. "That trap would destroy our island for nothing."

"Not for nothing," Aerax said. "No matter whether it would kill Goranik or not, the island must sink. But it is worth the attempt to take a demon with it."

Lady Junica frowned at him. "Why 'must' it sink?"

Aerax gestured to Tyzen. "He said that, ten years past, his mother heard a story that made Varrin into a monster. Who she heard was Icaro, telling to me the story of how Koth truly came to be."

Heart in her throat, Lizzan listened as Aerax told them what he'd learned beneath the crystal palace. She watched as disbelief and rejection chased across the councilor's expressions.

When he'd finished, Lady Junica shook her head. "You say that Varrin did not become a god?"

Bluntly Aerax said, "I say that all your family is imprisoned there."

She flinched back. Visibly shaken, she looked to Degg with an imploring gaze, as if asking him to tell her it could not be true. "Do you believe this?"

Gravely the other councilor said, "How can I not? The truth is in the King's Walk."

"The battle there?" Lizzan asked.

"That there *is* a King's Walk." Degg's jaw was set. "And that as every Kothan ruler nears death, they pass the throne to their heir and leave the island. Always before it seemed to me a ruler's wisdom to give over the crown before they begin to decline with age. But in truth, they were escaping the same torment that every other Kothan would know."

"So it must sink." With tears in her eyes, Lady Junica looked to Preter. "Unless you can think of any way that the souls can be freed but the island can be kept afloat?"

"Perhaps there is a way," the monk said slowly, his expression tightening. "But if what Prince Aerax says is true, then we may have it wrong. Why would Goranik send a few stone wraiths to slaughter those on the island, when there are thousands of generations of souls trapped there, and who can create an army of stone wraiths for the Destroyer? He would only need access to the chamber where they are imprisoned and some of your king's blood."

Lizzan felt all blood drain from her face. An army of stone wraiths, when only *one* had slaughtered a monastery full of monks. Against so many, even a dragon could not defeat them. The only hope was that Icaro and Koth were holding out against Goranik and the viswan.

"Could he be stopped?"

Preter nodded. "If the souls were freed before he cast the spell."

Abruptly she stood, Aerax rising beside her. A full turn of the moon still lay between them and the island.

And no time could they waste.

"Aerax and I will leave now for Koth." Heart pounding, Lizzan looked to Saxen. "Will you come with us? We'll find a horse and armor for you, because we may need your strength to defeat your father."

"If you will have me, I will come." Saxen rose from his bench, then turned back toward the table and ripped a leg from the roast to take with him. "For the ride."

Nodding, Kelir stood. "Let us all ride."

CHAPTER 26

LIZZAN

An empty road was still a dangerous road, and it did not take long to discover why. On his return to Koth from Radreh, Goranik had poisoned the forests and fields surrounding the road with spells that raised bramble beasts, reanimating the spirits of dead animals with wood and vines, as if the very forest itself came alive to attack them.

No more could Aerax and Caeb hunt, because every beast they brought down rose again. Only small animals did Caeb eat, for a bramble rabbit that a horse could stomp flat was easier to defeat than a giant sloth with long curving claws. Yet the forest was alive with predators that had no knowledge or care of spells, and prey was transformed into deadly predators themselves—from worms that became crawling twigs that would invade their bedrolls to shorthaired mammoths that became charging horrors of piercing thornteeth and massive treelegs.

Every day became nearly as harrowing as the monastery—though at least the bramble beasts could be defeated by blade and by fire. Still, it seemed to Lizzan that the full turn was spent racing north until they could go no farther each day, and then after a too-brief rest, they were racing north again.

It was with tears and sheer relief that she finally glimpsed in the distance the lake surrounding Koth. Under skies that were only yellow and gray since the eruption, the water seemed dull steel instead of brilliantly blue, yet she had no care at all . . . except that there was no escape from the bramble beasts, which meant that Goranik was also near to Koth.

At speed they rode toward the King's Walk, yet they had just crested the final hill when the sight before Lizzan struck her silent with disbelief.

So many rumors there'd been that Koth was abandoned—though it had not been when Aerax and the councilors had left, nearly two seasons past.

But it was.

In the outlands near the King's Walk, a huge swath of forest had been cleared, and the logs stacked in an enormous circle to create a high wall of timber. Inside the wall were tents packed together in rows—as if an army camped there. But Koth's army had never numbered so many. Instead it seemed that every Kothan citizen had sought refuge within those timber walls.

"What has happened?" Lady Junica looked ahead in horror.

"Let us find out," Aerax said grimly, riding forward.

They had nearly reached the wall when a thunderous cracking through the trees heralded the charge of a bramble beast—a longhorn bison that could knock a horse off its hooves before ripping it to pieces. With a roar, Caeb leapt upon its back, claws tearing the beast apart and fangs slashing until it was but a shambling collection of shredded greens and broken branches. Caeb swatted at a leaf that had peeled away from the bison's face and returned to trot alongside Lizzan and Aerax, and then a murmur from Tyzen set the remains afire.

"This way!" Toward them galloped a pair of soldiers in shining mail. "Prince Aerax! Councilors! This way!"

She knew the soldiers—Joha and Nil. Because she had no wish to fight with them, Lizzan raised the hood of her cloak, which had faded nearly to white on the journey from Radreh. Riding slightly behind Aerax, she slowed her mount as the soldiers fell in beside Lady Junica.

"What has happened here, soldier?"

"A demon came. No blade could harm him, no fire, no bludgeon. The king ordered us to evacuate the people and he retreated to the crystal palace with his guard. He is there now under siege, while we are under siege from these beasts," said Joha, his gaze searching behind them. "Does the Krimathean army follow you, my lady?"

"They have taken the plains road north. They will not arrive for another full turn of the moon."

Despair crossed the soldier's face. "We are near out of food. Whenever a group leaves to hunt and forage, only half their number return. We send out all the fishing boats we have, but they do not catch enough for everyone."

"We have brought friends who can help with the bramble beasts," said Lady Junica, gesturing to where the bison was but a smoldering pile on the ground. "But let us get inside that wall before another beast begs for a demonstration."

Together they rode past the gates, into air thickened with the scent of smoked fish and the stench of waste.

Lady Junica looked to Aerax. "This is not what we expected to find."

"If the king still holds the palace, this is better than what we expected to find," Aerax said. "But let us gather what information we can and meet at . . ." His eyes met Lizzan's before he looked to Nil. "Where will I find Yuna or Farzan, both of Lightgale?"

"Lightgale—" Nil's gaze narrowed on Lizzan before flaring wide with rage.

"Do *not* say what comes to your tongue, soldier," Degg snapped. "Answer the prince."

A muscle ticced in his jaw before he tore his gaze from Lizzan and settled on Aerax again. "They are likely at the far south wall."

"Your Highness," Degg added pointedly.

"Your Highness," the soldier gritted out, but no care would Aerax have for what the soldier thought, Lizzan knew, and had already turned away from him.

"We will meet there," Aerax said to the councilors, then shifted in his saddle to glance back at Kelir.

"We will find you by asking where your cat went," said the warrior, his shoulders covered by a light fur. No more did the Parsatheans wear only their linens, for though it was near midsummer, each day was colder than the one before—and it was often midday before they could no longer see each breath they exhaled. "First we will discover what are the defenses in this camp."

Aerax nodded. Quickly Lizzan urged her horse south with Aerax riding beside her, Caeb trailing behind. The expressions of everyone they passed seemed etched with misery, until they saw Aerax. Then hope erased the lines of despair on their faces, and joyously they called out to each other that the Krimathean army had come at last.

Throat tight and hood up, Lizzan said nothing. As they neared the south wall, Caeb loped ahead along the muddied path to search for her mother's scent. The tents in this area were not so tightly packed together, but only because here were the people that most of Koth did not want to see or hear or be near.

Caeb stopped before a large tent that seemed as if two had been stitched together. Heart thundering, Lizzan dismounted and then looked to Aerax when he said, "I'll tend to your horse. Go on."

The finest of all men. Swiftly she kissed him and then hurried to the tent's flap. Inside the air was warm and redolent with the scent of medicinal herbs, a fragrance that always powerfully reminded Lizzan of her mother's parents, and of days spent in their healers' chambers.

The tent was divided by a sheet of bark that had been flattened and pieced together with string—separating a healer's space from the living space, Lizzan realized.

Her mother bustled in from the living space, her black

hair simply braided, her tunic clean but her features thin and tired. Still her voice was as strong and brisk as always when she began, "My son is away, attending to a birth—but if your ailment is simple, I can likely treat it for you. Otherwise, give to me your . . . name. . . ." She stopped as Lizzan drew back her hood, her reddened hands over her mouth, blue eyes filling. "Lizzan?"

"I am here." With throat aching and her chest a solid lump of emotion. "I am here."

"Oh, you should not be, but I do not care." With a sob, Yuna flew to her, clutching her tight before drawing back to look up into Lizzan's face. "I am not sorry. But did anyone see you? They will not—"

"All is well." With a tear-filled smile, Lizzan glanced over her shoulder as Aerax ducked into the tent. "I am married to someone who is above Kothan law."

"Aerax." Yuna held out her hand to him, then instead flung her arms around him and held him tight. "So glad I am to see you both. All three of you," she corrected on a laugh when Caeb's big head pushed into the tent.

She moved aside the bark divider to offer them more room and continued, "Farzan is away. He is *always* away. No one has use for a magistrate here, but they all have need of a healer—though of course most will never admit who attended to them," her mother added wryly.

"And Cernak?" Lizzan asked, her heart aching.

Worry filled her mother's expression, followed immediately by the stout reassurance that Lizzan knew so well, as if her mother would make things be all right simply through force of will. "He is with the king in the crystal palace. But they must be safe. The island still stands, so they are safe." She shook her head. "But I do not know for how much longer we will last, here or there. The walls of this camp do not keep out the beasts that can climb, full half the people are sick with a cough, and food is more scarce by the day. And a message came by falcon two days past that there were cracks in the palace doors and to see if there was word of the Krimatheans' approach. But now you are here, Aerax. Do they come?"

"They are coming," said Lizzan, who could not bear to completely crush her mother's hope. "But we have arrived with warriors and a monk who knows of magic, and will see if we can stop the demon before that. First I need to know, Mother . . . where did Father come by this medallion?"

Her mother's lips parted as Lizzan drew the chain from beneath the neck of her tunic. Drawing closer, she whispered painfully, "I thought it was lost when your father was slain."

"It was," said Lizzan. "But Vela herself returned it to me."

Yuna's gaze shot to hers, as if searching for a jest. But no doubt or surprise did Lizzan see in her mother's eyes—as if her mother easily accepted that a goddess had spoken to her.

That did not seem at all like her mother, who had a magistrate's habit of questioning and interrogating the truth of everything.

"How did my father come by it?"

"He came by it through your soft heart." A sad smile curved her mouth when she rubbed the medallion between her fingers, as if caught by a memory. "He had gone with my parents as escort when they took their healing wagon into the outlands. I was not there, though I might have otherwise been, because I was heavy with Farzan."

Who was nearly four years younger than Lizzan. So little more than a toddling child she must have been. "This was during the Bitter Years?"

Her mother nodded. "Already you talked of becoming a soldier. You always talked of it. But Cernak was already on that path and we thought if you spent time with my parents, you might take an interest in healing. Especially after you saw how many needed it."

Something they had attempted for years afterward, too. "You thought my soft heart would sway me, even then?"

"We did not know then the depth of your stubbornness," her mother said, and grinned when Aerax grunted an agreement. But her grin quickly faded. "Everyone whom my parents passed in their wagon on the outland roads and every village they went to, they would ask if anyone suffered from an affliction so they might help. So when they came upon an old traveler sitting on a fallen log at the side of the road, you went up to them and asked if they had an affliction. And the traveler told you that they were in good health, but were fiercely afflicted by a bothersome fly that kept tickling their nose. A soldier then you were, as you went after the enemy fly until it was flattened."

"I have no memory of this at all," Lizzan said, and her mother laughed.

"Why would you? For you to stop and help someone is as unremarkable as the sun rising every morning."

"To someone who suffers the cold or fears the dark," Aerax said, "the rising sun is a remarkable thing."

"So it is." Yuna gave to him a quick smile, but then her gaze returned to Lizzan and her breath shuddered, as if in remembered fear. "Then the old traveler asked you to scratch an itch that the fly had left on their nose, for they could not. That was when your father saw that the traveler's hands were tied behind their back. He knew who they were then—and they were wearing their old and withered face, so if you touched them, you would be diseased. He shouted for you to turn away, that it wasn't safe . . . but you scratched the traveler's nose."

"Nemek," Lizzan breathed. Still bound by the hair Varrin had knotted around their wrists.

How many thousands of generations had they wandered in that way?

Her heart hurt at the very thought as her mother continued, "Your father was in terror. So he made the offering of a coin and put it into their bound hands, hoping that they would immediately heal whatever disease they had given to you, but they instead pinched the coin flat and plucked out strands of their silvery hair, for it reached in a tangle down their back."

Regrown, after Varrin had scalped them. But of course Nemek's scalp would heal, Lizzan realized. Easily they would heal themselves.

"From the hair and the coin, they made that necklace for you—and said to you that any soldier with such a soft heart would need a hard skin."

And so the necklace had saved her on the King's Walk. But it was not the medallion that had done it.

It was the chain. Lizzan nearly laughed. The chain that had almost choked her to death when it had caught on the woodstalker's talons and had not broken.

"But he did not give the necklace to Lizzan then?" Aerax asked.

Yuna shook her head. "He feared it was also diseased, for they had made it with their old and withered hands. But he knew better than to refuse a gift from a god, so he wore the necklace himself rather than give it to Lizzan, and always fearing the disease would come—though it didn't, not even when the red fever took my parents." Her voice thickened. "And never did we tell you, Lizzan, because we knew that you would take that diseased gift upon yourself."

"It was no disease," Lizzan told her. "Nemek's old face is the healer."

"But . . ." Her mother blinked. "That is not right."

"It is true. I met a woman who saw Nemek's birthplace. The beauty is the disease, the withered the healer."

Shaking her head, Yuna said, "It cannot be. Even in Varrin's story, he sees their withered face and knows he was betrayed."

"It was the healer who came to him in good faith. It was Varrin who betrayed them." At the sound of approaching horses, Lizzan caught her mother's hands. "And there is so much more I would tell you. But we have friends who come to discuss how we will destroy Goranik. Will you give to them a place here?"

"Always. Always, Lizzan." Fingers squeezing Lizzan's, Yuna looked to Aerax. "After her father and I spent so much time trying to separate you from Lizzan, you may not believe me when I say now that your marriage is the finest news I have had of late, and I am full glad that you found each other again."

"Always we would have," Aerax said, his dark gaze catching Lizzan's. "And I will allow nothing to separate us again."

Though he left the remainder unspoken, Lizzan heard what he truly meant. *Not even death.*

Lizzan full well agreed. Because she had no intention of dying.

And whatever battle lay ahead, it would be the demon who lay dead at the end.

With all the southern alliance party, the Kothan councilors, Saxen, Lizzan, Aerax, Lizzan's mother, and Caeb stuffed into the tent, they nearly stretched the sides at the seams. Which was how Lizzan felt, too, as she listened to the others share what they'd seen and heard. No more room was there inside her but a need to destroy Goranik, to finish what he'd begun at the King's Walk—and end the threat he still posed to everyone she loved.

"King Icaro and his eldest daughter remained on the island with the battle masters and full palace guard," said Lady Junica. "The queens and the other royal children are in this camp."

"Where the walls are hardly a defense," Kelir said. "They have barely enough soldiers to keep watch, and no proper weapons to fight the bramble beasts aside from a few axes. They are fortunate the demon didn't make revenants instead, or there would be no one left."

Ardyl frowned. "Why didn't the demon make revenants? They spread their corruption with a single bite, so these forests would have been teeming with the ravenous undead by now, and we would not have survived so many on the road."

"Perhaps Goranik can't," Preter said. "Those revenants are made when a demon's flesh and blood corrupt an animal's— but always those demons are reanimated corpses themselves. Here the demon inhabits living flesh."

"Then let us hope that also makes him easier to kill," Aerax said, his big body crouched in the corner of the tent.

Nearly sitting on his lap and with her fingers idly stroking Caeb's big head, Lizzan nodded. "Can the spell that raises the bramble beasts be cleansed from the forest?"

"It can," Preter said. "Though he must have cast it many times between here and Radneh. To track down the source of every spell would take time—but killing him will break the spell, as well."

"So they only need to hold out against the bramble beasts until Goranik is dead?" Tyzen asked.

The monk nodded.

"Then the question still is—how do we kill him?" Lizzan asked. "The Parsathean riders were united. If that is a requirement, then so we are united, too, hunched here in this tent and planning our attack." That drew a laugh, but she was full serious. "Queen Mala was on a quest, but also seeking alliances as she traveled—and she found one with the king of Blackmoor."

"And when my mother slew the demon-queen," Tyzen said, "it was the very beginning of the alliance that brought Parsathe and the five realms together."

"So that is a requirement met," she said. "And though your Parsathean queen has forbidden you from going with us to the island, you will be here protecting Kothans while the rest of us are at the crystal palace. We are united in the purpose of saving these people."

No laughter this time. Only nods of agreement—and then Kelir slanted a glance at Ardyl, who seemed to take that look as a prompt to say, "It is likely that Yvenne forbade us because she knew that if anything were to happen to us on the island, we would not know the comfort of Temra's arms. But we will take the risk."

Lizzan shook her head. "Better, I think, to stay and help

protect the walls." She looked to Aerax, who nodded his agreement. "Aerax knows the palace and is the only one of us who can open Varrin's prison. I wear Nemek's chain, which will help protect me as I protect him—and Hanan's blood runs through Saxen's veins. If we cannot do what must be done, better that you are here to help these people run."

Though his jaw clenched, as if unhappy with the answer, Kelir must have seen the sense of it. With a short nod, he agreed.

"What else have we to compare?" Lizzan asked. "One demon killed with a steel sword, another with an ivory tusk. It is said that Mala stabbed the demon's eye."

"After she first cut off its head," Seri put in. "When we were in Krimathe, at the feast that they put out for us, I heard her tell the story. She cut off the demon tusker's head, but still it kept moving. So she then stabbed through its heart, but still it continued trying to kill her. The eye was the final attempt."

Beside her, Tyzen sat up straighter. "My mother cleaved through the demon-queen's skull."

"So it is the brain that must be destroyed?"

"But the soldiers here said their blades could not even slice Goranik's skin," said Ardyl. "So it was true of the demon-queen, too. Many warriors attempted to. But only her daughter managed to injure her at all."

"Though not even right away," Tyzen said. "In our tower, my mother told this story to us over and over again—that she could knock the demon-queen back with a boot or a fist but couldn't slice through her skin. And my mother was desperate, because for four full days she'd battled the demon without a pause, and the demon's sword had often found its mark. So her body bled from a thousand wounds and she could feel herself failing, and said she was near death in that final rush, with her own blood streaming down her arms and dripping from the blade of her sword. She made a final prayer to Vela and struck—and her blade cut through the demon's arm. While it looked to her, stunned, she split its skull with a single blow."

"So we pray to Vela?" Aerax gave a short laugh. "But no power does the goddess have on the island."

Lizzan might attempt it anyway, but prayer was not what she took from that story. "So it can be harmed by its own flesh and blood? The demon tusker was killed by its own tusks. And a demon-queen was killed by her daughter, but only after the daughter's blood was upon the blade."

All looked to Saxen, who held himself apart from everyone crowded near him as best he could. In the full turn upon the road, rarely had he spoken, and never did he touch anyone. Even if someone merely handed to him a bowl, he took great care not to brush skin against skin.

A muscle worked in his jaw and his eyes closed. "So I am to be bled again?"

Lizzan's heart clenched. "I am so very sorry."

After a long moment, he nodded. "It will be for good reason. And at least it will be of my choosing."

"That cannot be how they killed the Scourge," said Seri. "It was made of volcanic rock, and had no flesh and blood."

Lizzan gave to her a dour look. "Do not pester me with complications, dragon-rider. Goranik is not made of rock, and the blood gives us a hopeful place to begin."

"So it does," she said with a sudden grin. "And if Ran Bantik killed the demon Scourge by waiting until a chunk of its body fell to the ground and then throwing the rock at its eye, perhaps that is why none of our songs say how it was slain. Instead of uniting, the tribes might have taken to throwing rocks at each other."

That image drew a few chuckles, and it was into the sudden lighter mood that Lady Junica said to Aerax, "If you succeed in killing this demon before he casts his spell, perhaps hold off on sinking the island so that these people can return for their belongings and—"

"I will not hold off," Aerax said.

She frowned at him. "I do not suggest that we leave the

souls imprisoned. I have as much reason as anyone to wish for their freedom. But if the demon is dead, then no immediate danger is there, and we might search for a way to free them without destroying the island and all that Kothans know."

"I will not wait," said Aerax again. "All of the island will be empty. No better time will there be."

"And you make this decision for all of us?"

"I do. For I know what will happen if I delay. There will be meetings about when it should be done, and forever that day will be changed and extended, because someone will not be ready. There will be those who begin saying it is all lies, that I only hope to sink Koth in revenge for when I was nameless—and others will believe it is a lie because they *want* to believe it is one, and because it is easier to ignore the souls in torment than to start their lives anew."

Lady Junica shook her head. "But it is their family and loved ones who are trapped, too. Kothans will not allow their suffering to continue."

Aerax broke out in a full laugh. "Let me tell you of the Koth that I know. It is a Koth ruled by fear and self-interest. What punishment is there for speaking to someone whose name is not written in the books? What punishment is there for those who refuse to pretend they don't exist or for saying their name? A lashing? Imprisonment? A fine?"

The councilor blinked. "You know very well there is no punishment."

"No punishment except the scorn of their neighbors. And yet I was a boy full grown the first time someone other than my mother spoke my name. All of my life, Koth would not even acknowledge a *child* with the simple kindness of seeing him, because they feared what others might say." His big hand curved around Lizzan's side, and with her heart aching, she linked her fingers with his. "But there *were* others who spoke to me. Because no fear did they have of punishment for hurting someone who did not exist. So when I was a boy, they would tell me to come near, to go to my knees and open my mouth, to bend and spread my cheeks. And when my mother went to a magistrate, no crime could be reported and no help could she get, for I was not a person. That is Koth. Not only the ones who would have abused a child—and those I learned to avoid—but also those who looked the other way. Those who said nothing could be done. You think I will let them decide the fate of those who are tortured and in pain? You think I will let them decide my mother's fate? These people who look away from suffering out of fear, or greed, or for their own comfort?"

Caeb snarled into the silence that answered that question.

"I will not look away," Aerax snarled, too. "And I *will* sink the island, and care not if all of Koth hates me for it and calls me a villain. They ought to be full glad that I did not sink it while they were still upon it."

Her expression taut, Lady Junica nodded. Beside her, Degg the Red rose and silently left the tent—as if in full rejection of what Aerax had said.

Perhaps they were not so united, then.

But even the others began to stir into conversation again, Degg returned carrying his pack—and dropped a leather pouch on Seri's lap as he returned to his seat.

"I believe those are yours," he told her.

The girl gasped, her eyes filling with tears as she withdrew silver claws from the pouch. She clutched them to her chest. "Wherever did you find them?"

"I stole them from the bathhouse," Degg said, and all went tensely silent. "After we secured Krimathe's help, the intention was to kill Prince Aerax on the journey home. Captain Uland would do it and make it seem an accident. But then the prince decided to return north on another road, the captain had to stay with the Krimatheans, and so it would fall to me. I planned to poison the prince's cat after he trusted me to feed him, and then I would lead the prince to him—and while he grieved, strike with those silver claws so that it looked as if he was killed by his own cat."

Who might have killed Degg now if not for the firm grip Lizzan had taken of his ruff . . . though she was tempted to let go. "Why?"

"He was always with the battle masters, and he'd never taken interest in courtly lessons—but of late, he'd been making more suggestions to the king . . . such as the evacuation. I believed he was preparing to kill Icaro and take the throne."

Lady Junica frowned at him fiercely. "Were you under orders?"

"I was not. But there are many of us who cannot bear the thought of a feral prince becoming Koth's king." He lifted his hands, shame heavy in his voice. "But it has become clear to me since that he is the finest of all Kothans."

"Lizzan is the finest of all Kothans," Aerax said, his voice a low growl.

Degg's throat worked as he nodded. "I only hope that, whatever we rebuild, it is worthy of you both and what you do for us now, as you face this demon. And I will accept whatever punishment you choose." He glanced to Seri. "For the theft, too."

His body tense against hers, Aerax asked, "Did you ever give to Caeb a poison?"

The man shook his head.

"Then I care nothing of what you do or what happens to you," said Aerax.

Lizzan cared. She frowned at the councilor. "Why did you not follow through while on the road?"

Degg sighed. "I came to truly like the cat."

Who no longer liked him back. And never would trust him again. And who might one day kill him for what he'd intended to do to Aerax.

Which seemed to Lizzan fair enough to let Caeb decide in his own time, but more likely a magistrate such as her mother would take up the matter if Koth and the realm's laws survived what came next. For now, they had more pressing matters to attend.

Such as deciding the best way to return undetected to the island—and how soon they would leave.

CHAPTER 27

AERAX

Aerax did not pray to Vela, but that goddess seemed to turn the night in their favor as he sailed with Lizzan, Caeb, and the Lithan prince to the windward side of the island. For they were helped along by Preter's wind, and though the moon was high and full, Vela's face was covered by a thick blanket of clouds and they approached the island under concealment of full darkness.

From the shore, they stole their way though a silent village to his mother's inn, where they would wait for dawn.

Never before had Aerax truly understood Lady Junica's desperate arguments to save the island. Yet within the inn, looking out to his mother's garden and thinking of how many times he and Lizzan had played within these walls, knowing it all would soon be gone brought a soft ache to his chest. And as he took her to the bed where they'd watched so many others, where Aerax had learned all the things he used to please her, it also seemed fitting that they would be the last, as if the purpose of this place had been fulfilled.

Unrestrained his heart was with every kiss and touch. Unrestrained his body was as she urged him inside her again and again, until they were utterly spent and lying quietly together.

It was near dawn when she slipped from their warm bed, and he heard the splash of water in a basin, saw the gleam of a blade as she shaved the sides of her head. A full Kothan soldier again, though they would leave all their armor behind. Leathers and furs did not make so much noise as chain mail, and it was stealth that they would need this day.

When she'd finished and gathered the crown of her hair into a tail that fell the length of her back, Caeb came to rub his face to hers, then growled plaintively. With a quiet laugh, she slung her faded cloak around her shoulders and left the chamber with the cat to let him out the door.

More slowly Aerax dressed, and found her standing at the open shutters overlooking the garden.

Where a soft blanket of snow covered the ground. Dumped by the same clouds that had covered Vela's face and offered such welcome concealment—as if already, favor was turning away from them.

"Lizzan," Aerax said hoarsely, gripping her shoulders and spinning her to face him. Her skin was bloodbare and her eyes haunted by shadowy fear, but the jut of her chin was as stubborn as ever as she looked up at him. "Let us abandon this place and head south."

She gave a watery laugh and cupped his jaw in her hands. "Run now, when all our friends will be killed by stone wraiths? As the Destroyer returns, we will look away from all who suffer, and sit content somewhere instead of fighting. Is that our path?"

It could not be. Gritting his teeth against the pain filling his chest, Aerax pressed his forehead to hers. "You must promise me—"

"Never to leave you?" Her thumbs swept over his cheeks. "I swear that it will not be willingly. I will fight to stay with you as hard as you will fight to keep me."

"Then promise to always love me," he said from a raw

throat. "For if I must fight to keep you with me, then I will. And I will do *anything*, Lizzan. Whether it makes me villain or monster. I will become anything."

And Aerax knew very well what he would become, after he'd heard the story of the chain Lizzan wore—a man no different than Varrin, or any of the snow-haired kings who'd lived before.

"And always I will love you," she promised, pressing her trembling lips to his. Then on a shuddering breath, she buried her face in his neck. "This snow may also be a gift."

A broken laugh shook through him. "How?"

"So that I will have something to drink as we make our way to the crystal palace. I took a sip from the wineskin . . . but it is not water anymore."

Because Vela had no power here. He stiffened. "And your necklace?"

"Still protects me, or I might have cut my head to shreds with that dull razor." Her arms tightened around him. "But let me tell you, Aerax . . . I want to drink all of the ale in that wineskin. *All of it.* I thought for certain that I did not thirst so much anymore after all this time. But instead of thinking fully of what lies ahead, I keep imagining how sweet it would be to feel that warmth in my gut again. To dull the edge of all this fear and worry. So I am glad of the snow, that I can leave the wineskin behind until Vela begins purifying all that I drink again. And I am sorry that I'm not as strong as I thought I was," she finished in a whisper.

"Not as strong?" He caught her face, made her look up at him. "Would you blame a starving man for craving the food that will ease the pain in his belly? You crave what once helped ease the pain in your heart. Now you are besieged by fear and worry, but you do not drink because you know the harm that may come if we face Goranik while you are drunk. So you are leaving it behind. That requires more strength than giving in."

A sobbing little breath broke through her lips, but she gave a quavering smile and kissed him. "You ease the pain in my heart, Aerax."

"Given a choice, no other purpose would I have."

She sighed against his lips. "But we are not given a choice. For you cannot look away from those in torment any more than I can run south." Tenderly she cupped his jaw, looked up at him. "Our path leads to the crystal palace. So on we go, to glorious battle, where my name will become legend."

And where he would never, *ever* let her go.

CHAPTER 28

LIZZAN

Sullen clouds crowded the sky as they stole their way to the heart of the island, where the spires of the crystal palace formed shining peaks over a fortress that had once crowned a mountain. Always before the palace had seemed so beautiful to Lizzan, filled with warmth whether catching the sunlight or moonlight, a symbol of strength and comfort, an example of all that might be accomplished through learning and effort and determination.

Yet knowing the truth of its purpose, she only saw the hard and sharp edges. To her now it seemed a cold and cruel place, built not so that Kothans would always look up and aspire to more, but so that all who ruled there could look down on everyone who would one day be trapped beneath its terrible weight.

But there was no one except Aerax, Saxen, and Lizzan to look down on now as they followed Caeb through the silent streets. Only once had they stopped, when the Lithan prince had gone into a blacksmith's shop and emerged carrying a heavy, long-handled hammer—as if he meant to crush his father's skull instead of stab his eye or cleave a blade through his head. Lizzan had no true care how it was done, as long as Goranik and his demon were dead.

They had been told that Goranik and the viswan monks had the palace under siege, and the last message the Kothans had received was that the doors were cracking but the demon had not yet broken through. As they crept closer, it became apparent that there was no one still outside the palace.

The crystal doors were shattered.

Aerax saw her dismay. "There are other defenses inside," he reminded her softly.

Lizzan knew. More doors, secret chambers, palace guards. But her brother was one of those defenses, and she could not bear to see him shattered, too.

As other guards had been. Her stomach tightened with dread as they started down the halls, the demon's trail easy to follow by the dead left in his wake. She knew that Caeb would warn her if he smelled Cernak among the bodies, yet still she could not stop herself from looking to each one, just to be certain.

They passed through a dining hall, where a dozen guards had fallen—and one of the viswan.

Never had Lizzan met one of the monks before. This one was a woman, killed by a crossbow bolt through her throat. Runes were tattooed with red ink into her face and arms. No armor did she wear, only blue robes, and she'd carried no weapon that could Lizzan see.

Saxen knelt beside her. "Her name is Perit. She always tried to take my seed after she made me bleed. And that is my blood on her face."

The tattoos. To enhance her affinity to natural magics . . . which might be why she carried no weapons or shield. Her spells might do both, as could Tyzen's fire or Preter's wind.

Saxen stood, put his boot on her head. And as easily as Lizzan might pop a grape beneath her foot, he crushed her skull.

"To be certain," he said, and continued on.

As Lizzan would not like to have a reanimated viswan at her back, she had no argument with that.

Scorch marks blackened another shattered door, and a guard burned beyond recognition. "I know where they were headed," Aerax said grimly as he passed through the door and on to a stairwell. "My uncle must have retreated to the chamber beneath the palace—likely fearing that if they were under long siege in another chamber, he couldn't cast the spell each day."

Lizzan nodded and they began to move faster, Aerax leading the way. "What defenses docs that chamber have?"

"Three blackwood doors guard the stone chamber, and in the stone chamber's heart is a crystal chamber that is keyed to royal blood. He and his guards would be safe within that, unless the demon shattered the crystal as he did the palace doors."

A small bit of relief slipped into Lizzan's heart. "It took him a full season to break through."

"And in that time, perhaps he learned how to more quickly shatter the crystal. But it matters not, because unless they took a season's worth of food into the chamber, the king would not survive that long." Aerax paused to look past the corner of a passageway before continuing. "If the viswan cast spells as Preter and Tyzen do, always they must first speak the words, and always they must breathe. Swing your blade for their throats and be quick."

Lizzan nodded. As they were no match for the demon's strength, she and Aerax had already decided that they would attempt to stop the viswan while Saxen tried to kill Goranik. Caeb would help her protect Aerax, while tearing apart anyone he could get his claws into.

Aerax slowed and crouched near the end of another corridor. A foul sensation crawled over Lizzan's skin—one she'd known before, the night at King's Walk, when she'd chased the wraiths into the forest and saw the demon-king waiting there. She could not see Goranik now, yet still she could feel him near, as if his corrupted power was a stench that lingered.

"We are near," Aerax said quietly, and held out one of his short knives to Saxen.

The man took the blade, and Lizzan saw how his hand trembled wildly before he gritted his teeth and made a small cut on his palm. His blood he rubbed over the wide head of his hammer, then gestured for Lizzan's sword.

"After you kill the viswan with this blade, only a trace of my blood may be left—but if you come face to face with my father, perhaps a trace will be enough."

To save her. Or Aerax, when Saxen slicked more blood over his knives. Then he spread more over Caeb's saber fangs. By the time that was done, the cut had healed.

"Let us hope that this will kill a demon," he murmured.

Pulse racing, Lizzan added quietly, "We are united . . . now give me a moment to pray to Vela. You both should, too. And Caeb."

Aerax grinned but obediently closed his eyes. As did Saxen. Perhaps the goddess could not even hear them from the island, but no chances would Lizzan take. She prayed fiercely until Caeb licked her face, and then no more time could they waste.

Chanting came from within the stone chamber. Silently they crept down the corridor, yet none of the viswan seemed stationed as guard at any of the three blackwood doors. All were broken as if from a single hard blow.

Preter had told them what to look for regarding the spell that would capture the souls escaping Varrin's prison in their new corrupted forms. An altar, a vessel, a conduit. The altar she could see beyond the crystal chamber, and it was just a simple slab of stone. The vessel was the material from which the wraith would take its new form, which looked to be a jumble of stones around the vase that would be the conduit. The vase was marked with runes, but the spell would not be complete without a snow-hair's blood— and without freeing the imprisoned souls, so they might be captured again.

But the viswan and the demon seemed done with the altar. Instead they surrounded the crystal chamber in a circle that included Goranik, and the demon's back was to the corridor as they chanted their spell to crack the crystal. Through the crystal walls, Lizzan could only see clouded shapes—at least a dozen. Mostly likely the king, his daughter, and the remaining guards.

So the spell was ready. Now Goranik only needed a snow-haired king or princess—or feral prince—to finish it.

Lizzan reached for Aerax's arm and squeezed. Wordlessly he shook his head.

He would not stay here in the corridor while she and Saxen and Caeb went in.

She sighed, and he brushed his finger against her chin. The chin that he'd told her that he'd always loved. She lifted it stubbornly, just for him. He grinned at her, filling her racing heart with unrestrained emotion.

Then, gripping his knives, silently and swiftly he went in with Caeb at his side.

Lizzan raced in, going left as Aerax went right, heading for the viswan in their circle. Goranik turned, and she had but a glimpse of the gray face that had featured in her nightmares just before Saxen slammed into him with such strength and speed that Lizzan felt the impact through her chest. Then her blade sliced through the first viswan's neck, and she spun toward the next as he fell back, chant over and desperately spitting out a spell that Lizzan cut short by jabbing the point of her sword into his throat.

She yanked it out and charged for the next, aware of Caeb's roar and a scream that ended at the rip of the cat's teeth—or Aerax's. More heavy thuds seemed to pound through the very air. She was around the side of the crystal chamber now and couldn't see what was happening between the Lithans or how far Aerax and Caeb had gotten, could see only the scrambling panic of the viswan who must have thought themselves so near to victory.

A blast of wind hit her face and she dove out of its path, whipping her dagger toward the nearest monk. She cared not if it hit a throat—she only had to break the viswan's concentration. A cry of pain ended the gale, and then Lizzan was on her feet again, charging toward the woman yanking the dagger from her side.

A flare of orange light and a wave of heat came from the other side of the chamber, and the stone ceiling shook with Caeb's roar of pain.

Saxen flew through the air and slammed into a wall. She heard the snap of bone but couldn't turn, stabbing through lungs that would stop a spell as effectively as through a throat. Saxen shouted a warning, but Lizzan's speed was no match for either a silver-blooded king or a demon. Pain ripped through her head and neck as Goranik whipped her aside by the tail of her hair. Another hard blow sent agony shooting down her shoulder and she crumpled to the ground next to Saxen.

Not a blow, but the impact into a wall. Gasping for breath, she crawled onto her knees, saw the shattered blade of her sword. Beside her, Saxen seemed a jumble of broken bones. Blood dripped from his mouth and his ears, and he still clutched the hammer's handle, though the thick wood was splintered and the hammerhead gone. The sharp end of a fractured bone pierced the flesh of his upper forearm.

"I will be up . . . in a moment." Each word sounded glutted with blood, as if his insides were as broken as his outsides.

They did not have a moment. His face singed bald, Caeb faced the oncoming demon, snarling. Behind him, Aerax tossed the body of the last viswan aside, then spit out the blood and flesh he'd torn from their throat. Gore covered his jaw and chest, and his dark eyes met Lizzan's across the distance.

Between them, Goranik paused and laughed. "A true bounty this realm has given." The sound of his amusement squirmed over her skin like a wet gutworm, and she knew not if his voice was his own or the demon's, or if there was any difference between them. "When I sent my bandits to attack your army, I had only hoped their sacrifice would create the ice wraiths to reduce your soldiers' numbers and ease my path across. Instead I discovered how many souls were locked away on this island."

Aerax's gaze hardened. "It was your spell that created those wraiths?"

That killed Lizzan's friends. Her father.

All of them trapped beneath this palace . . . and who Goranik would make stone wraiths of now, imprisoning them forever in that corrupted and twisted form.

She could not allow it. Lizzan's gaze sought her dagger. It lay on the floor only a few paces away. Could she reach it without Goranik noticing?

He seemed not to be looking at her at all, stepping nearer to Aerax and Caeb as he said, "Would that I had known how to make wraiths of stone then, and my task would have been completed two years past."

With Aerax's hand on his ruff, Caeb fell back a pace, his snarl deepening to a growl.

"You show your teeth, though they will do you no good?" The demon-king shook his head. "Join with me instead—for with silver blood flowing through your veins, you are more brother to me than that mewling boy is my son. Together we will serve the Destroyer and help him usher the world toward salvation."

Ice speared through Lizzan's heart. He was speaking to *Caeb*. As if he knew full well what the cat was.

As Caeb realized, too. His growl rumbled louder.

"Then you will bleed," the demon told the cat. "For you will serve the Destroyer's glorious purpose, one way or an-other. Your only choice is whether to be strong or weak . . . as the boy is weak. And did you truly believe you might stand against *me*?" His voice cracked like thunder, and Lizzan froze in place as he turned to spear Saxen with the fury of his stare. "From birth, you have been a sniveling waste, lacking true conviction—and now you are proved the fool I always knew you to be. You thought to attack me though you have been drained of what little strength you had? Clearly nothing of worth is left in you, and this time I will see you drained completely. After I have finished with these Kothans."

Which must not refer to Lizzan. As if she were nothing, barely did the demon-king glance at her before returning his attention to Aerax and Caeb. Fear thickened her blood until every beat of her heart thudded heavily in her ears. Icy sweat trickled down her spine. The demon only had to reach Aerax and he would have the blood to finish his spell. He would have a way to open the crystal chamber. And then he would have an army of stone wraiths that the alliance could not possibly stand against.

To prevent that, she'd been tasked to protect Aerax . . . yet this would have always been her path. And it was a path she gladly traveled.

Her life she would always give for his.

"Take this," Saxen rasped painfully. Beside her came the snap of bone, the wet tear of flesh, and agony scraping through every word. "Save them."

Into her hand Saxen placed the bone he'd ripped from his arm, still warm and wet. And where she knelt beside him, her white cloak was soaked in his blood. Once, Lizzan had said that this cloak would be dyed red with the blood of her enemies—with the blood of Aerax's enemies—yet now here it was soaked in the blood of a friend. This cloak that was not a true questing cloak, and not a true red. But if it had been, she might not have seen the way forward now. For without this blood, weapons were useless against the demon . . . and so were claws.

She gripped the bone, took the splintered handle that dropped from Saxen's mutilated hand and rolled it through the crimson puddle before surging to her feet.

"Caeb!" She charged the demon, throwing the hammer's handle over his head to Aerax. "The blood on my cloak!"

She whipped the fabric around the demon's side even as he turned toward her, and she was no match for his speed but the cat was, claws shredding through the bloodied cloak and into flesh. The demon screamed, striking at the cat as Lizzan leapt, stabbing the bone through the side of his neck.

There she clung, stabbing and stabbing and stabbing as the demon flailed and turned, as if trying to swat a fly from his back. An enraged roar joined Caeb's, and the demon staggered as a wet *thunk* sounded. Aerax. She gripped the demon's hair and yanked herself higher, then rammed the sharp end of the bone into his ear.

Goranik fell to his knees. Lizzan braced her feet against the floor again, saw Aerax at the demon's other side—the splintered handle jutting from Goranik's eye.

Caeb sank his fangs through the demon's neck, shaking the limp body viciously before tearing off his head. As it plopped to the floor, he dug his claws into the demon's belly and with a flick of his paw sent the body crashing into the altar. The rune-marked vase atop it tumbled over and shattered against the floor.

"Come now," said Lizzan, gasping for breath. "Now you are just playing."

The cat pounced on the corpse and tore off its leg. Shaking her head, she stumbled into Aerax's arms, unable to do anything but laugh her relief into his bloodied neck as he held her tight.

Then she took his hand and carried Saxen's bone back to him. "Will it heal if you put it back in?"

With a pained grunt, Saxen used the wall at his back for support as he shoved to his feet. "I know not if it will. Though if that was in his brain, I will not try until after I wash it."

Likely a fine idea. With the only clean spot on her tunic that she could find, she wiped as much blood as she could from Aerax's jaw. "You will terrify them all when you open that chamber," she said. "But they will finally know who you are."

She went with him, stepping over the bodies of the viswan littering the floor. With his own blood he opened the crystal chamber, and the sheer joy of seeing Cernak within made her head swim dizzily.

There were stunned stares, and grateful exclamations, and through it all she could only see her brother, holding his position as the king's guard but his eyes telling her all that he would have said, and that he was so glad to see her.

It was Aerax who remembered that Cernak was his keeper—and so served him before any other royal. To her brother, he gave the order, "Make ready to escort my uncle and the princess to the refuge. And take with you the Lithan prince."

King Icaro frowned, his features so like Aerax's but his manner now of a man wholly confused. "You would have me leave the island?"

Aerax nodded. "This demon-sorcerer meant to create an army of stone wraiths for the Destroyer. He did not succeed. But the next will come. And the next. And one day, you will not reach the protection of the chamber. Or they will steal the princess and use her to force you to open it."

Lizzan looked to the girl, who was not much older than Lizzan had been when first she'd met Aerax. Bravely she stood, nodding as her father claimed that never would they give in to such demands, that they would sacrifice themselves for all of Koth.

"And so you will," said Aerax with a touch of bitterness. "You will sacrifice her kindness and her courage when you tell her the truth of Varrin. Does she know yet what she will have to become? That she will have to be a queen who ignores the sounds of Kothans in torment? That she will have to be a queen who lies to all of her people? Will you tell her that her own mother screams because she died on Kothan soil during the red fever?" His gaze swept the guard. "Will you tell them the truth of what they heard in that chamber? Or will you have them killed for hearing it at all?"

The girl looked up to the king with lips trembling before she firmed them. "What is he saying about my mother?"

"He is saying that he wishes to free thousands of generations of Kothans who are trapped in torment," Lizzan told her. "And to make certain our people are kept safe from the Destroyer."

King Icaro's eyes closed. "I will do it. If it must be done, I will be the one to do it."

Aerax shook his head. "I do not trust that you won't delay at the last moment, or persuade yourself to continue as you have been. For ten years, you persuaded yourself every day to cast that spell."

Anger flashed across the king's face. "Koth ought to have time to prepare. It will be done, but we need time—"

"You have no time."

"And you are not the king." He looked to the guards. "Take the prince and his friends to the—"

"Do not make me kill them," Aerax interrupted softly. "And do not make me take the throne from you. Instead think of your daughter, and the burden you would put on her—and the danger that will come to her if this is not done now."

Expression torn, the king looked to her. Silently she gazed back, her eyes huge. Finally he nodded.

Aerax looked to Cernak. "As quickly as you can, to the king's yacht. I know not how quickly Koth will fall. But I will give you time to reach the ship . . . if you hurry."

Face bloodbare, her brother nodded before turning to the king. "Your Majesty . . . ?"

Flanked by his guards, the king strode from the stone chamber, holding the princess's hand.

Saxen limped after them. "I will make certain they do not turn around."

Aerax looked to Lizzan and before he could even speak, she shook her head.

"I am going nowhere," she told him. "My task is to protect you. So we will run together."

"Lizzan . . ." He appeared in agony. "We had a glorious battle. Go now while you can."

She laughed, shaking her head. "I do not know if it was glorious—but it won't lift the shame from my family. If my name becomes legend, it is only because we will be the villains who threatened the king and then sank Koth. I'm fair certain this is not what Vela promised me. So I do not think that I will die this day, after all."

Though Aerax looked as if he would argue, finally he simply pulled her close. "We will race for the King's Walk."

"We will," she agreed, then gently kissed Caeb's burned face when he pushed his head between them. "How much time?"

Never long enough.

Aerax did not allow her to enter the crystal chamber with him, saying that she already had too many screams filling her nightmares. She waited with Caeb, trembling violently as she waited for . . . she knew not what. A slow and gentle sinking of the entire island? Or the island tearing itself apart and falling to pieces?

It was the latter. Of course it had to be the latter.

The ground jolted and Aerax burst out the chamber, snagging her hand as they raced up the corridor. The stairs buckled and heaved. The walls cracked and a piece of the ceiling crashed to the ground in front of them. Together they ran, but knew not how they would be fast enough.

Until behind her came a roar, and Caeb's head shoved hard against her ass, nearly lifting her off her feet. Aerax gave a shout of laughter and in the next moment he tossed Lizzan astride the huge cat and leapt up behind her.

She had ridden Caeb before. Once. Swift she thought he'd been then, but such care he must have taken because she had not known what swift was. Desperately she clung to his ruff with Aerax leaning over her, shielding her body with his as they raced through the shattering palace.

Outside, the buildings shook apart, timbers falling into streets. Barely could she see, the wind ripping tears from her eyes, Caeb's powerful stride increasing pace until it seemed as if they were flying. Only twice he faltered, as a thunderous crack came from behind them and the ground seemed to drop out beneath his feet. Again it did, and when Lizzan turned her head she saw the water rushing in toward them, but the King's Walk was just ahead, sinking too, sinking but still above the waves.

She cried out as the earth ahead of them split, a gulf opening between the island and the Walk. Thick muscles bunched between her thighs and then they were truly flying as Caeb cleared the widening gap and continued on, with

Lizzan laughing wildly into his ruff and Aerax's laughter shaking against her back.

The bridge continued sinking, but by the time the water lapped at Caeb's paws they could have waded to shore. On solid ground, Lizzan slid from his back and hugged him with all her remaining strength, which seemed not much as she was still shaking so hard.

Aerax swept her up into a kiss, spinning her around and laughing—though from the nearby camp came wails of horror and fear as the Kothans watched their island sink.

That sobered them both quickly, and Aerax took her hand as they began walking toward the camp—where people had already begun spilling out and onto the shore, watching. In sudden alarm, Lizzan searched the forest for any bramble beasts before realizing they were no longer a threat.

Goranik was dead.

And the king's yacht had not yet reached the shore, but was near enough that when he and the princess came out onto the deck for all to see, a cheer momentarily broke through the grief.

She and Aerax dared not linger here for long. No doubt they would be driven out and shunned, if not chased down and killed. But this time she meant to persuade her family to go with her.

After Koth was gone. It was not completely yet. Lizzan paused to look out across the water. The peak of the crystal palace still remained above the surface, but it was slowly sliding deeper.

There Kelir and Ardyl found them, followed by Tyzen and Preter and Seri . . . and Lizzan's mother and younger brother. So she would not need to search for them, only wait for Cernak to arrive on the yacht. As he was Aerax's keeper, no desertion would it be if he went with them.

"Was it the blood that killed the demon?" Ardyl asked, never taking her eyes from the sinking spire as it fully disappeared, and Lizzan nodded.

"Or prayer. Or being united. I can't be certain which one

it was, but I think it was the blood . . . and Saxen's arm bone."

The warrior's gaze cut to her face as if to see whether that was a jest.

"Stabbed it right though the ear," Lizzan told her.

Ardyl laughed, and they both looked to the crowd when there was a sudden joyous cheer, though Lizzan did not see the cause. On the yacht, the king and princess stood in the same way they had before . . . though now they were turning, pointing back across the water toward the center of the lake.

Where Koth was rising again.

Or . . . a part of it was. Not the spires or the crystal palace. It seemed nothing more than the crest of a rocky hill that had breached the surface. Or as if perhaps the entire island had flipped over and now they saw the jagged remains underneath.

Those remains were headed through the lake toward them, water frothing gently at the forward surface. Not moving quickly, but coming.

Caeb snarled uneasily before butting his head into her shoulder, shoving her back away from the shore, then pushing Aerax. As if urging them to run again.

But the cat could not carry all these people.

"Preter?" Kelir stepped back, looking for Seri. "What is coming?"

"Something big." The monk said the obvious.

"Do you sense dark magics?"

"I sense the demon," Aerax said, jaw clenching. "The same as I felt in the chamber. Go with Caeb, Lizzan."

Run away from whatever true glorious battle was coming. A terrible ache filled her chest. Because she was not done. There was so much she still wanted to do.

But always this was the path she would have chosen.

"What happened below the palace?" Preter asked them urgently. "Was the spell completed?"

Lizzan shook her head. "It was prepared. The altar, the conduit, the vessel. But they had no blood from a snow-hair—and we killed the demon before he could take any of Aerax's."

"Did any blood reach the conduit?"

"Goranik's," Aerax told him. "But only after he was killed, and the vase had shattered against the ground. Then we were in the chamber for a while after. Long enough for the king to reach his yacht. Nothing did I sense of the demon then."

"Goranik," Preter said suddenly, his eyes squeezing shut. "He'd invited the demon into his living flesh. Perhaps that was who you killed—Goranik—but the demon fled his flesh. But then the demon would need another host, but could not take a dead body, for it would need to be reanimated with a spell . . . and Temra be merciful, there was a spell waiting. What was the vessel on the altar?"

"It only seemed like a handful of rocks."

"From Koth," Preter said. "Which had been filled for years with the essence of all those souls . . . and was suddenly empty."

Ardyl looked to him in horror. "You are saying the demon inhabits the island now? And that it is essentially a wraith the size of Koth?"

Wordlessly, Preter nodded.

"Then how can it possibly be killed? What is an island's flesh and blood? Do we do as Seri suggested and throw rocks?"

"Seri, Tyzen," Kelir said with steel in his voice. "Saddle your horses and race south toward the plains road. Warn the Krimatheans and anyone else who comes in this direction. The rest of us will attempt to keep these people out of its path."

Most of whom were still celebrating, for the demon was not rising quickly—as if it were walking slowly toward them but still in the deepest part of the lake, and only the top of its head could be seen.

Others were backing slowly away, as if becoming uncertain.

All Kothans who'd just lost everything they'd ever

known . . . and now it would rise to crush them. And likely some deserved it. Others would only care that so many people would suffer because now it would be their turn to suffer, too. But none of that mattered. Lizzan had not become a soldier so she could choose whom to save. She would simply save all that she could.

Aerax pulled her close, captured her face in her hands. His urgent gaze searched hers. "Run with Caeb," he said thickly, as if already knowing her answer. "I will see your family safe."

She shook her head. "We'll fight it. We'll kill it."

He went still. "Can we?"

"We can."

"Then tell me how I will do it, and go."

"Oh, Aerax," she laughed. "You tell me never to leave you, then keep trying to send me away. But I will fight to stay with you. Did I not promise that?"

"And I will fight to keep you with me."

"So we both will fight. But not each other," she added, her throat suddenly aching. "We will not fight each other."

"Not each other," he agreed, and kissed her so fiercely, so sweetly, even as the screams began behind them.

"It has eyes," Seri said with a note of horror. "So many eyes."

So many eyes. She looked up into Aerax's as his gaze searched her face again.

"How do we kill it?" he asked softly.

"With flesh and blood," she told him. "Yours and mine. Maybe also with a prayer to Vela, but most definitely together. And we will need swords or spears . . . and a boat, I suppose."

He nodded. "I will find them."

With another hard kiss, he strode off. Lizzan turned toward the water and her heart rolled sickly into her gut. If wraiths were twisted into their new forms but were still recognizable as once human, then she could hardly fathom what the demon's true form was. And all that was visible right now was half a head.

And a gaping mouth like a canyon filled with serrated teeth.

"Lizzan!" Her mother raced toward her, Farzan at her side. "Did you see Cernak?"

"He's on the king's yacht."

"On the water?" Terror in her voice, Yuna spun around. "Temra have mercy."

"They will reach the shore before it comes near," Lizzan told her.

"Then where do you go?"

"Nowhere. Aerax and I will fight it. As you can."

Kelir turned to her sharply. "How?"

"You cannot," Lizzan told him. "Though likely every Kothan can. How vulnerable it will be to people on the ground, however, depends on what lies beneath that water. If it is covered in eyes . . . a fine chance we have."

Though surely a brain would not lie behind all of those eyes, still they might hurt it. But more importantly, she saw not only terror in her mother now, but also hope.

Yet if all went well, the demon would be dead before it reached the shore.

Lady Junica came near, her gaze searching out Lizzan. "Do I hear that we can fight it?"

"I believe we can," Lizzan told her. "A demon can be killed by its own flesh and blood—"

"It is a rock!" called a man near Lady Junica whom Lizzan didn't know.

"That's true, but it is not *only* a rock." More of a crowd gathered now, and Lizzan could not see them all, knew they could not all hear her. She looked around, found a stump from one of the trees cut down to make the refuge wall, and hopped up. She turned to find Preter standing near, holding out a pine cone.

"Speak into that," he told her—and though Lizzan felt like a fool, she did.

"You can fight it," she called out, and the sound of her voice shot through the air, causing panicking Kothans to spin in her direction, others abruptly falling silent. The monk had cast a spell like the echo chamber, she realized—so that all she said came from every pine cone strewn across the ground.

"We can fight it!" she called out again. "A demon can be killed by its own flesh and blood. And you say that it is a rock, but it is not *only* a rock! For thousands of generations, as every Kothan was born, as all of you were born, your birth waters splashed on the ground. After the red fever, as the parents and children that were lost burned on their pyres, the falling snow turned gray with the smoke and ash and sank back into the soil. On the King's Walk, the blood of a thousand soldiers was spilled—they were your brothers, your sisters. Koth is not a rock. *We* are Koth! You have spilled your tears and sweat and blood onto that island. And so the demon that comes toward us is made of rock that is saturated with our blood and our flesh, and *we can fight it*!"

Cheers and shouts rose around her, and still she saw fear—but fear would also serve them well, as long as they were not ruled by it.

"If you cannot fight, or if you have children to protect, then by Vela—take them to where they are safe. But if you can fight, take whatever weapons you can find and gather on the shore. We will *not* let this demon destroy us."

And Lizzan would not let the demon destroy them. She tossed the pine cone away and Aerax was there, weapons in hand and a heartrending mix of pride and dread in his gaze.

"You will be a legend," he told her quietly.

Her throat burned and she took his hand. "Now a boat," she said, and looked to Preter. "Can you give us a swift wind as you did last eve?"

"You are going out to meet it?"

Lizzan nodded.

"By the time you sail that distance, it might have risen higher out of the water. Or it might simply swat your boat aside."

"True. But I cannot see many other options aside from waiting here on the shore." Where she truly believed it could be fought, but not before hundreds—if not thousands—of Kothans were crushed.

"I have an idea," the monk said. "For when we learn our spells and magic . . . we do not always practice responsibly."

Aerax frowned at him. "What does that mean?"

"Sometimes we jump off cliffs. You do not need to do that here," he added hastily. "But with a sail from one of those boats, I might get you across the water more quickly."

More quickly" was Lizzan holding tight to two corners of a square sail and Aerax gripping the other two corners, while Preter filled the sail with wind until it lifted them into the air.

"Hold fast!" Kelir shouted up at them, as if Lizzan had *any* thought of letting go as they rose higher and higher, swaying. From below came gasps, and shouts of encouragement, and Lizzan only wanted them to fall utterly quiet so that Preter's full concentration could be aimed toward their sail.

Oh, and they were *so* high. Lizzan squeezed her eyes shut.

"Do you pray to Vela?" Aerax called over the rush of wind, grinning.

Grinning. As if they were not hanging high above a freezing lake, heading toward a demon made of stone, with a hundred bulbous eyes and a cavernous maw created from nightmares.

"I am praying to Preter!" she shouted back, and his deep laughter in response was the finest sound she'd ever heard.

Until he called out, "I love you, Lizzan of Lightgale!"— and that was the finest.

Heart so very full, she looked to him as the wind whipped his snow-white hair across his face, memorizing every feature though she'd memorized them so many times before. Yet never had they been here before, so full of laughter and love and fear, for they both knew what lay ahead. And if this was the very last look she would have of him, then she would look her fill.

The laughter drained from his expression, leaving only love and desolation. "If you leave me, I will come for you," he told her thickly. "Wherever you go, I will find you, and we will be together again. Even if I have to rip you out of Temra's arms."

Vision blurring, she nodded—and then not much more could she say as the wind carrying them eased slightly, so that they began to drift downward. The demon had tentacles now . . . or antennae. They were still partially submerged so she couldn't be certain, but the enormous shadow beneath the water seemed to be moving slowly on at least twelve insectile legs. As they floated closer, the bulbous red eyes rolled upward, catching Lizzan and Aerax in their horrid gaze.

The antennae extended toward them, pincers at the end snapping, their reach falling short of the distance but filling Lizzan with new terror. Their sail began to drop toward the demon, faster and faster.

Abruptly new antennae erupted from beneath the water's surface, spearing toward them. Lizzan cried out, kicking at the pincers but missing, the sail wobbling wildly. With a slashing of the razored claws, it ripped a slit into the sail.

So fast they sank through the air that they were almost falling, straight toward the water in front of the demon, and then a hard wind caught their backs and shoved them forward, forward, until they bounced into one of the eyes and began sliding down its slippery surface.

"Hold tight!" Aerax shouted, still gripping the sail and using it like a rope between them to drag Lizzan back up to his side. "This eye?"

"Might as well try!" She drew a sword, the blade already streaked with the blood of a Kothan who'd volunteered theirs, and stabbed downward.

Fetid fumes poured out. A shudder ran through the demon that jiggled like custard through the eye, so that Lizzan had to cling to Aerax again for balance.

"It *hurt* it!" she cried happily—then screamed as their orientation abruptly changed, rising sharply as the demon stood up.

As if it had been crawling on its belly before. Sword buried deep in the jelly of the eye, Lizzan clung to the handle—and with her other hand desperately gripped the sail as Aerax slid down, his boots slipping on the smooth rounded surface that had seemed once at the top of the demon's head but was now at the back, and suddenly there was no eye beneath him and he dangled from the sail over the churning lake below.

"Climb up!" she shouted, then shook her head wildly when she saw his gaze go to her sword, which was slowly slicing through the jelly of the eye, drawn down by the weight upon it. "Climb up!"

He met her eyes. "I will come for you."

"Aerax!" she screamed as he let go, dropping straight down. With sobs catching at her throat, she watched him plunge into the water, then didn't breathe again until he surfaced, striking hard away from the demon, and a relieved laugh broke through the terror.

She'd always loved how well he could swim.

Gritting her teeth, she pulled herself up, using her second sword to stab deep and climb even higher. Two swords she had, and a spear at her back—the axe had fallen with Aerax. Each stab only pierced jelly, yet as she neared the reddened pupil, a pulsating mass she could see below it.

Gagging against the stench that poured out, she pierced the pupil and then sheathed the sword, reaching for her spear.

That she shoved deep, and a horrid screech ripped open the air. Faster the demon seemed to move through the lake, though she was so close to it no true view did she have of anything else—only the impression of too many arms and too many legs. With her foot, she rammed the spear deeper and cried out in horror as a mass of red worms sprouted through the bottom of the eye from the pulsating mass below. Like vines, they wrapped around her leg, tiny teeth trying to bite but skating across her charmed skin. Again she slammed her heel into the butt of the spear, hammering it in like a nail.

All went still and quiet. Then there was the sensation of falling forward, cushioned by the jelly in the eye, but still the demon's impact against the surface of the lake bounced her around, tearing her sword from her grip. Desperately she began to claw her way up as the water surrounded her, pulling against the worms that still wrapped from her ankle to her knee.

She gulped air as the sinking demon dragged her under, and then she curled downward, ripping at the worms with her fingers. So many there were, and her lungs were burning and heaving as she fought not to take panicked breaths.

So many worms.

Spots flared in front of her eyes. Her chest ached so badly, but Aerax would come for her. He'd come for her. She coughed and panic took her for an endless thrashing moment, choking on water, desperately fighting to reach the surface. Then no more did it hurt and she went still, marveling that the ache was gone from her chest, entranced by the pale streaming of sunlight through the clear water.

And there was Aerax, diving for her. Coming as he'd promised. Swimming closer, and a scream boiled through his clenched teeth as his gaze met her eyes. She tried to shake her head, to let him know that all was fine, but she could not move at all. Still trapped by the worms.

His warm hands caught her cheeks, his face utterly stricken, his kiss broken by another deep scream in his throat. Then he dove deeper, and she felt the tug and slash of his blade cutting her free of the worms. Catching his strong arm around her chest, he struck for the surface. He broke through and roared into the sky, a primal cry that was all grief, all pain.

She couldn't draw a breath to tell him she was fine. She couldn't turn toward him, take him into her arms and quiet the rough sobs that were her name as he held her close again, hot tears falling against her skin.

Then he gulped in a breath, fingers tugging at the chain around her neck. His voice hardened to steel determination. "I will do anything, Lizzan. Forgive me. But even a monster I will become."

Holding her, he turned onto his back and began to strike for the shore with sweeping one-armed strokes. Her head was lolled against his shoulder, her feet and arms trailing limply through the water, her gaze fixed up at the clouded sky, where lightning flashed and it seemed her father was smiling down at her, reaching out with his hand before another flash of lightning and the long sweep of a dragon's body flew her father away.

So she was dead. And soon silver-fingered Rani would come for her, too . . . though the goddess seemed at this moment occupied by the thousands of generations of souls released from Koth's prison.

Aerax's hold on her body adjusted, and then his arms came beneath her knees as he lifted her against his chest and strode out of the water onto the shore. In the distance she heard her mother crying, her brother Farzan's shout as Aerax laid her on the sand. His face came over hers, torment in his eyes. Then Farzan was there, hands at her throat, rolling her onto her side and pounding her back before setting his mouth to hers, blowing air that filled her cheeks while tears fell from his.

When he looked to Aerax and shook his head, her husband pushed him aside. Again he cupped her face, bending over her. "Forgive me for this," he said hoarsely as lightning flashed close, so close, and she could feel the steam of a dragon's breath.

Even though Aerax filled her vision, silver-fingered Rani was suddenly all Lizzan saw—black hair braided, eyes snapping with lightning and swimming with tears. Behind her was the dragon, his scales like flickering flames, glowing orange and red and crackling with heat.

"That is not the dragon we freed," Lizzan told her.

"That was not a dragon at all," the goddess replied, and

her voice was sweet and soft, like a nightingale's song. "I cannot take you with me while you are bound by Nemek's hair."

"And I am full glad," she said. "For that would be a very long way for Aerax to chase me."

Hardness crept into Rani's voice, no longer a sweet song-bird but a raptor of prey. "Another snow-haired man once tried to keep me with him."

"Varrin, the maggoty measle. So I have been told. The difference is that I don't want to leave Aerax—and that Aerax is nothing like that monster."

"That is not what he believes."

"Doesn't he?" A soft ache started under her heart. "He is full wrong. No more different could they be."

"Are they?"

"They are. Simply ask him."

Rani's smile was lethal as a blade. "Perhaps I will."

CHAPTER 29

AERAX

Caeb's rough tongue rasped over Lizzan's cheek, and the agony in Aerax's chest had him near to breaking when the cat nudged her yet again, as if trying to urge her to awaken. Full well Caeb had to know that no life was in her, yet he seemed as a helpless kitten, unknowing of what to do.

Aerax knew. Though he would be everything that he'd just destroyed. But if she came back to him? If she came back, he would not care what he'd become.

"If you do not remove that necklace, I cannot take her," Seri said, though it was not at all Seri's voice, and lightning crackled in the full black of her eyes.

"Seri?" Tyzen lurched for her, then stopped short at a lift of the girl's hand, the silver claws on her fingers sparking.

"You do not want to touch me now, young princc. For that will be a kiss you will not recover from." She glanced back as Caeb rose, snarling, and smiled at the cat. "Hush, beautiful one. Your snow-haired brother hopes to cast a spell to bind her spirit to her flesh, though water still fills her lungs and she will only drown again, in pain and panic. And though the cold water has slowed the dying of her brain, too far gone it is now. If you cast Varrin's spell to imprison her in this body, she will only know silent torture for the rest of her days. But you would have her with you. Is that not all you want?"

Burning agony surged up his chest, shuddering his breath through his clenched teeth. A body was not all he wanted. He needed *her*. Lizzan. His strong, generous, softhearted wife. The girl who had fearlessly said his name. The woman who had given her heart and her trust unrestrained. *Nothing* was Aerax without her.

"Will you be as Varrin, and trap her here in this way?"

Throat hot and aching, Aerax shook his head. Never would he imprison her. But she would not be trapped. She'd *wanted* to stay.

And he'd promised to fight to keep her.

The goddess came closer, wearing Seri's face, but nothing of the girl did Aerax see in her. "Will you have her rot?"

"I would have you find Nemek so they can heal her first," he said, his voice a shredded rasp.

Rani laughed. "Do you think they will trust you? After what Varrin did to them?"

"Tell them it is the girl who once killed a fly for them, and then scratched their itching nose." He traced shaking fingers down her still face. "Ask them to come for her."

"And will you trap them?"

"I will free them, too."

For a long moment the goddess stared at him, lightning firing through the black of her eyes. Then the girl collapsed to the ground, gaze fixed unblinking up at the sky.

"Seri!" Tyzen dropped to his knees beside her as Kelir grabbed her up against his chest, fingers pressing for the pulse in her neck. Ardyl sank to the ground behind him, her arms circling his shoulders and tears spilling down her cheeks.

"How fares our sister?"

"She breathes," the warrior said, voice breaking. "Her heart beats."

"Will you not move aside for an old traveler?" came a reedy voice from behind Preter, whose face drained blood-bare, then filled with joy, then slackened with disbelief as he made room for the withered figure with silver hair and travel-stained feet.

Heart in his throat, Aerax rose with Lizzan in his arms.

"And what am I to do with that pile of flesh?" Nemek asked him. "It is dead, and the heart has no spark."

"Can you not heal her?"

"The itch-slayer? She is within the bind of my hair, but not bound to that flesh. That, you must do."

Dread clutched at his heart. "With Varrin's spell?"

Nemek abruptly laughed. "He was a maggoty measle, true. Ah, very well. I will make certain she does not drown when you bind her."

"And her brain?"

"I will heal all of her. Now cast your spell."

The same he'd sworn never to cast beneath the crystal palace. Yet here, he would do anything. With his blood, Aerax made a lock of her necklace, and turned the key.

Her body convulsed and Nemek swiftly pressed their lips to Lizzan's, blowing softly into her mouth until her lashes fluttered. Aerax's heart near burst through his chest at the first glimpse of lake blue, and the first breath she took was deep and clear.

"Lizzan?" he asked hoarsely, and she smiled up at him. All the world seemed bright in that moment, his heart full—then abruptly clenching when he saw the tears swimming in her eyes. "Lizzan?"

She sat up in his arms, hands clutching his cheeks. "*Nothing* are you like Varrin," she said fiercely. "*Nothing.*"

"Except the face," Nemck said.

Aerax had no care if he resembled that monster. For Lizzan was here in his arms . . . and her scars were but faint marks. In wonder, he touched the side of her face. Always she'd been beautiful to him, always he'd seen these scars as a mark of her strength, yet since discovering how they'd also been her curse, he'd not viewed them the same way. Now they were all but gone.

Lizzan's fingers came up to trace the pale lines, and she asked thickly, "You took these away?"

"Never could they be fully erased, for the deepest scars left were on your heart," they said. "But the mark is a weight you should not bear. That is a mark meant for those who abandon their quest, and you completed the task my sister gave to you."

"So I *was* on a quest?" Lizzan asked.

Nemek smiled faintly. "I think not."

Perhaps not, yet it seemed to Aerax that a favor had been given—and ought to be returned. In full gratitude, he looked to them. "We will free you of those binds."

"And how will you do that?"

"In this way," Ardyl said, standing with fingers clasped behind her back. Slowly, bending and twisting, she worked her wrists under her ass, then down her legs and to the front.

Nemek cackled. "Do you see how old I am, warrior? Never could I do that."

"Then wear your young face," Aerax suggested.

And truly young and beautiful they were, with shining silvery hair, unlined skin, and a faintly disdainful twist to their smile. "I still cannot."

"We'll help you," Lizzan said, and Aerax reluctantly released her. "If you will allow . . . ?"

Lizzan went to their front while Aerax moved behind, and Nemek's hair shimmered like the stars when they shook their head. "The itch-slayer will be safe, for she wears my bind. But if you touch me, only pain you will feel."

"I know," Aerax said quietly. "So let us be quick."

Gently he lifted Nemek's slight form and a hot rash ravaged his skin, sinking deep and shaking his muscles with fevered fatigue. Agony spread through his gut as Lizzan carefully helped work their wrists under their hips. A cough racked his chest, phlegmy blood coating his tongue, and barely could he stand as Lizzan finally helped them bend to draw their wrists past their feet.

The moment Nemek's feet returned to the ground, Aerax fell wheezing, dying. Then the healer's withered hands touched his face and all the pain eased, the diseases vanishing.

"So much better this is," Nemek told him, though their wrists were still bound.

"Use your teeth," Kelir said from the ground, where he still held an unmoving Seri in his lap.

When Nemek tilted their head, Ardyl demonstrated by pretending to tug at the knot at her own wrists.

Hope filled their eyes and they clamped their teeth on the rope, tugging and tugging until the bind fell away. Then they sank to the ground beside Aerax, quietly sobbing.

Lizzan came down at his other side, and Caeb pressed forward, licking Nemek's cheek.

"Oh, beautiful one," they said quietly, trailing their fingers down his burned face, thick fur sprouting in their wake, before plucking the fallen silver braid from the sand and turning to Aerax. "You are no Varrin. All that he would imprison, you would free—and so no fear do I have to give this. Just as the itch-slayer wears my healing bind, so you would, too. In that way, you might always travel together."

Always. Emotion filling his chest, Aerax asked, "Will you tear it in half, so one might be Caeb's?"

Deftly their fingers pulled the strands apart. "At first touch it might seem to burn your skin, but that is only lingering heat from Enam's eye. No harm does it do." They gave both braids to Aerax, who felt the burn across his palm. "The silver makes a better necklace than belt—and when you are done traveling in this world, pray for me to come, and I will untie the knots you make. And now I also must be traveling on . . . though first I might wander through this camp."

Stopping first to drift their fingers over Seri's cheek. Aerax looked to Lizzan, who crawled into his lap to straddle his hips in the sweet, intimate way they'd always had.

Her palms framed his face as her gaze searched his. "Are you well?"

Throat thick, he nodded. Not full well. Never could he be again after seeing her in the water, staring sightlessly up at him. But in all other ways . . . "You are with me," he said softly. "So I am blessed beyond all other men."

Sweetly she kissed him, then laid her head against his shoulder. "And where will our path take us next?"

"Likely it will still be the path that Vela put us on," he told her quietly, as his hand stroked down her back. "For I still must become what I truly am. For although I am always fully yours, a new purpose I should have."

"And what is that?"

Aerax gave a heavy sigh. "To learn magic from Preter."

She drew back to look at him in full surprise. "Truly?"

"Truly. It is needed against the Destroyer."

"So it is." A full smile curved her lips. "You will be a fine sorcerer."

He groaned. "So many lessons I will have to take."

She laughed against his mouth. "Take them through a hole in a wall. You always liked those lessons full well."

So he had. And she had, too. With a grunt, he lifted her.

She grinned, holding tighter, her legs wrapped around his waist. "Where does our path take us now?"

"To the nearest tree out of sight of all these people," he growled softly. "And if any of them happen upon us, their own lesson they will learn."

"And so we will continue the Kothan tradition of always learning and improving." Mouth hot, she licked his neck. "What will you teach them? How to fuck your wife against a tree? How to make her scream?"

"That, too." Though that was not all that he would do. "I will show them how to love her, unrestrained."

"Oh, Aerax." She kissed him full. "They see that in *everything* you do."

CHAPTER 30

LIZZAN

Do you finally return home, then?" Lizzan called out as Saxen came her direction, leading his mount. A bedroll was tied to the saddle, along with new furs from his hunts with Aerax and Caeb. His arm had full healed, though not by Nemek—they had offered, but Saxen had not allowed even their touch.

"It is time," he said. "My father's warlords are no better than he. If I delay longer, there will be no Lith to return to."

"And the arrival soon of Krimathean warriors must have little to do with it."

He gave a rusty laugh. "You found redemption through courage and truth. I do not hope to find the same, but I have much to do before I let any Krimathean kill me."

As one sought him out now to do. Lizzan bit her lip. She'd not said anything of Laina to him, though that warrior hunted him now. Before, there'd seemed little point when they might not even survive the demon.

His eyes narrowed. "What is it?"

"I know a little of your path ahead."

"Then do not tell me. It has been many years since I could strike my own path. So let me discover for myself what lies upon it."

Lizzan nodded. "But I would ask two favors of you."

"Then I will do two favors for you."

She hoped it would be done as easily as he'd answered. "When we have defeated the Destroyer, there will be so many of his soldiers who will have no home to return to. I ask that you give them a place to come, for you may be one of the few who can understand how desperately they will need someone to take them in."

His throat worked for a moment before he nodded. "And the second favor?"

"You return home by the crossroads at Oana?"

"I do."

"Before heading east, go south to the river where a fisherwoman waits by a ferry. There tell her your story, and where you are headed, so that she knows that a son who once followed the Destroyer might one day stand against him."

"You speak of Ilris's mother?"

In the rush from Radreh to Koth, never had she time to share the story. "You've heard of her?"

"It is one of the few stories told over and over in the camp. That and the story of Lizzan of Lightgale."

Lizzan grinned at him, pleased. "I expect to soon hear fine stories of you."

"They can only be finer than the ones already told," he said before continuing on. "Safe journey, Lizzan of Lightgale."

She could not hope it would be fully safe. Not with the Destroyer still coming. Above the lake, the sun was setting in brilliant colors at the edge of the yellow sky. More snows had come, and already much of Koth had joined the rivers of refugees flowing south. Yet she and Aerax would soon head in the opposite direction, accompanying the alliance to the northlands, where they hoped to add the broken clans to the number who would stand against the Destroyer.

"Lizzan!"

She turned to see Mevida coming toward her, with Lady Junica at her side. The caravan had arrived at a wholly different Koth than they'd expected to find, and though their wagons could not support an entire realm, the supplies they'd shared had eased the camp's burden while everyone decided where they would go.

But she was surprised to see Lady Junica with her. "Did you not leave already for Radreh?"

Where the monastery might provide shelter for many. The royal family had already begun the journey. Mevida was soon returning there, too, and Lizzan's mother and brothers were joining their group.

"I have delayed to travel with your family instead of with the king," said Lady Junica. "He has tasked me to form a council to oversee the rebuilding of Koth. Obviously not much can be done until after the Destroyer comes, but that also means we have much time to plan . . . and I did not want to miss the opportunity of inviting you to join that council."

To rebuild Koth? Lizzan sighed. "What would it be rebuilt as?"

"What it was always meant to be . . . though in truth."

Without Varrin's lies. "Did you already ask Aerax?"

Lady Junica gave her a wry look. "Must I repeat his answer?"

"Was it more than a grunt of refusal?"

"Not much," the councilor laughed. "Though he did say that Koth should stop pretending to be what it is not. And I did not even truly know what that meant."

Lizzan shrugged. "Merely that Koth is not what it purports to be. The idea of Koth, where one might be anything one chooses to be, is a fine one. But simply saying it is true does not make it so. Always, it is a goal to be worked toward—with the full understanding that *never* will it be true. That there will always be someone who is working hard but still not achieving all they wish. So becoming what Koth wants to be is a struggle that is never finished."

"But it is a struggle worth the effort. And so yours is a voice we will need on the council."

"It is not," said Lizzan. "Because I said this to you, and you listened. And my story will be told over and over. But there are so many in Koth to whom no one listens. Begin with my mother, if you must, for she knows what it is to be the one who is ignored and forgotten and shunned. But there are many others whom Koth always forgets. Add those voices to your council, so they will be heard, too. For I merely need to speak to you, and you hear me, and take my voice into consideration. So I do not need to be on a council."

Lady Junica sighed. "So you also refuse?"

"I do. Though it does not mean that I'm abandoning Koth or her people. Always I would protect them. But Koth has left me with scars, and I am not full certain I wish to return to its arms until I see that true change is made . . . or if instead everyone will cling to the false image of Koth so hard that all will be the same."

Though she sighed again, Lady Junica nodded. "I will fight to see that it is not."

"And I look forward to seeing what you make of it." She hugged the woman. "Safe journey to you."

She continued on, beyond what remained of the walled camp, toward the camp the alliance had made. They would stay here until Riasa and her warriors arrived, but two of the Parsatheans were heading out in the morning with messages for their queen, and a few warriors had already taken to their beds. But she found Seri, Ardyl, and Kelir still at the fire, and joined them.

"The lesson is not yet finished?"

Ardyl gestured deeper into the forest. "We saw something afire over there not long ago."

But they must be returning, for Caeb trotted out of the shadows and headed for Lizzan, rubbing his face to hers.

"Were you singed again?" she asked, and he gave her a look of sheer disdain before settling in at her side. With a laugh, she scratched his ruff, fingers slipping across the silver chain looping his thick neck.

At the other side of the fire, Seri held the stem of a small wildflower pinched between her fingers. As Lizzan watched, the petals withered and Seri tossed it to the ground.

"Now me," Kelir said, holding out his hand to her.

Stubbornly, she shook her head.

"You hold death in your hand every time you hold your sword," he told her. "But you do not fear that."

"Because I know how to use it," she said to him.

"Through practice," he pointed out.

"Through practice," she agreed. "And how many times did I slip? But a slip with a sword is only a cut. A slip now, and I kill my brother. A kiss now, and I kill . . ."

She waved toward the forest, and Lizzan's heart leapt as it always did when her gaze found Aerax. Always she saw her husband first, though Tyzen and Preter walked ahead of him. On a sweet kiss of greeting, Aerax settled beside her.

"How go the lessons?" she asked him, and though Aerax grinned, Preter groaned in despair and dropped next to Ardyl.

"We will not survive the journey to the northlands," the monk declared.

Tyzen scoffed. "You boasted of jumping off cliffs. We will survive a jump from a tree."

Aerax would survive, regardless. She looked to him, at the silver chain that now held her braid pouch nestled in the hollow of his throat.

"When will we likely hear from my sister?" Tyzen asked Kelir. "Ferek and Raceni will not have to travel as far as the Burning Plains to reach her, I imagine."

"Yvenne and Maddek will likely have the message from Oana and be heading north soon," the warrior said. "They should already be in Krimathe by the time we return from the northlands."

"With so many stories we will have to tell them," sighed Seri happily. "The wraith, the dragon . . . and of Lizzan and Aerax killing a demon *twice*."

"Finally," Lizzan said. "I have a story worth repeating."

"But one I do not want to relive again," said Aerax, and

despite his light tone, she heard the agony that still lingered beneath as he remembered her death.

"You will not relive *that* again." Heart full, she took his hand, threading her fingers through his. "Even though the Destroyer comes. Because we will defeat him, too."

And because their story was far from done.

ACKNOWLEDGMENTS

I am eternally grateful to every reader who has enjoyed my work, but I have been particularly floored by the response to this series—thank you to everyone who took a chance on *A Heart of Blood and Ashes*, and I hope you've enjoyed Lizzan and Aerax's story, as well.

As always, thank you to my editor, Cindy Hwang, for her amazing patience and encouragement. To my agent, Nephele Tempest, who always smooths the way for me. The entire team at Berkley deserves a thousand rounds of applause for all that they do to make this book into a gorgeous package and to strengthen the story inside. This particular book had the additional challenge of being produced while the world around us went through a strange and uncertain time, and I'm writing this acknowledgment during a quarantine and lockdown—as the production and editing teams have been undergoing, as well, and yet this book is still making it onto the shelves. And I thank all of you so very much.

Turn the page for a look at the first
Gathering of Dragons book by Milla Vane

A HEART OF BLOOD AND ASHES

Available now!

MADDEK

C ommander!" A young Syssian soldier called out as Maddek rode toward the bridge. "Something's got the savages on the run!"

Her polished helm gleaming beneath the early-morning sun, the soldier pointed across the river. Maddek slowed his mare, his gaze scanning the opposite bank. This was a grim stretch of the Lave. On either side of the swift-flowing waters, sparse grasses grew on stony ground that buckled and heaved into hills and ravines. The Farians' hunting party was camped in one of those gullies, hidden from Maddek's sight—though he knew well its location and had posted soldiers along the riverbanks, eyes covering every route out of the ravine that the savages might take when they finally attempted to cross.

Covered in the mud they painted over their translucent skin, now Farians scrambled their way out of the ravine using all of those routes—but not in concerted attack. Instead they were as gutworms wriggling free of infested dung tossed on a fire. Some carried spears and spiked clubs, but most had no weapons, as if they'd been surprised in camp and chose to run rather than arm themselves. Faintly Maddek heard their urgent hoots over the rush of the river.

"A trap jaw?" Maddek asked Kelir as the warrior rode up alongside him. If one of those giant predatory reptiles attacked the alliance army camp, Maddek would not have reprimanded any soldier for fleeing there, too.

His second captain cocked his head, dark braids brushing his shoulders. "Too quiet."

So it was. A trap jaw was silent until it rushed its prey. Then it often loosed a trumpeting roar—one that would have reached them even over the sound of the river.

A handful of savages scuttled nearer to the bridge, as if preparing to escape across the water, though this side of the river was no safer for them. Two dozen of Maddek's mounted Parsathean warriors and a handful of soldiers waited to separate the Farians' hairless heads from their hunched shoulders.

In nearly eight years of holding the Farians at the Lave, Maddek had seen savages run toward death many times. Never had he witnessed a Farian flee from anything.

"There it is!" a soldier cried out.

Coming up the stony path out of the ravine. A siva beast.

Maddek exchanged a look with Kelir as the soldiers snorted with laughter. Though as heavy as a yellow tusker and as tall as a mammoth, a siva beast was docile as a milk cow. Usually it waddled along, a plated dome of armor over its humped back and protecting the sides of its belly, using hardened beak and curved claws to rip open rotten logs and dig up roots.

Yet there were few roots and logs here. The jungle where the siva beast must have wandered from was three days' ride downstream.

A hard, bloody journey for the siva. Gaping wounds on its leathery neck and legs showed signs of attack. Gore dripped from its beak.

As did green foam. Maddek tensed. "It is poisoned."

Kelir had seen the same. "Silac venom."

Stung by one of the two-armed serpents that swam the Lave. The Farians had been right to flee. That venom first weakened the serpent's prey so it could be dragged from the riverbanks and drowned. Most animals stung by the serpent didn't escape.

And those that did, didn't truly escape. They only staggered away, until the weakness put them to sleep—and they woke as if brainless, unfeeling of pain and killing everything that moved. Eventually they starved or died of wounds. But the siva's armor protected it from an easy kill, particularly from the Farians' primitive spears and clubs, so the best chance of survival was to stay out of its sight.

The savages weren't out of sight yet. If the siva made noise, Maddek couldn't hear it from this distance. Silently it charged, tearing open a savage with curved claws as long as daggers. Its strong beak crushed another Farian's leg as the savage tried to run away.

Maddek heard those screams. He also heard a young Gogean soldier nearby, his face bloodbare as he watched the beast attack the Farians.

"So we . . . let the siva kill the savages for us?" He looked to his companions hesitantly, as if uncertain whether to be glad the beast tore their enemy apart.

Although that question hadn't been directed at Maddek, he answered it. "Then wait for it to attack our camp? It does not care if we are Farian or human. It will kill us all," he said. "There are enemies, and there are monsters. Always slay the monsters first, because enemies may one day become allies—but monsters never will."

As the Gogean soldier would have looked upon Maddek as an enemy only a generation past. Perhaps even thought him a monster.

Color stained the young soldier's cheeks as if realizing the same.

Maddek drew his sword. "Kelir?"

The warrior hefted his axe. "Ready."

To the soldiers, Maddek said, "Hold the bridge while we are across."

He took a dozen Parsathean riders with him. Their hooves thundered across the stone bridge. Immediately the siva found new focus, growling wetly as it charged Maddek and his warriors.

Had Maddek known he would be facing a beast maddened by silac venom, he'd not have ridden his favorite mare to the river this morn. Yet there was reason she was his favorite. Though tall and muscular as all Parsathean steeds were, she was also nimble as an antelope. With the barest signal from Maddek, she dodged the siva's swiping claw. As soon as they were past the beast, the siva's attention shifted to Kelir and the warriors behind him. Maddek's mare swiftly pivoted and sprang forward with a powerful thrust of her hindquarters.

The siva's soft belly was too low to the ground to offer a real target—any warrior low enough and close enough to cut it open might be crushed when the beast fell dead. Yet Maddek had seen that every time the beast struck with its foaming beak, first it reared back its head.

Sword in hand, Maddek launched from his saddle. The siva's neck muscles bunched as it prepared to snap at Kelir. A grunt tore from Maddek's chest as he swung at the beast's exposed throat, laying it open with one powerful slice of sharpened steel. Blood jetted from the fatal gash. Narrowly Maddek avoided a blow from flailing claws, rolling out of the way across the hardened ground and coming to a quick stop in a crouch—face to face with a Farian that hid from the beast behind a nearby boulder.

Muscles coiled, bloodied sword in his hand, Maddek made no move. The Farian held a bone blade in its longfingered grip, yet the savage also remained motionless, near enough that Maddek could feel the hissing breath that issued from between its pointed teeth.

Mud covered its pale face. The savage's large ears shifted subtly—no doubt tracking his warriors' movements by their sound. All had fallen quiet behind Maddek. Waiting for his signal.

A signal would not come. He'd given an order that as

long as the savages remained on this side of the river, the alliance soldiers and Parsathean warriors were not to kill them except in defense of their own lives. Maddek cared not if the Farians overran the territory south of the Lave, from the Bone Fields to the Salt Sea. He would leave them in peace. Yet if they crossed the Lave, they would die.

Many *did* die. But this one hadn't lifted its blade toward Maddek, so it would not.

Slowly Maddek backed away, gaze never leaving the crouching savage. His mare nickered softly behind him. Eyes still on the Farian, he swung up into his saddle.

Kelir laughed at him as they rode toward the bridge. "Now you wait for that savage to attack our camp?"

Poking at him with the same words Maddek had said to the young soldier. Maddek grinned, for despite Kelir's teasing, he knew that the warrior would have made the same choice. Perhaps the savage would cross the river with intention of raping and killing every human it encountered. But Maddek would not kill even a Farian for what it had not yet done.

If the savage crossed the river, however—then Maddek would tear its head from its shoulders.

His attention was caught by the mounted figure watching them from the opposite end of the bridge. Enox, his first captain—who ought to have been at camp, sleeping in her furs after a night spent along the river.

Silver beads glinted in her dark braids as she cast him a dour look. "A thousand warriors you have at your command. Could you have not sent them to kill that beast instead of taking it upon your own head?"

Never would Maddek send warriors into a battle he was not also willing to fight. Nor would Enox. If Maddek had not been upon the Lave this morning, it would have been she who led that charge and felled the maddened siva. "Warriors accompanied me across the bridge," he pointed out. "It is no fault of mine if my mount was fleeter than theirs."

Her snort echoed Kelir's. Yet she had not come to reprimand him, Maddek knew.

Drawing his mare alongside hers, he asked, "What brings you?"

"Dagoneh has arrived with a company of Tolehi soldiers," she said, reining her horse back toward camp. "And a message for you from the alliance council."

Maddek frowned and urged his mare to keep pace. "What message?"

"He would not give it to me, but is waiting to speak with you."

Unease slithered through his gut. Not many years ago, he'd delivered a message from the alliance council, too.

Maddek had assumed command at the Lave eight years past. In the six years following, not once had Maddek journeyed home to the Burning Plains, until his parents had requested from the council a three-year leave, so that they might find him a bride and see him married. In his absence, Iova of Rugus had assumed command of the alliance army. Before even three seasons had passed, however, the alliance council bade Maddek to return to the river with a message for Iova—the Rugusian king was dead—and to resume command while that realm's affairs were sorted. Iova was to have returned when all was settled. Yet despite the passing of a winter, she had not.

Now the alliance council sent another message, and Dagoneh would not tell Enox what it was? That could not bode well.

Yet Kelir's mind had taken a happier route. "Perhaps they have finally found you a bride."

His parents. Though Maddek had returned to the Lave, a bride for him they'd still intended to find—one who might strengthen ties between Parsathe and the five realms that made up the alliance. A royal daughter, or a noblewoman.

Very likely a woman like Iova, who was not only a fine soldier but also aunt to the dead Rugusian king. If Iova had been younger, or if she'd had a daughter, Maddek suspected that he would already be married.

For all that it would be a marriage designed to strengthen

the alliance, however, never would his parents choose a bride unsuited to him. Though finding a warrior among the noble houses might prove too difficult a task, no doubt she would be honest, never lying or speaking with sly tongue, for she would become Maddek's closest advisor. If from Toleh, then she would be educated by the monks, with a mind both clever and fair. And as befitted a woman who might one day be a Parsathean queen—and if she wished to gain his mother's approval—she would be tall and strong and a skilled rider, and possess a heart that burned with fire.

Such a woman Maddek would be eager to meet—and take to his bed. For he'd been celibate after assuming command at the Lave eight years past, mindful of his parents' warning that when the High Commander of the Army of the Great Alliance asked someone to share his furs, there was not much difference between an invitation and an order. And during his short return to the Burning Plains, he'd taken no lovers. Not when his parents were already seeking a bride. Touching anyone else seemed a betrayal of the vows Maddek would make to that woman, and it mattered not that he hadn't yet met her.

A fine thing it would be, to finally fuck something softer than his fist.

So it was with anticipation that he rode into camp, where Parsathean tents made of mammoth hides and tusks housed the alliance army. Dagoneh had brought with him a hundred soldiers . . . as if expecting Maddek to leave with a large number of Parsatheans.

As Maddek would, if there was to be a wedding.

Yet there was to be no wedding. He entered the commander's tent with Kelir and Enox at his sides, and one glance at the Tolehi man's face told Maddek that he was not to receive news about a bride.

Dagoneh still wore his armor, yet had removed his helm, revealing his shaven head. Uncertainly he looked to Enox and Kelir before returning his solemn gaze to Maddek's. "Perhaps we might speak privately, Commander?"

As if fists had clenched around his lungs, Maddek told him tightly, "There is nothing you can say that they cannot hear."

Yet what Dagoneh did say, Maddek seemed not to hear. Not through the roaring in his ears.

Yet Enox must have also heard what Maddek could not accept. Fiercely she advanced on the captain, as if the sheer threat of her approach might force him to retrieve what he'd said and shove it back into his mouth.

"That cannot be truth," Enox spat. "It *cannot.*"

"It is." Grave and steady was Dagoneh's reply. "Ran Ashev and Ran Marek have returned to Mother Temra's embrace."

Ran Ashev and Ran Marek. The Parsatheans called them their queen and king.

Maddek called them Mother and Father.

All fierceness leaving her, Enox fell to her knees on a keening wail. With her fists she pounded the ground as if she might reshape the world, as Mother Temra had. As if she might shake her queen and king free of that goddess's eternal grip.

A harsh sobbing breath came from beside Maddek before Kelir threw back his head. The warrior's howl of grief sounded as if torn from a bloodied throat.

Maddek's own howl swelled in his chest, yet it seemed there was no release for it, the grief too deep, a cavernous hollow that had suddenly opened within him.

"How?" So empty was his voice, he knew not how Dagoneh heard it.

Yet the captain must have. With grim regret, the other man shook his head. "I have no answers for you. My message and orders from the council were so bare, I suspect they were sent to Toleh in great haste."

"And the messenger knew nothing more?" Maddek asked hoarsely.

"Only rumor that your queen and king were killed in Syssia. But I know not if it was bandits or beasts or illness, whether in the city or the outlands." Voice deep with apology, Dagoneh spread his hands. "I am only to assume command here and send you north to Ephorn."

To stand before the alliance council and learn what had killed his parents.

What had killed his queen and king.

In his heart yawned a great and painful emptiness, yet unreal it all seemed. Maddek knew the dangers that might befall a warrior . . . but could not imagine what had befallen them. His queen and king had been so strong, and such clever warriors. Unbelievable that they might survive Anumith the Destroyer, only to be killed by bandits.

So he would demand answers of the council. And if it had been bandits, Maddek would hunt down every single one of them.

Answers . . . and vengeance. It seemed that purpose was all that moved his feet. Each breath was a hot, shuddering agony. Maddek emerged from the commander's tent and a blurred sea of Parsathean faces was all he saw—warriors drawn by the sound of Enox's wail and Kelir's howl.

Three times he tried to say the words that needed to be said. Each time they broke on his mother's name. Yet it was enough. Understanding and grief slid like a blade through the warriors standing before him, shearing hearts open as Maddek's had been. On a deep breath, he gathered that purpose again.

Answers. Vengeance.

If they were to be had, then Maddek would have both.

In stronger voice, he called out, "Riders of the Burning Plains, make ready to fly north!"

The Parsathean army started out silently on their journey, grim-faced and grieving. Riding hard, never did they pause to hunt for meat or furs; their saddles were their dining halls, the cold ground their beds. Even battle-hardened muscles ached, yet no complaints had issued from the warriors' lips.

As the days passed, grief softened and song returned to

the Parsatheans' tongues, ballads that spoke of lusty warriors and legendary rulers—and of the goddess Temra, who
had broken through the vault of the sky and reshaped the
world with the pounding of her fist, forcing life to sprout
from the earth's barren face. Temra, whose loving arms
welcomed the souls of the dead back into her eternal embrace.

But silver-fingered Rani had carried Maddek's parents
into Temra's arms too early.

Though sorrow lay like stone upon Maddek's features,
even his granite mouth smiled again when the warriors told
their ribald jokes. Though his deep voice did not lift in
song, he felt the rhythm through his blood like the beat of
war drums. But his grief did not soften; instead the burning
need for answers and vengeance hardened around his be-
reaved heart like steel.

A full turn of the moon passed before the white stone
wall surrounding Ephorn's great city became visible in the
distance. Maddek often heard Ephorn's soldiers claim that
glimpsing the walled city from across the plain was akin to
gazing upon a shining mountain.

Maddek agreed that Ephorn could be mistaken for a
mountain—a pale squatting one, built upon a hill of its own
dung.

Walls should not swell any soldier's breast with pride.
Those walls symbolized fear, not strength. Ephorn and the
cities of nearby realms had built their walls because they
feared each other and feared their common enemies: the Parsathean riders to the north and the Farian savages to the
south. Yet the walls had not stopped generations of rulers
from conspiring and warring among themselves, had not
prevented the Parsatheans from invading and raiding their
cities, and had not saved them from the Farians who raped
and slaughtered their citizens.

And a generation past, those walls had not stopped Anumith the Destroyer, who'd crushed the cities' stone defenses as easily as he'd torn the hide tents in the Parsathean
hunting camps.

Walls were not strength. The alliance that had formed between the riders of Parsathe and the five southern realms in the wake of the Destroyer—*that* was strength.

That alliance was also why Ephorn's gates opened for Maddek upon his approach. The city that would have barred a Parsathean's entrance a generation ago now invited him in. The citizens would not as warmly welcome the Parsathean army that rode behind Maddek, however, so only three warriors accompanied him.

Beneath the shadow cast by the white wall, sallow-cheeked children played between mudbrick houses that only saw the sun at midday. No breeze stirred the stale air but for the wind created by the swift passing of Maddek and his warriors, their mounts' hooves clattering on the cobblestone road.

Visible beyond the clay-tiled roofs rose the shining blue spires of the citadel—and it was at the citadel where the splendor of Ephorn was put on display. In the great courtyard beyond the fortress's outer gates, lush gardens breathed their perfume into the air. Fountains splashed into gleaming marble basins. Market stalls boasted pots full of colorful spices and hung a dazzling array of silks. At the open tables, mead flowed like rivers to wash down mountains of roasted meats.

It was the city that never hungered or thirsted. Some said Muda herself favored Ephorn, so its fields always yielded a bounty and its wells never ran dry.

Maddek could not claim to know whether the goddess of law cared for crops and water, but he thought her favor had been helped along by Ephorn's location. Centered among the four other southern realms that made up the Great Alliance, Ephorn had not been raided or attacked as often as the cities on the borders. And most roads—along with the trade they brought—took a central route through the region instead of crossing Parsathean or Farian territory, so the merchants of Ephorn bought from foreign traders on the cheap and sold their wares to the other realms at a profit.

But perhaps they called that the goddess's favor, too.

Maddek passed through the citadel's inner gates and dismounted at the base of the Tower of the Moon—the tallest of the four great towers within the fortress. With sheer walls of seamless white marble topped by a sapphire spire that pierced the sky, the tower had served as the royal keep until the Destroyer had slaughtered the royal family. Afterward, though many nobles still lived, no one had taken the king's place on the throne. Instead the city had come under the protection of the Court of Muda and the fortress became the seat of the Great Alliance.

Here Maddek would find the answers he sought.

He glanced over at Kelir, who still sat on his horse. The big warrior's head was tilted far back as he took in the height of the tower.

A doleful expression settled over Kelir's scarred features when he noted Maddek's gaze upon him. "I have held the tales of Ran Bantik close to my heart since I was a boy. One day, I would have told them to my own children. But now I know them all to be false."

Tales of the legendary thief-king of Parsathe, who had long ago united the tribes that rode the Burning Plains. "Why false?"

"No one could have scaled *those* walls to steal the pearl from Ephorn's crown. Easier to scale a wall of greased steel."

"So it would be. But a man does not become a legend by performing feats that others deem easy," Maddek said.

"Climbing that wall would not be difficult. It would be impossible."

Maddek agreed. But a man also did not become a legend by doing what others deemed possible. "Is the feat not as impressive if he climbed the stairs?"

"How can it be? Shall I tell my children how Ran Bantik gasped for breath when he reached the top? Shall I describe how he must have clutched his burning chest as he stole the pearl?"

"If Commander Maddek were to race to the upper chambers, he would not be gasping for breath—and neither would I." This came from Ardyl, who had also dismounted and now looked up at Kelir with a frown creasing her black-painted brow. "Perhaps if you more often ran beside your horse instead of always sitting on him, you could also reach the top unwinded."

Kelir looked to Maddek as if for help, but Maddek had none to offer. Instead he could only laugh his agreement. Kelir's saddle would wear thin before his boots ever did.

"When I see the keep, I do not think of Ran Bantik," Ardyl added as she took Maddek's reins. The warriors would not accompany him inside but would remain in the courtyard with the horses. "Instead I wonder what sort of fools the royal family must have been. They built a majestic tower honoring the moon goddess, though it is by Muda's favor that they all prosper."

"What insult could that be?" Kelir frowned at her. "Vela gave birth to Muda. What daughter would not see her mother honored?"

Ardyl's response was a glance at the silent warrior mounted a few paces behind him. Danoh's feud with her mother was almost as legendary as any thief-king. Many Parsatheans claimed the only time they'd ever heard Danoh speak was when she yelled at the older woman.

Grinning, Kelir bowed his head to acknowledge Ardyl's point.

Movement on the tower steps drew Maddek's attention. A seneschal in blue robes approached—a wiry Tolehi man with shaved head and pursed lips.

Omer. Maddek knew him well. He'd first met the seneschal as a boy, visiting the tower while his parents spoke to the council. He'd spent a full morning in an antechamber with Omer watching him as an antelope watches a drepa—with trembling limbs and pounding heart, fearing the raptor's sickle claw that would spill steaming innards to the ground.

Though a sickle claw from Maddek's first drepa hunt had already hung from the leather thong around his throat, he hadn't spilled the Tolehi man's innards. Instead he'd eaten his way through a platter of roasted boa.

Maddek had pleasant memories of that morning, and of every meeting since. Even if the seneschal did not.

"Commander Maddek." Omer imperiously swept his hand toward the tower entrance. "The council is ready to receive you, if you are ready to be received."

The doubt in the seneschal's tone suggested that Maddek could not be. "I am."

The older man sniffed as Maddek joined him. "If you wish, I will escort you to the bathing chambers first."

Grinning his amusement, Maddek climbed the steps. "I do not wish."

There was no shame in smelling of horse, or in wearing the grime of camp on his skin. The duty of serving the alliance and protecting their people left his warriors covered in sweat and filth, and he would not pretend a warrior's work was a clean work.

As it was, the council ministers should be grateful he always washed away the blood of battle, or he would have faced them dripping an ocean of it.

With a sword's worth of steel in his spine, Omer tipped back his head to meet Maddek's gaze. "I would offer a robe so that you could clothe yourself before meeting the ministers, but we do not have any large enough to cover your mountainous expanse of flesh. But did I not see a mammoth's pelt rolled up and tied to your beast of a horse?"

Not a mammoth's but a bison's—and it was too warm for furs. The last frost had melted during their journey north, and Maddek no longer used his furs except to sleep on.

He said simply, "I am already dressed."

In red linen folded over a wide belt. The inner length of cloth hung to his knees. When it was raining or cold, he could draw up the longer outer length and drape it over his shoulders, but now it fell almost to the ground, all but concealing the soft leather boots that protected his feet and hugged his calves. The outer length of linen was split to allow for ease of movement, but unless he was riding or fighting, it concealed his skin as well as a southerner's robe did . . . from the waist down.

On this day, the sun was high and warm, so he needed no other covering—whereas Omer wore enough for two men.

The southerners did not just wrap their cities in walls. Their soldiers wrapped their bodies in heavy armor even when they were not in battle. The citizens wrapped themselves in cloth from neck to ankle, even on days when they needed no protection from the cold or wind.

An entire life they spent wrapped, as if for a funeral pyre.

Maddek spent his life as he lived it. For a full turn of the moon he had been traveling, so he was dressed to ride. He did not anticipate a fight, so he wore no armor, and his chest was bare aside from the leather baldric slung across his shoulder to carry his sword. No black paint darkened his brow. The only silver upon his fingers was the family crest circling the base of his thumb; he'd tucked away the razor-tipped claws that would drip with blood by the end of a battle.

Although he was a commander of the alliance's army, if Maddek had arrived looking as he did after a battle, he doubted they'd have let him through the gates. Many southerners within the alliance still believed the Parsatheans were little better than the Farian savages. The riders were still called raiders and thieves—and uncivilized.

Maddek had never known the raid. By the time he'd been old enough to mount his first horse, the alliance between Parsathe and the southern realms had been firmly established. But if civilization meant cowering behind walls, if it meant wrapping every bare stretch of skin in linens, then Maddek preferred to be a barbarian.

In a god's age, when their civilized walls were crumbling to dust, when the names of their civilized cities were forgotten, Parsathean seed would still grow strong amid the ruins.

Omer gave Maddek's bare chest a despairing glance before sighing and continuing across the marble floor inside the tower's entrance. In silence they walked, until they reached the anteroom outside the council's chamber.

There the seneschal quietly said, "It was with great sorrow that I learned what befell Ran Ashev and Ran Marek. They were always the most welcome of the council's visitors. Of those who knew them, there can be not one who does not grieve for them now."

Maddek inclined his head but made no other response, except in his gratitude to draw the red cloth up over his shoulder and drape it across his chest.

He had not yet learned what had befallen his parents. Maddek would not press Omer for answers, however. The questions that burned within his breast would be asked within the council chambers.

Nothing had been left unasked or unsaid between mother and father and son. Every Parsathean warrior knew life was too uncertain to leave important words unspoken. And since leaving the Lave, much time had Maddek to think upon what came next, beyond answers and—if needed—vengeance. To think upon what his parents would have wanted of him. When Maddek had last seen them, his queen and king spoke of finding him a bride and of strengthening the alliance between Parsathe and the southern realms.

Nothing was left unsaid, but there was much left undone. So Maddek would see it finished in their stead.